DIGGING
OUT

DIGGING OUT

KATHERINE LEINER

FICTION FOR THE WAY WE LIVE

NAL Accent
Published by New American Library, a division of Penguin Group (USA) Inc.,
375 Hudson Street, New York, New York 10014, U.S.A.
Penguin Books Ltd, 80 Strand, London WC2R 0RL, England
Penguin Books Australia Ltd, 250 Camberwell Road, Camberwell, Victoria 3124, Australia
Penguin Books Canada Ltd, 10 Alcorn Avenue, Toronto, Ontario, Canada M4V 3B2
Penguin Books (N.Z.) Ltd, Cnr Rosedale and Airborne Roads,
Albany, Auckland 1310, New Zealand

Penguin Books Ltd, Registered Offices: 80 Strand, London WC2R 0RL, England

First published by New American Library, a division of Penguin Group (USA) Inc.

First Printing, March 2004
10 9 8 7 6 5 4 3 2 1

FICTION FOR THE WAY WE LIVE

REGISTERED TRADEMARK—MARCA REGISTRADA

LIBRARY OF CONGRESS CATALOGING-IN-PUBLICATION DATA:

Leiner, Katherine.
    Digging out / Katherine Leiner.
        p. cm.
    ISBN 0-451-21160-X
        1. Accident victims—Family relationships—Fiction. 2. Loss (Psychology)—Fiction.
3. Women immigrants—Fiction. 4. Welsh Americans—Fiction. 5. Mine accidents—
Fiction. 6. Women poets—Fiction. 7. Wales—Fiction. I. Title.
    PS3562.E46144D54   2004
    813'.54—dc22   2003019336

Set in Sabon and Stone Sans
Designed by Daniel Lagin

Printed in the United States of America

PUBLISHER'S NOTE
This is a work of fiction. Names, characters, places, and incidents either are the product of the author's imagination or are used fictitiously, and any resemblance to actual persons, living or dead, business establishments, events, or locales is entirely coincidental.

In memory of

Miles Budd Goodman (1949–96)

Acknowledgments

I am deeply grateful to the following: My agent, Marcy Posner, whose enormous sensitivity, support and competence is boundless. My editor, Claire Zion, for her careful reading and intelligent notes. Tina Brown, for gathering the pieces. Regina Castillo. The Capelins lent me their beautiful home to write in for two summers in Durango, Colorado. Barbara Klema walked with me there, every morning. Julie Gates, Pat Nicholas and Mary Lee Gowland read early drafts. Bill Manning pushed when I most needed it. Sandi Gelles Cole gave me copious notes. My parents and sister, Stanley, Margie and Marie Gewirtz, did what most parents and sisters don't do: they listened. My children, Dylan Leiner and Makenna Goodman—are fast becoming my best friends. Jane Mendez. Miriam Nij. Naomi Gourley. Lynn Eames. Louise Edwards. David Field. Julien Gervreau. Dr. William Haas, who walks me through the mechanics and strategy of numbers among other rigorous mental activities. Dr. Helen Wolff and Dr. Thayer Greene, who helped grow me up. Joyce Ravid, my first NYC friend. Nancy Kramer, Ginko and Luna, for NYC solace and friendship. Christina Erteszek for everything. Leslie Lee. Barbara Symmons, my dearest Welsh friend. Michael Leiner, who long ago made Caerphilly, Wales, home for me. And last but really first, my Monday morning comrades, who read, listen and comment endlessly, and without whom my writing would never see the light of day: Janie Furse, Bette Glenn, Marilyn Kaye, Anne Adams Lang, Joanne McFarland, Lavinia Plotkin, Gretta Sabinson and Michele Willens. To all of you, my love and thanks.

AUTHOR'S NOTE

This book was inspired by a mining disaster that actually happened in Aberfan, Wales. However, I have changed the dates and the chronology to give my invented characters a chance to explore the impact of a tragedy of this magnitude in the world I've created. I offer this book as a tribute to those who survived and persevere.

Faith

I want to write about faith,
    about the way the moon rises
        over cold snow, night after night,

faithful even as it fades from fullness,
    slowly becoming that last curving and impossible
        sliver of light before the final darkness.

But I have no faith myself
    I refuse it the smallest entry.

Let this then, my small poem,
    like a new moon, slender and barely open,
        be the first prayer that opens me to faith.

                                    —David Whyte

DIGGING OUT

I always think I can smell death, feel it around a corner, see it before it happens. I am always waiting for it to strike. I live like a ghost-rider, galloping just in front of it.

—Alys Davies

PROLOGUE

"Come on now, Arthur, 'tis an absolutely miserable day out. Look there, the mist gathering so low in the valley. When I went out to fetch the milk bottles, I couldn't see my own steps back, and it's cold, like, too. Go on then. Have a look if you don't believe me. You can't make Alys go to school in this weather. She doesn't feel right, Arthur. She's still feverish."

"She's going, Rita. I've made up my mind."

The door bangs shut behind us. The hard drizzle pinpricks against my face. And the dark quiet is too cold and damp even for birds. I trail Da, slow, hoping he will change his mind and let me go home. It's not fair.

"Come along then, Alys. Don't dawdle now. You don't want to be late."

"Da . . ."

"Come now, it's the last day before half term. You'll have a whole week to get better in," he says.

And then I'll play with Hallie every day, I will. No one to stop me.

"Button up now, Alys. Your mam's right—'tis bitter. You don't want to catch your death, like."

At Hallie's, Da lets me go knock and we wait on the steps. Mr. Ames, who lives just down the road, appears.

"Trouble today?" he asks.

"Expecting some. Hope not, but I'm prepared if there is," Da says.

I want to turn home. Why is Da making me go? My head hurts.

My neck hurts. I wish Parry was walking me to school. He'd let me go home. He's a good brother like that.

Mr. Ames looks at his watch.

"It's half past the hour, man. We're late for the shift."

"Know it. You go, Ames. I'll be along," Da says, giving him a slap on the back.

Hallie comes out then, her yellow hair in pigtails tied with the red ribbons Beti just gave her when she turned eight a few weeks ago. I am nine months older. I hug her and her lunch pail digs into my side. "What you got there, Hallie?"

"It's a ham roll Mam made. Where's yours, then?"

"I was staying home again, but Da made me come out and I forgot it."

"I'll share mine," Hallie says, taking my hand.

Da reaches into his pocket and gives me a shilling for milk.

Here comes Evan.

"On my way to the mine," he shouts, waving at Da, looking like a ghost walking toward us in the mist. "There's my girl. Pretty as a picture." I look up quickly and smile at Evan, Parry's best friend. It doesn't seem like he is mad at Da, like Parry is. They shake hands.

I ask to see Hallie's ham roll, whispering in her ear, "Parry said yesterday Auntie Beryl was holding a sign telling people to take their children home."

"I saw it. What's it mean?"

I shrug.

"My da calls your auntie Beryl a 'do-gooder.'" Hallie laughs. "Says she's always getting into the middle of things, stirring things up, like."

"Well, she's not. She's just, well, she's Auntie Beryl, that's all. Gram says she's trying to make the world a safer place for us," I argue.

No matter what Hallie's da or anyone else says about her, I love Auntie Beryl, wild skirts, red hair and all.

But just now there is no one wild around or anyone we don't know. No signs. Just mams and das dropping off. Billy and Bonnie Sykes, Peter Davies, Sarah Keane, Lola Finnian making their way through the school doors.

"It seems quiet enough," Da says, pushing his cap back on his head, sounding pleased. I look up at him, a last try. He can tell I don't want to go in. "Remember now, 'tis the last day, today is, before break. And 'tisn't even a full day. You can do it. Off you go, now, Alys. Be a good girl, then."

His soft lips and rough cheek against mine as he kisses it make me feel better.

"You and Hallie walk straight home from school, hear."

In the playground everyone is talking about the fog. Mrs. Morgan rings the handbell, saying she thinks with all this fog it is as beautiful as it gets in the valley. We queue up in class order and the girls go through the side entrance straight to Assembly, me marching behind Hallie. It's Friday; we have Assembly Hall on Friday. We sing "All Things Bright and Beautiful," and then we go back to our classes.

Mrs. Morgan gives paints out to each of us. Bobby and Dai go out for the rain gauge. That's my favorite job. I did it Monday, before I took ill, when there had been three inches of rain. This morning, the gauge registers one and a half.

A call comes for "dinner children." These are the children who are getting milk. So I stand to give my shilling to the dinner lady, asking Hallie for hers.

"I'll do my own," she says.

"No, I'll do it for you, I will. You're sharing your ham roll."

"But I want to do my own," Hallie says. "I want to queue up. I'll do yours. You're the one's ill, like."

I try to grab Hallie's shilling from her. I want to fetch her milk to show how much I love her. I hold on to the edge of the coin, pulling hard as Mrs. Morgan calls out our names, marking the register.

"Come along now. One of you's enough," the dinner lady says, putting her arm around my shoulder. "No need for your squabbling, then."

In the hallway, everyone is talking. When Hallie looks away I pull her shilling so hard it falls to the ground.

"Look what you've done, now, Alys!"

Hallie is down on her knees searching when a terrible roar starts, screaming low over us, the roar swooping low to swallow me. Windows crash in, rush of black water, mud, a tidal wave. It comes and comes higher, higher, till I lose sight of Hallie.

I hear screaming. Then all around is black and still.

PART I

CHAPTER ONE

DURANGO, COLORADO
AUGUST 16, 2002

The darkness I wake to in the early mornings is hardly ever sweet. More often than not I awaken to the sharp pain of panic mixed with a maudlin homesickness, a longing for my beginnings, before all the trouble, a grieving for my past. It is what the Welsh call *Hiraeth*. No matter that thirty years have passed and I am more than six thousand miles away. I have tried to give up that other world, leave that long-ago time behind, staying with what is now. But my past is screwed down deep inside me. In these dark moments I feel lost. There seems nothing that can hold me or make me feel safe.

This morning, while first light edges the horizon, I do not immediately remember that I am in Durango. But as the brilliant Colorado summer sun shows through the white lace curtains I see at the foot of the four-poster bed, the plaid flannel comforter and the over-stuffed chair. I hear the river rolling over the boulders and I am reminded of all the years, all the sweet uninterrupted time Marc, Dafydd and I have spent in this cabin. Perhaps we should have kept it, taken out a second mortgage, borrowed from someone. After Hannah was born, Dafydd all grown-up, we sold it to Elizabeth, thinking we'd travel more, take long trips together. But somehow that hasn't happened yet. Marc's work and mine take us away from each other more often than we'd like. So sweet Elizabeth grants us usage rights whenever we are lucky enough to string a few days together.

I've been here for only twenty-four hours, and despite my abrupt entrance into the morning, I have already felt the tight muscles of my heart giving way and my breath going deeper. Even my voice last night sounded more sonorous. Lying here, I remember how I always feel an instant repair of spirit in Durango. So why is it such a bloody struggle to get here? I guess it doesn't matter. I'm here now. And ahead of me is a ten-day yoga retreat in Hesperus, the next town over, bordered by the La Plata Mountains and the ancient Anasazi ruins, said to be one of the most powerful energy vortexes in the world.

I don't really understand what an energy vortex is, but I believe in it, like astrology, numerology, tarot cards and psychic readings. For me, there is more than enough room for these kinds of possibilities, these mysteries.

Gram used to say I was born twice: the first time from out of my mam like the rest of the world, and then born again, straight out of the earth—in fact, dug out, saved. "You're special," she'd say, her fingers going through my long brown hair, making it feel like fine silk thread instead of a tangled bush of weeds. "Must have been saved for doing something truly exceptional."

Special. I've written three books of poetry. Is that exceptional? Despite what Czeslaw Milosz, the Nobel laureate, says about poetry having the potential to save people and nations, or what Stanley Kunitz says about poetry being the most indelible testimony we have of the adventures of the spirit, sometimes I feel my work is a wasting of words, nothing more than falling ashes.

When I am in Durango, it seems to matter less that at thirty-eight I have not yet done anything truly life-changing. Aside from my children, that is. In the heart of the Weminuche Wilderness, I am placed in a way I am not in the stark edges of Los Angeles.

For hours I've been listening to the rain beating down on the tin roof Marc and I laid the first year we owned this house. I smile, remembering our balancing act that day, yelling at each other from our opposite and precipitous rooftop spots.

"This is too much for me, Marc. This thing weighs a ton. Where should I put it?"

"Just hold tight, baby. I'm coming over."

"Omigod, I'm actually swaying. It's gonna pull me over the edge. Is that vertigo? Shit, I think I'm going to fall. Marc, really I'm not joking. I've always been scared of heights!" And dark places, murky lake waters, high waves, low waves for that matter, being left alone, you name it.

"Hold on, honey. I'm coming. Don't talk. Concentrate on your balance. Remember, 'balance is everything,' " he said, poking fun at my yoga practice. "If you start to fall, do *Trikonasna* or whatever that pose is called where you put your arms out and pump hard!"

Back then, I was certain Marc thought I was special, but in the last several years, something has changed between us. I think it started after Marc's mother's death, when he was understandably raw and oversensitive anyway. Then, after having done the music for the last five of Joe's films, he lost what he called "the big one," the one produced by DreamWorks Pictures, to someone else.

"The guy's not even a good composer. He doesn't do his own orchestrations. He can't conduct. Man, I thought Joe and I were just starting to understand one another! He knows I've got a million different styles. I know what he wants, for Christ's sake, or I thought I did." Losing Joe's film added to our already somewhat precarious emotional situation at the time, not to mention our financial picture, causing even more frequent misunderstandings.

I try not to think of our most recent confrontation, when Marc actually turned on the tape recorder behind the piano in his studio.

"I'm just going to do both of us a service here and tape this conversation, because it is so typical of the way we don't seem to get each other."

"If you do that, I won't speak," I said.

"Why not? It might give us a clue about things."

"A clue about what things?" I asked. "It's a rough time, that's all. Things are not perfect. What's the big deal, Marc? Let it go, as you would say."

"We have both let it go so much and so often now, that it's almost gone, Alys."

"I don't know what you're talking about."

"Alys," he said, shaking his head, "come on."

"I'm going to take a run." I started to unbutton my shirt.

He came over to me then, put his arms around me. "Let me do that."

It would have been so easy to just let him. To fall into that moment with him as we had before so many times. But I wasn't in the mood. I'd already decided that the only thing that could make things right for me was to get my endorphins going.

"Later," I told him, pulling away.

"Fine. I'll go smoke a cigar." He knew I hated his breath after he smoked.

"Whatever." I turned my back and walked out.

These last months we've actively steered clear of any further possibility of discord between us. We are careful with each other. Cautious to a fault. And we are both aware of it. I keep trying to convince myself that I'm just letting things between us be. But what I'm doing, plain and simple, is not dealing with it. Of course, neither is Marc. In the fragile moments between us, I am hoping for some easy way into our strain. Or more truthfully, around it. Perhaps we will simply grow out of this phase as we have others and into something else before too much more time passes.

Now, through the white lacy curtains and a thousand miles away from Marc, the whole wide-open blue sky of a Durango morning pulls me out of bed. I'm always eager to put these hard, wakeful hours behind me no matter where I am. And knowing that, I wonder why I have yet to find a way to avoid them. I've thought about taking up early-morning running—when it's still dark out, when I need it most. In Los Angeles I'd be in good company down San Vicente Boulevard and then along Ocean Avenue, even on the beach. I suppose there are good reasons not to run in these under-populated urban areas in the middle of the night, but people do it. Here in Durango I am never afraid of the possibility of intruders or even of running into wild animals, day or night. Two years ago, just starting out on an evening run, I spotted a large, blond mountain lion not far from the back deck. His face was the size of a dinner plate. I was surprised at how I wasn't at all afraid. In fact, I was amazed to find that I tried to follow him. I wanted to see him again, so I slept out on the deck alone, waiting, hoping for his miraculous return.

I pull on my running shorts, socks and sneakers. Outside, the early-morning air is soft against my skin, lilac-sweet. The crack of cicadas, like the earth's pulse, whirls through the wires of my own nerve endings. The low-flying buzz of a hummingbird, a horsefly—

each of them reporting their morning news. All of this, and the every-day possibility of an elk sighting, reminds me how much I love this place.

I walk for a while, trying to take it all in, looking and looking again at the wide, clear vistas of uncluttered ranchland. These views make me believe in the possibility of spaciousness in the mind, in the soul and in the heart. Two years ago a terrible fire on Missionary Ridge took over seventy homes and burned upward of sixty-five thousand acres, fortunately just missing our valley. The mountains around us have started to recover. I move into a slow jog down my favorite dirt road, the Animas River running next to me. Soon, I am sweating. Despite my lack of sleep, my muscles engage. After a mile or so I pick up the pace, running faster and faster.

As I often do at this point in my run, I begin to slip into silent meditation. I watch my breathing, the in breath, the out breath, the quiet way my lungs fill and empty, and I am grateful for the natural red-blooded feel of my life's promise. "Happy," as Rilke says, "to know that behind all words, the Unsayable stands; and from that source, the Infinite crosses over to gladness . . ."

Unfortunately, too often my mind clicks on to some desperate fantasy and sticks to it, and I must forcefully drag the wandering seat of my consciousness back to my breath. It is always one or another of my fears surfacing: Hannah being snatched on her way to school, Dafydd falling out of the air from a plane. Death by fire, falling, drowning—death by any means at any time, anywhere. Not proba-ble, not even logical, but the fears are always there, clutching and pawing, pulling me down. I have tried to work with these fears for years, but like my early-morning wakeful hours filled with longing, when fear shows up, it feels like my mind stretches over some long muddied lake. Although I try to rise above it, to hold some higher thought from entwinement, shrubs and sticks, to place myself on higher ground, I am always pushing against the rush of water for dear life. Running helps.

I've got my speed up. I am running so fast now, my hair is a dark mane flying out. As I break into a full lope, I feel Marc behind me.

I turn as though he might actually be there instead of where I know he is, home with Hannah, making one of his big breakfasts, reading the *New York Times*, a cup of black coffee and his morning pipe, cigarette or cigar. Reliable. Dependable. Sturdy. Always where he says he is. I hold my hand out to him, seeing him so clearly, it seems as if in that moment there is absolutely nothing between us besides our full, trusting hearts.

Another mile uphill and then turning back, like a speeding bullet, a beam of light, empowered. I call out, "Wonder Woman!" Strong thighs, heart and lungs push the hallucination, Los Angeles, Hannah and Marc aside. I am not thinking about my unfinished and fettered poetry galleys due to my editor at the end of the month. It is just me filling up with clean summer air, and the stark loveliness of parched fields, bleached white bones of long-ago winter months against the lush mountains. Yes, running has always helped.

Elizabeth's front door is open. The phone is ringing. I hear it stop. She shouts, "Alys, are you back?"

"I'm here!" I head toward the back deck to do a few yoga stretches, and see the kitchen table, where Elizabeth has left me half a papaya with a slice of lime. I am taking my socks off by the French doors when she calls out, "It's Phillípe."

Phillípe is Marc's partner and friend. There's something about him that makes me uncomfortable, always has. Until Elizabeth is in front of me and I see her expression I don't think about why he might be calling me here. She hands me the phone. "Phillípe?" I wonder if he's told her why he is calling.

Elizabeth shrugs and shakes her head. Her top lip, full and dashed with red lipstick, is quivering slightly. After she hands me the phone she leans her small, compact body against the plaid wing chair near me and gently holds my elbow. Things begin to move in slow motion.

"Phillípe," I say into the phone. Aha, he must be calling about his wedding. Of course, that's it. He's getting married in eleven days. Marc is his best man.

"Aly-ese," he says flatly in his French accent, pronouncing my name as he always does: wrong. Then there is a beat, a pause, just long enough for me to slow my breath, to begin to pull myself up tall, every muscle on alert.

"Phillípe? What is it?" The fear that's always just a swallow away suddenly rises in the back of my throat.

"Aly-ese," he says again, and I can hear the tears.

"Hannah?" I breathe out. "Phillípe, where's Hannah?" My hand grabs the shilling that hangs around my neck. I hold it, my life depending on it once again, as if Hannah's life depends on it now.

"Phillípe?" I push the back door open, step out onto the small wood deck, the sun above the tallest blue spruce. I look at the river, my heart beating so loud in my ears I can't hear anything else. From the inside out I'm pulled down, my breath sucked out. "Phillípe are you there? Tell me, Phillípe. For God's sake, tell me now!" My words echo inside of me.

"She's here. She's with me. She's safe." For one instant I am relieved, but then he says, "It's Marc." Phillípe is crying hard now, sobbing. I cannot speak, so I wait for him to say something more.

"He's gone," Phillípe whispers.

I imagine Marc at the market, in the studio or on a plane to Brazil.

I close my eyes. I know this cold darkness, struggling for air and light. It covers me. I cannot breathe.

And then come all of the details: How Marc collapsed against the door of Hannah's room, awakening her. How Hannah came out and saw him on the floor, dragging himself down the hall.

"Daddy, get up!" she pleaded. "Stop kidding around, please. This is not funny, Daddy!" she'd told Phillípe.

" 'I think I'm having a heart attack, Hannah. Would you mind calling 911?' He said it quietly. He said it so politely, Hannah told me."

And then, after Hannah called, she grabbed Marc up in her arms like they told her to do. "Daddy!" she'd shouted, and then she'd laid him back on the floor and began to push against him like crazy, like what she'd seen on TV, in what she hoped was the right rhythm.

I can see Hannah telling exactly what happened, every detail of it, for she is my orderly child—not messy, living in shades of gray like her mother.

"She tried everything, Aly-ese. Our little Hannah tried absolutely everything," Phillípe sobs.

And then the paramedics arrived and began to go at him with their machines and plugs.

"He was thirty-eight years old, for Christ's sake, and he'd never had so much as a bad cold," Phillípe says then.

"Phillípe, I need to speak to Hannah."

I want to rewind to the moment just after my run, before I opened Elizabeth's door, before I took my shoes off. Edit that instant. Stand at the door another moment, and this time not open it. Give me another chance and I won't open it, and none of this will ever happen. . . . My thumb and forefinger feel as if they have fallen asleep rubbing the shilling hanging from my neck. But I keep rubbing it, looking at the clouds, begging someone or something to give me strength. I have been here before, at this edge of myself.

"Mommy. Don't say anything, Mommy. Please don't say anything." I understand immediately. It is not my comfort Hannah needs. She needs her own strength. "Mommy." It is her midnight voice, the one that crawls into bed with us during the dead dark of her night.

"Okay, sweetie," I say, taking in another breath and trying hard to get control, to stop shaking, gather myself up.

"When are you coming home?" I picture her small frame, pulled up tall as she can, her rosy cheeks, and her long blond fringe nearly covering her blue, blue eyes.

"Soon. As soon as I can."

"What about Dafydd? Will he come too?"

"Of course, we'll both be there before dark." As if it's not as dark as she has ever known.

My mind is stumbling around trying to order things, to be calm while I am fighting for my own breath. "Darling, call Elodie." Elodie, one of my oldest friends, is also Hannah's godmother.

"I already did, Mommy." Her voice is so quiet. "She's coming to pick me up now." She sounds like she is twenty. I wonder if she is in shock. Oh my God, what a ridiculous thought. "I'm meeting her in front."

In front of what? "Where are you, Hannah?" I don't even know where she is. Jesus. My eight-year-old daughter has just watched her father collapse and I don't even know where she is.

"I'm at the hospital, Mommy. They say he died at the hospital. But I know he died at home, in the hall, near my room. I saw him. I was holding his hand. Before anyone came to help," she whispers. "I was holding his hand, Mommy. And I couldn't do the right thing to save him. I tried. I really tried. When they got there, they put machines and stuff on him. They weren't going to let me go in the ambulance, but there was no one to stay with me. I called Beti, but she wasn't home. Neither was Phillípe. So I had to go. I sat next to him. I followed them. I held his hand. I kept holding his hand even though it was really cold till we got to the hospital. Till they took him away. I tried to go with him. I wanted to go with him. I didn't want him to be alone."

After a pause, she says more firmly, "There's this nurse who came out of the emergency room after they took him in, and she wanted me to take a pill and said she was going to get a hospital therapist to talk to me. I told her I wasn't going to swallow it and I didn't want to talk to anyone but you. I'm not going to have to see him, right? The nurse can't make me see him, right?"

"The psychiatrist?"

"No, Daddy," Hannah says. I hear her deflate.

Oh shit. "No, no. No, Hannah. Not if you don't want to. I'll tell Phillípe. You stay with him till Elodie gets there—you understand? And when Elodie fetches you, you go home with her and stay with her, near her, within arm's length, okay? Not more than an arm's reach away until I arrive. That's a direct order."

From a distance this is all I can come up with, as close as I can get to folding her up in my arms.

"Okay, but, Mommy . . ."

"Yes, sweetie?"

"Where will they put Daddy? Never mind," she says at once. "I don't want to know."

"They'll keep him there, safe, until I arrive. I'll handle it, Hannah. You don't have to worry about it, sweetie."

"Just hurry, Mommy."

"I will."

"And be careful, really careful, Mommy."

"I promise. I love you, darling," I whisper.

"I love you, Mommy."

And the line goes dead.

I am suddenly very calm, making a list in my mind of what needs to be done first: I need a reservation to Los Angeles.

The travel agent says everything from Durango to Phoenix to L.A. is booked. "You can chance it. Go directly to the Durango airport, try to get someone to give up their seat. Usually, someone will, but if no one does, you're out of luck for today. The last flight leaves in half an hour.

"Your best bet is to drive to Albuquerque, fly from there. It's a little less than a four-hour drive from Durango. There's a plane that leaves in five hours. It has seats available. If you leave now, you can make it."

Elizabeth brings me a cup of tea while I throw things into my suitcase. She's under the mistaken impression that tea is what all the British drink in times of emergency. What happened to gin? Or better yet, Scotch? I smile and ask if I can have something a little stronger than tea. She puts her arms around me and I start to drain into her small, soft body. I gently push her away and shake my head. "I can't fall apart now. I just can't." She nods. I look for my baseball cap. I remember where I have put my dusty sneakers.

"I'll pack you some fruit and cheese for the ride," Elizabeth says.

"And some Scotch."

There have been some hard moments in my life, and I have faced them. I've had no other choice. I will make this call to Dafydd.

Dialing his number in New York, I imagine him there, in his office with a window, just twenty-two, hired straight out of college after a six-month internship in the legal department of Universal. He told us his bosses say he is smart and mature and learning the business well. He will go far and they want it to be with them. He called us last week to say he'd wrecked his knee playing soccer with a bunch of guys on a pickup team in Queens—and wondered if he should wait to have it fixed after Phillípe's wedding.

While the phone continues to ring, I picture Dafydd sitting at his desk, the signed poster of Antonio Banderas above it, his papers lined up neatly in piles on the desk and all over the floor. I remember Marc marveling at how tidy Dafydd's room was when he was a teenager.

"Should we worry?" Marc asked me once in Dafydd's presence. And then, deadpan, he'd asked, "Didn't Gary Gilmore always keep his room neat as a pin?" Dafydd got up from his desk and jumped Marc, throwing him to the floor, where they wrestled until Marc yelled uncle!

Six rings. Where is he? If that damn voice mail picks up, I'll scream.

"Dafydd Davies' office, Barbara here."

"Hi, Barbara. Is Dafydd around?" I ask as calmly and casually as I can, feeling my breathing beginning to change.

"Mrs. Davies, how are you? Just a moment, please."

Now I am hyperventilating, trying to get in a deep breath, but the air won't go past my breasts. How do I do this? How do I tell a son . . . ?

"Mom!" his voice comes on the line, excited. It cuts straight through my heart. "Where are you? I thought you were yogaing?"

I will ruin his day. I will ruin his life.

"I have awful news." I close my eyes and suck in as much air as I can.

"How awful?" Dafydd asks. I can hear his fear. I want to be able to say this right so it hurts him as little as possible.

"Really, really awful."

"Tell me fast," he says.

I use Dafydd's nickname for Marc when I begin to explain. "Marco's had a massive heart attack and he's . . . he's . . . he died."

The sound of his sorrow drags on forever like a mournful foghorn, like the soul-sad cry of a lone coyote, a sound he grew up listening to in our canyon, nightly.

I wait, closing my eyes, hand clenched around the phone, wishing I could hold him. Knowing that wouldn't be enough.

"Where's Hannah?"

"She was with him when it happened. Marco collapsed in front of her bedroom door. Now she's with Phillípe."

"I have to get some air, Momma. Can you call me back in five minutes and tell me what I need to do?"

Elizabeth lets me borrow her truck. Her brother, Ned, will return it next week when he comes in from Texas. He is a professor and teaches two classes in foreign policy at the University of New Mexico once a month. It seems everyone in Elizabeth's family is a teacher or a professor. Elizabeth teaches math at Fort Lewis, the UC campus in Durango. Her mother teaches at the high school, and her sister teaches kindergarten at one of the elementary schools in town. Before her father died, I think he taught, too. Ned will drive the truck up from Albuquerque and fly home from Durango.

Elizabeth helps me lift my suitcase and we put it in the back. She hugs me quickly and asks for the tenth time, "Are you sure you don't want me to go with you?" I shake my head.

I get in the car and roar out of the driveway, looking at the clock and beginning to pace myself. One hundred twenty-five miles to Albuquerque. I'll have to push it. Once I get out on Route 550, where there are long straightaways, I'll be all right.

I find the green bottle of single malt Elizabeth has put under the front seat. I pour a little into the tea to sip as I drive. Then I try to figure out the earpiece and how to use the cellular phone. First I call Dan Wolfe, our friend and doctor of twenty years. He tells me what he thinks happened.

"Fribulation," he says. "No pain, probably no fear. The brain has a way of shutting itself off when we're in that kind of physical emergency. It was fast. According to the paramedic report, he was already in cardiac arrest when they arrived at the house."

Hannah is right. He died at home in the hall in front of her. Lord. Somehow I have managed not to think about Hannah having to deal with Marc as he was dying. Now I let myself imagine the scene, hearing him fall, watching him pull himself down the hall, trying to help himself and at the same time trying to protect her from what he must have known was happening. I can feel the tears coming, and when they do, I cannot stop them. I pull off the road.

"There's going to have to be an autopsy because he died at home. It's a state law."

Autopsy? No. No. I picture Quincy cutting into Marc. The bright light over Marc's body, his barrel chest, bare and elevated—soft white skin, so little hair. He always wanted more. "Does it bother you that I have so little hair?" he once asked while we were making love. I wonder about his lungs, his kidneys, and liver. Will an autopsy tear him to bits? I sip the Scotch and remember *The Tibetan Book of Living and Dying*, how important it is to keep the body quiet, disturbing it as little as possible after death. I wonder how many people have already violated Marc's body. Is he in some deep freeze, his soul, frozen air, floating above it?

"No one is to touch his body until I get there. Will you see to that, Dan? Promise me," I plead.

On the highway again, it starts to rain, coming down on the

windshield in sheets like someone squirting a rubber hose full-force. This is what the newspaper must mean when it says the monsoon season has finally hit the southwest. I race through Bloomfield.

By the time I hit Cuba, New Mexico, lightning is breaking the sky, cracking it wide open, the rain now falling, fierce.

I stop for gas. As the rain beats down on the tin roof above me, I shiver. My hands are stiff, they are so cold. I catch sight of myself in the pump. Marc loved my hair, "rumpled after love," my "buffalo brown" eyes, "swan neck," bony shoulders, long-waisted back—his favorites. My uneven lips, bigger lower and disappearing top lip. Sultry. That's how he thought of me. Now all of me is slumped ragged, swollen eyes, a wrecked mess. I look as homeless as I feel. I start to cry, whimpering at first and then a full-out keen, falling hard against the pump.

"Ma'am? You awl-right? Anything I can do, ma'am?"

I shake my head. What can I possibly say to this nice attendant? I am icy cold, from the inside out—a temperature that is much colder than the human body should ever be allowed to feel.

Once on the road again, I try Dafydd's cell phone.

"Momma," he answers. "I've booked a flight that arrives at four thirty p.m. What can I do to help? What about phone calls from the car on the way to the airport?"

I can tell he is trying to pull himself together. I suddenly feel very tired.

"I'll meet you at home," I say. "Elodie's taken Hannah to her house. By the time I get in and fetch her, it'll be long after six. You should be home by then." We are talking business.

"Okay," he says and pauses. "Momma? How are we going to get through this?"

I swallow. For a moment I want to tell him just how afraid I really am. But instead, I say quickly, "We'll be fine. See you in a few hours."

After we ring off, I try Marc's sister in Los Angeles, but she's not there. Her message on the machine reminds me how Marc always referred to her as "My real mother." Nine years older, she had been the one to set his curfew, point him toward his first girlfriend, roll him his first joint. Some mother. "It's Alys. I'll call you later," I say. If I don't get out of Cuba fast, I'll miss the plane.

I reach Marc's sister-in-law in Florida. When she says hello, I can tell she is crying. Phillipe called her an hour before. Marc's brother is out of town. He'll be home tonight. "Come, please," I beg. "Bring the children. There's plenty of room in the house for everyone."

I call my sister. I call Marc's best friend in San Francisco. I call to make sure Hannah has been picked up by Elodie. I keep to the speed limit and continue to call everyone I can think of on the car phone. Each time I say Marc is dead it feels more unreal.

And the rain just keeps on falling, the sky so dark it doesn't seem to exist, the clouds so low I can't even see the mountains. I look at the clock. I wish I could go faster. For a moment I forget where I am going. And then it comes to me. *Home.* The word suddenly sounds so strange and empty. I say it out loud, like E.T. I want to go home. Phone home. But there is no one there. What will home be like without Marco?

I make Albuquerque, pulling in front of Southwest Airlines three minutes before flight time. A porter helps me with my bags and I beg him to call the gate and explain that my husband has died, my eight-year-old daughter is alone and I need to get to her in L.A.

"Sure," says the man I've cut in front of. "Why is it someone has always died when they're late?"

I turn around and glare at him. "How dare you?" I hiss, continuing to look straight at him, clenching my jaw, making two fists. For a second I actually think about punching him. Once when Hannah was three, maybe four, we'd been back east in New York at the Metropolitan Museum. A guard had caught Hannah petting a Rodin sculpture. He pulled her away and shouted at her. By the time I'd gotten to her, a crowd had gathered and she was petrified. I'd threatened the guard, told him I was certain there was another way to have handled the situation. Later, when I told Marc the story, he said I just should have hauled off and punched him. Even a small injustice would cause Marc's anger to rise. Right then and there he'd taught me the mean right swing that I often think about using, but so far haven't. Now I quickly turn away from the man in line.

In fact, they do hold the plane while I park the car. I race up the stairs and down a long passageway, through the metal detector to the gate, fumbling in my bag for my license and a credit card, giving up a metal nail file as the security people look over my shoulder. When I am on the plane, I thank the flight attendants and peek into the cockpit through the two metal safety doors.

"Fly carefully," I plead. Comfortingly, both pilots smile at me.

In my seat, I buckle up, and then begin to shake. I close my eyes. Since 9/11, I absolutely hate flying. Now there is a new reason to feel fear: I am a single parent. As the plane starts down the runway I look out the window and try to imagine Marc's soul in a better place. I think about his sweetness, all the good he has done, the stray dogs he has saved, his rose garden, the piles of music he's written, his children, rather than all he's left undone.

I glance at the woman sitting next to me. She smiles. I imagine her putting her arms around me, pulling me close, telling me, "Everything is going to be all right. Don't you worry about a thing. Not one little thing." She holds me, rocks me until I am calm and quiet inside. I turn toward the window. I hold my breath as the plane lifts off.

When the plane lands I continue to sit while most everyone files out past me. Finally, the flight attendant comes over and asks if I need any help. She has an enormous amount of hairspray in her hair. She runs her hand down her hairline and her entire blond flip moves up. I close my eyes.

"Are you all right?" she asks.

I nod, but I am not. I am pretending, smiling and pulling myself together in her presence. I don't want her help. In front of me a couple with a small child walks up the aisle. They are telling the child to hurry, but she is moving as fast as her small feet will travel. I follow them off the plane, using them as car lights in front of me on a dark night, trailing them. They are my guides. I follow them to the baggage claim, wanting my own mam, my da, needing them so bad.

As I drag my suitcase away from the terminal, the day is gray, gloomy. I stay off the freeway and drive the back way, through the Marina, down along the Pacific Coast Highway toward the most magnificent ocean view I've ever seen—anywhere. It is a road I've taken almost daily since I arrived in Santa Monica.

Through bumper-to-bumper Friday afternoon traffic and forty minutes later, up Topanga Canyon Boulevard, I pull into the long drive lined with eucalyptus trees circling Elodie's huge Mediterranean-style house. In the distance Hannah is jumping on the trampoline. She knows I hate tramps. In fact I've warned her several times about not jumping on the one here. Rolling the window down, I catch myself before yelling for her to stop, realizing that at least

Hannah has gone on with her day, isn't holed up somewhere or hiding out, hasn't downed a quarter bottle of Scotch. I am grateful for this moment of normality. I park the car and walk toward her. She jerks her head around at the sound of the car door. I know she sees me, but she continues jumping. I restrain myself. Right up next to the tramp, I put my hand out.

She stops but doesn't come over. She just stares blankly and then says, "Don't cry, Mommy. Promise."

"Okay." I know where she learned this.

What are you feeling? Marc asked after I'd gotten a letter from Mam saying Gram had died. *I'm okay,* I'd told him. *I'm okay, really.*

Hannah walks across the trampoline and takes my hand. I put my other one up and lift her down into my arms.

"I don't want to talk about it, okay, Mommy? Ever. Let's just try to forget about it. Please," she says straightforwardly. We hold each other. Neither of us cries.

By the time we arrive home, Dafydd is already there with dozens of others, standing in the middle of the group. I didn't expect there to be so many people. Actually, I didn't expect anyone but Dafydd. I recognize Alex and James, Dafydd's old friends from high school. Hannah runs over to Dafydd. He picks her up and wraps her in his arms. I let them be for a moment and then go wrap my arms around both of them. Dafydd is crying, shaking. "Don't cry, Dafydd," Hannah says. "Don't cry. It'll be okay."

As I look around the room, it seems like everyone we know in California is here, and they've all brought food. Every surface has something on it. I have had nothing to eat all day and have no stomach for anything now. I'm told that some of our oldest friends will arrive tomorrow from New York, Boston, Washington, London, Venice, Helsinki, Rio and Australia. Those here tonight have driven from the farthest California points. Some of these people I haven't seen in ten years. I try to smile and be gracious, but inside I am completely undone. Some part of me longs to be comforted, but I don't know how to ask for it.

I see Phillípe across the room. He rushes over to me, putting his arms around me.

"Hello, Phillípe," I say, stiffly.

"I'm so, so sorry," he says. "This is too big for us to talk about now. I hope you feel it was the right thing for me to invite friends?"

"Yes, of course, Phillípe. Thank you. I appreciate your being with Hannah." I am so stilted. He can tell.

"I will do anything for you and Hannah, Aly-ese."

Except remember how to pronounce my name. I feel mean.

Through the French doors that lead outside, I notice my sister. Everything about Beti is practical. She is sitting in Marc's chair on the deck, which under the circumstances actually bothers me a bit. Her hair is short and she has on a skirt and turtleneck. On her feet are Birkenstock sandals. "Health food shoes," Marc called them. I want Beti to take care of me, put her arms around me and make everything that's happened go away. But we don't have that kind of relationship. We've never had it—she is not that kind of sister. She has always given me a place to run to, but when I get there, she is too busy and scared herself to pay me much mind. Beti looks more haggard than usual. It takes a lot of work to do what she does: raise two children and run her tea shop. She is used to hard work and would know how to handle her husband's death. But Colin is here, rubbing her neck. Anwen and Morgan, who are grown now, sit cross-legged near Beti's feet.

Beti, seeing me stare at her now, smiles sadly. I smile back, briefly. A wave of fatigue flies in my face and I look away. My bones feel heavy, like fresh-killed elk bones hidden under winter fields, raw, not like the lightly bleached bones I saw this morning in the summer fields of Durango.

Someone hands me a cup of soup. If only they would feed me. But I haven't the strength to ask. I lean against the long pine table that Marc and I saved up for. "A Thanksgiving table," he called it. "Big enough to seat all of us. Your sister and Colin, their kids. Our kids. Our whole family. I want big Thanksgiving gatherings."

How many Thanksgivings did we actually have together? Nineteen? Lined up next to each other, they don't seem like very many. Now who will hold up the turkey while I stuff it?

I sip the soup until it is gone. My friend Connie pulls a rocker over and gently helps me into it. She doesn't try to have a conversation, just smoothes the side of my head and then takes the cup away from me, heading toward the kitchen.

My neck aches and my left arm is so heavy. I look at my left hand, at my wedding ring. With my thumb, I turn it around on my finger. It's too wide; it weighs me down. I am convinced the reason my arm feels so heavy is because of my wedding ring. But that's ridiculous. It is the thinnest band we could find. The night we picked our bands out, I was surprised at Marco's insistence that he wanted to wear one as well, because he never wore jewelry. "It's more than just jewelry," he'd said.

Looking around the room I see Lybess and Kenny—all the way from Oakland. We met them in San Francisco the first year we were together. Lybess is a film editor and Kenny is a violinist. Terry and Josie—we always looked forward to their Christmas party, the singing, the potluck, the kids. And there's Angela, such a fabulous Cuban cook. Almost everyone here invested as much as they could in her restaurant, Gaucho. So many familiar faces. Then it hits me square on why they are here and the tears start to fall. But Hannah has made me promise. I squeeze my eyes shut. I will not cry.

Before Beti left Aberfan to come to the States, she also insisted that I not cry. She tried to convince me that it was the right thing, her going. That I'd understand in time. "Don't cry now," she'd said. "There's no reason to cry, Allie."

When *is* it all right to cry? If it's not when your husband dies, or when your best friend dies, or when you are buried alive, when? I bow my head, hoping the tears will stop. But they don't. It surprises me when Beti comes over and sits down on the floor at my feet. She says nothing but the way she puts her head in my lap is reassuring. The weight of it makes me feel like I won't disappear.

Long before anyone starts to leave, Hannah finds me still sitting in the rocker and tells me she wants to go to bed. I notice the lime green sundress she has on. Did she have that on when I picked her up at Elodie's? I can't remember. Her blond hair is pulled back in a ponytail and her blue eyes look washed out, dark shadows under them. She doesn't look tired. Something else? Drawn? Vacant? I have never seen her looking like this. It frightens me.

"I want to sleep in yours and Daddy's bed," she says.

I nod and start to get up, patting Beti's head. She grabs hold of my hand and looks up at me. "Will you thank them all for coming, Beti?" I look around the room. "Tell them I'm very grateful, please."

She stands up, putting her arms around me. I hear her swallow. She pulls back. "You'll be okay." I almost laugh.

Before I start up the stairs with Hannah, Donald reaches out and puts his hand on my shoulder. His grip is firm, steadying. "Alys, you know how I loved him. I love you, too." He is Marc's oldest friend. Donald and Marco ate tuna sandwiches with the crusts cut off and rode horses over the flat, dry hills near their childhood home.

"I'll call you next week," he says. "When things have settled down a bit." Next week won't do. I need him now. I stare at him for a moment and then I turn away, starting up the stairs.

Halfway up, holding Hannah's small hand, I hear Dafydd. He calls up after us from the bottom of the stairs.

"Momma, are you all right?

I turn to look at his tall, slender body. How is his knee? My son's dark hair is buzzed short now, making his blue-green eyes look even bigger than they usually look. We haven't spoken much. Now I'm too exhausted to talk and too weary.

I say, "I think so."

"Is Hannah going to sleep with you?"

"You, too, Dafydd. I want you to sleep with us, too," Hannah says.

There is hardly a moment's beat. "Is there room, Momma? Do you mind?" His voice sounds almost as small as Hannah's. As if to explain himself, he adds, "Then Uncle Jack and Aunt Martha can use my room."

I know she needs my help, so I pull off Hannah's shoes and remove her dress. She crawls under the covers as I undress, putting on one of Marc's T-shirts. I throw Dafydd a T-shirt and a pair of sweats. He changes in the bathroom. Soon I am lying down between my two children, holding them, my arms wide feathered duck wings. I begin to hum the song Marc and I used to sing to each of them when they were tiny. Even after they have both shuttered down—Hannah next to me as close as she can get, and Dafydd on his side, back toward me, but still close, their small breathing sounds a comfort to me—I continue to hum quietly so as not to fly apart.

CHAPTER TWO

When first light breaks, I am staring at Dafydd's sleeping profile in the early-morning half-light, and I remember my dream:

> A meadow. At first I am alone. But then a figure way off in the distance approaches. He is somehow familiar. I raise my arm, about to wave, when he calls out, "Alys!" He starts toward me.
>
> "Alys, it's me, Evan."
>
> When he is in front of me, he says, "I've missed you." My eyebrows rise and I smile. "I have, you know. I've missed you every day of my life."

Certainly I have thought about Evan on and off through all these years. But I guarded against letting him in too deep or close. Of course it is obvious why I should be thinking of him now.

My breathing is short intakes of air. I close my eyes, trying to deepen it, and hear Gram's voice like a soothing mantra. *You do not have to think about the whole of life all at once.* I can see her standing by my hospital bed, feel her down deep in my guts like I did every lonely day after I knew Hallie was gone. Gram, how I wish she were here in the flesh with me right now. *Think only about the moment you are in. That's all, Alys. That's enough.*

The moment I am in . . .

I shimmy down the middle of the bed between my children and out the bottom. Everything in the room is just as it was two days ago, before I left for Colorado, including the pile of books next to the leather chair and Marc's clothes strewn all over the chair.

Downstairs in the kitchen everything is back in place. I feel comforted by our friends putting things right. My friends now. And I wonder if they will continue to be my friends. How often did we see Sarah after Matthew died?

The fridge is full of leftover cold cuts and pickles packed in Tupperware, aluminum and wax paper. There are several loaves of bread in the breadbox, Danishes and cakes in pink boxes. The food looks alien, perhaps even genetically engineered to look like real food.

The real food is the jars of raspberry jam from last summer that Marc, Hannah and I made together. They're organized on the inside of the door and labeled ALYS' RAZZLE DAZZLE in Marc's lovely, round cursive hand. My vision goes soft. I hold tight to the fridge door. He was so pleased with himself. Planting the raspberries had been his idea and last summer was the first they'd been prolific. His sweet smile, faded yellow T-shirt, tan arms holding a gallon tin bucket, a pipe in his mouth. I want to sink to my knees, but my children need me right now.

Should I make crepes for breakfast, Hannah's favorite? Or omelettes, always Dafydd's first choice? I stare into the fridge as the motor turns over for the third time. A stanza from a poem by Michael Leunig, which I'd used as a prologue in one of my first published books years ago, snaps into my mind:

> *When the heart*
> *Is cut or cracked or broken*
> *Do not clutch it*
> *Let the wound lie open;*
>
> *Let the wind*
> *From the good old sea blow in,*
> *To bathe the wound with salt*
> *And let it sting.*
>
> *Let a stray dog lick it,*
> *Let a bird lean in the hole and sing*
> *A simple song like a tiny bell*
> *And let it ring.*

*   *   *

A whole day goes by. In the night I awaken and don't remember anything beyond standing at the refrigerator, except for the terrible moment of viewing Marc's still body, the life of him so definitely somewhere else. I vaguely remember driving myself to the hospital, but Dan Wolfe had driven me home. He'd given me a sedative and I'd gone to bed.

On this morning, the second day of Marc's being gone, after breakfast, we all pull ourselves into our brand-new public roles of "Grieving Widow," "Man of the Family" and "Sad Little Fatherless Girl." A limousine picks us up. Someone, probably Ed Meyer, our business manager and Marc's executor, must have arranged everything. The limos, the three p.m. service at the Writer's Guild in West Hollywood. I guess I must have signed something at the hospital for the cremation? Notices I learn later went out in late editions yesterday of the *Los Angeles Times*, the *New York Times* and the trades. But it is mostly word of mouth that has gathered the large group already queued up outside the door. I have on a simple knee-length sleeveless black dress and a long strand of pearls that Marc gave me on one of our anniversaries. My hair is pulled back in a ponytail and I am wearing sunglasses. Hannah is angry that I am wearing black. She has on a hot pink jumper and a polka-dot skirt. Dafydd is wearing a white T-shirt and jeans and a navy blue blazer.

The car drops us at the building's austere entrance. My sister and her family are behind us in another limousine. Hannah, walking between Dafydd and me, sets the pace, moving too slowly for such a young girl.

In the lobby, there is a leather-bound book laid open for people to sign. "One-sheets" for many of the movies for which Marc did the music are displayed around the entrance, hung on the walls alongside the covers of his latest jazz CDs. A poster-size photo of Marc stares down at me.

"I haven't seen that one," Dafydd whispers. "It's a good one. He's smiling." Marc's hair had grown longish and his blond highlights are caught by the camera. He is tan and his hazel eyes shine. Several weeks ago, before he had it taken, I asked him if he was sure he wanted to wear a black T-shirt. He reached over, kissed me, and said, "All my Brooks Brothers button-downs are at the laundry." He never wore a button-down. Marc didn't own a tie, except for one of his father's, which he'd worn to our wedding.

We file past the doors leading into the auditorium. There is a "before performance" feel in the room. People are setting up speakers, pushing a grand piano to one corner of the stage, placing dozens of flower arrangements everywhere. The stage is covered with them. My nephew, Morgan, is passing out copies of a CD Marc put together only weeks ago highlighting his film music. Party favors. I wonder who made the copies. A photo of Marc on the cover has been added, and a poem called "Loving," which I wrote years ago, is on the back. I grimace and look away. I hear a high-pitched laugh, an octave on the piano, a few notes on the trumpet. Someone drags the lectern across the stage.

"Eddie. Give me more blue in the lights," says a voice backstage. "Testing . . ." The microphone. Marc would absolutely hate this to-do. He hated any fuss being made over him. I contemplate trying to stop it but can't think of how.

We sit in the third row. In front of us, all the cousins, uncles and aunts have turned around and are trying to get my attention: Marc's sister, his brother, their children. I want to escape the eyes on me, the grieving widow—to disappear from feeling or facing all of the difficulties that I know lie ahead.

The room is beginning to quiet.

"Mommy," Hannah says. "I have to pee." Behind me are the hundreds of people who have gathered and are now sitting down. I cannot ask her to hold it. She takes my hand and we inch our way out of the row and up the aisle. Almost everyone I have known since I've come to America is in this audience. People touch me, my arm, my hand.

Through the years, when I'd thought about which one of us would go first, it was never Marc. I have imagined Hannah's death in a million scenarios, and Dafydd's—but Marc was reliable, indestructible. Even though his father had a heart attack at thirty-three, Marc seemed ever present, indissoluble. I teased him about what he would do after I died, the kind of woman he'd end up with: big breasts, small waist, tight-bodice dresses and full skirts; a "Makola" woman buying all her clothes from that pricey shop on Madison Avenue in New York. She would be slow-moving, soft, easy, languid— the exact opposite of the intellectual, with my thrift store clothes and overanxious attitude. I was the one who pressed for wills, guardians for Hannah. I was supposed to be the one to go first. I don't want to be the one always left behind.

A week after the service, Dafydd goes back to New York. He will have his knee operated on there. "It will be easier," he says. "For the first couple of weeks, I'll have Barbara bring my work to the apartment. I'll be back in the office in no time." But he is back in L.A. with us the following weekend. "It's too hard being away from you right now," he tells Hannah. I know he also means it is too hard for him to be away from the town where the remains of Marc reside.

He takes a month off from work and has his knee operated on in Los Angeles. This is a good excuse not to get back to my own work. I have gone way beyond my editor's deadline on the poetry book. I can't face rewriting poems written when Marc was alive. I cannot work lines like: *"He moves toward the October of life"* or *"Setting ourselves like bulbs deep in hard ground . . ."* They mean nothing now. They are light, frivolous, stupid and empty.

Rather, I drive Hannah to school most mornings, come home and draw a bath for Dafydd, shop for food, cook breakfast and lunch for him, pick Hannah up at school, prepare dinner for all of us. I make extravagant meals, concoctions Marc would like: spicy shrimp with arugula; farfalle with zucchini, yellow peppers and spicy chicken sausage; chicken breasts stuffed with broccoli rabe; grilled lamb chops with roasted green figs; and pot after pot of mint chicken soup. This is something I can do. It is second nature to me. And I wait for the cooking to soothe me.

Mostly I think I am managing rather well. There are a few tricks that help—like setting the alarm but waking before it. A small thing, but it makes me feel I am in control. While brushing my teeth I tell myself to be glad I am alive. After some yoga, I pull myself together for Hannah and Dafydd. Getting Hannah off to school can be difficult. She's afraid things will continue to fall apart in her absence: Dafydd will disappear; I will die.

One morning the alarm beats me. Somehow it has landed across the room and under a cushion and has been ringing for over two hours. Dafydd is calling to come help him run a bath. I blur awake. The yellow numbers on the clock read eleven thirty a.m.

"Momma!" Dafydd calls again. It is impossible to pull myself up. I am waiting for someone to help me. I will never be strong enough to pull myself out of bed.

I lie in bed the next day, and the next, and then for the next two weeks. Hannah gets herself up in the mornings. Dafydd, struggling on his crutches, walks her to the bus stop. Later, he finds an empty bottle of pinot noir under my bed. I don't remember how it got there.

Dan Wolfe gives me Valium. He gives me Xanax. He gives me Prozac. I prefer a glass of wine or three.

One evening, after Hannah has made dinner—our third night of macaroni and cheese—Dafydd says quietly, "Momma, you're a mess. You've got to get some help, please."

Hannah is crying. "It's not fair," she tells Dafydd. "You have another father."

I am folding the laundry and eavesdropping on a conversation between them.

"What do you mean?" Dafydd asks.

"You know, that man Mommy lived with in Wales. The one who made you with her." She knows Evan's name but isn't saying it.

There is a long pause.

"But, Hannah, I don't even know him. I've never even met him. When I was growing up, Mom never even spoke about him. Marco was my dad."

"But you *have* someone else. You have another father."

"Hannah. Please listen to me. Come here." I walk to the kitchen door and peek in. Hannah climbs on Dafydd's lap. "Marco was my dad, just like he was your dad. It's true. . . . Evan is my real father, by birth and all. But when I was young, I never even thought about him. I've never known anybody other than Marco. For a while now I've been thinking I'd like to meet Evan someday, but it's just out of curiosity. Not to find another father. He'll never replace Marco. No one could, ever. Never."

"I'd like to meet Evan, too." Hannah's voice is almost a whisper.

"Well, maybe we'll do that sometime. Maybe we'll just bebop it over to Wales someday together and meet him."

"Yeah," Hannah says. "Maybe he could be both our fathers."

* * *

No matter how I try, I can't figure out why Marc died. He had high cholesterol but he'd been on cholesterol medication for about ten years. He watched his diet—olive oil instead of butter, lean meat, oat bran, grapes. Maybe it was because he didn't take vitamins except when he worked with his favorite director, which despite that final film had been quite a bit.

"Joe's into this new regimen." Marc holds out a small cellophane packet filled with vitamins. "Folic acid, B_{12}, multivitamin, calcium, ginko, ginseng, CO-Q_{10}, grape-seed extract. He's sending me a subscription for Andrew Weil's health newsletter."

Several years before, he started drinking red wine, specifically cabernet, because Joe said cabernet grapes inhibited blood clots or something like that.

This past April, Marc had his annual physical exam, which included a stress test. His blood was normal. His electrocardiogram was normal. His reflexes were all normal. Marc said the doctors gave him a clean bill of health. "I've got the heart of a twenty-five year old," he said, his hazel eyes beaming.

I feel Hannah standing at the side of my bed.

"I miss Daddy," she says.

The outline of her small body shows against the night-light in the hall. She is trembling.

"Get in, sweetie."

She comes into my arms and I pull her close. "I miss my daddy," she says again. "I'm the only one of my whole class who doesn't have a daddy." She moves closer and I rock her. "Sometimes when I wake up in the middle of the night, I see him. He is in the hallway outside my room. He is trying to get up, like he did that day, and I can't help him."

I want to tell her that everything is okay. But everything is not. I rock her until she falls back to sleep.

I begin to see a psychiatrist. I do it to get Dafydd off my back. The only other time I'd seen one was at Gram's insistence.

Dr. Jacobs is tall and thin, all angles. He has dark hair and a huge white toothy smile that spreads ear to ear. His round tortoiseshell glasses make him look even more nerdy than I've already decided he is.

"Of course you're depressed," he says. "Why should you be anything other than depressed? Your husband just died. He was your best friend, the father of your daughter, the man who helped you raise your first child. You're all alone in that now. You're going to have to figure out a new way to live your life. You're going to have to figure out how to swim. Of course you should be depressed."

Does Dr. Jacobs think this is making me feel any better? When I ask him, he tells me his job is not to make me feel better. His job is to help me identify the truth and begin to live with it. I wonder if it ever occurs to him that I am not ready just now to live side by side with this hard, cold truth. Perhaps I need a little more time in the denial stage. I get up and walk out, pulling the door behind me shut tight with decision. I am not going back. There are other ways to get through this.

At home I put together a spicy lamb stew with green olives, thinly sliced summer squash, a cucumber and yogurt salad. After pouring my third glass of cold Australian chardonnay, I sit at the dining room table with Hannah and Dafydd. I've cut some dahlias for the table and I have ironed the lace and linen serviettes. I've showered, washed my hair and put on a clean white blouse, black trousers and red lipstick. Dafydd and Hannah smile at each other and then at me, confident that their plan for getting me help has worked. I smile back at them and chew slowly, fifteen times per bite, still thinking about all the ways I can die.

The minutiae of Marc's death seem to keep me alive. I become completely pathological about these details. Something, somewhere has gone wrong. If he had the heart of a twenty-five year old, why did it suddenly fail him? It has to be someone's fault.

I work my way backward, studying all the paperwork from the hospital. I meet the ER doctor who worked on Marc. I meet the nurses. I ask them to tell me point by point, drug by drug, what they did for him, how they worked on him. I want to know how many times they used the "clapper."

I drive down to the fire station and interview the EMTs who were with Marc in our house and in the ambulance. What condition was Marc in when they found him at home? Was he conscious? Did he speak? Were there any last words? If I had been home, could I have saved him with CPR? How many minutes did it take them to get to our house? Could he have been saved if they had arrived sooner? Was there pain? Was there fear? Why did he die?

I call the pathologist who did the autopsy. He tells me eighty per-cent of Marc's left artery was blocked and thirty percent of the right artery, but the third artery and other vital organs had taken up func-tioning in their place. The pathologist can't tell me exactly what killed Marc. Nobody can. Twenty-five-year-old heart, my ass.

I call the cardiologist who gave him the thallium stress test. He re-minds me that Marc had failed the first treadmill.

At first I don't believe him. "Marc said he passed that test with flying colors, that you told him he had the heart of a twenty-five year old."

"It is quite common to fail the stress test, dozens fail each day. Often it is the machine's fault, a malfunction of some kind. So we did the test again, and just to be on the extra-safe side, with Marc's his-tory of dodgy genetics, we did a thallium treadmill."

I am totally confused. The doctor must be making it up, covering his tracks somehow to prevent a possible lawsuit, because Marc never lied to me. He would have told me about the machine screw-ing up, having to take a second test.

"But why would Marc tell me he had passed the test with flying colors if he hadn't?"

"Well, he certainly did fine on the second test, the thallium test," the doctor says. "Like I said, the first test is not nearly as conclusive."

I am stunned. "Are you sure? I mean, about the first test?"

The doctor says he is positive. He has Marc's file right in front of him, and he goes on to explain that often even a thallium stress test doesn't pick up the blockage, as this one hadn't. "Medicine's not per-fect," he says. "That's why we call it 'practicing.' " I feel like smack-ing him upside his head. It's grace that I've got him on the telephone and not in person. Why couldn't he "practice" on someone else's husband?

"So why didn't he tell me about failing the first test?"

The doctor actually laughs. "I can't help you on that one."

"So if he failed one and passed one, if you wanted to be so bloody *extra safe*, why the hell didn't you do a third test?" I yell into the phone before slamming it down.

I call Dan Wolfe again and again. Each time he tells me something different: his genetics. His diet. The fact that he smoked. Possible arrhythmia. He isn't sure.

I pace. I sit by Marc's side of the bed on the floor and read through all the books on his bedside table looking for clues. He was reading Simon Winchester's *The Professor and the Madman* and highlighted lines all the way through it. Ian McEwan's *Atonement, A Multitude of Sins* by Richard Ford and Bob Smith's *Hamlet's Dresser*. There is a stack of film scripts. I read every single one of the pages he marked. I throw the one book Joe lent him about health and aging through the window.

Searching through his calendar, I find he has appointments and meetings scheduled through January. On January 28, he has marked: *I's bill due?* Who is *I*? I don't know. My birthday is circled. He's got two trips to Brazil scheduled with Joe. I call Joe, who says he'll get his secretary to cancel Marc's flights and Brazilian appointments. I take our walks on the beach and in the hills. I weep.

Finally, after the morgue calls several times, I pick up Marc's ashes. Dan Wolfe arranged for the morgue and the crematorium. The ashes are in a small copper box. This has me confused. Marc was not a big man, but he was certainly too big to fit in this small space. I stare at the box. What am I to do with it? The man who has handed it to me puts it in a blue velvet bag with a pull string and asks me if he can walk me to my car. He smiles and I notice he has crooked teeth. He puts his hand on my shoulder and I curl down to avoid his touch.

"This is not my husband," I tell the man. "It can't be my husband. You have given me the wrong box. This is a mistake." I suck in a deep breath and stagger in the reception area of the funeral home, the bagged box between my legs. I am doubled over, and the pain everywhere is excruciating. The man puts his arm around my shoulders. The next thing I know I am in the car, the box on the seat next to me. Driving home, I wonder where Marc will live now. Where will we put him?

I awaken in the middle of the night, holding my heart. Working by ear in the darkness, I can still hear Marc's voice. It comes to me when I least expect it, like now, in the deepest, darkest part of night, wrapping me wild as he always did, his thick lips around my own, the sound of us knuckling me under, the pure outrageous sex of him. The base of my spine stretches up to him as if he is tunneled deep down inside of me. I move my foot to touch him and all there is is air. Where is he? Perhaps he is in the bathroom or downstairs banging out a tune? The possibility reassures me, like a soft, warm breeze of comfort. I struggle up then, the black waters colder as I come awake to the surface. I stretch my arm long across the bed, still digging out. Where has he gone?

As if it is the blare of the phone at some ungodly hour, I am shocked wide-awake. My heart sinks. All hope dies, and I am left bare in this moment of loss, realizing bare moment is all there is now. I grab hold of my heart again, cradle it gently in my hands.

Although Dafydd has been back in New York for only a week, he returns for Thanksgiving. There's a brace covering his knee and he is just beginning to move around slowly without his crutches.

"I'd like to walk on the Palisades," he says. It is a palm tree–lined pathway above the Coast Highway with a view of the ocean.

We drive over and walk for a while in silence, the perfect L.A. fall morning spread out as wide and blue as the Pacific Ocean. We can see twenty-six miles away to Catalina. I admire Dafydd's profile: his strong, angular jawline, his patrician nose, his high cheekbones. I love looking at him.

And then, as if he has somehow read my thoughts, unconscious even to me, he asks, "Do you ever think about my father?"

I feel caught. I look at him quizzically, pretending not to know he means Evan. As he gazes out to sea I am suddenly struck by just how much Dafydd really does look like Evan, and I realize I have been watching Evan all these years through Dafydd.

"What do you mean?" I ask, like the idiot I sometimes pretend to be since Marc died. So many questions I don't want to have to answer.

"Do you ever think about my so-called 'real' father? You know, what do you call him, my 'birth father,' Evan?" He stops walking then and shifts his sweatpants, which have tangled into the brace on his leg. Then he looks at me straight on and says, "I mean, were you ever in love with him?"

I am taken completely by surprise and am unsure how to answer him. On the face of it, it's a simple question. But based on my avoidance and secrecy about that time in my life, and the fact that in the past I have volunteered almost nothing to Dafydd, it's probably not such a simple question. His tone is insistent, almost angry. It is clear that Dafydd probably wants to know much more than he is asking.

As I think about it, it's rather unbelievable that through the years I've managed to get away with not having told him much about the disaster, or about Evan directly—and certainly not about my feelings for him. I have never even intimated to Dafydd how hard it was to leave my home: the light, the air, the mountains and, yes, mostly Evan. And I have never admitted I ran from home without letting Evan know I was pregnant.

I've not told Dafydd how hard it was to be pregnant at fifteen. I've never told him how Beti and Colin were so wonderful to take me in, and yet I could always feel their embarrassment.

Perhaps I should tell Dafydd that, along with everything else I am facing, I have actually been going over my long-ago past. I might tell him of the dream I had the night Marc died and that his so-called "real father" seems more present in my life at the moment than he has been since I left Wales. The truth is, even hearing Dafydd say his name sends a wave through me.

But instead, I answer Dafydd's question in the most basic way possible, giving him the simple answer. "Yes, I think of Evan quite often, and yes, I was in love with him for a long time." Even using the word *love* in relation to Evan sucks all the air out of me. I am close to panic.

"Have you heard from him recently?"

He knows about the checks that appear monthly, even now. Evan's "contribution," as he referred to it in one of his early notes to Gram passed on to me so many years ago. Dafydd knows also that Evan backed away because I wanted him to. This I've told him so that he would never feel rejected by his father.

"No," I say. "Why?"

"Well, I've been thinking about him. I'd like to meet him."

I remember the conversation I overheard between Dafydd and Hannah. Immediately there is part of me that wants to protect Marc's position in Dafydd's life. Ridiculous, but it makes me angry that Dafydd wants to meet Evan. I wonder if he has decided that his loss of Marc makes him need to place someone else there and Evan fits the bill.

But what is my anger all about? I was the one to sever relations with Evan, the one who left. Maybe the anger is because Evan gave up on me so easily. Still, I tell Dafydd what I know he wants to hear.

"I'm sure Evan would love to see you. He's always wanted to have the opportunity to know you." This is far more than I have ever given him of Evan.

"And another thing, Mom. You've got to snap out of this. The drinking, I mean. You've got to get back to work, your poetry. For your sake of course, but also for Hannah's. I can't keep flying back here as often as I have been. What about hiring somebody to help out? A nanny or a housekeeper, just for a while?"

I shake my head no. I start to turn away. "I can handle it."

"Mom. But you're not handling it. You're out of hand."

How dare he talk to me like this.

"I can't keep this pace up," Dafydd says.

I look over my shoulder. His eyes have filled with tears. "Please, Mom."

I turn around then and take him in my arms. We both cry.

When does this get easier?

This morning, more than two weeks since Dafydd has gone back to New York, our business manager calls to ask if I know a woman named Gabriella Purdue. I tell him she is a Brazilian singer Marc worked with years ago. Ed apologizes when he asks rather straightforwardly if I might have known what kind of relationship Marc had with her.

Confused, I repeat, "Marc worked with her years ago. She sang the title song for *The Yellow Door.*"

Ed pauses and then says, "She called this morning, to inquire if Marc had provided for her in his will."

At first I don't say anything, racking my brain. We had recently revised our wills, setting up a family trust for the kids.

"Gabriella Purdue called you? Why would she call you?"

"That I don't know, Alys. I thought you might be able to give me some answers."

"We haven't spoken to her in years." It must have been close to nine years ago that Marc did *The Yellow Door*. Why in the world would Gabriella think Marc had provided for her in his will?

I start to backtrack: Marc had gone to Brazil for the first time the summer before Hannah was conceived. Dafydd was at tennis camp, I was teaching that poetry workshop in Vermont. Marc had planned a month in Rio de Janeiro around our schedules to record an album of Brazilian jazz as well as the title song for *The Yellow Door*.

"I don't know what this is about, Ed."

"Alys, I feel terrible being caught in the middle. I feel awful that I am the one who has to bring this to your attention. But I've no choice."

Around the edge of my mind, I hear Beti's long-ago whispered warning about Marc and me spending time apart and how dangerous she thought it was. How many times had Marc gone to Brazil since his first trip? Dozens. He'd done several Brazilian albums. So it was two, maybe three times a year. Oh shit, maybe it was more.

"What did she say?"

"She said Marc told her that, if anything ever happened to him, she should call me. That I would see to it that she was looked after. She has a lawyer in Rio that feels she is due something. I didn't know what to say, Alys, or how to handle it. I thought perhaps you might be able to direct me. I told her I'd get back to her."

I am sliding, my mind swirling down.

It is routine now. At around two a.m., Hannah gets into bed with me. Tonight I hear her padding up the stairs. In her long white nightgown, she stands ghostlike for a moment at Marc's side of the bed. Although the light is not on, I am awake.

"Get in, Hannah," I say quietly. Her hands and feet are cold. She moves close to me and puts them under mine.

"Is it okay?" she asks. "Is it okay that I'm here?" She knows I don't sleep very well and she worries she is disturbing me. Since the phone call from Ed, I have been displaced, short-tempered, confused and angry though I am not sure with whom I am angry. Hannah has picked up on all of it.

"Fine," I say. I am glad she is here to fill the empty spot. I rub her back until I hear the soft, even breathing that lets me know she is asleep. In the morning, as always, she asks, "How in the world did I get in here?"

I say, "You walked."

"I don't remember."

"That's okay. I like it that you show up in the middle of the night. You're always welcome."

She smiles and says, "You're always welcome in my bed, too."

"Thanks," I say.

I think about how young she is to be going through all of this. Just eight. I remember the lonely, terror-filled nights for me at eight. I am glad to be here for her. I am glad to be able to comfort her, remembering how my own mam couldn't comfort me.

"I'm sure I don't know what Ms. Purdue is on about," I tell Ed when we speak again.

"What do you want me to say to her?" he asks.

"Just tell her . . . tell her you didn't get ahold of me."

Trying to remember exactly how many times and how long Marc stayed in Brazil, I look over his calendar, go over his receipts for the last two years.

After the first trip when Gabriella recorded "And Then There Was Love," Marc hadn't mentioned her. Was that good or bad? Had he nothing to hide or everything?

I call Phillípe. "Something rather unusual has come up. I wonder if you might know why Gabriella Purdue would be calling Ed Meyers?"

"Ah," Phillípe says. And then nothing.

Shit.

"Are you in touch with her?" I try to sound casual.

"Well"—he pauses—"yes, I am."

"So?"

"I, ah, don't know what to say," Phillípe stutters.

"Have you spoken to her recently?"

"I have."

"So?"

"Well I called her, of course, to let her know about Marc's—"

"Oh," I say too quickly. I am cold. That same death-defying cold that I've known since childhood. The blood gone from my fingers. Dizzy. "When was that?"

"Several months now. I don't remember exactly. Not long after it happened, I guess."

"Oh." The light in the room seems darker. Sucked down, I hold on to the arm of a chair as I slip into it. "Were Marc and Gabriella in touch?"

"I think they were," Phillípe says. Now I can tell for sure Phillípe knows more than he is saying.

"So?" I ask again.

"So *what*, Alys?" Phillípe answers almost angrily.

"So why did she call Ed Meyers, Phillípe? What's going on? What aren't you telling me?"

"Aly-ese." I hate his goddamned French arrogance, his phony-baloney French bullshit. I've never trusted him. I asked Marc a million times what he saw in Phillípe.

"He's a class act," Marc had said. "And a good musician and my friend."

"Shit!" I scream into the phone, suddenly seeing it all.

"Aly-ese, I don't want to get involved in this. I can't."

"What do you mean you don't want to get involved? You're obviously already involved and Marc's not here now, in case you haven't noticed. It's just you and me and now Ed Meyers. So you better tell me. Do you hear me, Phillípe? What is it exactly you're afraid to get involved with, Phillípe? What was it between Gabriella and Marc?"

Phillípe doesn't answer.

"Come on, Phillípe. What does she have on Marc? Tell me why Gabriella is calling *my* business manager. Why does she think Marc provided for her in his will?"

And then I ask the question I've been afraid of. "Was he having an affair with her?"

Silence on the other end.

"Phillípe, answer me!"

"They have a child together, Alys. Gabby and Marc have a child Hannah's age," he says in a resigned voice. "Maybe she's a little younger."

Dark. I can hear someone far away calling, "Sir, help me." I cry out the same thing but my mouth, my nose, my ears are full of cold, thick stuff and nothing comes out. I can't breathe well. The air won't go in too far. My arms are pinned to my side, but I can still feel the shilling in my hand.

CHAPTER THREE

Mam calls me home from Hallie's. I hear the bell loud and clear. We are in the middle of playing dress-up in Hallie's attic, our favorite game. Hallie's long blond hair is pulled back, and on top of her head is a crown we made with aluminum paper and hair grips. She has a white petticoat pulled up under her arms, and she is wearing her mam's red high heels. The petticoat keeps falling down because she doesn't have bosoms. Hallie says she's glad. "If you have bosoms, you can't sleep on your tummy. Can you imagine? I could never fall asleep on my back." Finally we hike her petticoat up with a tie from an old bathrobe.

I have on a pink tutu that is kind of small on me. And of course my hair is in a tight bun. I even have pink tights. We are pretending to be famous Russian ballet dancers, which is what we are going to be when we grow up. We have made a pact. We are going to live in Moscow and dance in Red Square.

I love playing at Hallie's house because her mam never bothers us. She lets us alone for hours. Sometimes she'll even set a snack outside the door for us: milky tea, Marmite and butter spread on sweet biscuits. Only a whisper through a crack in the door to tell us she's brought it up.

Hallie's mam and da never holler at each other. In fact, they are lovey-dovey, kissing all the time. Niko, Hallie's brother, is still really little. He stays out of our way mostly. Maybe once or twice a visit, he will crawl up the stairs and push the door open. We see him stick his head round, but he never says anything. He is just two.

Hallie lives down the row, three houses away from mine. When my mam wants me home she rings the bell. It is my gram's bell from when she was a little girl, the same one her mam used to call her home, a large bell with a black wooden handle. It is so loud you can hear it down the road.

I love when Gram tells me the story of her mam, Great-gram, and how she used to live on a farm way up in the high country, North Wales. Real farm people, they were.

"They had so many sheep on their hillside, lambs in the spring of course, covering everywhere like white tulips. They needed two sheepdogs to fetch them in at night. And huge mountains, not measly hills like we have here. In the winter they are always covered in heavy snow. One time, my da took me up to spend the whole summer with his people. Left me there all on my own. They are the ones taught me how to milk a goat and dig a potato. I'd be out first thing in the morning till last thing at night, the stars lighting my way home. I remember that summer as if it was last week. The wildflowers were over my head and I used to lie down in them and watch the clouds scudding across the blue like it was the ocean."

The way Gram's parents met is my favorite story, and I make Gram tell me again and again.

"Great-granda was with his da. They'd come up the mountain to try and round up some men to work the new mines in the valley here. Great-granda was coming out of the pub the evening they arrived. He was tall and handsome, a strut to his walk."

I love this part. Gram's voice gets real deep when she gets to this part in the story.

"He almost bumped headlong into Great-gram. Imagine it. She was walking home from a friend's house in a fluffy pink dress, her hair piled high on her head. It was love at first sight for both of them. The bad news was, three days later, Great-granda had to go back to Merythr. Great-gram tried to talk him into staying, but he was already working in the mine here and couldn't."

So Great-gram wrote long romantic letters to Great-granda every single solitary day for months, getting answers back each day.

"And I guess when you are in love the way they were in love, after a while letters, even long poetic letters, just aren't enough. She couldn't stand being without him a moment longer. So, without telling a soul, she took a horse from the barn, saddled it up and, with only a change of clothes, food for one day and her Bible, rode off through the mountains, telling herself it would only be for a fortnight. But fourteen days later she wrote her parents, telling them she was staying in Merythr Tydfil for good." Gram gets a faraway look in her eyes when she tells the story.

"So you see, girl, farming's in my blood," Gram says, pointing at the lush earth she calls her "Victory Garden" of tomatoes.

And I know my granda must still be in her blood, too. Because even though he's been gone for fifteen years, Gram still says, "It'll always be him and only him that I love."

I don't know much about Mam's family. Except that her mam had died early on of tuberculosis and her da had remarried and Mam never much liked her stepmother. She didn't talk about them much and we never saw them. I have her mam's hair, she says. Unruly and dark.

By the time I get home from Hallie's, there is a crowd in the kitchen. My older brother and Mam, Gram and Da. Auntie Beryl is there, too, in one of her wild full skirts and her jangling earrings, gypsylike, her curly red hair tied back in a scarf. I love it when she comes down the valley for a visit. It isn't often enough for my liking. I'd be happy seeing Auntie Beryl every day, and I know Gram would be, too. But that isn't possible since Auntie Beryl lives way up in the Brecon Beacons and doesn't drive. She takes a coach everywhere.

Gram and Beryl have been friends since they were my age, best friends like Hallie and me. When they want to tell secrets they speak to each other in Welsh, both having learned it when they were little.

"It's a sadness not to be able to speak it round the house nor in the village now, regular like. Back home, we all spoke Welsh."

And that's not all. Gram tells how Auntie Beryl's family had a whole flock of sheep when the two of them were little. And Gram always says she was needing that kind of wilderness, and so whenever she was around they let her help herd those little lambs. Auntie Beryl sold the sheep and the farm after her parents died, and moved up the valley because of a broken heart. Gram never actually says how it got broke, but I think it was something having to do with a man.

When I come in, I can hear the whole group of them arguing in the kitchen. It seems they are always arguing these days, especially my brother, Parry. Used to be whenever you saw Parry he'd be quietly drawing up a storm, or painting a portrait. Now he's hardly home for meals and his papers and canvas lie in a pile. Auntie Beryl and Gram are both unhappy Parry gave up the offer for art school.

"It's a real shame, 'tis," Gram says. "Don't like him joining up in that weary work down the mine one bit. Don't care what Arthur says. It's dark and depressing and it will bleed Parry's spirit. I'm sure of it. No talking to either Arthur or Parry, though."

"Sell his paintings, he should. Not his heart," Auntie Beryl agrees.

"I'm not that good, Beryl. It'll wait. Seems to be more important matters at the moment than watercolors," Parry tells her.

I can see Parry now, pushing his fingers through his thick yellow hair. "Why is it you won't listen to reason, Da?" He is pacing round the kitchen and seems frantic, like Hallie's kitty gets when we manage to trap him in some corner, the way the kitty turns his head round and round and then back again, looking for some way out, but not finding one.

I miss the old Parry, walking me and Hallie to school every day, having time to do that. He doesn't tickle me or play hide-and-seek. He doesn't even smile much anymore, either. Yesterday when I asked him to twirl me, he was stiff.

Right now he's on about another slag heap that was supposed to have slipped up the Rhondda in the forties.

"You read it killed a child. And more recently, what about that other slide up there? When it slid, the force of it took down the skating rink. What makes anyone think you can pile slag so high near where folks gather, and it'll be a safe hill of coal trash? Coal slag piled that high is dangerous no matter where it's piled. Jesus, Da, you can still see the gap 'tween the buildings on the main road," Parry says, shaking his head like that might clear everything up. "This isn't like you. Mam promises you're a man of reason. So come on now, Da. Show us some reason!"

It's the same stuff over and over, day in and out, 'bout the National Coal Board being bandits and Da trusting them over Parry or Auntie Beryl.

Mam stands like always 'tween Da and Parry. She stretches her hands out on Parry's shoulders, but he jerks away.

Sometimes the yelling is about whose responsibility 'tis, Da's or the coal board's. Or how Da isn't listening to Parry, or Parry's acting like a bully. Today they are yelling about the man from the coal board who was sent round to check if there was a creekbed beneath the coal tip where the men are piling the slag that's behind the school. Auntie Beryl says the inspector was a lazy sod for not really doing his job right, or he would have found the dirty spring. She is telling Parry to get the men to strike.

"A strike will put pressure on them, Parry. Talk to them. Most of them are fathers. Tell them they've more at stake then just their jobs." Her eyes glow like two bright flames against her red hair. Auntie Beryl looks as if she is on fire.

But Parry needs no pushing. He's wanted to strike since first the rumors started that the tip was in danger of collapsing. But Da doesn't want to go up against the coal board.

"What's happened to you, man?" Parry says. "What's happened to the da that used to stick up for what's what? I want to know where that man has gone. I want to know where my da is."

"Parry, stop it. Get ahold of yourself," Mam says. "I might ask you where my sweet boy is. The boy that thought your da could do no wrong. He is only doing his job, protecting his men—who you are now one of, in case you forgot—as well as protecting his family." Mam looks over at Da. "Right, Da." Her voice is shaky. "Go back to your painting, Parry. You'd be better off taking that offer from the university. You are happier when you are painting, regular. Leave this fight to your da."

I think Parry is starting to cry. His eyes are red-rimmed and full of tears. But then I can see that it is rage. Gram comes over and stands next to him, her hand holding back Parry's arm.

Just then Beti comes in through the kitchen door, not knowing what's what and unbuttoning her cardigan like it was a normal afternoon with everyone gathered in the kitchen having a cup of tea. She smiles at Auntie Beryl across the room.

"Ta, very much for the Welsh cakes, Gram," she says, handing Gram the empty plate from out of her tan satchel. "I ate every single one at work."

My sister is all the way through her schooling. She is the eldest, ten years older than I. Two years older than Parry. She's never around, hardly, and has no time for me or Hallie when we try to get her attention. She loves Colin. In fact, Beti would live at Colin's if Mam let her.

"Set an example for your sister, Beti," Mam always tells her about things concerning Colin. I never know exactly what she means about that or anything. Mam and Beti puzzle me. I want to be able to read their minds like I can read Gram's.

Mam doesn't even say hello to Beti. The talk keeps going on about mine stuff.

"Colin says he won't walk," Beti tells Parry. Colin and Beti are engaged. "I don't blame him," she adds. "You're asking a lot of the men, Parry."

"Where'd you come from, anyway?" Parry asks, looking over at her. "No one asked you for your input, Beti. Colin's a bloody idiot, he is. You can just go to your room, like. We don't need you here, pretending you know what's what."

"Parry, stop it! Colin's a good man, he is, and Beti loves him," Mam says.

"They're both bloody fools," Parry says, turning his back on Gram and Beti.

"Well, I'll be off to Colin's, then," Beti says. "I'll tell him what you said, Parry. I'm sure he'll be very pleased. We're all incredibly pleased with how bloody fierce you've become. It does us all a world of good. What I wonder, Parry, is what you're really afraid of. The mining work's not big enough for the likes of your anger. Sorry, Mam. I can't stand this rubbish or the way you both let him go on about it." She shakes her head in Parry's direction.

I want to go with her bad as I've ever wanted to do anything. I don't feel well. My tummy is hurting and my arms feel heavy.

"I'll come home after supper, Mam. Maybe by then you will have sorted this all out and there'll be some quiet."

"Not bloody likely," Parry says, throwing his arms away from Gram's hold and making a fist. "Shit! What is it with you two? For God's sake, Mam, you're not gonna tell me you're protecting Da's retirement over the possibility of God knows how many lost lives?"

"Jesus, Parry," Da says under his breath. "Get control of yourself. You're over the top, boy. Like I've told you half a dozen times, the National Coal Board is neither my friend nor my adversary."

"You can't be in the middle," Parry says. "On this one you've got to take a side—the right side."

"But they should be," Beryl says on the tail of Parry. "Your adversary, I mean."

"Well, Beryl, they're not. They are merely my bosses. They pay me to walk that middle line."

"Oh, Arthur. Dear, dear Arthur. You can't know what you're say-ing. Wait a moment. Follow me, bear with me." Beryl straightens her-self up tall as she is, which is taller than Da. She rearranges her skirt and pulls her blouse down tight.

"Let's just say for the moment, Arthur, Rita, that there is a stream running beneath that particular tip as some say." I lie down on the floor, the cool lino against my face. There is a breeze coming in from under the kitchen door. "That in fact, the flooding we experienced be-fore is due to runoff from underground that streambed."

"We've been over this, Beryl, get to the point," Da says.

I wish I had stayed at Hallie's. Wish I hadn't heard the bell. Why did they even bother calling me home? None of them have noticed me. I want some tummy tea and a biscuit. I pull myself up off the floor and try to be noticed.

"Just exactly where do you think all that muck is going to go? On the off chance that indeed there is a streambed under that tip, and it does slip, well, it comes down straight and it comes down fast, Arthur. And the only thing 'tween the top of that tip and Moy Road is the school. Can you imagine what that would mean? On the off chance, that is, Arthur, just let your mind go."

Auntie Beryl seems worn-out. Her voice sounds hoarse. Her beau-tiful smooth skin seems loose and saggy.

"Those are your facts, Arthur. I know them. Parry knows them. We've already handed the headmistress a petition stating the danger. But we won't be able to close the school down unless we get the NCB behind us. We need your help."

She pauses, waiting, I guess, for Da to say something. He doesn't. So she says, "But mind you, if I have to talk to each mother and fa-ther myself, you better believe I will. Because you listen here, Arthur. My facts say there is indeed a spring underlying that tip and we are standing here right now not doing a bloody thing, when it could go any moment, and it scares the life out of me. But it's not my life, Arthur. It's Alys' life at risk and the lives of all those children at Pant-glas School. If something happens to even one of those children, could you live with it, Arthur?"

By this time I am up close to the group of them, and I bury my face in Gram's neck. Auntie Beryl is scaring me.

"Rita," Da says to Mam. I look at Da. He looks at me and shakes his head. "Do you think I would actually allow Alys to go to school each morning if I thought there was any real threat of that tip slipping? Please, Rita." Da runs his fingers through his graying hair, then bows his head. He puts his elbows up on the table and buries his face in his hands. "She's my daughter as well as yours."

Mam comes away from the sink to Da. She puts one hand on the back of his neck, the other on his shoulder. She says softly, "Well, how do you explain the slimy black muck Alys tracked in the same day Mrs. Symmons complained her daughter walked through it on her way to school?" She sits down and turns to face him, putting the washing-up rag down on the table.

"I just don't know." Da shakes his head. "I can't explain anyone else's experience, Rita. I 'spect it's hysteria. You know how women and children in groups can get." His head is still down on his bent arms.

"Arthur, please. It can't just be hysteria, all of us begging you here. You can't really mean that we are all just hysterical?"

"What I mean is that all of us are under such enormous stress that we're not coping properly. I think it means we should let things go a bit. See what happens," Da says, looking over at me again. "Let's not go over this any longer."

"Mam," I say quietly from behind Gram. "I'm not feeling well."

Mam pushes away from Da and sighs. "Come, Alys, let me feel your head, then. Don't be standing on the cold lino with no shoes, like." Mam puts her lips on my forehead and I can feel the soft flick of her hair on my face as she moves her lips around.

"You've got fever." Mam touches the back of my neck. I want to stop the bad feelings 'tween Mam and Da. I want Mam to let me stay home from school. I want Parry to get along with Da. I want all of this to go away and the house to be quiet like it was a long, long time ago when there was no trouble with the tip.

"Right. I think you do have fever. That's all we need now, a sick little girl." She hugs me up a little. "Now upstairs and in your jammies and to bed. I'll be there in no time with a cup of tea. Choose a book and I'll read you off to sleep. Go now, Alys."

As I drag my feet out of the kitchen I hear Mam say, "I hope you're right about all this Arthur. I only hope you're right."

I am home from school for almost a week. My sore throat and cough won't go away. I've had fever for three days but now it is just the sore throat and I feel yucky.

Parry is glad I am home. "Keep her in bed, Mam. It's the safest place for her right now."

"Parry, you can't go on like this, ramming your point home to Da. He's doing his best."

Sometimes when Parry is around it feels like there's not enough air.

"Your da knows what's what with that tip. He's said so and he ought to, like. If you're to continue down the mine, you need to let Da worry about that tip."

"Yeah, right," Parry says, making a snorting sound that looks like his anger escaping from a red-faced balloon. He shakes his head. "He ought to know what's what, and he actually does, though he won't act on it. Mind you, it comes out in the end same as not caring. It's like with the mural I painted on the side of the school. Remember, Mam, a few months back? He will never admit how much that mural, showing the hardships of a miner's life, helped get the boys and him our pay rise."

The mural is huge and Parry painting it had made Da angry. Da said it could have cost him his job.

"You're either a painter or a miner. You put us all in jeopardy by being both."

But the mural is still there on the side of the school, the three paintings: the big black mine, a miner sick in bed with black lung, a man under the wheels of a mining cart. The man under the cart was the way Granda died. Gram had told me the story after Parry finished the mural.

When I am sick, I want to be in the parlor, where the telly is. But it's a rule. The parlor is saved for best. There's nothing to do. I am making stories up in my head about being rescued by a handsome prince on a horse or by a friendly giant and riding away real fast from this family. I am counting black sheep backward from one hundred. I can't read, my eyes hurt too much. There is absolutely nothing else to do. I miss Hallie.

"Can Hallie come over after school today?" I ask.

"If you're not well enough to go to school, you're not well enough to have a friend over," Mam says sternly.

"But I don't have fever anymore."

"We'll see what the day brings."

The day doesn't bring Hallie.

The next morning Da comes into my room. When he leans over me and feels my head, I can smell the soap on his hands. Those hands of his, never quite clean, rough as dry cement and the black coal dust always under his nails.

I don't open my eyes. He shakes me lightly with those hands. "Get up," he says, softly but firmly. "You're fine. You're going to school today."

I sit up slowly. Da seems so tall from where I sit. Part of me wants to feel fine but I don't. "I'm dizzy," I say.

"Dizzy doesn't mean sick," he says. "Get up now and have a wash. Your mam will be making you breakfast and she'll be getting your dinner ready in your lunchbox. I'll walk you to school." His mind seems made up.

I move slowly. When I go to the toilet I feel really dizzy. When I swallow, it feels like I have knives in my throat. I practically crawl down the stairs. Through the crack in the kitchen door, I can see Parry and Da. But this morning they are not yelling for a change. At least not yet. Mam is at the stove, with her back to them.

"Rita, I'll be taking Alys to school myself. It won't do for her to be staying at home with all the commotion going on down there. We have to set an example, like. And that's the final word." Da raises his thumb and nods.

Da puts his cap on and turns to Parry. "I'm tired to the bone of you always being on the other side. Sometimes I think it's just to rile me. Try to distinguish yourself in some other way, Parry."

Parry clenches a fist and moves toward Da, but Da puts his hand up. "No more this morning. I've had enough."

"What kind of example do you think you're setting?" Parry's loud voice makes echoes in my achy head. "Stupidity is all I can see."

"Yours, boy," Da says.

"I'm not listening to you like you're not listening to me."

"Another word and you can find somewhere else to live."

"Arthur, please," Gram says, coming down the stairs into the kitchen. "It's too early in the morning for this."

"You're gonna throw me out. Is that it, old man?"

"You push. You've been pushing me hard for some time now. More, it seems like, since you decided to quit your painting and go down the mine."

"Now, Arthur, don't say something you'll regret after," Gram says.

"Parry, Da, leave it alone, please," Mam adds.

"I'm in the wrong job—that's for sure," Parry almost spits. "Going down the mine was for you, Da. So I could be just like my da. Walk in my old man's footsteps. But I don't want to be like you anymore. And truth be told, I'm bloody sick of myself. If I stay around this house, I'll turn out just like you, Da. Scared to do the right thing. Fuck you, Da. Fuck you and your tip. Fuck that filthy mine that sucks us all dry. And most of all, fuck whatever the fear is that's got hold of you." Parry turns his back and slams out the kitchen door.

I come down then and lean against the door. "I still don't feel well. I can't swallow and my head is hot. Please don't make me go to school, Mam."

Mam wipes her hands on her apron, comes over to me, feels my forehead with the back of her hand and then reaches down and kisses it. "You do feel a little warm, girl. Arthur . . ."

Da turns away, ignoring Mam's pleas. He speaks into the air. "I felt her head a while ago, and she's fine. She's going to school."

"You know, Da, sometimes I wonder about you," Mam says. "There must have been another way to have handled Parry, like. He's trying to help."

Da turns his back on Mam and Gram and goes to the kitchen sink to wash his hands. "Alys, eat up. We're going in five minutes."

"Come on now, Arthur. 'Tis an absolutely miserable day out. Look there, the mist gathering so low in the valley. When I went out to fetch the milk bottles, I couldn't see my own steps back, and it's cold, like, too. Go on then. Have a look if you don't believe me. You can't make Alys go to school in this weather. She doesn't feel right, Arthur. She's still feverish."

"She's going, Rita. I've made up my mind."

Chapter Four

October 20, 1972

The door bangs shut behind us. The hard drizzle feels like pinpricks against my face. And the dark quiet is too cold and damp even for birds. I trail Da, slow, hoping he will change his mind and let me go home. It's not fair.

"Come along then, Alys. Don't dawdle now. You don't want to be late."

"Da . . ."

"Come now, it's the last day before half term. You'll have a whole week to get better in," he says.

And then I'll play with Hallie every day, I will. No one to stop me.

"Button up now, Alys. Your mam's right. 'Tis bitter. You don't want to catch your death, like."

At Hallie's, Da lets me go knock and we wait on the steps. Mr. Ames, who lives just down the road, appears.

"Trouble today?" he asks.

"Expecting some. Hope not, but I'm prepared if there is," Da says.

I want to turn home. Why is Da making me go? My head hurts. My neck hurts. I wish Parry was walking me to school. He'd let me go home. He's a good brother like that.

Mr. Ames looks at his watch.

"It's half past the hour, man. We're late for the shift."

"Know it. You go, Ames. I'll be along," Da says, giving him a slap on the back.

Hallie comes out then, her yellow hair in pigtails tied with red ribbons Beti just gave her when she turned eight a few weeks ago. I am nine months older. I hug her and her lunch pail digs into my side. "What you got there, Hallie?"

"It's a ham roll Mam made. Where's yours, then?"

"I was staying home again, but Da made me come out and I forgot it."

"I'll share mine," Hallie says, taking my hand.

Da reaches into his pocket and gives me a shilling for milk.

Here comes Evan.

"On my way to the mine," he shouts, waving at Da, looking like a ghost walking toward us in the mist. "There's my girl. Pretty as a picture." I look up quickly and smile at Evan, Parry's best friend. It doesn't seem like he is mad at Da, like Parry is. They shake hands.

I ask to see Hallie's ham roll, whispering in her ear, "Parry said yesterday Auntie Beryl was holding a sign telling people to take their children home."

"I saw it. What's it mean?"

I shrug.

"My da calls your auntie Beryl a 'do-gooder.' " Hallie laughs. "Says she's always getting into the middle of things, stirring things up, like."

"Well, she's not. She's just, well, she's Auntie Beryl, that's all. Gram says she's trying to make the world a safer place for us," I argue.

No matter what Hallie's da or anyone else says about her, I love Auntie Beryl, wild skirts, red hair and all.

But just now there is no one wild around or anyone we don't know. No signs. Just mams and das dropping off. Billy and Bonnie Sykes, Peter Davies, Sarah Keane, Lola Finnian making their way through the school doors.

"It seems quiet enough," Da says, pushing his cap back on his head, sounding pleased. I look up at him, a last try. He can tell I don't want to go in. "Remember now, 'tis the last day, today is, before break. And 'tisn't even a full day. You can do it. Off you go, now, Alys. Be a good girl, then."

His soft lips and rough cheek against mine as he kisses it make me feel better.

"You and Hallie walk straight home from school, hear."

In the playground everyone is talking about the fog. Mrs. Morgan rings the handbell, saying she thinks with all this fog it is as beautiful as it gets in the valley. We queue up in class order and the girls go through the side entrance straight to Assembly, me marching behind Hallie. It's Friday; we have Assembly Hall on Friday. We sing "All Things Bright and Beautiful," and then we go back to our classes.

Mrs. Morgan gives paints out to each of us. Bobby and Dai go out for the rain gauge. That's my favorite job. I did it Monday, before I took ill, when there had been three inches of rain. This morning, the gauge registers one and a half.

A call comes for "dinner children." These are the children who are getting milk. So I stand to give my shilling to the dinner lady, asking Hallie for hers.

"I'll do my own," she says.

"No, I'll do it for you, I will. You're sharing your ham roll."

"But I want to do my own," Hallie says. "I want to queue up. I'll do yours. You're the one's ill, like."

I try to grab Hallie's shilling from her. I want to fetch her milk to show how much I love her. I hold on to the edge of the coin, pulling hard as Mrs. Morgan calls out our names, marking the register.

"Come along now. One of you's enough," the dinner lady says, putting her arm around my shoulder. "No need for your squabbling, then."

In the hallway, everyone is talking. When Hallie looks away, I pull her shilling so hard it falls to the ground.

"Look what you've done, now, Alys!"

Hallie is down on her knees searching when a terrible roar starts, screaming low over us, the roar swooping low to swallow me. Windows crash in, rush of black water, mud, a tidal wave. It comes and comes higher, higher, till I lose sight of Hallie.

I hear screaming. Then all around is black and still.

Dark.

Hallie. Hallie.

"Sir, help me!" A voice. Far away, underground, not Hallie. I try to call out—but no sound comes. No sound. Something tight, up against me. Pushing into me. Thick, cold. In my mouth, my nose. I blow, cough. Nothing happens. Thick stuff. No air. Can't breathe. Pinned tight. Arms can't move. Legs hurt. Blurry. Cold, wet. Someone screaming . . . "Help me! Help me!"

*   *   *

I wake up in a strange bed, hooked up to wires and tubes. A dim light in the corner of the room. Seconds pass and Gram is there, hanging over me, patting me. "Ssssssh," she says. I smell her talc.

"It's all right. You're safe, Alys. You are safe."

"Where's Hallie? Where's Hallie?"

Gram pats me still and whispers, "Ssssssh." But I can't stay still. Finally, she gets into the bed with me and pulls me into her arms, rocking me. "Don't move now, Alys. Ssssssh."

"Where's Mam!"

"It's all right, dearie. Your mam is with your da. It's all right. She needs to be there now."

I cry, my whole body shaking so hard my bones feel like they've come loose. I cannot stop. I am wet and so cold. Someone comes in and turns on another light, brighter. She has on a small white cap. I am rolling my head from side to side.

She bends over me. "I'm Nurse Banwell," she says.

My chest hurts, my stomach. I am still crying and she is so close, her hot, sour breath on me and she is smiling down at me as if everything is okay. She has large yellow teeth and bright red lipstick. I might throw up.

"I'm going to give you a little jab in your bum. Don't you move now and it won't hurt a bit." She wipes me, my mouth, my hands. "Soon you'll go off to sleep again. Your gram will be right here. She'll be right next to you all through the night. You sleep well now, and don't worry about a thing. You're fine," she says. "You're safe now."

Don't want to sleep. Need to find Hallie. I just want Hallie, that's all. Just Hallie.

Before I can say stop, I feel the sharp jab.

I can't say it out loud, but I'm thinking that I might swallow my tongue and choke. I need my hand so I can hold my tongue, keep it from going down my throat. "Gram . . ." I try to raise my body so I can see the other children. My eyes are blurry. My head, so heavy. There are voices, whispering, fading into each other. . . .

"Gram, where's Hallie, please?" My own voice sounds funny.

"Don't talk anymore, Alys dear. Just close your eyes and have a little rest now."

I am trying to remember . . . the small sound of Hallie's shilling hitting the floor. A ping, and then, "Look what you've done, Alys!" So angry at me. Hallie's shilling. Dropped it. Don't have it. No, don't have it now. But I have my own. Hallie's mad. The wave coming toward me . . . the thick, black wave covering . . . "Hallie . . . don't be mad at me!"

When they take me home from the hospital two weeks later, Mam and Gram make my bed up in the parlor so I will be near the telly and the electric fire, and close to the kitchen. Everyone trying to get my mind off . . . It is still really hard to sit by myself. Mam makes me chicken soup, but she doesn't have time to sit with me. She tells me she is sorry but she's trying to help out in the village. Each time she leaves the house I am afraid she will never come back. I make do, staring as the light changes through the stained glass window, the colors a prism of comfort.

Gram tells me Mam is working with some of the other mothers. Helping them clean house and cook because they are so broken after all they have lost. Gram tells me to be patient with her.

When she's not working down at Hoover, Beti reads to me. She is reading me *Love Is a Many Splendored Thing*. Beti wears short skirts and sleeveless low white blouses just like the girl in the book. And sometimes you can see her bra strap. She is so pretty, Beti is. I love the way she smells, too. Lemons. She tells me not to read ahead. Mostly, I don't. She and Colin bring me a stuffed cat to cuddle and boiled sweets to suck on. Colin massages my feet.

The house is so quiet without Parry. He's taken to staying at a girl's house, name of Gillian. Mam doesn't like her at all. Calls her a scrubber. I want to ask Mam what that is, but I don't.

Finally, a few mornings, Parry sneaks in when Da's gone, bringing me coloring books and Smarties from the shop. He says over and over again how sorry he is about Hallie. He sets up his easel and lays out his paints. It is almost like the old days when I was little and he was always around, sketching me, sketching Mam, telling jokes. But in the end, he crumples up his sketch papers and tears his canvas from the easel.

Evan comes too. He brings me stacks and stacks of library books. Sitting close, his dark hair longer now and his blue eyes so bright. He reads me poems by Idris Davies, who he says was a great poet and lived just round by Rhymney. They are beautiful, and I remember the lines "Let rapture conquer sadness, / For life is but a day; / Let there be love and laughter / Oh hearts, be glad, be gay." One thing is for sure: I won't ever be happy again. I can't imagine it. No. I can't imagine what I will ever do without Hallie.

It's been three weeks since the tip slid. One evening Colin stops by to pick up Beti and I hear him say that tomorrow there will be a service for all the children—a mass funeral, he calls it.

Gram makes our supper. "It's nothing fancy, a pot of soup. Really just potatoes, carrots and onions boiled up with lamb bones, but you're welcome to stay, Colin."

Mam sits, not like her, letting Gram serve us at the table.

It tastes like dishwater to me. I don't dare complain. But I can't swallow proper, like.

He stands at the door. Da, towering over us with his hands in the pockets of his wooly gray cardigan. His hair gone long and wild. His beard, scruffy.

"I can't go," Da says quietly to all of us. "Besides, someone needs to stay with Alys."

I wait. I am waiting for some nice word from Mam. But she doesn't even look up.

But Gram does. She says, "Arthur, you must. I'll stay with Alys. It won't do for you to stay behind."

"What about you, Beti? Why don't you stay with Alys? I'll go with Da. He'll need me," Mam says. "I'd appreciate that, Beti, I would."

Beti looks at Da, and then she looks at me. She puts her hand on top of Colin's and says quietly, "I need to go. Colin's little cousin Peter was among them. . . . I want to go, pay my respects, like. Sorry, Mam." She takes Colin's hand, and biting her lip, she starts to cry and quickly looks away.

I start to cry, too. I can't help it. I've only been home from hospital a short time, still with nightmares: the sirens, the wet, cold muck, the sight of parents digging wildly for their children and no Hallie. I am still mostly in a wheelchair and the arms of it get in the way of the table, so I have to reach way over to my soup bowl.

Da comes full into the room then and stands next to me. He pats me lightly on the head and leans over, picking up the spoon, feeding me the soup. I swallow hard and look up at him. His eyes are full of tears.

"It won't always hurt this bad, Alys," he says, looking me straight in the face. "It won't always feel this hard." He pats my head again and his hand falls to his side, limp and useless. He turns away and starts to sob. Long, heaving sobs that make his whole huge body shake, lifting his hands to cover his face.

Mam starts to cry. She is so small, like a bird. It is the only time since everything has come apart that I've seen her cry.

And Da doesn't go to chapel. He stays home with me, sitting in the parlor, me propped with pillows on the settee, him with his hands 'tween his knees and his head down, the low mist and fog outside settled once again just like it had on the day of the disaster. And it is so cold, the draft coming in under the doors and through the cracks of the windows. I pull a blanket round me tight as I can. I wonder if I will feel this cold in my bones, in my heart, everywhere, for the rest of my life.

We listen to the broadcast of the funeral. "Lord Jesus Christ, we tenderly commit the bodies of our dear children to the ground. Earth to earth, ashes to ashes, dust to dust. All in all, one hundred sixteen little hearts . . ."

I keep my eyes glued to him, missing most of what Reverend Land says—except for the bit about "No one knows why some are taken and some left behind, and though it seems useless and without meaning, God works in mysterious ways. We must, in the face of tragedy, above all else, keep faith and, more importantly, hope. Especially for all of us left behind, in particular the children who were spared."

Da looks up at me then, and with the back of his hand, he wipes away the tears. "Sorrier than I've ever been about anything, ever, I am about this, Alys. Please believe me."

I don't know what to say.

Da closes his eyes.

It is so quiet. The arguments making the noise of our house for so many months, over. Nothing the same. Mam, Gram, Parry not painting and thrown out of the house now. Hallie gone forever. Everything ruined.

But he is my da. I look at him. The deep lines on his face. The dark under his eyes. He is my sad da.

And then finally I say, "I do, Da. I believe you."

He raises his head, looking surprised. He reaches out his hand and touches my foot. "Ta, Alys. Ta, very much."

CHAPTER FIVE

FEBRUARY 1973

Although Da goes to the mine, he hasn't been out in the village for a long time, months and months. He is a ghost, coming up behind me, scaring me with his own silence.

Mrs. Elwood stops by to see Gram and I hear her say, "Keep him away for as long as you can. They are vicious about him. Can't see that he will ever be forgiven. Not in this village, with so many families having lost children, him being the tip manager and all."

Parry, too, coming round early one morning. So quiet, like a low growl, he says, "You killing bastard. All of them dead because of you."

"Did you come round just to spread your hate?"

"And my germs," Parry says, spitting on the ground near Da's feet and turning to walk away.

From then on, the house, except for the telly, is even quieter. Mam and Da hardly speaking, me tucked up in the parlor, a mangled mess, inside mostly, a stomach injury, my pancreas, and a broken leg. But nothing as bad as the memories.

I miss Hallie. I miss everyone. Peter, Emma, all of them. There is no one left who knows me. Even Evan can't help.

"Up in the cemetery," he describes the way the white arches standing next to each other look above each grave. "Touching each other as if they're holding hands. So many of them, side by side, it stops your breath. The silence of them all there together is overwhelming."

*   *   *

Closing my eyes, I can still see Hallie, just there. Next to me. She is mad because I've knocked the shilling from her hand. She is bending down to fetch it. "Look what you've done now, Alys!" she shouts. When I squeeze my eyes shut tight, Hallie is still there with me. Alive. And then I imagine what would have happened next. She would pick the shilling up. She would pretend to be angry. "Now *I* will get our milk. You give me your shilling right this moment, Alys." And I would smile and give it to her, because she is the strong one, she is the one who always gets her way. And I would back up and the roar would start and I would duck and the muck would flow over me. Not Hallie. It would be me gone, and Hallie saved.

Each night after dinner, Mam does up the dishes and Da sits at the far end of the kitchen reading his *Echo,* all duty between them.

"Going to bed, Rita," he says when he's finished reading. Mam nods, her back to him as she dries the dishes. She tidies up the house, has a conversation with Gram, sees me off to bed before she goes to their room.

One early morning when I am needing Mam, I find her asleep on the daybed at the foot of their bed. It is too short for her, so she is curled up like a cat. Somehow I know that this is where she sleeps now. I lie down on the floor next to her and watch her. I wouldn't mind staying there all day, forever. The floor is cool and hard. It doesn't move.

It takes me six months to recover the full use of my arms and legs. I am in the wheelchair for at least two months. In school no one wants to push me in the chair. Mr. Odell has to tell someone to do it, else I would just stay in one place all day.

There are others left from the middle and junior schools, about fifty in all but only five from my class. First we are shuttled to Mount Pleasant, where we share space with the middle and infant school there. Then a new school in Aberfan is built down the road. All of us go there, different ages but in the same one room. There is a darkness like someone spread a black cape over the whole town.

One evening after supper, a rock comes sailing through the window of our parlor. A crumpled paper is wrapped round it, and when Mam smoothes it out, she reads, " 'You better look after your daughter. Why is she alive when ours are dead?' "

Mam drops the rock like it is on fire and grabs the paper up in her hand, scrunching it back into a crumpled ball. She shakes her fist at Da and says, "What have we left? My God, where have our lives gone? Whatever will become of us?" She glares at me like I have done something awful, too.

But what have I done?

"Alys, it's not your fault," she says, but she is still glaring at me. "They are just mean and jealous because you are alive and theirs are not." Mam turns her head, her hand over her mouth. I know she is crying. Could she know about me grabbing Hallie's shilling? Maybe that's why she can't look at me, or hold me. Maybe she thinks it's all my fault, Hallie dying?

"Please, Mam, will you sleep with me? I am so scared."

"Go on now, Alys. You're fine on your own, you are. Pull yourself together. You are lucky to be alive." If that is so, then why do I feel like I am down a dark tunnel, all by myself?

Some nights I awaken and don't know where I am: the hospital, the parlor, or Gram's bed. "Mam!" I cry out. Finally Gram puts a small night-light in my room. But even with the light on, I cannot close my eyes for long.

At school, some of us talk about the trouble our parents are having. Most everyone left has lost either a brother or a sister. In one case, Gwynth, who stayed home ill that day, has lost two brothers and her father, who had walked the boys to school.

We are the only family to lose no one. It seems like Mam should be glad. But she never smiles. And she never touches me.

Nine weeks after the funeral, there comes a knock on the door. It is a man from the National Coal Board, who says he has a check for fifty quid. "Fifty quid?" Mam asks. "What for?"

Turns out to be it is a sympathy payment from the coal board. Even those who have been spared get it.

Mam shouts at him, "You son of a bitch. You take your money and stuff it if you think the price of a child's life, or any life, is worth only fifty quid! Take your fifty quid and bury it under the tip. Buried alive is what the death records should show. Buried alive by the National Coal Board is what I want written on those death certificates!"

And then she is down on her knees, pounding the floor, the man from the coal board standing there with the check in his hands. I want to help her. I want to kneel down and hug her, protect her. But I can't. I am too afraid she will tell me to go away.

In April, Gram leads a woman into the parlor. I am still using it as a bedroom during the day. Her hair is curly. I can see through it when she stands in the light of the open door.

"Alys, this is Dr. Kowal. She's come to talk."

Dr. Kowal smiles at me.

"You sit down, Dr. Kowal, and make yourself comfortable. Are you chilly? D'you want me to turn on the electric fire?"

I don't know why this doctor is here, but she is making Gram nervous.

"No, no. I'm fine. I'm warm enough, really." Dr. Kowal unbuttons her cardigan. "Don't you worry a thing about me, then, Mrs. Davies. I'll be fine as I am."

"I'll just go make us a cup of tea, then." Gram winks at me and backs out of the room.

"Now then, Alys, you're looking fine. How d'you feel? Some of the other children are complaining of headaches and nightmares. D'you have any of these complaints or any others?" She pulls the heavy rocker up next to my bed and takes a pad of paper out of her bag. "Anything at all?"

I'm not sure what she means. Is she talking about my body aches? Her breath smells like sour milk. I don't know how to answer her, so I say, "Well . . . it's my leg, mostly."

"That's to be expected, though, isn't it? You were seriously hurt. Your body is still recovering. What I'm talking about right now, Alys, are your feelings about everything that has happened. Is there anything that you need to speak of that you haven't been able to talk about yet? Something that might be giving you nightmares or making you uncomfortable in the daytime even, or causing you worry and keeping you up?"

One side of Dr. Kowal's lip is higher than the other. The more I look at her, the more I want to be able to tell her something, but nothing comes out. I can't say anything about the way I feel. In fact, I don't really know what I feel. How can I explain about the roar that builds in my ears just before I fall off to sleep? I move my lips and take a breath in, but nothing comes out about Mam and Da, and how the shouting 'tween Parry and Da has stopped now, and how he is gone mostly from the house, and I am more worried about that than I was about the hollering.

I can't say a thing about how I won't let myself rest too long on thoughts about Hallie, 'cause if I do, I feel my chest filling up with so much sludge I know I will never be able to breathe again, and what I want, really, is to be as stone-cold as Hallie. I can't say anything about how heavy every muscle in my body feels all the time.

"No." I smile. "Everything seems okay, now." That's what I tell Dr. Kowal. "I'm fine, now."

She reaches out and pats my hand and then she digs in her bag and pulls out a blue notebook and a new black felt tip.

"Well," she starts, "I hope you won't mind me saying something that helped me back a while ago, after I lost someone close. She was older and all, and I was older, too. But it was still a terrible loss for me. My friend and I talked every day the whole of our lives. Forty years." She hands me the notebook and then the pen.

"Sometimes there's just too much to say about what you're feeling. And if you try to say it out loud it doesn't cover all that you are feeling, really, because your mind gets overloaded and it all wants to come out fast—in a flash—and perhaps it won't make much sense to someone else. But if you were to write it down—just a thought, here and there, or a whole mouthful when you feel like it—then it will be out of your body, and somewhere safe where you can look at it and see it and maybe understand it better. Sometimes if you write down the things you're feeling it even makes it easier. Easier to feel those hard things."

She puts her hand on my shoulder. Firmly. I want to tell her how nothing she has told me is the same as losing Hallie. Nothing. She doesn't know at all how I feel.

"You're a brave little girl, Alys." She looks at me for a long moment, waiting, I suppose, for me to say something. I don't. Then she looks at her watch. "I have to go now, but I'd like to come back and talk some more if you'll let me." She reaches into her bag again and pulls out a small card. "I'm on the telephone. 'Tween now and when I come again, if you ever want to talk, just ring me."

Later, when Da's out, Parry and Evan come round. Evan's furious about what's what at the tribunal.

"It's horrible. Horrible! All of them talking about it again like when it first happened. What can they be thinking, to bring the surviving children in front of them, to tell them what? So cruel. What does their presence do besides tear our hearts out again?"

Parry leans up next to him. "Doesn't matter, Evan. It's done—don't you see? Da. The NCB. They're to blame. No amount of white-washing'll ever cover it up. We're all together on this, man. We're all together."

"But it's not your da, Parry. It's the NCB—period. Get it straight, man. You got to take the high road on this one and stop pointing the finger at your old man. Your da couldn't make that final decision. It wasn't up to him."

Parry shakes his head. "Sure, Evan. It's all bullshit at this point, anyway. Most of the children in this village are already dead. Can't get them back, can we?"

Parry's voice has an edge now all the time. Beti told Gram that he'd been drunk in the village on Sunday.

Evan puts his arms around him. Parry's head goes back and he sucks in some air. The vein in the middle of his forehead stands out.

"I want that time back. Before. I would be stronger, fight harder, convince them. If only I could have done something different. Da."

Evan and Parry are the same age, seventeen, but Evan's been on his own for two years, since he came to Aberfan, and he seems so much older than my brother, who cries all the time now.

"I can't stop, Evan. I think about it over and over, what I could have done differently. Maybe I just should have killed him?"

"Don't talk nonsense." Evan pulls Parry to him again.

"Maybe I just should have got myself a gun and killed him."

A week later, Evan tells me, "They've decided to move the tribunal to Cardiff."

"Surely my brother won't be able to go now." I knew none of the men Parry and Evan's age could afford cars, and Cardiff was a long way. I was thinking that was probably a good thing.

"That's the point. And we need his fire more than anyone's, we do, and his loud, strong voice. Parry has become the spokesman for the village. Angry as he is at your da, if he's not at those tribunal meetings, the blokes from the NCB will smooth things over, try to make it look like your da didn't give them proper information."

My eyes narrow. I don't understand.

"Your da's the one who was communicating with the NCB. They are going to try and make it look like it was your . . ."

I put my hands over my ears.

"Alys."

I keep my hands there and shake my head. After all the weeks and months of shouting in the kitchen, I can't listen anymore.

"Alys. I don't think your da was to blame. But it's complicated."

I keep shaking my head.

"It's just that we need Parry, and it seems like he's given up."

I was glad Gram came in then and offered us tea.

At the end of June, eight months after the disaster, we finally hear the findings of the investigation:

" 'Blame for the Aberfan disaster rests upon the National Coal Board. This blame is shared, though in varying degrees, between the NCB headquarters and the South Western Divisional Board,' " Gram reads me from the *Echo*. "So that's that," she says, patting my knee before continuing.

" 'There was a total absence of tipping policy and this was the basic cause of the disaster.

" 'Our strong and unanimous view is that the Aberfan disaster could and should have been prevented. We are not unmindful of the fact that strong words of calumny have been used against the NCB and a few of its employees. But our report tells not of wickedness but of ignorance, ineptitude and a complete breakdown in communication.' "

Chapter Six

The Tibetan Book of Living and Dying says that in the first forty-four days after a death, one must think wonderful thoughts about the deceased. One must do good deeds in the name of the dead. Lucky for Marc, forty-four days have long passed. If he weren't already dead I would kill him.

I go through Marc's drawers looking for something that will give me the truth. Now he's a stranger. Nine years of lies and deceits. I feel mortified, remembering how I once wanted to tell a friend whose husband was having an affair, "You don't know because you don't want to know." Either my self-absorption has been stunning or Marc was a bloody good actor. How could I not have known about Gabriella? And a child, for God's sake—how could he? Knowing my pathological reaction to abandonment, how could Marc, of all people, do such a thing not only to me, but to our children?

I find his frequent flyer miles. He has 339,876 on American Airlines, and half that many on Continental and Delta.

Does the child look like Hannah? Shit, this is just unbelievable. I feel so used. So ashamed. My God, what will Dafydd think? Marc was his idol.

I find a handwritten list of all the securities we have. Was he counting up our assets? Marc has also noted the money Evan sends me for Dafydd and the five hundred dollars I send to my mam and da each month. Maybe he was trying to figure out how to split things up. Maybe he was going to ask me for a divorce.

I try to think back to the way he acted when he returned from his Brazilian trips, or at least the last one. But it's all a blank.

Does the child look like Marc? In the moment I can't even seem to conjure up Marc's face.

Conversations come to mind: "I wish I didn't have to be away for so long. . . . I wish you and Hannah could come with me. We could rent a little place in Bahia for a week or two . . ." What if I'd said yes? What if I'd gone? I think about whom I can tell. There is no one I want to know. Not Beti. Not Elodie. Not even Elizabeth, who knows everything about me. This is too shameful, unspeakable. Another person might go to a therapist, spill out this ugly, bilious secret shame. But not me. I will keep my mouth closed so the sludge will not drown me.

I hate Phillípe, because he knows the real story. He would have seen them together through the years. A wave of nausea passes through me and I feel like I might faint. I crash through the French doors to the small deck outside Marc's office. The waterfall I had built for his thirty-fifth birthday is on. I splash some water on my face.

I imagine Marc and Gabby in some romantic little beach house in Ipanema, the baby running on the sand, Marc watching from the porch, Gabby with her long black hair and low-cut dress on his lap. I imagine Marc holding Gabby, telling her how much he loves her.

The first time Marc invited me to Brazil, Hannah was just a few months old. He'd said, "Alys, 'And Then Came Love' has won Best Song of the Year on the Brazilian charts. Come with me to the award ceremony." But I was feeling guilty enough about leaving Hannah to teach a class at UCLA Extension three times a week. Brazil would have meant at least four full days away from her. I was still nursing. Shit, why didn't I go? It was an award, for Christ's sake. A big award. I could have taken Hannah. But what could he have been thinking? Surely Gabriella was already pregnant. Perhaps back then he was still looking for a way out of their affair? Maybe my going with him might have changed things.

I picture parties they gave together to which all the Brazilian singers and musicians I'd met through the years must have come. Obsessively I list them: Ivan Lins, Dori Cayummi, Joao Bosco, Oscar Castro Neves, Tio Lima. Their faces come up like portraits on their

CDs. Gabriella in the kitchen throwing together one of her simple pots of fejuada. Latin women have always made me jealous—their ease, their beauty, even their accents. They seem to know some secret way into a man's psyche. I hate Gabriella for allowing this to happen, for the pain I feel, for what it will do to my children. I could never do this to another woman. Never.

Beti takes Hannah for two days. I stay in the house for most of it, having a "lost" weekend. On Sunday night before dinner, Beti, Colin and the kids drop Hannah back. I have managed to clear out most of the wine bottles and the debris in the fireplace where I have burned most of Marc's clothes. I open the door and Hannah holds out a Christmas wreath in her arms. When she sees my uncombed hair and shabby pajamas she says, "Mom, have you been in bed all weekend?" She backs away as if I smell or have some contagious disease. She drops the wreath on the coffee table and pulls the drapes wide. Then she opens the windows. "We need a tree. The house is so gloomy and quiet all the time. I can't stand eating here. Let's go out for pizza."

"I don't like pizza," I say.

Beti, who has brought in Hannah's duffel bag, says, "What does it matter? You don't eat anything anyway. You've lost so much weight you're just skin and bones."

I look at the skin on my arm and how it droops. I should do some yoga. Maybe run. But so should Beti. She's gained weight, and her clothes are so maternal. It's none of Beti's business how much I weigh.

"Thanks for bringing Hannah home, Beti," I say as graciously as I can, walking swiftly back toward my bedroom. "We've plenty of food in the fridge, Hannah. You'll find something to eat."

"I'm calling Dafydd," she says, storming over to the telephone. "He needs to come home."

"Don't you dare, Hannah," I shout.

"What happened? You're acting so crazy, Mommy. You've been acting crazy for days and days. Weeks. Totally nuts. You're scaring me." Hannah starts to cry.

It's true that, the day before Hannah left with Beti, I broke the dishes Marc's grandmother had given us when we first started living together. And the day before that I'd taken a pair of scissors to the

Dora Carrington drawing I bought Marc when he turned thirty. Not to mention tearing up the photo of the two of us sitting on the piano at the Ritz taken on our first trip to Paris.

Beti tries to comfort Hannah, but Hannah has never liked to be touched except by people very close to her: me, Dafydd, Marc. My sister doesn't take rejection well, even from a distraught eight year old. Her expression is sullen as she begrudgingly waves good-bye and too carefully closes the front door.

Of course I won't tell the children about Gabby. I'm not only too ashamed for myself but also for Hannah. Her father was as unfaithful to her as he was to me. How many other things in my life have I not noticed or ignored or, even worse, missed completely?

Phillípe and Ed Meyers leave messages. I don't return their calls.

When I close my eyes, I can feel the wet, cold slurry in my nose and mouth. I can't imagine why I've been saved.

Several days later, Hannah asks me if I know CPR.

"If you'd been here that morning, could you have saved Daddy?"

Is this a veiled accusation? I'd like to tell her that knowing what I know now, I would have thumbed my nose and walked away. But I am a better mother than that, if only a little.

Instead I try to comfort her, rise above my own pain. "Everyone did everything humanly possible." I remember Gram's comfort when I'd asked her why if God were so great He would have killed Hallie and all my friends. I put my arm around Hannah. "Perhaps Daddy did all the work he'd come to do in this life more quickly than all the rest of us."

"So where did he go? Where is he now?"

Probably burning in hell for living a double life, I think.

"I don't know. I don't really understand that part. Perhaps no one understands that part until it happens to them."

Hannah comes home from school and tells me she wants to move. She hates all her friends. They are all snobs, she says. They are all mean. There is not one of them she likes. I try to listen calmly.

"I want to move to New York. I want to be near Dafydd." When I press her for more details, she says that one of her friends said whenever she wants anything, Hannah uses her father's death to get it. "Sandy says she doesn't even believe my dad is dead. 'Your parents are probably just divorced and he lives somewhere else.' She thinks I just made it all up."

The next morning she refuses to go to school. I let her stay home. She seems angry. All morning she stays in the den, watching TV. I wonder if she intuits my complicated, negative feelings and they make her angry.

"I wish Rosie O'Donnell was my mom," she tells me when I peek in to see how she is doing. "At least she's good at working everyone's problems out." She glares at me.

At eleven a.m. she comes into my office, where I am still in my pajamas pretending to work. "I've made myself an almond butter and marmalade sandwich. Can you drive me to school?" Her clear resolve buoys me.

Later, I call Ed and tell him in no uncertain terms to call Gabriella Purdue. "Tell her there is nothing for her in Marc's will. Nothing. Tell her to leave me alone."

I shower, put on makeup, go into the kitchen and cut up potatoes, carrots, and onions while a small hen defrosts. I make corn bread stuffing with chili peppers and a yam soufflé, orange and cranberry sauce, sautéed greens with turnips and a double fudge cake. When Hannah comes home from school, I look at the cold bottle of chardonnay standing in the fridge. I don't open it. Hannah is in her room standing by her stereo. When she sees me outside her door, she comes into my open arms. I hug her close, very close.

CHAPTER SEVEN

The fifth spring after the disaster, the playground is finally finished. It's at the bottom of the road, below where the school area once stood. The parents' group lays a lovely lawn and puts in a yellow slide, blue swings and a roundabout. They plant a lot of trees, small and so spindly I don't see how they will ever live through a winter let alone grow big enough to climb—which is what everybody has in mind. And even if they do, who will climb them? Seems like a waste of money. But Gram says it's not only for us few left, and the memory of those who perished, but for future generations.

I tell Mam and Da I don't want to go to the dedication, but they are making me. The whole village is turning out, they say. Gram gives me a small package, and when I open it, there is a pink mohair sweater she has been knitting. It is so pretty, I think it is worth going to the ceremony just to wear it.

When we get to the playground, Da is talking to Mr. Ames and a group of parents. Mam is passing out chocolate biscuits. Gram and I are standing alone. I see Sophie Greenway, who is never very nice. Her long blond hair is done up in a braid with a ribbon running through it. Sophie tells me she likes my sweater. Then she turns her back and looks away. She's younger than I am and she has a crush on Oscar Jeens, who is my age. Oscar Jeens likes Sondra. I don't care about any of them.

Most evenings now, Evan comes to supper. Gram and I have come to expect him. Sometimes she leaves us alone. We talk about everything and I find myself asking him the most peculiar questions.

"What about your mam and da? Why don't you see them? They must feel like all the folks here, like they've lost you. You could be like Parry, not the same anymore. Don't you think they worry?"

"Nope," he says matter-of-factly. "We don't see eye to eye. That's why I left. And I'm never going back."

I want to ask him why they don't see eye to eye, but his tone suggests it isn't something he wants to talk about.

"My life is in Aberfan now. No matter how bad it has been here, this is my home forever."

So many ways Evan and I are different. If I could, I would leave Aberfan tomorrow. I dream about getting away from the terror of that morning. Night rises up in me like a dragon breathing hot fire, the flames licking me, pushing me toward their hot center, ready to swallow me whole. I want to get away from Mam and Da, who, like most of the villagers, stay so stuck in their loss they might as well be up in the cemetery along with the children.

Now the streets are deserted. The only noise the roar and screech of the bulldozers up the mountain as they pull the slag from the killer tip bit by bit, pile by pile into their huge shovels. "The Cleanup," we call it. Dr. Kowal has come back again and left sedatives for sleeping. Gram hands the little red tablet to me with water, and when I can't swallow it, she crushes it and mixes it with a spoonful of clotted cream. Even now, at thirteen years old, I still don't sleep alone, and it is still Gram beside me most nights, her back up against mine. I continue to wake in the middle of the night, screaming.

Everything else has changed. Not just Mam, Da and school. Everything. All the rules. Even the simple things. Before the disaster, every night we'd all have tea together. Now Da doesn't get home from the pub till late, and by then, Mam has already gone off to bed in Parry's old room.

Seems to be the same in the village for everybody. "No one helping others like before. Too much grief set in stone," Gram says.

And Evan hovers over me, like he's afraid something's going to happen to me. It feels as though he is standing guard over me.

"How do I know if you are all right, Alys? You've got to talk about things, not keep it all inside."

"I'm fine, Evan. There's nothing wrong."

"I'm not so sure it's such a good idea, you spending so much time at the Joneses'."

I baby-sit for little Niko twice a week. Of course he still misses Hallie, and anyway, he's used to me being around all the time. At the end of a visit, Mrs. Jones always gives me a pound note. I pretend to hand it back but she won't take it. "It gives me a break," she says.

"Why do you think that it's bad, me being at the Joneses'?" I ask Evan. "I'm thirteen and I need money."

"It's not about your age. It's just that they might be needing a little space now that time has passed. You know, to try and move on. And you, too."

"It's not bad for me. Mr. and Mrs. Jones are almost like parents." In fact I wish Mam and Da were like them. There's nothing for me to worry about at the Joneses'. When I go over they welcome me. "Alys, come in, come in," they say. "We've a nice pot of tea ready and I've just made Niko some toasted cheese sandwiches. There's one here with your name on it." No matter that Hallie is gone and they are still so sad—they always make room. No one asks me any questions or makes me talk when I have nothing to say. We are just being together quietly.

"But it must be confusing to little Niko," Evan says.

"Little Niko is not so little anymore," I remind him. It's Evan who is confusing. He turns up at the oddest times, out of nowhere, always worrying. It makes me feel cornered.

Fall is here again and the hillsides are turning from dark green to the dried bloodred of bracken. It's been five years since the disaster. I walk along the top of the hills, making my own way on the same paths I used to run with Parry before everything fell apart. Sometimes I pretend that nothing has happened and everything is good, like it used to be. Safe. I cling to the familiar sight of smoke from the mine curling into the sky, giving us something to look at besides mile after mile of the dark bracken hills.

I remember Parry asked me once, "Imagine living in a city, Allie, where there are cinemas, restaurants and a dozen bakeries to choose from and not one single solitary hill. Just buildings, skyscrapers and lifts that take you to the top, where you can look out over everything and see right where you are in the world."

I laughed and said, "No way. That's not my world. I want to live here forever and ever."

That was the way I felt then. When life was perfect. Now I am sure the only way I'll ever be able to live is to turn my back on everything I have ever known. Because nothing else seems to help this intense pain.

I am just coming into the house and see three suitcases queued up next to the door. Beti has on her nice black trousers and a dark green cardigan Mam gave her three Christmases ago. Her black knit beret, all the rage, is clipped to her hair at an angle. As usual, she looks pretty. When I'm twenty-three I want to look like her.

"Oh, Alys. I'm glad you're home." She comes right up to me and puts her hand on my shoulder, squeezing it a little. Then she hugs me.

"I'm going to the States, Alys," she says in my ear.

I don't believe what she is telling me.

"I'm ever so sorry to be leaving you, your only sister and all. But we've got to go. Colin and I have been thinking about it since the disaster and now we've decided."

I step back, away from her.

"Don't be mad, like. I've no choice, believe me." She puts out her arms trying to move closer to me.

"You save your tuppences and before you know it you'll have enough to come and visit us." She grabs me by the arms, pulling me toward her, hugging me. I can feel her heart pounding.

"Don't cry now, Alys. Colin and I need to start our own lives like, away from here. Far away from all of what's happened here. We can't seem to move ahead. We've tried, but there's no way. Not like Evan, who wants to get his teaching credentials and work with children, right here. There's nothing like that for us. There's no way you can understand it now. I don't expect you to. But you will, like. You will, Alys. Someday you'll understand. Please don't cry, lovey."

I do understand. Right this very moment, I understand.

"Let me come with you," I plead. "Please."

Months pass and I have been saving all the money Mrs. Jones gives me and I am running extra errands for Gram and Mam. I stuff the pound notes in a pillowcase, storing them until there is enough for plane fare.

"It is such a long way," Gram says, trying to talk me out of it. "Wait until you're older." I've not told her yet that it won't only be for a visit.

Meanwhile, Parry doesn't go near the mine after the tip slips. After all these years, Da is still convinced he'll be back. "Da believes with all his broken heart," Mam says, "that all Parry needs is time."

"The mine is in him, like it's in me," Da says, hopefully. "Work is the only way through this."

Mam glares at him. "Give it up, Arthur. Parry will never go underground again."

And he doesn't. After he quits the mine, he works wherever he can: Blackwell's Chemist, delivering prescriptions; the Aberfan, pouring drinks. Then he lands a full-time job at the Hoover factory.

"At least it's regular, like," Mam tells Gram.

"But the boy's drinking," Gram responds. Her eyes so sad. "He needs some kind of help, he does. He doesn't have it in him to help himself."

Even I can smell the stout on his breath.

"I think it's sneaked up on him," Evan tells us. "I'm not sure he even knows how much he's drinking."

Gossip travels back to us. We hear that Parry's girlfriend, Gillian, who took him in after Da threw him out, has told Parry if he doesn't stop drinking he'll have to live somewhere else. Parry's boss down by Hoover gives him a flat-out warning. He'll get the sack if he doesn't stop dead out and right away.

"How can he not know he's drinking too much if everyone else knows it?" I ask Evan.

"When you wake up drunk and just keep on drinking, it's hard to know when you're drunk and when you're sober," Evan says.

Later, Gram and Evan think I'm catnapping though I'm really on the staircase eavesdropping. I hear Evan say, "It doesn't seem he cares. When he gave up his painting, we should have known things were going wrong for him. Sometimes I catch sight of his eyes when he doesn't know I'm looking. He is so sad and I'm not sure what to do about it. He doesn't seem to be able to get by the disaster, even a little. No relief, even all these years later."

"We need to do something," Gram pleads. "I can't stand it."

"I wish I knew what to do," Evan says.

I beg Parry to come home. "You can have your old room back. It'll just be temporary, till you're back on your feet. Gram and I will see to you and fix you up. Please let us help. Da won't bother you a bit. He's gone first thing in the morning anyway, and doesn't get home till way after dark. He's even said it's fine for you to come home for a while," I lie. "He's sorry, Parry, about chucking you out. He hasn't said so right out, but he acts like he is. Give him a chance, Parry."

But Parry won't come home. Finally, Evan convinces him to stay at his place. But that doesn't seem to help much.

Evan begins to confide in me like I am one of his peers even though he is now twenty-two and we are eight years apart. "After all you have lived through, you qualify as 'experienced.' " He says I'm one of those people others refer to as "wise beyond her years."

Evan tells me one night, "Parry came in past midnight and fell onto the couch dead drunk. I could smell it on him in the morning when I went off to the mine. His boss has given him one more chance."

With Parry at Evan's now, I stop by regularly.

"Parry. Parry." I rub his neck. "You can't keep at it like this." He smiles up at me and laughs, pushing my fringe off my forehead. "Don't you worry your pretty little head over me, now, Allie. I'm going to start to paint again. Right. That's what I need to do. That's what I'm missing."

Soon Parry just stops showing up at work.

Evan's continued patience with him doesn't surprise me. The way he cares about Parry, worrying after him, fixing him meals, getting him up in the morning, is consistent with how he helps me sort through my feelings. And who knows how many others he helps?

At first I am stopping by only once a day. Then I am dropping over before school and again after. Pretty soon I am helping Evan with dinner, because he is studying for the teaching exam. And I am doing Parry's wash, spending as much time at Evan's as I can, glad to be away from my own depressing and lonely house as often and as late as possible.

One night while I am at the sink washing up, Parry dead out on the couch, Evan says, "Nothing seems to help him."

"I know." I am looking over at Evan, but he is staring at me.

"But it's incredible having you here," he says. "I mean, for me. I didn't realize how lonely I was, before you . . . and Parry started hanging about with me."

I swallow, understanding how he feels but not knowing what to say. Everything is so quiet I hear the clock on the stove ticking. There is something in me then that wants to lean over and kiss him and I almost do. But instead I blurt, "Well you must surely miss your parents and everything."

"No, Alys, I do not miss my parents." He throws the towel down into the sink. "I definitely don't miss my parents. I'm sure we talked about that." Turning away he adds, "I've got to be up early tomorrow."

The night of my fourteenth birthday is the last night Parry, Evan and I are all together. The two of them are waiting when I come out of school. For a change that morning, I've done my hair up in a French twist and put a little rouge on my cheeks, pink on my lips. When they greet me, Parry is quiet. His eyes roam, not focusing. Evan has one arm balancing Parry and the other behind his back, hiding something.

"Give 'er the flowers," Parry slurs. "Go on, lover boy, give 'em to her."

"For you, Alys," Evan says shyly, presenting a bunch of flowers. "One to grow on. They're from both of us, actually," he says quickly.

My hands fly up in front of my mouth, hiding embarrassment, hiding my smile. It is the first moment I know I love him.

That night the cold chills the bones. Evan lights the fire and serves Parry and me in front of it, the two of us on torn cushions, the stuffing coming out.

"A birthday celebration!" Evan has prepared my favorite meal: leeks and parsnip pie, crème caramel for dessert.

"So easy to please, your sister is," Evan teases.

"Are you inferring I'm not?" Parry pretends his feelings are hurt.

Afterward, after he clears all the plates away and we drink our white coffee, Evan leans toward me and looks me straight in the eye but says to Parry, "You know, I love your sister, Parry. I will wait forever if that's what it takes for her to love me back, I will."

The next night I am home. It has just gone dark when Parry comes round. I know Parry must stand out front of the house and look for telltale signs of Da being gone before he rings the bell.

He is drunk and swirling. He's come by to see Mam. She is in the middle of putting tea on. He grabs her up as he always does and whirls her around. Even drunk as he usually is, Parry always makes Mam laugh.

"My old mam!" he says. "Still as pretty and sweet as ever. How d'you live with that bastard, Mam? How d'ya put up with 'im?" His words are all slurred.

"Parry, you mustn't go on about your da now. Too many years gone by and there's enough muck between the two of yous as it is. It wasn't his fault, like. Everyone in town 'as forgiven him. And now you too must or your anger will eat you alive."

He puts her down then and kisses her on both cheeks. "You're the best, Mam. You're the only chance that murderer has for redemption."

"Go on now, Parry. Talk to your sister, boy. I imagine she's missing you as much as any of us."

I am jealous of Parry. No matter what he says or does, drunk or not, Mam looks at him as if he is some prize. She loves him the way I want her to love me.

Parry sits down in the straight-backed chair next to me, leans over and pushes my hair out of my eyes. "You taking good care of Mam then, Alys?"

I nod. I wonder why he's acting like I hadn't just seen him over at Evan's the night before.

"She's taking good care of you. I can see that," he says, looking at me as steady as he can. "You're as beautiful as the moon, you are. No wonder that cad of a bloke 'as been tumbling over you since you were toddling. Problem with Evan is 'e's never 'ad any brothers or sisters of his own. You look after yourself with 'im. The gentle bloke you see and hear is a front. He's really a wild man, 'e is."

"Parry!" Mam says sternly from her place at the sink. "You're talking about a girl just turned fourteen years old. Alys has as much interest in Evan as she does with the likes of you, she has!"

"It's not Alys I'm worrying after. 'Tis Evan," he teases. "Should have heard him talking at her birthday dinner, then."

He reaches over and puts both his hands over mine. "Look after yourself, Alys. You've always been my heart. You've all the possibility I never had. A born poet you are, and the guts to continue at it. Someday your poems will be in books, they will. You'll be reading them in front of large crowds, just like Dylan Thomas did. Gram and Beti, they'll be there for you. They love you like I do. With everything in them."

I wonder what Parry is on about. Beti, of course, is long gone from the house and in the States.

"Well, well, if it isn't our laggard," Gram says, walking into the kitchen just then. Parry puts his arm out and grabs her.

"Oh Gramo! Come sit on my knee, Gramo. Let me kiss your neck!"

Gram blushes a deep shade of red. He loves Gram as much as I do. Maybe even more. She comes over to the table and says, "You're not driving, are you?"

Ignoring her, Parry says, "You're in charge of Alys. Right, Gramo?"

"No one's in charge of me, Parry," I pipe up.

"Your da will be home any moment. He won't like seeing you in this condition. In fact, none of us like it," Gram reprimands.

"Oh, now, Gramo." He chucks her under the chin. "Not to worry." But he looks at his watch and then gets up. "I love you, Gramo. I love you with all my evil little drunken 'eart." He kisses her on both cheeks.

"Bye-bye, baby," he says to me. "I'll be seeing you." And he salutes me, our secret salute since I was little. We'd seen it in an old Shirley Temple movie when Bojangles saluted Shirley.

And then to Mam: "Don't let the ol' man pull the wool over your eyes." He stumbles to the sink where Mam is and kisses the back of her neck.

After he is gone out the door, I feel panic, and run after him.

"Wait up!" I yell at him, running as fast as I can, my arms waving wildly at him like I am still a young child. The road is slippery. It has been raining pretty near all week and the winds are high. It is dark enough that the bright light from the streetlamps and the glow from the mine across the river cast an eerie orange light. The coal tips down Merythr way stand like guards. I know Parry is off to the pub. He doesn't turn around as I pull up next to him and shove my arm through his.

"Allie, you've got no shoes on. You'll be stubbing your toe if you aren't careful, like, and you're bound to catch your death of pneumonia."

I don't have anything to say. I just want to be with him. Mam always says I am the only one can calm Parry down. She says Parry's anger boils up in him like a kettle of water on the high burner. He is just looking for a place to let off steam.

When I won't be shaken off so easy, Parry starts a soliloquy.

" 'e's not a bad man, Da isn't. 'e's just afraid. And it's what done us all in. Never stood in the light of his own truth. Can't 'ate a man because 'e's known darkness all his life, can you, Allie? 'e's been workin' in that mine so long it's blinded 'im. I should never 'ave joined up with 'im. Should've taken that scholarship. I'd be painting now.

"Go on, you get, Allie. You don't want the ol' man coming home and finding you gone." He pulls me up to him then, and gives me a tight squeeze. "You'll be all right, no matter what. You remember that, Allie."

I don't want to go. Don't want to leave him, but I turn and head back down the road.

The next night, Parry is dead. He hangs himself from the big tree at the top of the cemetery behind the hundred sixteen white arches. Da finds him as he is walking home from his own rounds at the pubs. I know Parry meant for Da to find him because it is the path Da takes every night of his life.

Da calls the police from the little house in the cemetery. They come immediately, cut him down and bring him home. Mam answers the door. At first Da can't bring himself to tell her. Then he bows his head and says, "I've brought your son home," his whole body heaving with sobs.

I am upstairs, and run down. Mam holds the door open wide, the cold rushing in after them. They carry Parry's body inside and put it on the settee in the parlor. Mam watches and doesn't shed a tear, just covers Parry over with an afghan. Gram comes down for only a moment, stares at all of us, goes back to her room and shuts the door. I cannot bear another moment in their house. And I am out, running so fast through the cold, straight to Evan. He opens the door, and I collapse in his arms. I can't go home that night. And then, I think, I can't go back at all. And mostly I don't, except for the small funeral and reception, and a couple of times each week to check on Gram.

Six months later and I am still suspended in a gloom so overwhelming that often I feel as if I am floating. Although I am alive, most of me feels nothing. As time moves on, part of me thinks Parry's death might in some small way be a relief to Mam. Now there are no further confrontations between him and Da or me and her. Perhaps it gives her something in common with the rest of the villagers. Now Mam has lost someone. She has lost something real she can point at as evidence of her own grief. Strangely her spirits seem to lift. Mam joins the mother's group that meets each week. She has become one of them.

But she still keeps her distance from me.

I tell her the *Echo* is printing one of my poems. In fact they want another one and have some interest in a regular weekly poem.

"That's nice, Alys," Mam says, with no expression at all, either on her face or in her voice.

I tell Gram how jealous I am of Parry. Up on that graveside with all my friends. I don't want to be here, alone. I don't know what to do now. There seems no reason to be here or anywhere.

One early morning I ask her, "Gram, tell me why Evan couldn't save him?"

"Oh, Alys. Don't you be blaming Evan. No one could save that boy. There, there, Alys. At a time like this, it's just living moment to moment, waiting until the pain has a chance to settle. That's all you can do. Not all at once, but there's still a whole full life ahead of you to live."

But I am so depressed I stop going to school. Evan doesn't try to convince me otherwise. I am either at his flat, or he is with me at home. He is always around, and it's as if we are watching each other, looking after each other, waiting to see what the other one will do.

And then one night, I am off the couch and sleeping with him, next to Evan. His arms around me, night after night, but not making love. It's more about comfort for both of us, our sleeping together. More about Evan taking care of me, and me letting him.

In the middle of one terrible, stormy night, I wake up cold and shaking. For a moment I don't know where I am. I reach for Gram and Evan says, "Are you all right?"

I am half asleep and still confused and out of nowhere I ask, "Why did you leave home, Evan?"

"Oh, Alys," he says, turning over. "It's the middle of the night."

"Tell me, Evan."

He sighs. "It's not a question for the middle of the night."

"Please."

"This is not something I am proud of, Alys."

"Tell me."

He sighs again. "When I was fourteen, my mam got pregnant." He pauses, as if he might not go on. But then he says, "To my da, it was a surprise. They were old to have more children. Neither of them expected it. I was their only child." He pauses again, this time longer.

"Go on, Evan. Please."

"I always wanted a sister or brother more than anything. I guess my mam always wanted more, too, and apparently she had secretly tried with no success. When my da found out she was pregnant, he wanted her to have an abortion. I'd hear them arguing, my da saying how they couldn't afford it and how much time it would take out of their lives. Then the baby was born and it turned out to have a disease, a bad disease. She was hydrocephalic. That's when the baby's head gets huge and fills with fluid. The doctor told my parents it was fairly common in South Wales."

And here he takes another breath, long and deep, the escaping sigh loud. When he resumes, his voice is softer, almost a whisper. "It was a baby girl. They named her Nellie. She was cute. I couldn't tell that her head was bigger than it should have been. A couple of times I sat in Mam's rocking chair and rocked Nellie while she drank her bottle. And the next thing I knew, the baby was dead and my mam was crying round the house, not speaking to my da. One night I heard them arguing and she was calling him a bastard and a baby killer. I knew immediately what had happened.

"So the next morning I got up as if I was going off to school but I just kept on walking. I hadn't planned it. But I knew I was never going back. I put them out of my head and soon they were out of my heart. When I got to Aberfan, first off I met Parry, who told me I could get a job in the mine. So I went to the mine and signed up straightaway. Soon enough, Parry and I were having our lunch together every day. Your brother embraced my friendship. Never asked me a single thing about my past. He just became my friend . . . my best friend."

I can feel his body beginning to shake and I know he is crying. His sobs are having a strange effect on me—it is the saddest story. And to know how long he has carried it with him, unshared, is even sadder. We are each filled with so much pain. I am relieved to hear him cry.

We fall asleep finally and in a dream I have gone to Evan's house for lunch. He makes me a toasted cheese sandwich with tomatoes. I offer him a bite, but he has already eaten. Sitting in the straight-backed chair, I take my shoes off. Evan is in football shorts sitting across from me. Without thinking, I put my bare foot on the back of his calf. I can feel the long hair on his leg with my toes. I laugh and rub my foot up and down his leg, thinking about how I can get him to kiss me. I have always wanted him to kiss me, even when I was little.

He takes my foot in his hand and starts to rub it. I go all soft in-side. We look into each other's eyes while he continues to rub my foot. Slowly his hand slides up my leg to my knee. Letting my leg fall gently into his hand, he pulls me toward him. I wrap first one leg and then the other around his waist. I unbutton his shirt. He reaches toward me and lifts my hair, wrapping it at my neck in a knot. He kisses my neck. I want to tell him to love me, pick me up and take me to his bed. As though he can read my mind, he picks me up and takes me to his bed, where he undresses me, looking at me all the while, my breasts, my tummy, as he folds my clothes, placing them neatly at the foot of the bed. I am naked in front of him. But I can't move. I wait for him. After several moments, he starts to cry. He just stands there and cries.

I wake up. It is still dark. I reach my arm out and find Evan's leg. He sleeps in his boxers. I feel the smooth inside of his thigh. I move closer, putting my leg over his. He stirs, slightly. I touch his stomach, the silky hair on his chest. I roll onto him and slowly begin moving my hips. My eyes adjust enough to make out where I touch my fingers to his lower lip. I kiss him. He opens his eyes.

"Allie, what—"

"I want to make love to you, Evan."

"Sweetheart, are you sure? "

"Yes. I want this, Evan. I really do."

After that, I spend as much time as I can in bed with Evan. Some-times it is the sweetest love I can imagine. And sometimes I cannot get enough, and I beg him to do it again and again, pushing him until we are both exhausted, falling into dreamless sleep.

"I love you, Alys," he says after one of our longer mornings. "But there's something else going on here for you. What is it? Please talk to me."

But I cannot.

I cannot tell Evan how before we made love I was fading away. There was nothing left for me to hold on to. I was like the rest of them in the village, lost to myself, lost to everything. Now the only thing that makes me feel alive is when he is banging away inside me, me rising up to meet him, the hard throb of him. But I also know it will not last. Because if Evan could not save Parry, he can never save me.

As the days move forward, it is clear as the morning light that I must leave Aberfan soon.

I write to Beti in California. She has a tea shop now, and Colin works construction. They have been there almost two years, married and settled with one child, and another on the way. I remind her that she said I might come. I could help her with the children. I tell her that I really need to come as soon as possible, that I am desperate. I have saved enough money. I post the letter, and without telling Evan what I've done, I wait. I wait for a long week. The week turns into a fortnight, and then a month passes.

I write in my journal or a poem here and there. And whenever I can, I cook, and sometimes I'll use the broom and dustbin or Hoover round the kitchen. I've totally given up school, though. My books and notebooks are half under the bed and strewn across the floor of the small bedroom. Evan, so sweet, never says a word about the mess I leave.

"I've given notice at the mine," he tells me. "I can start teaching next fall if I go to school full-time and finish getting my teacher's certificate. I am ready to start a new life here, and I want that life to be with you, Allie. Not marriage, not yet. I know you're not ready for that, still young and all, fifteen. But a commitment to go at life together. I love you," he says. "Someday this village will heal and we will have helped."

I cannot answer him. When he leaves, I put on a loose pair of his trousers, a mackintosh and wellies, and I walk out the door and up behind his flat toward the hills. It is drizzly, still dark, and the dampness chills me. I walk with my head down, straight up along a narrow path some shepherd must have tramped out a long time ago, an old stone wall on my right. I bounce my bare hand along it. The whole of Aberfan is laid out like a toy village with Merythr Tydfil off to the right, Mount Pleasant in the distance.

I have spent my entire life here, every moment, the beauty in me like blood. But I cannot live here anymore.

I've known I am pregnant for a while. I've not had my period in two months. For a brief moment I'd considered an abortion, like Sophie Greenway did when she got pregnant and it turned out not to be Oscar's. But I can't.

No one knows, 'cepting Gram. I don't show much at all. But I will soon. If I am going to leave it must be sooner rather than later.

Now I know for sure Evan will never leave Aberfan. I am amazed how he is able to dig into his life, trying to build something new out of rubble. I know many of the villagers have done the same, as the full rows of terraced cottages queued up next to each other remind me. To me, there seems no difference 'tween the row upon row of white arches in the cemetery and the terraced houses below.

The letter from Beti finally arrives, telling me I can come.

"But he'll be wantin' to marry you, then," Gram says one morning when we are out walking. "Not just out of duty, mind you, but because there is so much love between you. You've both a responsibility to the child."

I start to cry. Of course there is love between us. I've loved Evan since I first met him. Forever. But at fifteen, what do I know of duty or responsibility? Besides, I can't think about love now. I have been planning another life since before Beti left, and neither Evan nor this baby can get in the way of that. Nothing can. I have to leave. If I don't leave Aberfan, I will die, like Parry. I cannot raise a child between my own endless grief and the town's grief.

In the dark early mornings, when I'm not at Evan's, I crawl into Gram's bed there in the attic, and she rubs my back while I cry.

I've told Auntie Beryl, too.

"Are you sure you want to have this child, Alys? There are other ways to deal with it," Auntie Beryl reminds me.

I shake my head.

"It will take a lot of strength to raise a child alone, and it's not something you can change your mind about in the middle of the lake . . . or whatever that old adage is, you know what I mean, once the baby is here," Auntie Beryl says.

"I'm having the baby."

"Then why not stay here and let Evan have a chance at raising the baby alongside you? He'd be a fine father."

I cannot tell about the wall of darkness I slam up against when I think of staying here. I can't talk about it. I am leaving Aberfan. Alone.

When I finally tell Mam I'm pregnant, her anger is like steam, quiet and barely visible and in each breath, every word and action toward me from then on. I am on my way. They will let me go. In fact, they'll be glad I am going.

The night before I leave is another wet, moonless summer night. I walk the high pathway above the village for that last time, remembering how my heart used to lift looking at the way the shadowed hills roll into each other, blindingly green in the spring, and then the dark rich brilliance of the autumn colors. Whenever, whatever season, how I loved the soothing night rainfalls. I owned it all and remember how I'd told Parry I would live here day in and day out, loving this land forever. It seems a long-ago time now.

Tonight my walk around the village—past Marty's Greengrocery, the chemist, Bethany Chapel, the narrow cobbled streets—I feel it all as an endless path of heartbreak. I come up on the side of Moy Road that looks directly over at the huge vacant area where once Tip Number Seven stood. That slag heap was tall and black as the shadow of any mountain, deadly for all of us, killing some of us all at once and the rest of us little by little.

Each anniversary, when the whole town gathers at the cemetery to lay wreaths in front of the white arches, reviewing our losses, I feel like I am living those losses for the very first time. I will be gone before this year's anniversary. And I hope to put the memories of this time far away.

Now, as I look at where that tip stood, it's as if it was never there, the spot as innocuous as any other grassy sloping field. The truth is they might as well have left it just as it was after the disaster—we are all buried by it anyway, and at least we would have been able to see what ruined us.

Rain pelts against me as I start down the hill. I reach home, drenched to the bone.

"Who's there, then?" Mam calls as I come in.

"It's me." I wonder if Da is still out.

She comes from the kitchen, wiping her hands on her apron, her face pinched into a scowl. "Where've you been, then, Alys? You're like some wild wet dog, showing up every once in a while. It's late, like, and you, in your condition. I thought you were staying at Evan's tonight?" She comes right up to me, putting her hand on my tummy. "And the rain teeming . . . You've got to look after yourself now, you do. It's not just you anymore. You must be sensible, Alys."

For a second I feel she might be softening to me, and to "my condition," as she calls it. But then she says, "Although I must admit 'tis better that you take your walks at night, like, so as the neighbors don't get a good look."

"Mam, please."

"It's not like your da and I haven't been through enough as 'tis."

"Mam, do we have to get into that now?" I turn my back on her and start toward the stairs.

"It wouldn't hurt you none to give us some thought, like. It never occurs to you that we are still suffering, then? No matter how many years pass, our pain is still raw. There isn't a day your da doesn't go out of the house without the blame of the whole village staring him straight in the face, like. Da, ghost of himself, choking on his own grief he is. We are still in a terrible way about your brother. And now we have to live with this . . ." she says under her breath, pointing at my stomach. Right then another woman might have begun to cry, but not my mam. "It's too much to bear, just too damn much."

"Well you won't have to bear it much longer. I'm off with first light tomorrow." And now I tell her what I have not admitted before. "And I won't be back. 'Tisn't a visit I'll be making. I'm going for good." I wait a beat, searching her face for any reaction, but there is none. Either she does not care or she pretends not to, which is even worse.

Anger sucks me up like smoke, but I turn and talk straight to her, speaking my own truth for a change. "And what about me, Mam? What about me? You think any of this has been easy for me? You think I like what I've had to live through? You and Da separate from each other since the disaster. Me living here without a loving word 'tween us for all these years. Cold stares as if I am to blame for all our past. Needing to stay at Evan's in order not to end up like Parry. None of it's been easy for me, you know. "

"Don't raise your voice to me, young lady."

This is all she will give me.

The next morning, with only a bit of blue in the otherwise gray-black sky, I leave the village, my heart hardened, and board the coach to Cardiff, the coach that will eventually take me to Heathrow Airport, and finally the airplane to America and Beti and Colin's house in California. As each green field turns into the next, I don't look back.

CHAPTER EIGHT

SANTA MONICA, CALIFORNIA
NOVEMBER 1979

Three afternoons a week I work at the Tudor House, Beti's tea shop. We dress up in Welsh outfits, heavy, short, tweedy cotton skirts and white blouses with puffy sleeves. Beti pays me six dollars an hour and the other waitresses and I all split the tips. On a good afternoon I can make thirty dollars in tips alone.

Paintings of the Welsh countryside decorate the walls, along with muted tapestries and a collection of wooden love spoons. Two tall antique dressers covered with Welsh plates, cups, saucers, teapots, brass bed warmers and trivets make the shop into what an American might expect to find in a Welsh village home.

I work hard. When my mind wanders to the far corners of my heart, I drag it back to the washing up, the sweeping, serving the customers.

During long walks in the morning and late afternoon, I breathe in everything new around me. I love California, its bright spacious light, warmth, the way the sun rises over the mountains, the glowing explosion as the sun sets into the sea.

There are many moments each day when I know I've left a good part of me back in Aberfan and taken with me so much of its darkness and cold. Early mornings, before I pull myself out of bed, it is hard to remember why I left. Evan's face and smile swim up and threaten to pull me back to my own hilltop. Most of me still wants to be home.

I am now huge with child. I'm getting used to stares from the customers, and the other day one of the busboys asked me how long I'd been married. My new friend Elodie doesn't seem to care that I am pregnant. As we work together, every time she passes me, she rubs my tummy, saying, "Maybe I'll get lucky!" In some rather American way, her yellow hair, the way she teases, and her easy manner remind me of Hallie.

When I'm not at the tea shop, I look after Beti's children, Anwen and Morgan, a sweet, well-behaved, towheaded set. Anwen, at two, and Morgan, at just eight months, are not yet old enough to appreciate their Welsh roots, but we do. Tricky as it will be, Beti, Colin and I agree to protect them and my child to come for as long as we can from the darkness of our own desperate past. And yet we are singing the Welsh lullabies and telling them of the land's beauty, the changing drama of the sky, our strong history, lest we forget the strengths of our own Welsh hearts.

When I first arrived, Beti wanted to concoct a story for her friends about how my husband had died in some horrible car crash. I'd not had a chance to tell her about my pregnancy before I left home. Selfishly, I'd not given a thought to how embarrassed she might be by it.

"Allie. You don't generally see pregnant fifteen year olds in Santa Monica. This is a pretty conservative little town." As if it's commonplace in Aberfan.

Finally we decide to say nothing about my past. No excuses or inventions about my pregnancy. Better not to have my child living with some outrageous lie that might catch up with either of us.

Six months later, I have gone sixteen and Dafydd is just five months old when I start up at the high school. During the school day, Beti baby-sits Dafydd. In the afternoons, I watch all three children. It's a huge relief to be back writing poetry again, and reading it aloud to more than just my reflection. I like my English teacher, George Marx, a tall, bent, scruffy, gray-haired man who smokes between classes and smells like it. He expects a great deal from us. Occasionally he will tell me that I am using idioms or expressions in my poems that are utterly British. "Revise. This is America!" he says.

Our current assignment: Write about some specific day-to-day challenge in your life and what would happen if that challenge was removed.

I've finished the first draft of the poem when the doorbell rings. The mailman delivers a large registered envelope for me from Gram.

She writes at least once a month, but this is a large packet filled with several letters.

September 5, 1980

My darling Alys,

Things here are mostly as they were. Your mam and da are struggling, but doing better. Your da is still going down the mine daily. Your mam is working with the children's centre. She is part of a committee trying to raise money to build a swimming pool. I am hard at work on my Victory Garden and Beryl is on a committee dealing with acid rain and ozone problems.

I know you've not wanted to hear from Evan. But he has asked me to send these letters on to you. Forgive me for causing you any pain, but I feel I've no choice but to send them. I will write again soon.

All my love,
Gram

There are dozens of letters. The part of me that doesn't want to read them battles hard with the starving part that grabs a handful, sits down and tears the first open. I trace my finger over Evan's strong, bold print:

October 28, 1979

Dear Alys,

Where are you? Gram will not say. What am I to think about your disappearance? One day you are here and the next gone. Why? Please, Alys, I love you!

Evan

Two months later:

December 10, 1979

Dear Alys,

How could you leave me knowing you were going to have my baby? I have made Gram tell me about him. I don't know what I have ever done to deserve this kind of treatment. This is torture.

Knowing all you know of my life makes me think a part of you
must have gone mad.

Evan

Finally, the last one I am able to read:

April 11, 1979

Alys,

I don't understand what is happening. I have tried every which
way to sort out what you might be thinking. When Gram first
told me, I felt if you had time away to gather your own thoughts
and your own feelings around you, to grow up a little, you would
know how important it is to be together, here in our home, our
village—both for us, for our baby.

I cannot imagine how you have talked yourself into believing
that raising our child alone is better than raising him together. It
is far more than just selfish.

How can you be so cold, so heartless? For so many years we
have all missed the sound of children, their spirit. And now you
have taken the possibility of mine away. I despair every moment of
my day, losing you, my best friend, my lover and now my child.

It is as if Evan is sitting right in front of me, his voice, anger. His
hurt is so clear in his letters. I can hardly bear up against all I have
forced on him because of my own desperate needs.

With all we have been through, I would never have thought
you of all people could be so cruel.

I almost tear the letter up before reading the last paragraph:

Though it is utterly clear we will not meet again, I still want
to contribute to Dafydd's maintenance in some manner. It is en-
closed. I will send more when I can.

May you have as much difficulty living with your hardness as
I am.

Evan

I cannot respond to him. Instead I write to Gram, reminding her simply as I can:

> It is not because I don't love Evan that I left. It is not because I don't long for him, miss him every day of my life, that I don't write. Please, Gram, help me let Evan go.

That September, during a lunch break in the second week of school, Elodie takes me out of the queue and drags me over to the table where Marc Kessler is seated. He is one of her best chums.

"He wants to meet you. He has a crush on you," she teases.

"This is Alys," Elodie says, pushing me down on a seat next to him. "Alys Davies from Wales."

He is handsome, dark, smiling. I am impressed first by his blue collared shirt, with the sleeves rolled up to his elbows. This seems so American. Under his stare I am suddenly shy. Then he stands up and puts out his hand, a small hand, with a broad palm and strong grip. Holding on to him, I grow calm and quiet inside.

"It's a pleasure," he says. "I've been watching you. I like your accent. If you're from that part of the world you must know Shakespeare like the back of your hand." He takes my hand and turns it palm down. "I've been waiting for a girl like you all my life," he teases.

He is the same age as I am but a year ahead of me in school. Our getting to know each other is a slow process, both of us cautious, reticent.

It takes me six months to bring Marc over to meet Beti and Colin. I am afraid if he visits the house he'll think I am some kind of scrubber, what with having a baby, me having just turned seventeen. But when I finally do, Marc smiles and says, "A baby. Man, that's probably a lot more responsibility than a dog, huh?" Adding quickly, "But he's certainly cuter and he probably doesn't know how to bark yet?"

I laugh, waiting for him to say how young I am, or how could I ever let it happen, and where is his father—for him to judge me. Instead, he merely picks Dafydd up and gives him a little cuddle. "We're gonna be great friends, right, boy?"

Of course I am relieved that he doesn't question me, yet I also wonder why he doesn't. He knows nothing about my prior life and it doesn't seem to matter to him. He seems to care only that I'm different from his other friends—wild long hair, long skirts, my accent, which he comments on endlessly, making me read Shakespeare out loud.

"You are an intriguing foreigner, a secret."

Now Marc comes over to Beti's house nearly every afternoon. We sit for hours on the front porch, in the back garden. He talks about growing up on "the ranch." How he helped the Mexican laborers who came in illegally for the summer months to pick grapefruits and oranges. How he'd ride his horse over the dusty hills to meet his friends under an old willow. He has blue ribbons and trophies from summer rodeos and holds the ranch record for saddling and unsaddling a quarter horse.

"The downside about those ranch years was when the cattle were castrated. I'd go watch. Those workers would make a big deal of cutting the balls off and then they'd fling them at me. Said it would make a man of me. What it made was a vegetarian for so many years I can't count. I've only just begun eating meat again."

Marc notices views, the skyline, sunsets and the rich deep purple bougainvillea that grows outside my sister's house. He talks about his feelings, tries to get me to talk about mine.

Reading my latest poem, he challenges my use of adverbs. "Very," he says, "is a useless word. It actually lessens the power of the word it stands next to. Mark Twain always said, 'If you see an adverb, shoot it!' What's bigger than big? 'Very' doesn't make it bigger. What's more beautiful than beautiful, except for you? See how very stupid 'very' is? Dafydd is big. You are beautiful."

"*You* are brilliant," I tease. But he does seem to know everything. He seems so secure, solid—romantic, too. I forgive him his arrogance.

Dafydd looks forward to showing off for Marc, roaring round the cement patio on his Big Wheel, throwing himself up on Marc's lap, where he falls asleep, comfortable as a cat. In those moments my mind brushes up against thoughts of Evan. Marc says it makes him feel alive to be around us, makes him feel useful.

I begin to let myself feel protected, to convince myself that my past is past. Life is so different here, the weather so beautiful. Easy.

On the front porch, in the back garden, at the market. How can Evan, Gram, Mam and Da survive here when I have been reinvented?

For his senior project, Marc decides to set music to *Our Town*.

"God, I love this play," he whispers, leaning over me at the rehearsal—my fourth time seeing it with him.

"This is where I want the voices to really build—after she's chosen the time in her life which has been most precious to her—and she's back in it for just that moment. I want voices, a cappella, rising over this speech. Alys, try to imagine."

And then Emily says, "Oh, earth, you are too wonderful for anybody to realize you. Do any human beings ever realize life while they live it—every, every minute?"

"That's the spot. Right there," he says.

As the rehearsal continues we both watch quietly. I think about Hallie and for just a split second I allow myself to imagine her my age, still alive.

Later on, Marc leans over and whispers, "If you got to choose the time when you'd come back, Alys, when would it be?"

"Right now," I say, without a moment's hesitation. "Right this very minute. Sitting next to you, enjoying your brilliance," I tease. But mostly I mean it. Mostly in Marc's presence I feel shielded from harm. Except for the part that is always waiting for the next tip to slide.

Marc laughs, softly touching the top of my hand.

As we grow closer, Marc shares more details about his family. He was born in Santa Monica, lived near the beach, went to a small grammar school where he learned to play the piano at an after-school program. His father had a heart attack when he was six and that's when they moved to the ranch.

"It was my dad's idea. He wanted to make our lives smaller, give us space, quiet. Probably thought it would give him more control. But we were miles and miles from the ocean, so at first I hated it. My mother hated it even worse than I did. She just kind of stayed around the house doing nothing while my dad went to the office each day to sell insurance and I went to school.

"I'd get home from school and she would complain about everything—the town, the people, my dad. In her awful need, she confided things to me that she shouldn't. She didn't seem to notice that I was only seven. She complained nonstop about not having enough money, yet she never worked a day in her life."

"But she raised three children," I say. "That must count for something."

"It counts. But, Alys, she was really smart. She read a lot, published essays in the local paper. When she was a teenager she studied art. All of us, including her, would have been happier if she'd had a life, some kind of real job."

"What about your sister and brother?"

"Well, my sister's nine years older than I am. When I was growing up, I looked up to her. She was my hero. Basically, she told my mom what to do about everything, including me. In high school, she saved money from after-school jobs and bought a convertible Pontiac. I remember her riding around with the top down and bright scarves on her head and patent leather pumps. She had them in every imaginable color lined up in her closet. She and her girlfriends would tool around, Bob Dylan and the Beatles blaring from the radio. Sometimes she'd let boys a lot older drive her car. I was just a nuisance. I was only cute when she didn't have to baby-sit, when I left her alone. She paid me to stay out of her way with Dots and Jujubees.

"My brother's six years older. When we lived on the ranch, he played baseball and was always at practice or playing with the kids who lived down the road. Mostly what I remember is that he had firecrackers and a surfboard.

"Once my parents let the two of them baby-sit together. About twenty minutes after they left, my brother and sister tied a rope around my waist and swung me from the chandelier in the main hall.

" 'This will keep you in one place till Mom and Dad get back,' they said, slamming the front door on their way out."

"And what about your childhood, Alys?"

I avoid talking about my own past.

Marc invites me to his senior prom. I shop for a prom dress and find the perfect one—sleeveless and slinky black. When I slip it on and pose in front of the mirror, I admire my body, more of a woman's body than Elodie's or the other girls in my class. I guess having a baby has done that for me. I wear Beti's pearls and black shoes with just a hint of a heel. Pink lipstick. Marc picks me up in his father's old blue Volvo, surprising me with a small bunch of flowers behind his back. I am reminded of my fourteenth birthday—the last I spent with both Parry and Evan. Marc holds out orange poppies, sticking me when he pins them to my dress.

"Ow."

"Oh, Alys, I'm so sorry." He slips his hand under my dress to fasten the pin at the top.

"It's all right." My knees go a bit weak, at the warmth of his hand against my breast.

Dafydd, at the door watching us, says, "Can I go?"

Marc pats him on his head, Dafydd's hair still nearly white, saying, "Not tonight, boy, not tonight. Your mama and I are going out on a real date tonight, alone. No kids—not even you, the best kid of all."

Before the prom, we stop at the beach, take our shoes off and run from the parking lot through soft sand to the water. I spread a blanket so near the water's edge that we can feel the mist. I want to take my dress off and run into the waves. Marc's brought a fifth of bourbon, two glasses, a bag of ice and some cola. As he pours us drinks, he says, "Man, look at that sun." Huge, bright orange, slipping behind the horizon into the deep green sea. Neither of us says much more, but when he brushes my hand, I shiver. He has touched me a million times but I have never felt quite like I do in that moment. Then, for just an instant when I look at him, I see Evan. My God. I close my eyes, breathe in, the feeling of Evan sweeping through me. For a second more, I keep hold of him deep inside me. When I open my eyes, Marc is staring at me.

"You look terrific, Alys."

Hours later, at the Beverly Hills Hotel, we dance every dance together, ignoring people who try to cut in. We hold hands during dinner. I touch his knee under the table.

A month later, when Marc is supposed to go off to college in Ohio, he transfers to UCLA. We find a small house in Point Dume, near Zuma Beach, overlooking the ocean. I have one more year of high school.

Two years later, while making dinner one night, Marc proposes to me.

*   *   *

Before long we are in our third house together. Although this one is small, we own it. Already it is piled high with books and CDs, our kitchen bulging with the latest equipment. I am becoming quite a good cook. Dafydd's cleats and soccer balls are spilling out of his room into the living room. Marc has made the garage into a music studio and I use the small laundry room for my office.

Sometimes Marc complains about how long it is taking for each of us to establish careers that give us enough time and money to do anything other than work. I remind him that when we met ten years ago we looked at a ski vacation as something only very rich people with a lot of freedom could ever afford.

In March, Marc and Dafydd go off for spring break to Utah for a weeklong ski holiday. I decide to stay home, hold down the fort and use the time to begin studying yoga and meditation.

I hate the cold. Marc does not like meditative exercise. He hates silence. He tells me that he thinks my world is getting smaller while his is expanding to the four corners. After he and Dafydd return from their trip, I go on my first silent retreat. While I'm gone, he writes a score for a movie about a man who leaves his family to climb Mt. Everest. When I get back, he goes off to Brazil. I start work on a new book of poetry.

Beti worries about these separations. "It's not normal," she tells me, "for couples to be away from each other. You've already spent two months with him here, you there and vice versa. And now he's going off to Brazil for a fortnight? Anything might happen."

"What could happen?" I ask. "We've been neck to neck for so many years we look like the winged staff of Mercury."

In June when Dafydd goes off to camp, I am scheduled to teach a monthlong workshop in Vermont. Marc plans to go to Brazil again.

We are in bed; he is on top of me. We kiss. "I'm sorry I've been so cranky. I'm tired, I guess," he says. It feels like a half-assed attempt at an apology for the argument we'd had yesterday. "I hope time away from each other will give us some perspective," he says. "I hate fighting with you."

The argument started because I had stood in front of his piano while he was working, waiting till he looked up, and then asked him to listen to a poem I'd written in the middle of the night. He put his hand over his brow and rubbed his face, sighing deeply, clearly put out by my having interrupted him. I ignore it and read him the poem. He looked up and said, "I don't like it." Looked at me square in the eyes. "Maybe it's because I don't understand it. Maybe I've never understood your poetry."

"What?" I am so shocked, so hurt. I understand the true meaning of "taken aback" because I feel so pushed off balance, I nearly fall.

"Oh, Alys, I don't know. I . . . I . . . I'm just tired of being your constant audience. You have editors who understand your every nuance. I don't know enough about poetry. I'm not even sure I like words."

I know anger is not the right response. It's childish, but I am furious, thinking about how many of his rough scores I have listened to: "Allie, do you mind just coming in here and listening to this theme . . . ?" Like *I* know music? Like *I* can read music? The only thing I know how to play is the radio. But I have still listened to his work, critiqued it as best I can. I don't understand why all of a sudden he seems so touchy about mine.

I explode out of his studio, through the yard to the kitchen. I make lunch and eat it, pouting and alone. By the time I finish, my anger has turned to disappointment. And by the time I've done the washing up, I realize I should never have interrupted him. His work time is as precious as mine. I apologize and so does he. But there has been damage done. I can feel it.

We speak several times while he is in Brazil, short conversations, slightly removed, about our work and letters we've each received from Dafydd. Brief exchanges of information. It's awkward and sad. I think about how to make it right between us.

A month later, I pick him up at LAX. He looks tanned, his hazel eyes gleam. He looks down at his sneakers when he tells me, "It was a good time."

"I missed you. I thought a lot about our life together, our family." What I don't tell him is how I have decided to have his baby. We have talked about it and not talked about it for ten years. He has always wanted a second child. Because of my deepest insecurity of losing a child in some unprecedented way, or of rocking my own sketchy equilibrium, I have been afraid. Now I am sure it is the one thing that will smooth things over. I am convinced it will make things right between us.

When I hug him, he is reticent, tight shoulders, stiff neck. I give him one of those quick nurturing massages lovers exchange without thought and kiss him lightly on the mouth. I whisper, "Let's go home."

Later, when we make love, I can feel him holding back. But I don't and I realize I have forgotten to put in my diaphragm. A month later I take a home pregnancy test and it is positive.

Marc and I sit shoulder to shoulder just above the hard line of wet sand. Hannah has just had her sixth birthday. We are watching her in the sea, up to her knees. She shrieks as she falls face forward into the shallow shoreline of the waves.

"Do you think she's ready for piano lessons?" I ask, leaning over to smooth suntan lotion on his back.

"Oh, I don't know." He tilts his head and squints to watch a gull.

"She's asking for them. She wants you to teach her."

"Not me." He sounds emphatic. He bats a wasp away angrily. "I'm not a teacher. I'd ruin it for her."

"Why do you say that? You're a wonderful teacher. You've got patience. You've got—"

"Forget it, Alys. I'm not going to teach her. Why should I chance it? I'm not even sure she's ready."

"Well, how will you know?"

"She's six, Alys."

"Why are you getting angry, Marco?"

"I'm not angry. I'm just tired. I wish I could just listen to the waves break and watch our daughter without planning for her future. It's Sunday. Let's just give it a rest."

But he is angry. He has been short-tempered and angry with me for a while now.

PART II

CHAPTER NINE

Eight months later and Marc's ashes are still in the box, sitting inside the Chinese cabinet in the dining room. I had this idea we would scatter them in the garden on the first day of spring. But Dafydd isn't available and Hannah doesn't want to do it without him.

How can we move forward without Marc's body put to rest? I feel him watching me all the time. Several weeks ago I came downstairs naked, cutting through the dining room on my way to fetch the morning newspaper, and actually covered myself as I passed the mirrored cabinet. "I hate you," I said out loud, shaking my fist at the cabinet doors.

I insist the "flinging," as I call it, must happen soon. I tell Dafydd and Hannah enough time has passed and we need to do something with their father's remains. It is unsettling for all of us. But it feels false, my trying to press them. They are not yet ready. Perhaps none of us is ready yet to let Marc go.

One morning after Hannah is off to school, I come in from the garden to find four messages on my answering machine. The first message is a voice like velvet, lush and sexual like a baritone sax, rolling her *r*s thick as tar on hot cement.

"Alys, please, it is Gabriella Purdue. It seems unfair that I have to be tracking you down. I know it is hard for you to understand my life with Marc, but losing him is perhaps just as difficult for me as it is for you. I know Phillípe has told you Marc and I have a child together. She is just eight. But I want to talk to you, to see you. I have not spoken to anyone about my life with Marc except Phillípe. Marc and I kept our life extremely quiet. Please let me speak to you. You can reach me at . . ." And then she signs off with "I am begging you to call."

So the child is a girl. Another daughter.

Aside from everything else, this woman must have no sense at all. What if Hannah were home? What if she were standing next to me when I played my messages? My body temperature has risen at least ten degrees. I pace, want to scream, shake someone. Marc. Gabriella. Both of them. I am ashamed of the intensity of my anger and my jealousy, knowing I should at least care about the child. The little girl is innocent and she is Marc's flesh and blood. But because she is connected to Gabriella, she doesn't seem innocent. I punch the DELETE button and don't listen to the rest of the messages. I break a glass while doing the dishes and leave the broken pieces in the sink.

Ed Meyers has told me Gabriella called him more than once requesting I ring her, threatening to come after me if I don't. Friendly. Phillípe, too, passed on a message that Gabriella wished I would ring her. Her call on the machine this morning is more than an intrusion. It is an invasion.

My lawyer assures me in no uncertain terms there is no way in the world Gabriella can extract money from Marc's estate, either for her or her child. The trusts Marc and I created for each other and the children are the final word. Binding, irrevocable.

Hannah asks me if she can spend a month—"four weeks, exactly"—at camp. "Alone. I can do it. And I want you to take me and pick me up," she adds.

Deerwood Camp is outside Durango. It is the same camp she spent two weeks at last year. But last year Marc and I were at Elizabeth's, our home away from home, close by.

"I swear I won't get homesick. I just know I won't."

She is certainly in better shape than she was eight months ago. In the weeks soon after Marc's death, Hannah wouldn't even talk to her best friend, Heather. She wouldn't return her phone calls or see her. Last week she played at Heather's twice and slept over on Friday night.

I suppose I am still afraid for her to be out of my sight for such a long stretch. What if she has one of her nightmares or sleepwalks? What will happen to her without my ever-present watchful eye, my constant warnings? I'm not sure how Hannah is really dealing with her loss. At the moment it seems to be a little-by-little letting go. But I still worry about some major explosion, some huge emotional reaction when I am too far away to be of help.

I have to admit that part of what really frightens me is what *I* will do without Hannah's steadying presence in my life. Four weeks is a long time—an eternity for me to be on my own, without my safety net.

But Hannah is so intent I agree to let her go. I wash her clothes, taking each piece of clothing from the dryer, each garment larger than last year: wooly long johns, knickers, a pile jacket, T-shirts, shorts, rain pants and jeans. I sew name tags into each piece, wishing I could sew one on her arm, tattoo her, implant a locator chip— any kind of protection against loss.

While packing her purple trunk, I say a silent prayer over each item. "Keep her safe, keep her safe . . ." I put in Winnie-the-Pooh, stamped postcards, seven little knickers with the names of each day of the week, each wrapped separately in colored tissue. And finally a flashlight and a small Swiss Army knife—presents she will find from time to time. She catches me putting a photo of Marc in and asks me to take it out. "I don't want to think about Daddy," she says.

Having not flown since Marc died, at the airport I force myself up to the role of "the good mother," the calm mother, taking her child to camp. No one knows anything about our lives. No one knows what we have been living through. In public we are ordinary folks with quotidian problems, and it feels good.

On the airplane, seat belts fastened, Hannah confides, "I'm afraid of flying."

"Don't be. It's safer than any other form of transportation. It's much safer than driving." I don't believe a word of this, of course. I close my eyes and say a prayer.

In Phoenix we change from the large plane to a sixteen-seater, so small we have to bend down to get through the door. We've flown on these planes a hundred times and I know it might be rough, especially over the Rockies. When the plane starts to waggle about, I breathe deeply. When we reach peak altitude and the plane dips a bit, I clutch Hannah's arm.

"I'm used to it now," she says confidently, adding what Marc might have said: "Just pretend you're on a bucking bronco."

"Yeah, right."

Safely in Durango, I rent a car, and an hour later we are at Deerwood Camp with dozens of other parents and kids who have flown in from all around the country. We shake hands, help to make beds, mill about uncomfortably, and then it is time to say our good-byes.

"Don't cry, Mommy, please," Hannah whispers when she sees my eyes fill and I pull a tissue from my sleeve. She sounds like Mam and Beti. "This is a good thing. I'm going to have fun!" I smile through my tears. "Write in your journal, Mama-loo. When we meet up in four weeks I want you to be able to remember every single moment so you can fill me in." I know she is mimicking me.

"But seriously," I beg, "if you should get homesick—write me, okay?"

Hannah smiles and waves.

"I'll miss you!" I manage to choke out. I take a long last look at her before turning and walking down the dusty hill past the mess hall and the swimming pond to my rented car.

Before going to Elizabeth's for the night, I take a walk along *El Río de las Ánimas Perdidas,* "The River of Lost Souls," better known in Durango as the Animas River.

On this soft, warm summer day, the sky seems to be everywhere. I reach my arms up as if to touch it. I wish I were staying longer than just the night. I wish I were going off to camp.

Near the river's edge, I pick up a river rock, smoothing it between my fingers. When Marc and I first came to Durango, we picnicked right here, in this very spot. We'd just seen the cabin.

"If we can get a loan, let's buy it. We can spend Thanksgivings and Christmas, Easter break and summers. It'll be good for our writing. It'll be good for our lungs. It'll be good for our marriage," he'd said.

Our marriage. I hadn't known just how much trouble our marriage was in. I throw the rock into the river, aiming at nothing, throwing it straight and hard.

The next stone is small and sharp.

Our first Christmas we'd cut a tree from the woods out back and dragged it to the house, making a trail through the deep, newly fallen snow. "You want to tell me again why we had to cut one so big?" Marc asked breathlessly.

That had been the first time Hannah saw snow. I'd found little tin candleholders and brought them with us and put candles on every arm of the tree. When we lit them several days later, one of them caught fire; before long one side of the tree was aflame.

"I guess your instinct was right. If we'd cut a smaller tree, we'd have nothing left. Good choice, Alys." Marc laughed. Fortunately, he'd bought a fire extinguisher, which we'd put next to the tree.

This stone follows the first into the river.

It catches the current, then disappears. So quiet, wind through the trees, the soft swing of tall blades of grass, the full sweep of life around me. Just now there seems such a sweet purity to it all.

Each of us collected rocks. Marc's collection was the largest. They lay in ceramic bowls on every surface, and we'd left them with Elizabeth when we sold her the cabin. That last summer we had a discussion about the difference between a rock and a boulder. I thought a boulder was a huge rock. Marc told me that a boulder was any rock that was moved from the parent rock by weather or any other natural force, and was bigger than a breadbox.

I reach behind myself and pick up a larger rock and heave it into the river. What a satisfying *plop*! One by one, twenty rocks, heaved with all my might. We'd been together for twenty years—twenty good years, I'd thought. Who can I trust now?

Walking away from the river, I look around, hearing the sound of Marc's voice, loud and clear. *I love you, Alys,* he says. Of course, there is no one there. "No one but the River God," Hannah would say. I look up at the bare, burned limbs of the tree Hannah and Marc named the "Buzzard Tree." It is covered with huge, crouching black buzzards, their red-crowned bald heads shining under the glaring sunlight. Their slow downward dive for flesh makes me cringe. I clap my hands, causing most of them to spread their wings wide and fly off. Then I put my palms together and bow low to the River God and to my memories of Marc, and I walk away.

I spend the night with Elizabeth. This is our first time together since Marco's death. Although I've often considered confiding in her about Gabriella—even had the phone in my hand to call her—I can't go through with it. Elizabeth has her own deep feelings for Marc, who had been her friend for nearly all the years he and I had been together. In fact, her being in Durango is because of Marc.

"It's an easier place to live. You don't need as much money, and it'll be a change for you," he'd told her.

After Elizabeth graduated from high school she left Texas to seek fame and fortune in Los Angeles. I had just quit working for Beti. Elizabeth took my job. We've been friends since.

Recently, Elizabeth had a brief affair. Too late, she learned her lover had invented everything he had told her about himself. Too late she learned he was a married ex-con who had gone to prison for fraud. One of the reasons she misses Marco so much is because of his honesty. How can I ruin him for her?

Elizabeth serves up her amazing Guatemalan rellenos with lots of roasted hot peppers and guacamole, one of my favorites. We sit contentedly under the black-and-blue sky, watching our shadows grow longer on the surface of the Animas River, roaring just feet away. She has opened one of her precious bottles of Chianti Riserva, and when she raises her glass, she says, "I predict a trip over the big waters, where you will find . . ."

I look over my wineglass. "Don't say 'another man.' "

"You've got something against men?" she teases. "No, I don't think this is about a man. Actually, I was going to say, I predict you will find *yourself*."

"Ah."

Elizabeth claims to be psychic, has studied tarot cards for years. "Remember, it's in my Indian blood."

I laugh, loving her good intentions. "Okay, Elizabeth, who exactly is this sitting across from you if it isn't me?"

"Oh, it's you all right, Alys," she says. "But I'm talking about what's going on inside you." She tilts her head as if I am acting silly and must surely understand what she's on about. "Or perhaps what's *not* going on inside of you," she adds. "Correct me if I'm wrong, but you've been 'outside of yourself,' as k.d. lang would say, for a long, long time."

"Outside of myself?"

"Don't you think? Not just in the last year because of Marc, but ever since I met you. Part of you living and the other part of you always off somewhere else pretending at life?" She knows quite a lot about my childhood, the disaster, my lack of relationship with my parents, Evan.

"I feel like you're on the verge of something different. I don't know. *Profound* maybe. Perhaps you're ready to fly."

"Literally or figuratively?" I am trying to throw her off my trail. "Exactly how do you know this, Lizzie?"

She shrugs her shoulders. "It's just a feeling. A hunch. You know how I am about these things."

She's empathetic in the deepest sense, and her ability to share in my emotions, thoughts and feelings is of course one of the many reasons I love her.

We are quiet for a long time as we eat her rellenos. She talks about her new work aiding elderly people in need, many of them Alzheimer's patients.

"I think I've finally found a place for myself in the world." She seems calm and happy. How lovely to be so content alone.

I raise my glass. "I love you, Elizabeth."

Back in L.A., I sort through the stack of mail waiting for me and discover a letter from Mam. It could only mean trouble. I haven't had a letter from her since Gram died. Of course I knew Gram was dying. We continued writing to each other since our first letters after I'd left Wales. A month before Hannah was born, I'd had a letter saying she felt she was "on to greener pastures." I'd wanted to see her, desperately, and actually bought a plane ticket. But in the end my doctor said absolutely not. I was too close to delivery.

In her last letter, she'd written:

No need, Allie. I'm not afraid. I'm ready. I've been ready for a long time. Beryl is with me. I love you in the deepest part of my soul, and even with you a million miles away, you are also here with me.

I felt Gram's death. In the middle of the night I awakened and sat bolt upright. Marc awakened and tried to comfort me. "Gram has gone. I'm sure of it." And then I felt her with me, Marc's hand, suddenly hers. He turned over, closer to me. Before long I was fast asleep again. Mam's letter arrived a few days later.

This time there is no premonition. With Mam's recent letter in my back pocket I walk out to the deck. If it's bad news, I want to have the Pacific Ocean in my view. The warm sun makes me glad to be in southern California, even alone. On this quiet morning, hummingbirds cluster at both feeders, a red-tailed hawk circling above the Torrey pines.

This past year I felt like I had disappeared, just as I felt when I moved from Aberfan. In those first months here in Santa Monica I was so utterly depressed. The obstetrician assumed the depression was caused by my fluctuating hormones. But I knew it wasn't the baby moving in me causing the weepiness, the constant metallic taste in my mouth, the hole at my core. It was all of my past losses. When Marc died, it felt the same. I was no one again.

Perhaps Elizabeth is right. Maybe I will have the chance now to make myself up anew.

I shrug and take the letter out of my pocket.

Dear Alys,

Da is ill. He wouldn't want me worrying you. Doc Rogers says his lungs aren't all that bad, considering. They're filling up with liquid. They might hold out for a few more months. But I can see his strength ebbing. His appetite is not good. Seems like he's given in to it. I'd say Da is worse off than Doc Rogers is letting on. As you know, Beti came at Christmas with Colin and the children. I know he'd like to see you. I don't mean to be putting pressure on you, but I thought you should know.

Love,
Mam

Since I'd left Wales, the closest I had ever come to going home—besides the time just before Gram died—was while Marc and I were in Ireland staying near the Rosslare Harbor. He was working on a film. Over breakfast one morning he said, "I looked at a map, and you know, it's a straight shot on the ferry to Fishguard. We could rent a car, drive up to Aberfan."

I didn't look at him. We'd had an agreement. I'd said no conversation about my parents. Back then, he knew I couldn't handle reminders of home; my contact with Beti was the one exception.

Later that morning while hiking to the top of an overlook, I could see the tip of Wales. In a flash some part of me unlocked, and light—through a crack not more than a keyhole's worth—moved in. When I returned to the hotel I dialed Mam and Da up. I let it ring three times, my heart wild, before I carefully put the receiver back in its cradle.

This is our dream house. The house we had bought, big enough for grandchildren. Marc's and my fourth and now last house together. Our beautiful canyon. The view is broken only by the towering old redwood tree planted long before Marc and I bought the house. It stands rooted, taller than anything else in our garden. How many times have I looked at that tree and wondered how it felt to be the only redwood for many miles? The people who built the house had terraced the garden and planted some of every kind of tree that grows well in California. Torrey pines, a stand of scrub oak, eucalyptus, a birch, a sycamore, a gingko, orange, grapefruit, lemon, avocado—the California woods. But it is this one tall redwood that is my towering strength. That tree has heard my poetry and helped me hold my tears.

I make my way down the narrow back steps into the heart of the garden where the azaleas are falling off their bloom, seven different kinds. At one time I knew all their proper names. Now I don't remember any of them, but I can smell the huge purple ones whose blossoms look like babies' hands and bleed when I break the flower from their stems. Their sweet smell permeates the whole garden. Walking among them, I pull the dead leaves and wilted flowers and push them into the pockets of my trousers. I love this garden. I planted a good portion of the flowering plants just after we bought the house.

"Alys, the house is a wreck. Leave the garden alone for now." Marc was exasperated. We'd bought the house—a "handyman special"—and planned to renovate everything before we moved in. Marc wanted my attention inside. But even before we closed, I'd come over with my hoe, saw, hackers and shears. I cleared out all the dead plants and pulled shrubs and bushes up by the roots, piled them high. I'd cut back the ferns and the vinca to nothing, torn out the dead cactus and ivy by the roots. I'd pruned the orange and lemon trees myself.

"Come on, Alys," Marc begged. "What about Hannah's room? What about our bedroom? Our offices? We aren't going to live out here, Alys." In the end, Marc gave up and joined me. He'd put in a small rose garden and two pepper trees at the far end of the property.

Had I ever seen Da ill? I can't remember he'd ever had so much as a sleep in, even during his bouts of catarrh. He was always up and out by the time I'd started off to school. Even after the disaster. Even on the weekends, he sometimes worked the night shift. I'd find him in the kitchen, early morning, leaning against the table, drinking his cup of tea and reading the newspaper by the back door, all six foot of him bent over it. He'd look up and smile at me. "Alys, you're up early."

Now I run down the narrow garden path, faster and faster, the wind pushing me. I grab the redwood and hang on. I want my da.

Later that day while I am going through Marc's desk, my nerves still jagged, my mind full of the past, the phone rings.

"Hello," I say, hoping it is Elizabeth. Knowing her incredible power of telepathy, I'd thought about calling her just after I read Mam's letter.

"Alys?"

Oh, Jesus, it's Gabriella. I consider hanging up. In fact, my arm is in motion.

"Don't hang up, please," she says.

Caught. "Gabriella," I say slowly.

"Thank you," she pauses, catching her breath. "I have wanted to speak with you ever since Marc . . ."

Her voice is so full-bodied, so genuine, it is like she is standing in the same room with her hand on mine. I soften for a moment, then remember her relentless harassment of Ed and her messages on my answering machine.

"I've not had a soul to talk to, except Phillípe, and he's never been terribly behind us, as I'm sure you know. Now he says he feels squeezed in the middle."

In my darkest moments, I have imagined Philípe pushing Marc full force to take the Brazilian leap to love, abetting their connection.

"I need, so much, to talk with you. Not to hurt you, not to make a problem. Is it possible, Alys, for us to meet? These matters are so difficult over the telephone coming out wrong sometimes, and I would like to be able to talk about them to you face-to-face. You see, if you give me the chance, I will explain . . ." And here she goes silent again and I can hear the hands-over-the-phone muffling of her tears. "I am planning a trip to Los Angeles as soon as there is work for me there. My manager is working on it."

I am silent.

"Actually, the truth is, I have not been able to work. My daughter has needed me close at hand. I know you must understand that situation. You and I, we have a great deal in common. I would like to meet you again. To talk about them, our children."

"No," I say, slamming the door on this idea.

Another moment of silence on her end. "We must sort this out," she says, equally firm. "Isabel and I are having a hard time of it."

Isabel. One of the names Marc had wanted to call Hannah.

"I have no family here. I have no one to turn to. The way Marc spoke of you, and Hannah . . . can you understand that I feel as if you are my family?"

A chill runs up my spine. I hate Marc, furious he has put me in this situation. I reach into the bottom drawer of his desk, where I know he hid his cigarettes. I shake one out and light it.

"I don't believe there is a way to sort this out, Gabriella." I say her name slowly, pronouncing each syllable. "In fact, please stop calling. Leave us alone."

"I cannot. Marc had another family. You must recognize us. Our daughters are half sisters. Marc would have wanted us to work this out," she adds.

Inhaling deeply, I explain, "I don't know what you mean by 'working this out.' I'm sure had Marc wanted us to work it out, he would have directed us. Don't you think?" I watch the smoke as I exhale. I can be so cold. "I mean, nine years is enough time to have figured something out," I say rather calmly, considering the circumstances. The cigarette has made me dizzy. I need to call Elizabeth.

"You should know that Marc never had any intention of hurting you," Gabriella says quietly. "You were not to know about us unless it was absolutely necessary. Now it seems necessary."

"Not for me." Inhaling the cigarette, my jaw clenches, my body is stiff. I feel like there is a metal rod tied up against my spine. "You both must have thought me an awful fool." I am surprised I have admitted this to her. Nine years.

As I stub the cigarette out on one of Marc's crystal paperweights, it occurs to me how stressful it must have been for him. The lies he had to tell. The lies he lived. No wonder he smoked and was on edge most of the time. Had he planned to keep the two of them from me forever?

"How did you manage for as long as this without my finding out?" I ask.

"I can hear how angry you are," Gabriella says. "It was just something that happened. We didn't plan it and we certainly were not trying to make you look or feel a fool. That was the last thing Marc wanted, believe me. He loved you dearly."

"Now that's a comfort." I almost laugh.

"Obviously I've had more time to get used to this. Please let me tell you how it happened. Perhaps when you hear—"

"I can't listen anymore."

Her tone changes. "If you won't let us in emotionally, perhaps you might be willing to help in other ways. You see, Marc was paying for Isabel's school as well as our mortgage. I've had to take a sizable loan against the house and I've run through most of it."

Ah, finally, there's the money issue.

"Oh my God, Gabriella. I happen to have a family to provide for, too. I'm sure a singer of your caliber makes a lot more money than a poet. Forgive me, but I cannot talk any longer. I must go."

As I put the phone down, I remember Marc's calendar. *I's bill due* jumps out at me. Why should I have to give her anything? She has already had more than her fair share. And our daughters most certainly do not need to know one another. How in the world would I explain to Hannah that her father had lived a double life? Am I supposed to bridge the gap between her and her "half sister" by explaining that when he was in Brazil and couldn't come to her parent/teacher conference, or missed it when she starred in *Ramona Quimby*, it was not really because he was working, but that he was in Rio with his other daughter? For that matter, I wonder how Gabriella had explained this to Isabel.

While I stand by the kitchen window hunched down, unable to move, my arms crossed over my chest, the phone rings again. Two rings, three, four rings—the machine picks up.

"Alys, I know you are there. You absolutely must help me, Alys!"

I vomit into the sink.

CHAPTER TEN

For the next twenty-four hours I stay in bed, sleeping on and off, getting up only to go to the bathroom. My body is so heavy. At five thirty a.m. the great horned owl hoots. I have not heard it in years. Marc had thought he was gone for good. But he is back, just outside my window in the same eucalyptus he was always in.

I lie perfectly still, thinking that what I have really wished for most often this year is to just lie down flat as a rubbed stone at the bottom of some river, the water rushing over me, smoothing my edges, all memory of heartache pulled out with the rush of the current as it empties itself. And in the end to rise like that owl and eye the water's surface, shining, its pull, wild with life, my own. Water over water, words over words, water over words, words over water—the persistence of that rhythm, the sound of life beating in my own ear. Collect yourself, it says. Pick yourself up like a prized pebble along a riverbank. Hold yourself lightly, letting the cool river wash over you. You are worth keeping.

And that is an example of the kind of awful, overwritten nonsense I have been committing to paper in the wee hours of the morning since Marc died.

In the morning, I am certain I must see Da, yet the thought of leaving the country while Hannah is at camp seems terrifying. But melodramatic as it seems, there is no other choice. Da's time is running out. I get up, shower, make myself a cup of milky coffee and, without a moment's hesitation, pick up the telephone and make a reservation using most of my accrued miles, for tonight's red-eye on American Airlines to London. I remember the Angel Hotel; Da and I walked by it when we were in Cardiff together. As if I've done it a thousand times before, I call and make a booking to begin the following afternoon. Then I arrange for a car to pick me up at Heathrow Airport and drive me down to Cardiff.

Finally, I call Dafydd at work.

"Dafydd Davies," he answers on the first ring.

"Hi, sweetie."

"Hi, Mom," he says in his work mode, talking quickly. "Did you get Hannah off to camp?"

"I did."

"How'd it go?"

"Fine. Everything's fine. It looks like she's going to love it. I met her roommate and helped make her bed. She'll be fine." How can I leave her? It's crazy to travel so far away. What if she should take ill?

"And how are you?" he asks. "Alone for the first time, maybe ever?"

"Well, actually, I'm fine, too." Interesting that he should notice that it is in fact the first time. I wonder if he is worried about me being alone. "In fact, I'm going to Wales tonight." Only half of me believes it.

"Wales? You're joking, right? I thought you were never going back to Wales?"

"My father is ill."

"Oh." He pauses. "How ill?"

"I don't know. My mother says she can't tell how serious it is," I lie.

"Do you want me to go with you?"

"Oh, sweetheart, I think I should do this on my own."

"Well, I'd like to go, really. You know I've been thinking about it. I'll take a long weekend. It's a good time for me to take off here. I'd like to meet my grandparents. I'd like to meet my father. I'd like to know what part of me is like them, Mom."

I flinch. His father. "You will, Dafydd. You absolutely will have a chance. But not now. Next time, okay?"

"Oh, come on, Mom. You really want to go alone? You being there would make it more comfortable for me. It would be great."

"No. I think I really do want to go alone. I can't tell you why. I don't really know why." And then I add, "I guess I need to."

"Okay. But it doesn't seem exactly fair."

Another pause.

"Dafydd. This is not about being fair. He's my father and I haven't seen him in twenty years."

"Yeah, I can understand that. It's about the same deal for me." I hear his anger, covering his disappointment. I almost relent, but then he says, "Forget it. But if you change your mind, I'll come. All you have to do is call."

"Dafydd, thanks." I am relieved. "I appreciate that. I love you."

"I love you, too, Momma. Be careful," he says.

As I imagine getting on the plane, taking off, arriving in London and driving down to Cardiff, my stomach muscles tighten.

What clothes should I take? I have not been in Wales in more than twenty years, not since I was four months pregnant. What will we all look like to each other? Jeans, T-shirts and hiking boots, a long cashmere dress and cowboy boots, an old army jacket of Marc's. It'll be cold and damp even though it's summer. Pushing the fact that I will be thousands of miles away from Hannah out of my mind, I throw things into my suitcase like time really is running out.

I call Beti. "I'm going home."

"To Aberfan? Are you serious, Alys?" Same reaction as Dafydd.

I try not to be defensive. "Yes, I am serious."

"Well, that's wonderful. You'll make Da so happy. He's wanted to see you for so many years. But you must be nervous about seeing them, after all this time. Are you?"

I tell her I am mostly worried about being so far away from Hannah. "Remember, she's at camp."

"Oh, of course. Since you've decided to go, try not to worry. If anything comes up, you know I'll be glad to deal with it. I'm sure you gave them Dafydd's number but please give them my telephone number as well."

"I really appreciate that, Beti. Thanks."

"How long will you be gone?"

"About ten days."

I ring off before she can ask me any other questions. Although admittedly Beti has always been there for me in a pinch, I know it's been hard. Through the years I've gotten used to our cool manner of relating. Our shared genetic code. Since Marc's passing, she seems to want to help in some new, more comforting, way. Perhaps because of Hannah. But still, we don't talk much. One of our commonalities seems to be we don't like to look back. Beti left Aberfan as quickly as she could and doesn't like to be around anything that reminds her of it. And I'm one of those "things" that force her to remember what she fled.

I wish I could leave without telling Hannah. She will only worry about my being so far away from her, in another country. The directors have asked parents not to call. Letters and faxes are okay. I leave my hotel number as well as Dafydd's and Beti's with one of the directors, letting them know that both Dafydd and Beti should act on my behalf in case of an emergency.

I try to fill my mind with more innocuous thoughts, wondering what Cardiff is like now. After all, it is the capital of Wales. I never spent time there except that once, when Da took me in cousin Greg's car to see a celebration for Prince Charles. It was years after the Prince's investiture, two years after the disaster. "A kind of prebirthday celebration," Da said. "You don't turn ten every day!" No one else would go with us. Parry had moved out and Mam said she had no desire to go to "that stinkin' Cardiff." Gram was up valley with Auntie Beryl for a few days since Beryl would no longer come to the house because of Da.

I was glad to be alone with him. The day was sunny and warm; cousin Greg's car smelled new. We kept all the windows open as we drove out of Aberfan, along the old familiar roads bordered along with the high full hedges, toward the cutoff to the M4.

The motorway was the widest road I'd ever been on: two lanes of traffic going in both directions. As we got near to Cardiff, the traffic backed up for miles. In the end, we couldn't even get close to the castle where the festivities were being held.

"Oh, well, we're here. We might as well enjoy ourselves." Da realized my disappointment.

We parked about two miles from the city center and walked along the dockland Da called Tiger Bay. Fishermen were everywhere, with their nets and burlap bags full of fish. The fishy smell stayed stuck up my nose the rest of the day. The crowd was so thick, I feared I could be lost forever if I let go of Da's hand. From the direction of the castle we could hear a band.

On the drive home, we stopped and had lunch at a pub in Pontypridd where Da knew the owner. I sat outside while Da had a quick beer inside and ordered our lunch. On that sunny day, I pretended my life was as normal as those of the other children playing on the grass.

That memory seems to take me through the rest of the day, all the way to the airport. But by that time I feel like I've had six cups of coffee. I am shaking like a rattlesnake about to strike, and I've a headache from clenching my teeth. On the plane I am seated next to an attractive older man, about sixty, white hair slicked back. He's wearing a blue pinstriped suit. He smiles at me as I buckle up. I return the smile but look away, out the window, not intending to spend the whole trip chatting with him. I quickly put on my earphones and turn up the volume so I am wrapped up in the *Goldberg Variations*.

The flight attendant offers me a glass of wine, which I gratefully accept. After several sips I put my head back and breathe a little more evenly until suddenly Gabriella comes to mind. I am furious all over again. She was not just my husband's lover; they shared a life, a house, a child. They shared part of my life. Everything she had with Marc meant there was that much less of him for me, for us. The really terrible truth is that, for all of those years, I had not known how much more there might have been of him. The question now is, how can I make all of this go away before Dafydd or Hannah gets wind of it?

When the plane starts down the runway the fist of fear lands a sudden punch in my stomach. I close my eyes, imagining myself running next to the plane and as it lifts off the ground, I lift, too. A small voice inside tells me I am going home. Aberfan. When we are at a cruising altitude, I ask the flight attendant for another glass of wine.

I sleep on and off for most of the eleven-hour flight, missing dinner and breakfast. When I awaken the flight attendant is bringing around hot towels. The earphones are still plugged in my ears, and when I remove them, the pilot is announcing we will be landing at Heathrow in twenty-five minutes. As the plane banks to the left, a patchwork of land comes into sight. There seems no color in the world like the deep green of Britain. My stomach reels with a mixture of excitement and overriding anxiety and fear.

I am glad for my British passport. There is a long queue at the customs windows, where those with American and other foreign passports must stand.

Marc always wanted me to become an American citizen. I used to kid him that it was mostly so we could stand in the queue together.

As the automatic doors slide open I see a tall, suited man holding a sign that reads MS. ALYS DAVIES. In jeans and a sweater and Marc's army green bomber jacket, I suddenly feel underdressed.

"Hello, Ms. Davies. I'm Tom Jenkins. How was your flight, then?" The lyrical rise and fall of his Welsh accent makes me smile with pleasure and disbelief.

"Lovely, thank you." I don't give him my backpack. It looks so scruffy alongside his neat black suit and white shirt with the starched collar that, when he offers to take it, I smile and shake my head. After we collect my bags, he leads the way through the tunneled maze of Heathrow's bowels toward the car park. When the doors open, the familiar smell of diesel and the damp, thick, cool morning air take up residence in me.

Mr. Jenkins brings the car, and as I start to go round to the front passenger seat, he says, "Sit in the back, Ms. Davies. I think you'll find it more comfortable." I pile into the backseat of the gray Daimler, a little embarrassed to be making my reentry in such an extravagant manner.

The ride home is alternately bone-deep familiar and completely strange. We pass field after field of the black-and-white Jersey cows that Gram so longed for. But the small lone stone white farmhouses of my childhood memories have mostly been replaced by larger factory towns. Ridiculous things pop into my mind, all of them about food: treacle, tiny Brussels sprouts, new potatoes, courgettes, rhubarb pie with dollops of Devon cream thick as butter, gooey chocolate puddings and trifle. I realize I am hungry.

It is about two p.m. in Colorado. I wonder what Hannah is doing. Should I have taken her and Dafydd with me? Mr. Jenkins barrels the car forward. Thankfully, he doesn't try to make conversation. I just let my eyes wander over the scenery and the backside of village after village as we eat up the miles.

Two hours later we cross the Severn Road Bridge with its sign that reads WELCOME TO WALES and, under that, CROESO I GYMRU. I roll down the window and in the rushing wind I swear I hear the rise and fall of a hundred Welsh voices, their melodious ringing piercing me to the marrow. I try like mad to hold the tears back. Mr. Jenkins sees me in his rearview mirror.

"It's been a long time since I've been home. I guess I'm a little overwhelmed."

"Oh, I thought you might be from these parts, like."

"Up the valley, actually. I haven't been home in more than twenty years."

Mr. Jenkins nods in the mirror. "Whereabouts?"

"Aberfan."

Silence.

And then he says, "Not the easiest place to have been from."

I have forgotten that most everyone around my age would have heard of Aberfan.

I do not know downtown Cardiff well enough to determine if it has changed, but the number of people we pass on the roads tell me that, if once it was a small city center, it is now a large and crowded one.

As we pull in front of the hotel, I remember that when we'd seen it on that day so long ago, Da had called it the poshest in the city.

I walk up the marble stairs and into the spacious, slightly faded lobby to find the check-in desk. Mr. Jenkins refuses a tip, saying, "That won't be necessary, Ms. Davies. It's all included. Will you be desirous of my services before your return to Heathrow?" I shake my head, explaining I have rented a car. He hands me his card. "I live close by, if you need anything. Anything at all."

"Welcome home." He bows to me, tips his cap and starts to turn away. "Do you mind me asking a personal question, like?"

"Not at all."

"I knew a boy once from Aberfan name of Parry Davies. Is he in your family? I lost track of him after my parents moved us away from the valleys."

He catches me completely off guard and for a moment I just stare, trying to remember Tom Jenkins from way back. And then, breathing in deeply, I say, "No."

I haven't actually talked about Parry much since I married Marco. Even before that, when it was fresh, I tried not to talk about his death. And now, it seems, I still can't say much.

He nods at me awkwardly. "Small world sometimes. I just thought I'd ask."

I look away, hiding whatever trace there might be of Parry in my face.

"I'm around if you need me. Don't forget now."

Before going up to my room, I fax Hannah: *Have arrived in Cardiff, Wales. Thinking of you!* I push all of the numbers and watch the paper being pulled through the machine, feeling far, far away.

In my room, I throw the drapes open. Next door, Cardiff Castle looks like something out of a fairy tale, beautiful, with its turrets and balconies, the vines growing up the sides. In fairy tales, the castle is the stronghold, where everything inside is magical. But I've learned there is no fairy tale castle and no life is untouched by hurt or harm.

I fall asleep for several hours, and when I wake, my muscles are cramped and I'm feeling starved. Probably because of the long flight, lack of water, time change and, most of all, the distance from home and Hannah. My head is splitting. After two aspirin and some yoga, I remind myself that there is no past for me in Cardiff, and Aberfan is still a day away. Today can just be tourist stuff. The guidebook on the coffee table includes a map. Before I can change my mind, I dress and grab my backpack. Out of the hotel and onto the road, I turn right and walk up St. Mary's Street, hit again with the familiar smell from childhood. Diesel oil. The castle towers behind me.

The next few hours are full of the business of getting organized, changing money, remembering to cross on the left side of the road, getting oriented. I feel irresponsible and guilty remembering Dafydd's response and me not wanting him to come. But I remind myself it is as necessary for me to be on this sojourn alone as it is for Hannah to be at camp.

On the other side of the guilt a certain freedom rises. Until yesterday there hadn't been more than twenty-four hours since Marco's death that I'd not thought of him. Today he slips a little farther away.

With the *Western Mail* under my arm, I move through a low stone archway into a corridor with shops on either side. A Welsh mall! I find a table in the back of a nice, dark pub where the ceilings are so low I almost have to stoop.

"Special's steak and kidney pie and a glass of red wine for four pound fifty pence," a short redheaded waitress practically sings in her Welsh accent. For dessert I order my favorite, crème caramel, and when it comes I am overwhelmed with a sense memory of my fourteenth birthday, when Evan served the rich toffee-colored sweet to me and Parry.

I spend the rest of the afternoon exploring the wide streets, where red double-decker buses and square-backed taxis move bumper to bumper amid diverse crowds. Cardiff could be any sophisticated European city. In the distance is the sea. I pass an Indian takeaway, where the smells of cumin and cardamom immediately make me want to eat again, a fish-and-chip shop, a mosque, a Jamaican greengrocer, a Greek Orthodox church and a tattoo parlor. A left turn down Boulevard de Nantes and I am completely lost.

A queue of British Navy men walk toward me. Hearing Mam in my ear, I can't decide if I should run or stare. For her, Cardiff would always be famous for its "grotty feeling round the edges. It's the sailors. Don't like the place a bit."

Little by little, I feel my family beginning to take hold of me. I am not more than fifteen miles from where I grew up. Perhaps if I'd known a real city was so close, I might not have run so far as California. Hah! The truth is, back then, sometimes even California didn't seem far enough away.

On the right, a huge rugby stadium called Cardiff Arms Park sits next to the Taff River, which I remember starts way up the valleys, beyond Aberfan. "Hey, little Taffy. D'you want to go catch a couple of two-eyes?" I remember Da asking Parry. "Taffy," a nickname for a Welshman, and "two-eyes," Da's shorthand for fish. Occasionally I've used Taffy as a pet name for Dafydd.

After climbing a steep stairway to the top of a lookout tower, which a sign says was built by the Normans, I get a clear view of the hills and up the valley, where I will head tomorrow. I shiver. But today there is nothing but the sights and smells of Cathedral Road, Llandaff Cathedral, Howell's Department Shop, Cathays Park and Butetown—along the sea with its sailors, small houseboats and tugboats stretching off in the view. I am on holiday.

In the evening I change my clothes and walk to a bookstore, where I buy Margaret Drabble's latest as insurance against any possibility of a long, lonely night. Then I hail a taxi that drops me at a small, four-star café recommended in the guidebook, order a glass of French chardonnay and Dover sole meunière with chocolate mousse for dessert. The fish is flaky and the mousse is perfect. Halfway through my second glass of wine, I remember tomorrow's drive home and my stomach tightens. Will I even be able to find my way?

Back at the hotel, I call Hannah's camp. "There was some homesickness for a few days," the director says. "But it seems to have subsided," he assures me. They are watching her closely. She is out on a horse ride and won't return until it is early in the morning here.

Since I am traveling abroad, they agree I can check in periodically by phone. My fax has already been placed in Hannah's mailbox. The director promises to give Hannah my love and kisses and tell her I will call again.

I pull back the curtains, open the windows and turn my lights out—leaving me with only the illumination from Cardiff Castle.

From bed, I watch HTV, the Welsh-owned station, fascinated that the program is in Welsh.

Sometime much later, I awaken and the television is still on but there is no sound, just a lineup of color bars. Following a homing instinct, I reach over the bedclothes, searching for Marc. The numbers on the digital clock read four twenty-three. It takes a moment to remember where I am.

My mind starts to tumble over all the terrible possibilities of what Gabriella might do in her frustration to get to me. I don't know her well enough to know if she is vindictive. If she wants to sue the estate she can probably find a lawyer who will take her case. Marc's music was popular in Brazil and I guess she could even sell the story to some sleazy writer at the Brazilian equivalent of the *Enquirer* or the *Sun*. It's the kind of gossip that could ruin one's privacy. No mother would expose her child to such filthy publicity, would she?

The last time I saw Gabriella was when the Brazilians were in town for the U.S. opening of *The Yellow Door*. I didn't notice that she and Marc paid each other any particular attention. Hannah would have been about a year old. And their child—I run through the math quickly—my God, Gabriella was pregnant.

That night our friend Shata and I had put together an unbelievable Indian feast, unusual and spicy. Memories of the evening seem
consumed by food and the weather, which I remember was also
rather unusual for L.A.—a cold, rainy night. We built a fire in the living room fireplace and after dinner we gathered round it. It was a
pleasant evening with lots of Portuguese and English mixed together,
hysterical laughter. Late in the evening Gabriella sang, Marc playing
the piano, the rest of us filling in with guitars and percussion. I
sensed nothing. Not a thing. No stolen glances or quick caresses. But
of course I wasn't looking.

Shit. I shake the covers off, scream into the pillow, "You bastard!" After throwing the pillow on the floor, I pace around the
room. What really was going on in our relationship those last eight
years? Now nothing is as it seemed. He had another wife! It's still so
unbelievable. I continue to go back, rethink, remember everything.

The last time we made love was the night before I left for Colorado, the night before he died. Marc was tired, complaining of a migraine headache. He had gone up to bed before me. When I climbed
in, he was already half asleep. I rubbed his back, his neck. He rolled
over onto me and kissed me. We made love, both of us halfheartedly.
After we were through, he said, "I love you, but my head still hurts.
Sorry." And then he was out.

Next door, I remember a radio came on, loud, blaring rap music.
I was afraid it would wake Marc. I dressed quickly and in a rage ran
downstairs. For the whole year, workmen had been building a tennis
court next door. I yelled at them that morning for playing their music
so loud and taking up every spare inch of space in the canyon with
their trucks, their tools, their music. Though the crew had gone for
the night, the radio was blaring at full volume on its own. Obviously,
someone had decided to retaliate and had set the alarm. Fuck them.
There was a padlock on the gate, so like a cat burglar, I scaled the
chain-link fence that separated our properties, and when I was on the
other side, I ran over to the black boom box and kicked it hard,
kicked it again and again, smashed it until it was on its side, quiet,
dead. Then I stood for a moment in the dark, completely out of
breath, examining the view the Larkins had of our property—our
swing set, our vegetable garden, our huge pepper trees. They could
see right into our kitchen. And then I looked at the skeleton of their

tennis court as it hung out over our canyon, ruining our view. The Larkins had promised Marc when they finished, he could use the court anytime. Fuck them, too. I was glad I killed the radio. I had scaled the fence back to our property just as the neighborhood patrol car drove past.

At nine o'clock room service arrives with my breakfast: Welsh cakes, white coffee and half a grapefruit, along with my ancient but newly shined-up cowboy boots, which I'd left outside my door. There is also a copy of the morning's *Western Mail*. Biting into the buttery Welsh cake I glance quickly at the headlines and read:

Longtime Aberfan Resident, Gavin Ames, Loses Final Battle Against Cancer

Gavin Ames was Peter's father. Mr. Ames was sixty-seven, the article says. Younger than Da. The funeral service is to be this afternoon at two o'clock.

Hallie is mad for Peter Ames. She sits next to him in school. She turns the color of pink tulips in spring when she sees him on the road.

We follow him down Moy Road and all the way to the overhang. He whirls around and sees us. He smiles back at Hallie. "I see you there, Hallie. I do. I'll be tellin' my da if you keep following me!" he laughs.

After the disaster Mrs. Ames comes round the house to show us a picture Peter drew. She is one of the only ones who comes round regularly to see Mam and Da. Mr. Ames, too. They don't care that the rest of the village blame Da. Mrs. Ames is like a tiny sparrow with tightly curled hair. She cries at the kitchen table while Mam makes her a cup of tea.

"He didn't want to go to school that day. He didn't," she says. "He'd been unwell all the day before, snively like, and I'd made him go off anyway. I pushed him, like. What kind of mother do you think I am, telling him to behave like a man when he was only a little boy, with a cold, snot even? Could he have known? Could Peter have had some kind of feeling or dream, a premonition, something?

"The night before he'd drawn this picture," she says, holding out a small drawing. The picture, done with black crayon, is of an airplane with the initials NCB written on it. Below the airplane is a row of terraced houses queued up just like the ones we all live in, and the school. The houses are crossed out and smudged over. The tip is in the picture and it clearly has run into the school. Above the picture Peter wrote the words "The End."

" 'Twas a warning, it was," Mrs. Ames sobs. "I only found it after. If he'd shown it to me then, I would have known, or at least I could have had the chance to know."

"My God, Molly," Mam says. "It's not your fault, like. No way you could have known even if you had seen the picture. Don't go blaming yourself!"

Poor Mrs. Ames died a few years after the disaster. Mam said she'd died of a broken heart.

> During the seventy-six-day tribunal, Gavin Ames fought for truth and justice.
>
> He was the one appointed chairmen of the Residents and Parents Committee to look after the three-million-pound memorial relief fund that was donated from the government and concerned people around the world.
>
> Last year he saw his efforts rewarded with the return by the government of £150,000, which had been snatched from the disaster fund to pay for removal of the slag heap lying above the village.

Soon after the funeral, Hallie's mam helped form a committee made up of all the mothers in the village who had lost a child. They decided the tip must be removed. Its presence was too ghastly a reminder, and everyone wanted it gone, fast. The village felt the cost to remove the tip should be the NCB's responsibility. But the NCB wouldn't pay. In the end, years later, the village was forced to take the money for the removal from the relief fund referred to in the obituary.

Da had said, "Gavin'll see to it we get that money back. Don't you worry 'bout that. Gavin won't let them beat us out of it."

Da had been right.

I decide to try and make the funeral.

The concierge tells me my rental car is parked in the lot in back of the hotel, a small blue Ford. Pulling the seat forward and looking at the map, I chart my course. The A470 goes all the way up into the valleys. I move out of the small drive and maneuver the car onto Westgate Street, then right, past the castle, bearing left onto Kingsway, which runs into the A470.

Out the window I notice all the road signs are written twice, just like the WELCOME TO WALES sign—once in Welsh and again in English. The village names, of course, are only in Welsh, and each seems familiar and holds some memory. I crank on the radio to David Gray singing "My Oh My."

I pass a sign for the village of Rhiwbina. I remember after the disaster, Gram said how Hallie's mam went to see Alex Somner, who lived in Rhiwbina. It was said Dr. Somner had powers. He worked with spirits.

Years and years later Marco was working on a musical about the supernatural. He'd brought home a stack of books about hypnotherapy. It turned out Dr. Somner was world renowned for his work with dreams and hypnotism, specializing in past life regression. Experts, well-known psychologists and psychiatrists believed he had the ability to get in touch with "the other side." Gram said Dr. Somner helped Mrs. Jones find some peace with Hallie's passing. In fact, Mrs. Jones told Gram that Dr. Somner had made contact with Hallie. I wonder if he is still alive. I should scout him out, see if he can help me make face-to-face contact with Marc so I can let him know what a wretch he is and that he'd better find a way to get Gabriella off my back, quick.

Several miles up the road from Rhiwbina is Tongwynlais, where Gram had known the owner of a small antique shop who had a daughter my age with long, curly blond hair like Hallie's. After the disaster Gram took me round to play with her several times, hoping, I suppose, we would make friends. But it didn't work—she wasn't Hallie. Finally, Gram gave up.

And then comes Caerphilly, known for its eponymous product: dry, brittle white cheese. I hated it when I was little. Now I love it and buy it whenever I come across it in specialty stores in Santa Monica.

I see the sign to Mount Pleasant and know I am close. My tongue goes dry, and I'm having a hard time swallowing.

"But I don't want to go to school in Mount Pleasant, Mam. Please don't make me."

"Alys, it's not up to me, like. That's where they're putting you all for now, so that's where you're going until they build a new school. The coach is waiting now, Alys. Get along."

The kids are not friendly to us. Evan says it's because they don't know how to speak to children who have lost so much. It is too hard for them to sit next to us in the classroom and to play with us on the playground, to pretend we are all the same. They know we are different and so none of them can figure a way to make believe otherwise. Yesterday one of the other children told me he'd never known anybody who had died, especially never another child. He wanted to know if all my friends had died or just some of them.

Turning off the main road onto a narrow one lined with hedgerows on both sides, I pull into a turnout to check the map and steel myself. The clock reads eleven forty-five a.m. Having bought a packet of cigarettes before leaving the hotel, I rummage in my bag for one, light it and breathe in deeply. The whole world goes dizzy.

I prop myself against the car, inhaling the cigarette as well as another smell—sweet, almost like dried blood, or decaying bracken—and then I recognize it: coal. Someone on the mountain is burning coal.

Beyond the hedge, the continuous rolling green hills are dotted everywhere with sheep, hundreds of them. Away in the distance behind a high stone fence is a small cottage. The sky is still intensely blue but the clouds are beginning to move in, and against the blue, their white is mesmerizing.

I think of the Santa Monica view: the summer smog hanging in front of our deck, the jammed four-lane freeways, the noise, the dirt and the crime.

Lawrence Durrell has written that each of us has a home landscape, the place we return to in our mind's eye whenever we contemplate our own beginnings. It is Wales that appears in my dreams. This subtlety of color, the roll of these velvety green mountains one into another, the soft cloud swirl of the sky—this is the scene of my young psyche. But on the other side of that youthful and innocent affection is the intensity of having had the earth move against me. My love and loyalty for this land will always be colored by how it betrayed me.

And here I am again, my whole emotional world turned upside down. All of what I thought I'd built in these last years and counted on as steady and secure has fallen away.

CHAPTER ELEVEN

The road is narrow and it takes some concentration as I parallel park opposite Bethany Chapel. It's not until I shut the door that I remember home is just a block away. A hearse pulls up in front of the chapel that long ago was the place we all returned to again and again, each anniversary of the disaster.

I know there are twenty-four steps leading into the chapel because every Sunday of my childhood I counted them. Standing next to the door are Mr. Mecca and Mr. Fowler. Memory is a wondrous thing. Mr. Mecca was my Sunday school teacher. In our youth he was very thin and wiry. Hallie and I called him "the thin man." He's put on weight and lost some hair. Mr. Fowler lived the next road over and had a boy about Parry's age. His wife left him several years after the disaster. He and his son were living together when I went off to America. Like a child thinking nothing ever changes except my own world, I wonder if they are still living together. I nod at them as I pass but they don't really look at me. I choose a seat in the back near the door.

Reverend Land stands behind the coffin, hands folded in front of his robe just as I remember, though of course he looks much older. Mrs. Land worked at the post office and they had three, maybe four, kids. Two of them died in the disaster: Bobby and Polly. Polly was in my class.

I am floating. My hands and feet are cold. I watch each person file in, hoping somehow that my mother won't be one of them.

After a while the Reverend clears his throat. "We are gathered here today to honor the memory of Gavin Ames."

As the reverend talks, I sense a presence behind me, and I am terrified it might be Mam.

"It's me." First there is her familiar voice, and then the sweet mint smell of her. Auntie Beryl folds me up in her arms like I am a small child, kissing my cheeks, and pushing the hair from my face. My chest feels like a bear is standing on it. The tears start falling and I don't even try to brush them away.

"Your mother told me about Gavin. She was going to try to make it today," she says, glancing around. "But I guess she thought better of it and stayed home with your father." Beryl is so casual it's as though it was only yesterday or a week ago we saw each other last. She carefully lowers herself, using my right leg as support, and sits down. Her hair is no longer red, but it is still untamed, escaping from her bright scarf, and she is still chewing her peppermint gum.

She settles back in her seat, taking my cold hand in her warm one and giving her full attention to the Reverend.

Holding tight to Auntie Beryl's hand, I feel the same strength and security I felt from her as a six year old.

"Gavin will be buried up in the cemetery next to his son, Peter, and his devoted wife, Gladys. His sister wants those of you wishing to come round to the house afterward to know you are welcome."

"Well, that's that, I guess," Auntie Beryl says. "I don't think I'll go up to the house. Will you?" she asks as she starts to get up. "Or will you be going straight to see your parents?"

"I don't know," I answer quietly, part of me feeling guilty as if after all this time I should go immediately, and the other part of me not yet ready to confront them. I seem to need more time to adjust, to walk around, get my sea legs or something before I enter again into their world.

"Well then, if you've a motorcar I'd love a ride home, if you wouldn't mind terribly. Save this old body from having to trudge on the coach."

Following her out, I glance down and notice she's lost her ankles—the shape of them, I mean. Everything seems to have slipped a bit. Gram used to say Auntie Beryl had the prettiest ankles in the Rhondda Valley. At parties we'd all watch her pull her skirts way up high to show them off when she danced. She seemed so ageless with her red hair, dramatic clothes and flamboyant ways.

Just before we pass through the door a voice behind me announces, "Come Home Again to Thee." And when the singing starts, I stop to listen as the choir's voices blend and rise together. And then, so clearly, as if he is standing next to me singing in my ear, I recognize Evan's.

"Oh my," I say under my breath, but loud enough for Auntie Beryl to catch. I am stunned by how much he looks like Dafydd. He is standing on the raised platform in front of the choir, conducting, heads taller than everyone else, his thick head of dark hair gone gray around the edges, and even more handsome than I remember in his black suit as he throws his own head back in song.

Auntie Beryl smiles, touching the back of my neck gently. "I thought Gram might have told you. Evan started the choir a few years after you'd gone," she says quietly. "It's saved us, really. All of us. Brought us back to our own spirit, he did. And him to his, I suspect." She pats my arm and looks at me sadly. "He was a bit of a wreck after you left."

So many years ago, and now still when I see him, it is the same. It can't possibly be love after all this time, can it?

"Do you want to stay?" Beryl says in my ear.

I shake my head, trying to get clear, wondering if I will be able to move from the spot. I feel frozen, glued to him even from a distance.

"Come along then. We best get out of here before the crush. Plenty of time to hear the boys later. Evan calls a practice twice a week down the rugby clubhouse."

I am grateful that Beryl takes charge. She guides me out of the chapel and down the stairs as if I am the old woman.

As we walk down the road, she explains how when she saw me in the chapel she deciphered either I'd seen my parents and already had a row, or just arrived.

In the car, she says quietly, "You're still in love with him, loved him all along, then?"

I'm off my guard, but I know my feelings are more complicated than a simple yes or no. "Don't be silly, Auntie Beryl. How could I possibly know? It's been a million years."

"Well," she says simply, "I don't notice that any number of years changes the way I continue to feel about William—dead or alive, that is."

"William?"

"Don't tell me your grandmother didn't speak about my William? Can't believe that. But then perhaps I'm the big mouth. Your gram was always so bloody discreet and perfect." She laughs.

"I didn't know." But in the back of my mind I do remember Gram telling me Auntie Beryl's heart had been broken long, long ago.

"It's been over fifty years now, and I can still remember the moment I laid eyes on him. No question for me about it being love at first sight—none at all." She puts her arm around my shoulder. "And I saw it in your eyes today, Alys. A million years or not, everything about your expression changed. Perhaps you're not even aware of it?"

My face gets hot. "I think there are different kinds of love, Beryl, don't you?"

She shrugs. "Different kinds of love? Don't know about that. I've only had one."

I feel light-headed as I drive out of Aberfan and up the same roads I had so often taken on the coach with Gram to Beryl's.

And then Beryl is off Evan and on about all the other people she'd seen in chapel, like Mrs. Bramfitt, who owns the grocery shop, and how Mrs. Bramfitt and her husband have managed to save enough money so they can retire next year. "They'll be moving to Jersey. Been trying to get out for years, they have.

"And Mr. Delvin—you remember, don't you? He's the school janitor. Did you see him, Allie? Don't have a clue how he managed to get there today." She shakes her head. "He loved all you children, he did, the first to help with the rescue work after the disaster. Must have been that, because he never drank before and now he's become an old drunken sod. Spends most of his time in the pub doing it up, or down by the chapel, repenting. And what about Max Riley, then? He's on his fifth wife—I think he is. Fourth or fifth, anyway. They keep throwing him out because he's so unlovable, always got to have his own way, never lets on to any of them that he loves them. 'No heart,' the last one said straight out." In between Beryl's observations and small talk, she directs me from one narrow road to another until we are on a straightaway up through the mountains.

She tells me about the last weeks of Gram's life. How she hadn't wanted to go to the hospital and Mam hadn't the strength to look after her and so, being of course her dearest and best friend, Beryl took her in and nursed her till the end.

"Which was exactly what the old girl wanted anyway. She was always so afraid of hurting your mother's feelings. 'Specially near the end. She wanted to be the perfect mother-in-law. She would have come to me sooner if she'd figured a way. She knew my cooking and she liked my fire. So in the end it all worked out for her best." Beryl had an ambulance bring her round less than a fortnight before she died, and tucked her up in a bed she'd put in front of the fire. She fed her and read to her and helped her die.

"Your gram ate a small dinner at noon. Let's see, I think I made her chicken soup with braised leeks. And after I read a few Blake poems to her, she went down for her afternoon sleep and she never awakened. That's how I'd like to go. Of course I 'spect that's how we'd all like to go." She pauses, taking a breath in, and puts out her hand and pats my knee.

"I wish I'd stayed in touch, Auntie Beryl. But somehow I just couldn't. I always felt like we spoke through Gram. And sometimes it was hard even to keep in touch with her. I think after she died, it was just easier not to stay in touch. I know that sounds awful—it *is* awful."

"Oh, don't you worry yourself, Allie," she says, looking up at me with her bright eyes. "I won't say I haven't missed news of you, but I should have written you. When your gram was alive, she shared all your letters with me, and we talked endlessly about your having left here. We both agreed you knew yourself and how much you could take, and we were both proud in a sort of lonely way you'd had the courage to leave. Now there seems so much to talk about.

"Do stay for dinner, Allie. Or . . . will you be going now to see your parents?"

"I s'pose I should. But I'm suddenly so tired. Jet lag, I guess."

"Stay, then. It's already close to four."

I thought about the large bathtub back at the hotel, and the soft, clean sheets. A queasy scared feeling sits in the middle of my abdomen and is the stall that keeps me from my parents. Perhaps my nerves will be better in the morning, probably a more appropriate time to descend on them.

I follow Auntie Beryl up the familiar pathway, overgrown with huge pink rhododendrons and red rosebushes in full bloom, the overwhelming smell of feverfew and pennyroyal as I crush their leaves under my shoes.

In the cottage, I am immediately comforted by how nothing much has changed. Beryl stokes the fire to a full roar and starts the teakettle. The day is not chilly, but I remember Beryl always has a fire going, which I appreciate.

The open kitchen stretches into the parlor and the fireplace is the focal point. There are glass bottles filled with rice, beans, pasta and spices on every shelf near the sink. Everything is just as I remember: every surface covered with small bric-a-brac, and along the windowsill a collection of miners' lamps and other mining tools. There are small colorful throw rugs on the wood planked floors, an overstuffed settee and several rockers close by the huge stone fireplace.

"Take your shoes off, dear, and pull that chair up in front of the fire. It won't be a moment till the kettle's boiled."

"Let me help you," I offer.

"I'm not so old I can't still make a cup of tea. Dusting and mopping is another story. Not enough time left in my old life to do that anymore."

"Auntie Beryl," I say, "please don't talk like that."

"Well, it's true, dear. There are better ways to spend whatever time is left me."

I walk around the room, looking at everything, touching it all. Near the dining room table, under a window, is a small bureau, on top of which is a framed photo of me when I was about six, wearing a pair of plaid overalls I remember well. I am waving at Mam, who was taking the photo. Next to it is another one of me with Dafydd when he was about six. I remember when Marc took the photo in Paris. We'd just eaten the most delicious breakfast. "Croissant!" he had said to Dafydd—instead of "cheese"—to get him to smile. Dafydd could never get enough of the buttery treat. Next to us is a portrait of Parry in his mining gear, a grin so wide and angelic that for a moment I can't believe he'd ever been so angry.

Beryl catches me looking at them. "I have all your gram's photos and most of her things. Shawls, tapestries—they're strewn everywhere round the place." She motions with her hand. "Your mother felt I should have them and your father agreed. I've got some packed away for you whenever you're ready for them."

Beryl puts the teapot, a creamer, two cups and a plate of biscuits on a small table near the fire.

"So you've come to see your old da now, have you?" She tilts her head curiously in that way she has of asking a question when she really wants to tell you something. "You shouldn't be too hard on him, you know." She gives me a look I can't quite fathom, remembering how she felt about Da back in the bad old days. "It wasn't his fault, really, the disaster, like. I'm sure you remember those terrible conversations between your Da and me, Allie. The ones in the kitchen?"

"I do." I remember like it was yesterday.

"I wish I could take them back. I was so angry. Beside myself, really. I blamed your da for everything. Don't misunderstand me. We all needed to blame someone. It was all just too terrible. But I let the villagers put all the blame on him, too."

Auntie Beryl lowers her head and pours out the milk into each cup, and then the tea, passing me my cup and the sugar.

"You see, there was no one person to blame. Your da actually did his duty by calling in the NCB. And the NCB sent all kinds of experts, who said there was no stream running under that tip. Even though your da didn't really believe them, he had no choice but to continue to follow their orders and haul the slag out onto that tip. There was no other way for him. After your gram got me to settle down and look at things, I was finally able to see this. That was one of the wonderful things about her. She helped me see things differently just by getting me to settle down."

I was confused. "I know I was only little, Beryl. But I had big ears. I heard you." Why was Beryl trying to sell me this new bill of goods?

"Now, now, Alys." She shakes her head. "You go relying on only the facts and you're going to get half the story, and half the truth. But there are other things that figure into the whole story and I've learned they are even more important than the facts. They fill in where the facts fail us." She pauses and looks at me. "Oh, Allie. You look like you could use a little air," Beryl says brightly.

I don't want to admit how tired I am. I feel like I need to have a lie-down for, say, about a month. In fact, my shoes feel like they are full of lead.

"Come on, I've something to show you that might explain part of the story—at least my part."

Beryl pulls herself up and grabs a shawl from a rocker by the fire. She wraps herself in it. "Do you need one? We've only a little walk up in the back."

I shake my head. The fire has warmed me. I follow Auntie Beryl out the back into the small overgrown garden. The air is cooler than it was an hour ago and it actually picks me up a bit.

"My poor rhododendrons are in need of some TLC and some training, cutting back and discipline," Beryl points out. "But I seem to have lost the touch, or maybe in my old age I've become disenchanted with sharp corners, discipline. I don't want to cut anything back anymore. I seem to want more wildness around me rather than less."

At the back of the garden is a small wooden gate that closes Beryl's property off from the acres of farmland behind it. She tells me she built the gate to keep the neighboring farmer's sheep from getting into her garden. One summer two small lambs found their way in and ate all the newly sprouted greens Beryl had carefully planted in the early spring.

I breathe deeply, the smell a familiar combination of sweet moldering bread mixed with wet coal. Its sharpness rubs up against my memory of childhood.

"Do you remember when you and Hallie spent the day here that long-ago time? I knew she'd snuck out." Beryl laughs.

It is Saturday. Parry gives us a ride up. It is gray and damp, but mild. He has lent me a rucksack and I have organized a picnic. Two sandwiches, sliced cheddar and tomato with hearts of cress on buttered brown bread. No crust on Hallie's. Two apples, two oranges and a waxed bag full of crisps that Mam hid behind the jar of marmite in the larder. Sticking my finger in the jar, I lick off a mound of the dark, bitter molasses.

In the car, Hallie confesses, "I didn't tell them. If I told them last night, they wouldn't let me go."

"Hallie!" I scold. But I know she is probably right. Her parents don't own a car and they don't like Hallie going too far away.

"I have half a chocolate bar and a pile of sultanas," she says, proudly thrusting the brown bag for me to stash in my rucksack.

At Auntie Beryl's, Parry goes inside to talk while we race through the back gate and straight up the path to search for goosegogs.

Hallie finds them first, but actually what she finds is blackberries. By the time we start back to Auntie Beryl's, our fingers are stained purple.

"How will I ever explain this to my mam?" Hallie says.

Through the gate, to the left a few hundred yards up, is the pond, and next to its edge, a white heron, sitting tall and elegant. Several dogs bark and a bull stares us down. There is a farmer pitchforking fodder.

"Don't mind them," Beryl tells me, waving to the farmer. "The bull's actually friendly. We're going just up here, not too far now."

She waves me over to where there is a clearing and a breathtaking view out toward the whole mountain range of the Brecon Beacons. And there, under a stand of beech trees, looking over all of it, is a small weather-worn gravestone. Beryl motions me over and when I am closer up, I see that the engraving on it is:

WILLIAM ROGER NOLAN
1924–1964
IN LOVING MEMORY

As if on cue, the wind begins to blow and Auntie Beryl's skirt flies up. She pushes it down and draws her shawl tighter around her shoulders. Quietly she bends to her knees in front of the stone and bows slightly, then closes her eyes.

I don't know exactly what to do, so I follow Beryl's example, staying slightly off to her right. After a moment she opens her eyes and smiles at me.

"If you haven't already guessed, this is my William."

Amazed that she's got him in her own back field, I don't know what to say, so I nod.

"He was an extraordinary man through and through, he was. Half his family came from the Gower Peninsula—in the Welshry— and the other half from these parts and farther north. All of them were farmers.

"William used to tell a story 'bout how as a child he was always fascinated by a faraway light in the sky. It was the mine's fire. And in the winter, when the dark fell early, he said it seemed like the whole sky was ablaze with it. When the winter wind rushed across here and his da's fields heaped full of rotting swedes as it always did in the fall, that smell of decay carried into the farmhouse. And William's mother would start a small fire from damp logs. He'd tell me how after they'd cut enough chaff for the next day, he would sit by that small fire, longing for the heat and brightness of the fires he could see out the window, in the distant valley of coal mines.

" 'Want to be in the works, like,' he told his mam, meaning the coal mines, of course. At the time it was the Bessemer Works in Dowlais that was lighting up his sky.

"And so when he was nearing his sixteenth birthday, he left home loaded into the back of a neighbor's cart pulled by two horses, taking him to Treclewyd. I can still see him in my mind's eye—that lovely boy he must have been—so keen to start out on his own.

"And that's where it began underground for William, and like most miners he moved from one mine to another. And despite the dirt, the dust, the gas, the dark, damp, belching black of its insides— he was thinking he'd found his true love. Until me." She laughed.

"But that's another long tale I wish had been years and years longer. The reason I'm telling you all this is to try to explain why I was so angry at your da. You see, I'd been through the bureaucratic stubbornness of the National Coal Board with William. It was all happening just like it had ten years before. Oh, not the same accident, but the same stupid pattern of blaming everyone, pointing fingers and not really doing anything to stop an imminent disaster."

"But if Da knew there was a spring . . ."

"He couldn't really do anything—don't you see, Allie? It was out of his hands for two reasons. One, because he didn't have the power. And two, he wouldn't go against the NCB because of who he was. Your brother would have and tried to—but your father is a proletariat Welshman through and through. And despite whether or not he questioned the possibility of a spring, at his core he believed what the powers told him to believe. He assumed that his superiors were superior because they knew more. William did the same, and I was as angry at him back then as I was at your da."

The wind was blowing hard now. I had to strain to hear her.

"But 116 children, Beryl."

"I know, Allie. With William it was twenty men and half the mine caved in on them, all of them leaving families and lovely lives to be lived. The NCB had told them just the day before that the mine shaft was as safe as being in bed. Almost forty years ago I lost my William and all the possibilities of life with him because of the carelessness of the NCB. I railed at your da and anyone else who would listen because I'd seen it before and knew it could happen again."

I remember that Gram's husband had also died in a mining accident. So many did, I guess.

"And what about Parry?" I ask. "You said he would have done something and actually tried to?"

"About mine issues, Parry was fearless. In a way, he had nothing to lose. I've thought a lot about Parry and his anger. I think initially he went down the mine because he was not yet certain that his artistic talent could support him. Someone had probably warned him about having a real job. Since your da was his idol, he thought he'd give the mine a try. It was natural for Parry to follow in his footsteps even though the mine was not in Parry's heart as it was in your father's.

"And then when all the business with the creekbed started and your da wouldn't take a stand against the NCB, I think Parry was so disappointed in his position and that he couldn't convince your da to do 'the right thing,' Parry's anger took over and he put his art on the back burner. And then after the disaster, he just couldn't get back to it."

"So time passed," I said. "And he became more and more depressed and angry, and then the drinking, and he must have felt there was just no way out."

"Exactly." Auntie Beryl nodded.

"He must have felt he had failed in every way."

Auntie Beryl was quiet. A light drizzle, mist really, began to fall. Before long my face was wet. I was remembering what a good artist Parry had been.

"I used Parry's anger to try and rally the other boys to go against your da and strike the mine. I pushed Parry to try and sway your da to go against the NCB. It's a terrible thing I did. It was like throwing petrol on a fire."

"Is it true that Da didn't believe in Parry's painting?" I asked.

Beryl shrugs. "I'm not really sure. I suspect that being an artist wasn't something your da thought about as a serious career. Maybe the mere fact that he didn't push Parry to accept the art scholarship he'd won was proof to Parry that he didn't take his ability seriously.

"Or maybe it's as your gram said: at the core, Parry didn't believe in himself."

I think about how hard it has always been for me with my poetry, and how despite all the rejections I've had, I continue to write, convincing myself that it matters and that someone is listening, but also because I seem to have no choice. I have to write. The pencil makes it into my hand despite me.

It is really raining now and it's hard to tell if my face is wet from the rain or tears.

I watch Beryl close her eyes again, and then, placing her hands prayerlike, at her chest, she bows slightly toward William's gravestone for the final time.

"It's getting late. I've worn you out, Alys. Forgive me. I do go on. Your gram used to say I could talk anything to death."

I laugh.

"Shall we go back in and have some supper before we drown out here? I've a nice lamb stew simmering since morning."

CHAPTER TWELVE

Auntie Beryl sets the table up in front of the fire. The bowl of lamb stew is succulent and comforting. She tells me that it is local lamb, and the spicy flavor and green olives were Gram's recipe. I don't say so, but I know it well and I smile, thinking how I thought I'd invented it. She always had a flair for cooking, which must have come from somewhere beside her Welsh roots. And then Auntie Beryl changes the subject.

"So did you know that Evan bought a little cottage just outside of the village? Perhaps you even know it? Up on the ridge, it is. Large piece of land behind it that looks out over all of Aberfan and the valleys east of it. He's done it all up, I'm told. Teaches at the new school. Oh, you know the new school, 'spect you went to it, after. It's not so new anymore but we all still call it that.

"I heard he had a woman in his life, for quite some time, in fact." She looks at me after she's delivered this news, but I manage not to show anything.

In fact, Gram mentioned it years ago in a letter. I was surprised at the time how disappointed and jealous I'd felt. But like anything else I'd heard about in Aberfan, I put it immediately out of mind. Hearing it now, I am embarrassed that I still feel jealous.

"So it's not just only your da you've come to see?" Beryl has somehow caught me but I ignore it.

"Well, of course Mam, too. And you. I'm needing to make some peace with all of this. It's too long I haven't been willing to face everything here."

Beryl smiles.

"What?"

Beryl pulls her chin in, making a funny face of disbelief.

"Oh no, you're meaning Evan?" I laugh out loud. "Don't go on about Evan again. You are wicked, a troublemaker if ever there was one, Auntie Beryl. Even when I was a child, Gram warned me against your shenanigans."

"Shenanigans? I saw your face today, Allie, clear as the noon-bright sun it was."

"What you saw, Auntie Beryl, was surprise. Oh, maybe a bit of shock—I'll admit to that. I hadn't been prepared to see him at that moment, that's all."

"I think thou dost protest too much. . . ."

And before I say another word, Beryl changes the subject. "Stay the night, Alys. It might be better to see your parents first thing to-morrow? I 'spect your father might be stronger in the mornings. A good night's rest will put everything in a cheerier light."

Too tired even to feel guilty, I get in the hot steamy bath Auntie Beryl draws me in her old clawfoot tub. But first I call the Angel Hotel, knowing full well there will be no messages from Hannah, but just in case, just to be on the safe side.

When I get out of the tub, the sheets and blanket on the guest bed are folded back and on the pillow is a small black box in which there is a wedding band and a note: *For you, Alys darling. With all my love, Gram.*

Before Beryl tucks me up and turns the light off as she often did when I was little, I look at my own left hand, the marriage finger empty of Marc's ring. I took it off at home before the driver fetched me for the airport, before I'd left Santa Monica. As I study my hand and the deep indentation the ring has left, I wonder if I ever felt about Marc the way Gram felt about Granda.

Left alone in the darkness, I slide over the day. In retrospect, per-haps I should have forced myself to go directly to Mam and Da's. Though being with Beryl has made me feel more secure and grounded than I did earlier.

I know I have only scratched the surface of my deeper feelings about home. The anger is still all there. Still blaming Mam after all these years. Why? She suffered as much as any of us, perhaps more. Leaving Aberfan, I was as glad to get away from her as Da. Not writing them protected me. Sending them money each month, same as Evan sent me for Dafydd, took care of some of my guilt about not being in contact. After the first check, Da had written me back to thank me, a nice note, but I had answered only by continuing to send a monthly check.

After Hannah was born, Mam wrote to congratulate me. Her never having acknowledged Dafydd's birth made this acknowledgment seem like another of her judgments, and I was angry all over again.

The next morning Beryl cooks a feast: rashers of thick bacon, sausage, fried eggs and grilled tomatoes. Even fried bread. "I remember how you loved it when you were small. I 'spect you'll be doing some visiting today, so you can take the Welsh cakes to eat on the road. I'll pack them up after they've cooled." She adds casually, "How long will your visit be?"

I've taken a long sip of the hot, rich coffee from the beautiful china cup. "Another week or so."

She notices I've put Gram's ring on the index finger of my left hand. "It looks pretty, if not a bit strange on that finger. Why don't you try it on your right ring finger? Is it too big?" Not waiting for an answer, she says, "Your grandmother would be pleased that you like it. You know, it surprised me how she never worried over you. But she didn't. She just seemed to know you'd be all right. When I asked her how she knew that, she said it was because of the way, after the disaster, you instinctively knew what the Joneses needed, and the courage you showed in the face of all you were feeling."

I look at Beryl quizzically. Did I feel all right? Had I ever really been all right?

Suddenly, out of nowhere I remember Dafydd's sixth grade graduation. As Dafydd's friends were crowding around, congratulating each other, talking about what they were going to do for the summer and about what middle school might be like. I started to cry. But it wasn't about how proud I was of Dafydd—though of course I was—it was about his crowd of friends. About how they were all there together, growing up together. I felt so sorry for myself at that moment, that I'd never had a sixth form graduation or that there were only seven of us left in the class. And then I was instantly so ashamed at feeling sorry for myself and not being able to enjoy Dafydd's moment. Marc sweetly put his arms around me and asked, "What's going on, Alys darling? Can I help?" And I couldn't answer. It felt too dark and the loneliness was so overwhelming that I couldn't speak. I waved him away. He'd looked at me sadly and left.

"Perhaps I don't mean all right," Beryl says as if reading my mind. "But rather that you've survived your past. Perhaps that's closer to it. Yes, that's probably what your gram really meant."

If that was what Gram meant, is it enough to just survive one's past? It hardly seems like living.

"Turns out I'm the worrier, Alys. I'm the one who always worried there'd been so much pain in our lives, so much loss. But your gram argued, 'Out of loss grow the very things that give us strength and joy. Just on the other side of loss,' she'd say, 'is joy.' "

Marc had certainly given me joy. But perhaps I'd not been able to show him the kind of lighthearted joy that he deserved in return. Without my even being aware of it, maybe my pain and sorrow had seeped into our lives on every level.

At the end of breakfast we clear the dishes away and Beryl sends me off with a bag of Welsh cakes and a thermos of milky tea.

"The thermos is so you'll have to see me again before you leave," she says, leaning her compact body into the car and kissing me on the cheek. "I love my thermos." She winks. "Don't run off to the States with it. Oh, and don't wait too long dear to grab on to love. It doesn't come around that often. I can tell you that for sure."

Once in the car, I find myself wishing I had asked Beryl not to tell Mam I'd gone to see her first. I am feeling uncomfortable now about being here for a full day and not contacting them. But of course Beryl will do precisely what she wants regardless of what anyone asks her. Hallie might have grown up to be a bit like Beryl.

"If you should see Evan, tell him he owes me tea!" she calls out after the car.

The mountains are a dappled mustard color in the muted sunlight as I retrace Beryl and my tracks back to Aberfan. In an unearthly sort of way, the motorcar seems almost to be driving itself. But I am still not ready to go home, and so pass right by our road and continue up and around until I can see the whole of the valley below me like some Tinkertoy setup. On Bryntaf Road, just above the cemetery, I park, but it takes me a while to move my hand, to open the door.

Finally I push the dead weight of the door and step out. And there they are in full view, the rows of familiar white arches joined like outstretched arms. The strange, comforting curve of each one—Hallie, Peter, Suzanne, Polly, all of them there together, their memory filling me up with the deep ache, and loneliness of being here without them. Thirty years and six thousand miles have shielded me from the daily emotions of living next to this loss. But standing here now, it all but bowls me over. And it is not just the loss of Hallie or Peter or Parry, or even the other 116 children who lie in front of me, but of all we might have been.

I fall onto a weather-beaten bench that affords me a full view of the cemetery and the mining works below, closed down and quiet now. In the opposite direction is where the tip once towered and, below it, the spot where our school used to be. The place is peaceful, really, if you don't know the history or where you are or what you are looking at. All the trees have grown, filled in, and the bushes are fuller.

The graves seem endless, row upon row. Once I spent the entire day looking for Mam's mam. Mam had always said that they made a mistake and buried her in the wrong family plot and none of her children, including Mam, had had the strength to have her dug up and reburied. Now I don't remember where she is. Or for that matter, where Parry lies. The tree where he'd hanged himself had been cut down before I left. Evan had seen to that. He warned me so that I could come and watch if I wanted. Mam watched. For her it must have been like watching a murderer being executed. I couldn't. It had been one of my favorite trees: an old sycamore, its branches high and sturdy. Parry and I used to jump and try to touch its lowest branch as we passed. Once we'd even had a rope swing in it. After Parry's death, in some strange way it was a comfort to me.

But I don't remember this bench. If it is new, who would have put it so close to where the tree had stood? Evan had seen to so many things for all us, even arranging Parry's burial. Had he for some inexplicable reason put the bench here?

Like everything connected to Parry and his death, I've gone over the what-ifs so many times. The recent conversation with Beryl has given me more information. It's true that he was young and smart with great possibility. How did he get himself so trapped that he couldn't see any other way out? With so much already lost in all our lives, how could Parry pile more on us? Maybe the answer really is as simple as Parry looking at his life and only being able to see everything he would never get right.

Down walking among them, I can see and feel Peter, Donald, Matt, Priscilla, Daniel, Johnny. Those arched white gravesides like closed doors. This is where they live now, their neighborhood; these graves are their homes.

I kneel at the side of Hallie's grave, wondering what it would have been like for us to grow old together as Gram and Beryl had. There is a fresh yellow rose on Hallie's grave—her favorite flower, I remember. Maybe her mam comes each morning. How does she bear it?

I think of Hannah, who has already been through so much herself. I cannot imagine life without her. I think of Mrs. Jones and how she had probably envisioned Hallie's future. Hallie wanted to be a ballet dancer. How many lessons had she missed in the last thirty years? How many recitals? Perhaps Hallie might have changed her mind a million times about what she wanted to be when she grew up.

And unbidden, Isabel sneaks in.

I walk back down the line of children into the middle of the cemetery, past the huge old mausoleum that towers over all the graves and marks the cemetery from a distance.

A quiet rain begins to fall. One thing I know for sure is rain, its steam rising off the cement walkway, the cold gray smell and the wet-tear feel. Of course it hardly rains in Los Angeles, but Marc loved the rain. He worked better on rainy days, the white noise making things quiet.

Hannah loves rain, too. As a child, she'd pull out her blocks and build bridges for hours.

Dafydd loves to nap on rainy afternoons.

For me, the rain is the primary memory of my childhood. Hallie once said, "I think rain must be God's tears."

And I replied, "Then in Aberfan, He sure cries a lot."

The trees now tower above me. Their presence makes the place seem friendlier. Near the cemetery entrance is the small stone office. I touch the shilling around my neck. The door is shut, but I knock and an old man in bibbed dungarees peers out at me.

"Good morning. Sorry to disturb you." I wipe the tears from my eyes and pull my hair back. "I'm wondering if you could tell me where Parry Davies is buried? I can't seem to find him."

He looks me straight in the eyes as if trying to place me. I'm sure he's seen these tears and others like them day in and day out in his job. He points up to the left of where we stand, then pushes the door open. "Let me show you."

He leads me back up one of the paths and around till we are standing in front of a small headstone.

"Thanks," I tell him.

"No problem."

Alone again, I read:

PARRY DAVIES
1956–1978

There's not a word of who he was in the world. Nothing about Parry's battle or his gift as an artist.

After I'm gone, and Evan, and all our respective families—the "disaster generation," as we are sometimes referred to—who will ever know Parry?

Then I see Gram's place next to him. Her headstone is larger than his and a small rosebush is planted next to it. Carved in the stone is

ROSEMARY LYNN DAVIES
1904–1994

And under that,

LET THE RIVER RUN THROUGH US
AND EMPTY IN OUR HEARTS.

It was a line from one of my earliest poems.

Gram seemed to know Parry best and to perceive his true nature. Gram was always there for me, too. Always.

Perhaps Beryl is right: Parry hadn't consciously made the choice not to paint, but had just gotten caught by the swift movement of bad luck.

I walk down Moy Road and over the footbridge into the village proper, with its shops and narrow walkways. Past the Welsh Church and the Catholic Church, then turn on Aberfan Terrace Road.

Coming near the new school, I hear the children first. Then I see them, bright colors whirling. Evan is standing at the far corner of the blacktop, surrounded by them. His back is to me but I would know it anywhere. He must feel my eyes on him because he turns and looks out over the children's heads directly at me. The longer I stare at him the more I let myself remember. I think of my brother and imagine what I have never allowed myself to imagine before—Parry hanging, feet so close to the ground he almost doesn't die. Almost. And of all the emotions I might feel, rage dominates. No matter what Gram tried to teach me, and even after all the years of living away from here, part of me still blames Evan. Parry was living with him. Somehow he should have found a way to help him. I remember after the funeral I wanted to shout at him, "It's your fault he died. You should have saved him!" But instead of dealing with my feelings, I ran.

Evan touches the top of one of the boys' heads, saying something to him, and starts to move around two of the other children who stand between us. I can feel myself begin to back up inside, and I actually take a step backward, two steps, then turn and walk quickly away. I can't stop. I break into a jog, then a full-out run.

Fear.

Would Parry have come to his end if he hadn't been afraid to live his own life? Perhaps his fear had slammed up against him like a closed door and left him with no place to turn. Had fear kept Da from acting against the NCB? Certainly fear had led me away from my own sadness and grief, as well as from Da, Mam, Gram and Evan. It led me to California and Marc and another life while I was still smack in the middle of this one.

Beti and I always felt we had no other choice but to leave. The truth was, each in our way, Parry, Beti and I had all deserted. Only Evan chose to stay. Evan had been here every minute of every day. He'd held Da's hand, comforted Mam and visited Gram. His work with the choir had helped the town to resurrect itself. In the end,

Parry had broken his own heart, and then certainly all of ours, Evan's included. In this way, I guess all of us had been betrayed by him.

When I have circled round the cemetery and am back at the car, my breath is pushing my lungs and my heart beating hard against my ribs. Will I continue to run for the rest of my life?

Catching my breath, I drive to the top of my favorite hill, a view of all of Aberfan. If I've got the place right from Beryl's description, Evan now owns this meadow. Folding my arms and standing stock-still for a long time, I listen to the wind, and it steadies me. From the corner of my eye I see the cottage and the silver Cortina parked in front of it. Then I see Evan, walking up the hill toward me. I fold my arms and stay my ground.

"I was wondering if you would come to see me," he says simply. Although he is clearly not overjoyed to see me, I am surprised how the sound of his voice immediately soothes me, catches me by the hand.

"How did you know I was here?"

"Here? On the hill, in my back meadow? Or here, in Aberfan?" Now that he is close up I can see his hair really does have gray all through it. In fact, it is mostly gray. His pale smooth skin is almost wrinkle-free. His eyes seem to gleam behind his glasses, and his lightly lined mouth is still full.

"I am totally embarrassed," I tell him.

"Why?"

I have forgotten what it feels like to have him speak to me. I have forgotten the thrill of his full attention.

"My behavior a few moments ago, running off like that—I don't know what came over me. I just suddenly had to get away."

He tilts his head and looks at me challengingly. "Seems to be my experience with you."

"Omigod, Evan. That was quick, but not entirely fair."

He sighs, kicking the ground in front of him. "Perhaps you're right. We can leave it for now, anyway."

I'm grateful for the reprieve, although it has stirred my own anger.

"I saw you in chapel yesterday. How do you find your mam and da?"

"I've not seen them yet."

"Really? Do they know you're here?"

"No."

"Your mam told me she'd written you. She didn't think you'd come. Actually, neither did I." He stretches his neck from side to side as if trying to crack it and then sits on the edge of the nearby wooden table. "*They'll* be glad you've come."

"Clearly you're not." I am happy though that he still sees my parents, figuring in my absence that he might not.

"It's not that I'm unhappy to see you, Alys. It's just that I've put you behind me, if you know what I mean. It took me some time—in fact quite a lot of time. But, well, let me be clear. I've put *us* behind me." His anger is overpowering.

I try to ignore it. My hand goes to my shilling again. "What about the bench?" I ask abruptly. "Who put the bench there?"

He looks confused.

"Bench?"

"In the cemetery."

My question seems to disarm him. He takes off his glasses and rubs his eyes gently as if I am taking him back to a place he has not visited in a while. He looks at me sadly, the energy between us changed.

"Your father."

I am quiet. Perplexed. I was so sure it had been Evan.

"It was your da built the bench. Out of the tree . . . Seems he'd managed to keep part of the tree after I'd cut it down. It was the year you left. It took him ages to make it. And then, according to your mother, he dragged it up the path by himself and put it where it is now. Imagine—the weight of it is something. Until recently, at some time of every day you could find your father sitting up on that bench."

We both stand stiffly, looking at each other.

He sighs. "I can't believe you still blame me. You do, don't you, Alys? For letting it happen. Parry's death. You always blamed me, didn't you?"

He takes in a deep breath, running his hand through his hair, kicking the grass. He squints like he is trying to get me in focus, dig into my thoughts.

When I don't answer him, he asks, "How long will you be staying, then?"

Although it's not a lot, I feel my insides soften some. "Here? On top of this hill? Or in Aberfan?" My voice is shaky.

"Oh, Alys." He shakes his head and air escapes through his teeth. "*You* are the quick one, Al."

I almost smile. "About a week."

He nods.

"Beryl told me you bought the cottage."

"I did."

"Is it as nice as we thought it might be—you know, back then?"

Our eyes meet briefly.

"Would you like to see it?"

CHAPTER THIRTEEN

Evan leads me down the hill and onto a pathway made of flag-stones.

Above it are flower beds filled with tall orange poppies, their wide black eyes huge; cow parsley and yellow marigolds; lavender asters; mounds of honeysuckle growing over the side fence; and ivy. I wonder if it is deliberately haphazard. I think it must be.

The cottage has a Dutch door and the top is wide-open. As he pulls the latch on the bottom and I go in ahead of him through the mudroom and another open door, I realize how nervous I am. I am trying to contain myself. The immediate feel of the place as I look around is that it is delightfully warm and gracious. Two leather chairs flank a huge open fireplace; books, magazines and papers are piled everywhere; a small wooden table with four chairs around it; a chandelier with six candle lamps—each with its own small, opaque shade—hangs over the table; a waist-high wooden sideboard; and a Welsh dresser with delicate blue and white plates arranged on it. An open window is framed by brilliantly flowered drapes.

"This is the dining room, although I use it for everything."

I am pulling down the sleeves of my cardigan.

"Are you cold? Shall I light a fire?"

"I'd love that."

"A cup of tea? Or a glass of wine?"

"Wine would be lovely." My knees are shaking. I turn around, admiring everything. I wonder how much of the cabin was decorated by the woman with whom he lived, perhaps still lives? I stand awkwardly in one place.

Sensing my discomfort he asks, "So what is it?"

"Nothing. It's beautiful."

"But?"

"It's just that . . . What I mean is, are you living here alone?" He looks at me quizzically. "You know, is it all right for me to be here?"

He seems confused. "What do you mean?" he asks. "Oh, I get it." He shakes his head in disbelief. "You think a woman decorated my home. You can't imagine that a man, let alone I, could do it. Is that what you're getting at? Certainly if Beryl told you I'd bought the cottage she must have told you I live in it alone."

My turn to shake my head, embarrassed at how cold he continues to be, and feeling completely caught out by him. Of course Beryl hadn't come clean about him living alone. Though it stuns me how relieved I am that he is. However, now I am angry at Beryl stirring things up. She wanted me to be jealous.

Evan moves over to a wine rack tucked among some bookshelves. "Do you like red or white?"

"Red would be perfect." I am uncomfortable to the point of anxiety. I don't know how to hold my body or what's going on inside of it.

He opens the bottle and, taking two glasses from a shelf behind him, leaves it for a moment. Then, moving over to the fireplace, Evan puts some kindling and newspaper in it, several logs, and strikes a match and blows the flame into action. I watch him, his movements easy and fluid.

"Where are you staying?"

"Well, last night I stayed with Auntie Beryl, but I'm actually staying in Cardiff at the Angel Hotel. My luggage is there. I didn't expect to stay with Beryl last night. It just sort of happened. It's taking me longer than I thought to get to Mam and Da's." I am struggling. I don't know how to behave. I stare at Evan. He looks so much like Dafydd.

No doubt feeling my eyes on him, he glances up at me. "What? Did Beryl not tell you something else you are wanting to know? You keep looking at me as if you are expecting something else, someone else."

"I was actually thinking how much you look like Dafydd."

"I rather think it's the other way around, don't you?" He smoothes his hair, looking sort of haughty. "That, of all things, must have been rather disconcerting for you through the years."

"No," I probably answer too quickly, and then can't think of what else to say. I am beginning to realize just how far out of my mind I had to put Evan in order to go on, and what price it has cost us now. "It wasn't exactly disconcerting. It just was what it was."

"And what exactly was that, Alys?"

"It was, I don't know, just normal. Dafydd was Dafydd." But there's the anger and hurt in his eyes again and I know I haven't really answered his question. I stop myself from saying anything more that might somehow sound glib or superficial.

He fetches the wine and glasses, placing them on a low table in front of the fire.

"How is Dafydd?" There is more than a touch of hostility in the question, and it feels like he is holding it tight so as not to let it take control of him. He hands me a glass of wine.

"After your gram died, I lost contact with most news of the two of you. Of course your parents didn't have much either. Last I heard, you'd finally married—Marc, is it? And had another child? I've always been curious as to why you never asked me if your husband could adopt Dafydd." Now the hurt is harder to ignore, but I don't know what to say, so I say nothing. The silence is deadening.

"You're right. I did marry Marc." And then I look directly at him when I deliver my next line. "But he passed away almost a year ago." I almost add, *And guess what—turns out he had a whole other family.* I shudder, holding back my tears. This is the closest I have come to confiding my discovery. It makes sense to me that it would be to Evan.

"Oh, Alys, I'm sorry. I didn't know."

"Hannah is almost nine now."

He stares at me sadly. I might be imagining it, but there seems to be just the barest hint of relief that I pick up in his body when he adds, "I had absolutely no idea. None at all. I'm rather surprised Beryl didn't say."

"She didn't know. Anyway," I continue, moving quickly by Marc's death, "we never spoke about his adopting Dafydd. Marc and Dafydd had a very good relationship. He would have liked to adopt him, I'm sure, but it never came up. He never even asked. We talked, though, about what it would mean to him when Dafydd asked to meet his birth father."

"Birth father? Hmm. That's kind of clinical. Makes me sound like some prearranged petri dish donor, doesn't it?" He rolls his eyes.

"Well, I certainly didn't mean it that way, Evan," I say defensively. Nothing is coming out quite right. "It's just that Marc knew there would come a time when they would have to face you in some way. It's not like he didn't want Dafydd to know you."

"Big of him."

I suspect I'm getting just the tip of the iceberg from twenty-odd years of anger. "Frankly, I suppose it might have been easier if he had adopted Dafydd."

Not only do I feel we are stalemated in anger and defense, but now I'm beginning to wonder how I might gracefully leave the cottage. My discomfort level is too high.

"So why didn't you suggest it?"

I shrug. What truth can I offer him? "I'm not sure. Perhaps because I didn't want you entirely out of my life," I admit rather boldly, having not really thought about it. "Or maybe because adoption would have meant having to have contact with you, and I wasn't ready for that, either. I don't know, maybe both."

His next question, of course, might be: *And you're ready now?* Which would really put me on the spot, completely corner me. But he doesn't ask, though he looks at me as if he might.

I change the subject quickly. "So did you buy the cottage from the same people who lived here when we used to trespass on that back meadow?"

"Trespass? That's a funny way to look at our outings. I never felt we were trespassing. I remember those as innocent picnics, Alys. The two of us wanting to share a meal." There is a softer, more familiar illumination in his eyes, the bright light I remember like a Fourth of July sparkler. "I'm sure the Whites loved our comings and goings in their field, knowing we were innocent as the day was long."

Now I'm not quite sure if he is kidding or not, but I say, "Oh, right, Evan. Would you like to explain all that groping and bustling about we used to do, then? As if no one in this cottage might have looked out the window at any moment and seen us, full daylight, rolling about in the middle of a wide, clear-mowed meadow, for goodness' sakes. What do you think we must have been thinking? Do you think we thought we were invisible?" The memory seems to move me from a solid state to a more liquid one.

"*I* wasn't thinking." Evan's sudden smile makes me blush to the roots of my hair. "As far as I am concerned, it *was* innocent, Alys. Simple. That bustling and groping about, Alys, was love. At least for me, it was."

It is a tense, uncomfortable challenge, even more so than the rest have been. I am unable to respond, afraid I will lose it completely.

A few seconds pass and he turns to look at me, quietly. Almost apologetically he says, "Let's not fight. I suspect we have a day or so to work out what we might feel about all of this?"

I nod.

"How've you coped with your loss of Marc?"

"Well, I don't know exactly," I begin tentatively, wondering if this is a trick question. "I guess I've just sort of moved through one hour at a time. Now there are full hours, three or four of them together, when I don't think of him at all." I look down. "Sometimes it doesn't feel much like he's gone."

Evan nods and looks away before continuing. "You know, the people who lived in this house had five children. When I bought the place, there were two bedrooms on either side of that six-foot stone wall and no inside loo." He runs his hand through his hair. "Occasionally I walk around this place and I'm embarrassed at how much space I have. This fireplace was covered up with Sheetrock and an electric fire—their attempt to modernize. Yet when I moved in, the cowshed, which is now my parlor, still had a thatched roof. Mrs. White even offered me the cow."

"Hmm. I don't see you with a pail and stool." My small attempt at some levity.

"You're right there. I couldn't be bothered to milk it. It would have meant getting up an hour before I do now to get off to school," he says seriously. "You might remember I like my sleep." And then he blushes.

In fact I do remember having to push him out of bed in the morning, pulling the cozy away from him, rolling over onto the warm spot his body left after he'd gone, his smell, lavender. My turn to look away, also remembering the heaviness in my chest at his leaving me for the day and my inability to pull myself from the bed.

"So, when will you see your mam and da?"

"I meant to go round directly after Mr. Ames' funeral—I really did—but then I took Beryl home. I don't know. I guess I'm having difficulty diving into all of what that means, just yet. I should probably go round now, before I completely chicken out."

He runs his fingers through his hair again. "Your mam's told you, of course, how ill your da is?"

"She didn't say exactly how ill." I want his take on things.

"Well, I saw him three days ago. You remember how close your da was to Gavin Ames? I went round just after I'd heard of Gavin's passing, to let your da know. He was in bed. Barely looked up at me when I told him. Not at all like him. Your mam said Doc Rogers told her it was just a matter of time. That's when she let me know she'd written to tell you. I know he'll be glad to see you."

"I hope so." I wondered if Da, too, might be angry with me.

I move toward the kitchen, which is small, rows of ragged paged cookbooks on a shelf, and an iron rack hanging from the middle of the ceiling full with pots and pans. It is so like my own at home it is eerie.

"May I look around?"

"Oh, sure," he says, still rather coldly. "It's a bit of a mess."

In fact it's not. Clearly Evan hasn't changed in that way. Housekeeping was always his way of keeping control. Two stools are pushed under a small wooden counter near a sink filled with breakfast dishes. There are three oil paintings: one each of a fish, a tomato and a bunch of grapes. On closer inspection I see that they are Parry's. I am surprised. Parry had destroyed most of his work when he finally refused the scholarship. Over the kitchen sink a window opens to a view up the whole valley toward the Brecon Beacons. Cooking a meal here with this view in sight would be lovely.

On the refrigerator are a lot of photographs. I am surprised to see a very old one of Evan and me on a picnic a while before I left. I am so young, pregnant actually, but not noticeably. I can remember the day, how dizzy and nauseous I felt. I wore a purple-and-white dress I still have in a trunk somewhere in my garage in Santa Monica. Evan is in jeans, his hair longer than now, a day or two of a beard started. He has his arm around my neck, his hand reaching almost to my breast. I remember we'd asked an old gent just happening past to snap the photo, and afterward, we had kissed long enough to make us both decide it was time to get home. I feel my shoulders soften.

There are others of Dafydd. One when he was very little, perhaps about three. One of me holding Dafydd's hand, the two of us standing in front of the Eiffel Tower. I have a copy at home. And another of Dafydd when he was about twelve, standing in front of our house in Santa Monica, both hands in his pockets. It was the day he'd gotten his driver's license.

"I guess you got the photos from Gram?"

"I did."

The pain I have caused him crosses his face and I can see that the lines are there because of that pain.

There is a photo of Parry in his mining clothes. I must have been near him when the photograph was taken because he is giving me our private salute. One of Gram much older than I remember her, with her arm around Beryl. It is not surprising that there is nothing of Evan's family. I wonder if he is still not speaking to them, or still hasn't forgiven his father for his newborn sister's death. Such a horrible story that I plied from Evan that middle of the night. Oh, that we could all forgive and straighten out our pasts as Evan has so neatly organized his kitchen.

A long, quiet moment stretches between us. He is still so handsome in his tall, lean, muscular body.

"After you'd gone away, I'll admit I was so done in I was almost nonfunctional. Gram told me your letters were full of lines written by the poets you were reading. One night when I was down the pub, more than a bit in my cups, I sat next to a man who taught poetry at the university. Over the weeks and months we got to be friendly and I told him about you, mentioned some of the poets you were reading. Next time we met up, he had a book for me by Robert Creely. He lent me another and then another, till it became a regular thing between us."

He leads me out of the kitchen, down two stairs into what he still calls the cowshed. The floors are puzzled together with irregular pieces of flagstone and covered with two large Kilim rugs. The stone fireplace at the far end of the room is surrounded by books, and books fill every other surface in the room and are piled high on the floor and in the corners. I run my hand along their spines, noting they are mostly history, architectural and photo books. I see novels and two or three rows of poetry—among them, *Ariel* by Sylvia Plath.

"It was what we had between us, Gram and me. I told her stories about Parry's last days, and she gave me news of you. It was a trade for us during a difficult time. Perhaps we were both a little obsessed with the two of you," he admitted. "Our grief took us over. Looking back, I guess I'm grateful in a way. Poetry opened up a new world for me. I actually teach it to the children now."

Then, changing the subject once again, he asks about Dafydd. He wants to know how he did in school, what his interests are, whether he is athletic, does he body surf, what is he doing now that he's out of school. The questions come quickly with a certain abandon that he hasn't shown up till now, as if they are unconnected to anything else he might feel and have just been waiting to tumble out.

And finally he asks, "What does he know about me?"

"I've not told him nearly enough."

He waits for me to go on.

"When he was small, I deposited the money you sent into a savings account. When a goodly sum had gathered, I invested it for him. By the time he was ready for college, it paid for a good portion of his education."

"Glad I could be helpful. Did you tell him where the money came from?"

"Of course I told him. He's enormously grateful."

He waits for me to say something else. "Was that it? No such thing as a thank-you note in the States?"

It's true, I never insisted Dafydd write to Evan—a thank-you note or otherwise. I didn't discourage contact, but I didn't encourage it either. And after a while, as the years passed and the checks kept coming, I'd often let months go by before I mentioned to Dafydd that I'd received another one. It was easier for me. I take a deep breath in and close my eyes for a moment, realizing how much finagling I did, so as not to have to face my past. Then I look up guiltily at Evan.

"He wanted to come with me on this trip. He wants to meet you."

"Hmmm." Evan stares, blinks and then looks away. "Well, that's something, I guess." He shrugs. "You'll have to excuse me, Alys. Part of me can get right back into the hurt and anger. It is so huge. I can actually feel it starting in my solar plexus. It's wretched." He tilts his head. "I've had to really battle not to despise you for what you did."

I am cornered. His anger is brutal. It makes me ashamed.

"And I have. Battled, I mean," Evan continues. "And mostly I'm okay."

"I wish I could have done things differently, Evan. But I couldn't." I am defensive, my tone flat. It's the wrong thing to say in the wrong way. I know it. He clenches his jaw and starts to turn away. But what exactly is the right thing to say at a time like this?

"Every time you came up, everything else came up with you. I would feel like I was smothering all over again. I mean really, the cold, wet sludge appeared and seemed like it was everywhere. I had to shove you down. I had to go. If there had been another way, I would have stayed. It was not just some fly-by-night whim that made me leave, Evan. I dragged myself away from you. I was so scared. I didn't have a choice. When I got to the States, I just blocked you out."

"Sounds like it was pretty easy for you. Blocking me out."

"Are you not listening, Evan? I don't expect you to forgive me, but at least you have to hear me. It was the single hardest thing I have ever done in my life, leaving you. You must believe me. Now, at least maybe I can be of some help in getting you and Dafydd together. If you'll let me."

He stares at me, and another audible sigh escapes. "Well, there we have it." He turns away. "A plan will have to be made!" He glances at his watch. "Oh my, look at the time. I've got choir practice in half an hour."

I don't know what else I can say. Another moment passes before he turns back to me and straightens up tall.

"Alys. I'm sorry. I really am. The thing is," he starts, looking down at my feet. "I don't want to drag it all out again, for either of us. But not to talk about it would be false, don't you think?" I actually nod. "I'll try to go slowly, okay? I don't want to dump all my anger on you at once. You'd be running off again."

There's nothing else to say at the moment. It is utterly clear the pain I have caused him is not something for which I can lightly apologize.

"Would you like to come to choir practice?" he asks quietly. "It goes about two hours. You could stay as long as you like, because it can get tedious. We go over the same song again and again. Don't feel the least bit shy about leaving. You could have a look around the old neighborhood. We could meet afterward and go to the Black Cock for supper?"

The Black Cock Inn is the pub down the road from Evan's house. It was "our place," the one we'd gone to after our visits to the meadow. We'd sit close and eat chicken curry without the watchful eyes of the village, since the pub was ideally out of the way. Evan had actually kissed me for the first time at the bottom of the pub's drive.

If it weren't for his residual anger still hanging all around him like some fog cloud, I might imagine he's asking me out on a date. But I think this is nothing more than Evan trying hard to be courteous. And it is fine with me, a relief. I feel so battered by his anger. So I am tenuous about his dinner invitation. The guilt, sadness and shame he has elicited from me now lies on top of my own anger and disappointment toward him. I don't answer him about dinner.

We walk down the hill, a wide-open space between us. "Beryl says you owe her tea."

He smiles, a real smile, unforced, immediate. "You know she comes to my class occasionally and helps out. She works with the slower ones, helping with their sums and their reading. She's terrific with them. They're very fond of her."

I'd love to tell him how she tried to make me think he was still living with someone, tried to make me jealous. But I don't. There is little doubt in my mind Evan would not get any pleasure out of Beryl's shenanigans, and frankly, at the moment, neither do I.

Once we reach the rugby club, Evan points to a chair in the back of the large room with windows overlooking the road. The room has a bar with stools in the front. Liquor bottles sit on a shelf against a mirror. As the choir members pile in, taking off their cardigans and caps, some of them nod to me, or look and quickly turn away. I am the only woman in the place.

After several moments, Evan raps his knuckles on the podium. "Okay, men." In unison, they all stand. "Don't forget about your breathing, and to bring the sound up through your diaphragms. Sing it out. We've got a visitor here all the way from the States to impress."

As they begin their scales, my spirits seem to fly on the back of each note. Their voices rise in song, and so, somehow, does the small amount of hope that still lives in me. Every once in a while one of the men turns around and stares, perhaps trying to place me.

"Let's do 'We'll Keep a Welcome.' "

> *Far away a voice is calling,*
> *Bells of memory chime . . .*

I recognize the song immediately, one of Da's favorites, and Parry's. I bow my head, silently singing every word along with them:

> *Come home again, come home again,*
> *They call through the oceans of time . . .*

It is all I can do not to break into song myself, for this is the song of my childhood; in it I hear Da, Parry, Mam, Gram, Hallie, all our neighbors and friends, the theme of why I've come back. I dab my eyes and my running nose again, hoping this choice of song is his way of trying to show some forgiveness. But then I could be reading in what I would like him to feel.

After a while, as Evan suggested, I sneak out for some air, feeling the cool beginning of evening on my skin and relief to be out in the open again. Funny how neither distance nor death seems to change the way the heart remembers.

The sun has dropped, leaving the sky dramatically streaked with yellows and reds. When we were young, it seemed like summer's early-evening light lasted forever. It didn't get dark until past ten. We'd all be out in the road, dozens of us chatting each other up, playing SPUD and hide-and-go-seek, our parents calling us in only when the dark curtain of night was fully drawn. Now, probably out of some long-buried habit, I catch myself walking up the road, toward home, quickly passing Peter's house and Hallie's so I won't change my mind. Then I am standing in front of my own, the whitewash looking dingy and the doorframe smaller than I remember. The front stoop barely a foot wide. How had Hallie and I played our expansive game of dolls on it? How had we built our castle out of the huge cardboard box that our new Frigidaire came in? I can't believe it is the same stoop where Gram brought us hundreds and hundreds of toasted cheese sandwiches. The wood door looks as if it hasn't been painted in many years. But the brass knocker is shined bright.

I stand in front of the door, waiting for the courage to knock, wondering if Da will be in bed, Mam catering to him as always but still not really talking to him. Will I remember them? Not what they look like, but the real them, their smell, the feel of them, the way they were—the way we all were—before our lives were taken from us.

I drop the knocker, my heart going wild. The door opens and it is Mam in a flowered dress I actually remember. Surely it can't be the same dress, can it? She is smaller and thinner; her thick dark hair has gone gray. It is parted in the middle and the sides are held back with long grips. I take all of her in like I am a camera's lens.

She smiles and says, "Alys. You've come." The way she says my name feels like the hug she gives me when I dream of her. It's what I wanted after they dug me out, longed for every day afterward when I was with Gram and not her. "He'll be so happy to see you."

I step forward and put my arms around her, hugging her frail body. Tentatively she returns my embrace.

"You look all grown-up, then, Alys. Come in, come in. I'll make you a cup of tea."

Walking into the small front hall, everything I left behind comes back: Mam's tidiness, clean and spare, the wood floors mopped to a shine. I think of the mess of my own house, dishes in the sink, cereal boxes on the table, papers, manuscripts and newspapers everywhere. I follow her into the kitchen, where near the door sits the low table Da made. I notice the brown speckled lino he laid on the floor a million years ago is intact. The room is plain and the paint job faded, but the late-afternoon sun streams through the window, casting its warmth over everything. I can see Mam has already started to put together their supper, cutting up carrots and potatoes on the dark maple wood chopping block near the sink as the kettle simmers on the cooker.

We don't speak at first. It is not exactly uncomfortable. It is the way I remember us. Mam goes about getting a bottle of milk from the fridge, and her good teacups down from the cupboard above the stove, making me feel even more the guest. It's been a long time since I've seen a glass bottle and I remember the cold, cold milk. On the wall is a drawing I did when I was six, its colors faded and edges curled. It is a vase with six flowers, one flower for each of us in the family, every petal outlined in dark crayon. I'd been so proud of it. There is nothing else on the walls.

"Thank you for coming," Mam says from her spot near the cupboards. "I know it's far and terribly expensive." She moves around gathering faded cloth serviettes and plates. She looks up and smiles at me. "He's had a good day, today. You'll see. He's napping now. After a while we'll go up. He likes to eat early. That's why I'm already at it here.

"Last week he was only able to stay in his own bed. But this week he's been staying the day in Parry's room, because it's warm. You remember how the sun heats it when the weather's good? At night, he's back in his own room. Evan hooked the telly up in Parry's room. It makes it nice for Da."

She brings the cups, milk pitcher and sugar bowl to the table, then returns to the cooker and pours the hot water, a little first to warm the pot, followed by four teaspoons of tea and the rest of the water.

"I remember," she says, smiling. "You like it strong but milky."

She seems tired. Wrung out. But Auntie Beryl is right. Even though she is still mostly all business, there is something softened round her edges, an acceptance. She brings the teapot to the table with a small plate of chocolate-covered digestive biscuits.

"How are you, Mam?" I ask, pressing, wanting to pull something more from her.

She looks up, teapot in hand. "Oh, I'm all right. Holding up, like, you know. Some days easier than others, I guess," she sighs. "Glad to see you, I am. I was hoping you'd come. It's been such a long time." She smiles.

"It has," I reply, wanting to hear her say how she has missed me, beginning to let myself feel how much I have missed her. But neither of us says anything. There is another of those awkward moments of silence between us. "I probably should have let you know I was coming."

"Oh, I didn't expect that. I'm just glad you're here."

As she sits down and pours the tea, I ask, "When did Da last see the doctor?"

"He came round yesterday. Said he'd stop back this evening. I was thinking it might be him at the door."

"What did he say yesterday?"

"Blood pressure's normal. Heart's still beating good enough. He's weak. All things we know. But he does seem better today." She sounds hopeful. "Breathing is smoother. Not so raspy, like. And he's not complained of any pain today, although he doesn't have much of it anyway. That's a good sign, I think. Don't you?"

That seems a hard question to answer, assuming Da has emphysema or lung cancer, like all the rest of them who took ill and worked in the mine. In the old days, the term "black lung" used to cover it all. But I nod, sipping my tea. She's made it just like she did when I was small.

"Good cup of tea," I tell her.

Mam smiles and passes the biscuits.

Now I am waiting for her to ask me something about myself. Anything. About Dafydd. She must know about Marc's death. I'm sure Beti would have said something. But Mam doesn't say a word. Now it comes back to me that Auntie Beryl said she hadn't mentioned Marc's death to her. Now, instead of anger, I feel hurt. Does Mam still not care enough about me to ask how I might be doing since Marc's death? We sit quietly in the kitchen and drink our tea as though I live down the road and have seen her only yesterday.

"The weather's been good," she says, then. "We haven't had so much heat and sun in a summer for a long time."

Why do I need more response than she can give? I am here for her. For Da. In the distance I hear a bell.

"That's Da. I've given him Gram's bell to ring me when he needs something. He'll be wanting his dinner, which I've not finished making. Would you like to go? Give you a moment or two on your own with him, dear. I've told him I wrote to you. He won't be completely taken off guard."

"Okay, I'll go up." My neck and back suddenly stiffen as I pull myself from the chair.

"Tell him I'll be up directly with his broth."

How easily we seem to have fallen into our old roles. But it does feel a little different, as if somehow Mam needs me.

As I start out of the kitchen, I think of all that remains unsaid between us. When I was little, I wanted her to know what I felt—to hold me. Now I want her to make up for that lost time, to have really missed me and for me to feel it, to ask me about my life, my work, my family. To want to know me. Perhaps the loss of Mam in my life is why I try so hard to be there for Hannah.

Before I start up the stairs, I turn back to the kitchen, peering in, my hand on the doorframe. "Mam."

I surprise her. She looks up, concern in her eyes. "Oh, Alys, is anything wrong?"

"No. I just wanted to say that I'm awfully glad to see you."

She smiles shyly, tilting her head. "Why, that's just so nice of you to say, Alys. Thank you for telling me. You go on up now, dear." She waves, turning back to the stove top. "I'll be up in a moment, I will."

Seventeen stairs up to the empty hall, and the worn carpet leading into Parry's room. As I place my hand on the knob I remember all the times I'd just burst into Parry's room. *Don't you knock?* he'd say.

"Da?" I say quietly. "It's me, Alys." I peek around the door so as not to startle him with an abrupt entrance.

"Alys?" he says. "My Alys?"

I stand for a moment just through the door, looking at the room, half expecting to see Parry. But there is nothing of Parry left except for the brightly patched comforter on the bed. The walls are bare, the desktop empty except for the small TV.

Da is propped up in Parry's single bed on two pillows. I go over to the bed and put my hand on his covered feet, which are under the comforter. The room is hot. He struggles to pull himself toward me but it is too much for him, and he collapses back onto the pillow.

"Hello, Da," I say, eyeing the oxygen tank next to him, my own breath coming with some difficulty now.

"Oh, my sweet Alys." He talks slowly, a lot of breath between each word. "How good of you to come all this way." He motions me to come closer. "Did you bring the little one I've heard so much about? Dafydd?" He slowly pulls his body so he is sitting and can see me more eye to eye. "I 'spect he's not so little now. I'd like to meet him, I would." He takes a breath in. "Your gram went on about him endlessly, she did. And you've another one? Hannah?" Now he is breathless.

I sit on the edge of the bed, feeling as if I am holding back decades of tears. Although Da's mind seems clear, his body is half what I remember, his high cheekbones jutting out, his complexion yellow-gray. My heart sinks—and then I see there is still some life shining in those strong steel blue eyes. Parry had those blue eyes and Beti, too. Mine are the flat drab brown of my mother's eyes.

"Alys dear," Da says. "Forgive me for not writing after your husband died. Marc. Each day now, I meant to."

"Oh, Da, I've missed you," I say suddenly. It surprises me; it seems a lot to say out loud. But I want to say more about all I have been through without him. I wish he'd known Marc, been there when Hannah was born, been able to see Dafydd and Hannah together. He has missed my life and I have missed him in it.

He puts his large, thin hand over mine. "I've missed you, Allie dear."

I can hear the rasping in his chest. He closes his eyes and within seconds he is snoring. After a few moments, I gently pull my hand away. His eyelids flutter softly but don't open. Through the window it is getting darker, the sun setting lower on the horizon.

I tiptoe out Parry's door and take the last five steps up to my own room. I open the door carefully, remembering to lift and push so it doesn't creak. It seems just as I'd left it. The books on the small shelf, my pillows on the bed, the small hook rug Gram made for me on the floor. On my dresser are photos of me and Parry as children.

I hug myself and start to cry, the silent sobs coming from the dead sea of my now open heart. Part of me wants to lie down on the bed and never get up.

Once my body stops shaking, I open the dresser drawers and see they are filled with Mam's clothes. The long cupboard is filled with her housedresses and shoes, the spring smell of her enveloping me. This is her room now.

I hear the knocker go downstairs and I quietly close the closet door, switch off the light and make my way back down to Da.

At first it is an unfamiliar voice with Mam's on the creaking stairs, but as they get closer, I recognize Doc Rogers. He looks older, of course, slightly bent, but there is the same comforting manner and cheerful smile I remember. Just after the disaster he came every day to see me, always with a kind word of encouragement. The last time I saw him was a few weeks before I left for the States.

I come out of my corner and put my hand out to him.

"After all these years, only a handshake, Alys?" He pulls me to him, putting his arms around me and giving me a tight hug. "How are you then, my little one? You're looking beautiful as you always did, like." He pets my cheek and looks at me straight on, smiling. "Come to see your old da, eh? Well let's see how he's faring tonight, shall we?"

Da pulls himself up in the bed and says brightly, "Fine, William. I'm feeling just fine, I am. How could I not?" He nods my way.

Doc Rogers takes his stethoscope out of his small black bag and sits down on the edge of Da's bed.

"Oh, there's the door again. Can't remember when we've had such a crowd," Mam says, slipping out and down the stairs. Moments later, I hear Evan's voice on the stairs.

"You'll never guess, Alys," Mam says as she reenters the room, smiling wide in my direction. "It's Evan." She waits to see my reaction. I smile at Evan, guilty now for not having come straight here. Mam looks at me, then Evan, confused.

"This must be more than just a coincidence?" she asks.

Evan puts his head into the room. "Doc Rogers," he says, shaking Doc's hand. "How are you this evening, Da?" And then he nods at me. "I actually had the good fortune of running into Alys this afternoon."

"Oh?" Mam asks.

"Well now, Arthur. What do you say we have a look at you?" Doc Rogers asks. "Won't take but a few moments," he tells us.

Mam leads us out. We stand at the top of the stairs, waiting.

"And how've you been, Evan?" she asks. "I haven't seen you in a time, now."

"Just fine, Rita. Isn't it nice to have Alys back with us?"

She nods. She is distracted. Mam looks at the door. "What d'you think Doc's looking for?"

Evan puts his hand on her arm. "Probably just wants a moment alone with him so he can have a close look. Nothing to worry about, Rita, I'm betting." I am touched by the affection between them. He looks my way. "You okay, Alys?"

"I'm just a bit ragged."

Mam leans against the wall looking worried. "He's taking a

rather long time of it," she says. "I hope nothing's wrong." As if everything had been just fine before Doc Rogers closed the door.

Another few moments pass while we all stand quietly looking at each other. I am uncomfortable in Evan's presence and hope Mam didn't take too much notice about my having met up with him first. Then the door slowly opens and Doc Rogers emerges.

"He's just tired, is all. He's slipped off to sleep. Do him the world of good, it will. Just leave him be. I gave him something light so he'll sleep through the night. He should, anyway." He puts his arm around Mam and looks at me. "How long are you in for, Allie?"

"About a week."

"I'll see you again, I 'spect. And I'll be looking forward to it, too." He smiles and starts down the stairs. We follow. "Call me if you need me, Rita."

When we are at the bottom of the stairs, Mam looks at us, her face full of worry.

"Evan, be a sweetheart and take Alys for supper, will you? I've suddenly not the strength to do too much more tonight." She puts her hand over her eyes. Her shoulders hunch forward and she sighs. "I just don't think I'm up to anything."

"Mam, let me help."

"No, no. I'll be all right, I will. After a little sleep myself, I'll be fine." She smiles at me sadly. "You understand. I'll just go back up now, if you don't mind, and have a few hours. I try to sleep when he does." She nods, putting her hand on my cheek. "I'm glad you are here, Alys."

"I don't have to leave."

"You go on now," she says. "I'm sure you both have a lot to catch up on."

"I'll come round early tomorrow," I say.

"We'll be here," she says, up the stairs now.

Before we leave, I sneak a peek behind the closed door of the parlor. It is in shadows as the last light of day streams through the stained glass window that comforted me as a child. The white porcelain dog and the two brass candlesticks that belonged to Gram are still on the mantel where they always sat. There is nothing at all on the walls, not even one of Parry's paintings. It remains sterile, unfriendly and formal. There are so many unpleasant moments I spent in it. I still wonder why when we were children, they put the telly in this room, which we used only on rare occasions. So many things they did for show. It should have been in the kitchen or up in Parry's room, as it is now.

Evan follows me out, shutting the door behind him. Once outside, I pause, shaking my head as I look up at the lighted second floor, so many conflicting feelings.

"Amazing," I say.

"What?"

"I'm just surprised she didn't want me to spend the night. She didn't even ask where I was staying."

Evan says, "I wouldn't be too hard on her. 'Specially now. She may have thought you were staying with me."

He is such a paradox. His cold intense anger toward me and his gentleness and warmth toward my mother.

"I'm not trying to be hard on her, Evan. I'm just trying to understand things. I've spent a lot of time lately thinking about why I had to leave and how it must have affected everyone: you, Gram, Da and Mam. At the time I couldn't dwell on it—I just had to go, quick as I could. I can see how much damage it has done. I can't imagine how I'd feel if Hannah or Dafydd left me like that. But if they did and then came home after a million years, I sure wouldn't want them running off again so fast, even for the night." I am thinking out loud, probably not even making a lot of sense.

"But you are not your mother and she is not you. Give her a few days to get used to you being back. You saw her as we left. She's a mess. She probably needs to privately refuel."

"I'm sure you're right. I'm just impatient, only having these few days to cover so much ground."

Evan's expression changes. Even less friendly. "A few days? What can you possibly accomplish in a few days? You can't really expect too much of anyone, can you now?" The bitterness in his tone, the harshness, is back.

"Evan, now what have I said?"

"Well, help me out, Alys. If you're only home for just a few days, during a time when your mother is having to deal with your father's imminent passing—no easy thing, as you know—you can't be expecting her to entertain you. In fact, you probably shouldn't expect anything."

"I don't expect her to entertain me." He is attacking me again.

"So what exactly do you expect?" He throws his hands up in exasperation, looking at the sky, maybe at the North Star just come out.

"Well, I don't know. I don't really expect anything. I just want to be here. To see Da, to—"

"Do you think that you can just go away and not make contact with any of us for years and years, and then show up for three minutes and expect your mam to welcome you home with open arms?"

"Evan, I can't believe that after all this time and now I'm finally here you choose to yell at me because of how long I'm staying?" His anger toward me is all around him.

"I'm not yelling."

"You are. Perhaps we shouldn't talk about this in the middle of the road."

"Why not? What difference does it make where we talk? We've got so little time, better take advantage of every moment, middle of the road or not." He turns to look at me.

"There's no way we can have a reasonable conversation about anything. You're so angry with me." I look up at him, biting my lower lip. "Jesus, Evan. I've at least tried to explain—I have."

Evan sighs.

My upper lip is trembling.

He turns away. "Okay. Okay. You've made a point." When he turns back, he says, in a softer tone without looking at me directly, "The truth is, we all do love you, Alys. Your mother, your father, Beryl and I. I'm betting you'll get more than what you need from your mother if you give her half a chance, a little patience, and a lot of understanding, despite how long you stay. These are hard times for her."

"And what about you, Evan?" I can feel the tears behind my eyes. I am determined not to give in to them. "I may have made a point, but you've kind of ignored it."

"No, I haven't. I just don't want to delve into it in the middle of the road," he says.

"Hah! See what I mean!"

He rolls his head and a smile of sorts appears at the corners of his mouth. "Caught."

I clear my throat and swallow through the tears. "Can't you see I am so sad about everything, Evan? There doesn't seem anything I can do to make the past better. Despite the fact that I'm only here for a short time, I am here. We could take a stab at it."

"A stab?"

"You know."

He looks at me quizzically.

"We could try to at least have a conversation that's not edged with innuendo, sarcasm and anger. These are hard times for all of us, it seems."

A moment passes. Evan nods.

"Truce?" I put out my hand.

Another moment passes.

"Truce."

We shake.

Chapter Fourteen

No one else is on the road. As evening begins to settle, lights go on in the terrace rows. Evan shows me a dirt path he's found, a shortcut that leads up to the field behind his cottage. We branch off before reaching the field, heading instead toward the pub. Bending low under a weeping willow, I notice how the light is muting from twilight to dusk, our shadows growing, a full moon giving us more than enough shine to see our way. We come out from under low-hanging branches into the lights from the pub.

Evan asks quietly, "I would actually like to try and understand why you left me, Alys. Could you be more specific? Because I thought our being together—I mean, you sleeping at my flat—had helped."

The question, so sudden and coming out of the quiet after the show of his anger, takes me aback. Part of me is almost afraid to answer him, as if he might be setting me up.

"Of course it helped, some. But it wasn't just you, Evan. It was everything. It's been so long I don't know if I can really explain it. It was so many things. My relationship with Mam, my anger toward Da. You saw me—I wasn't functioning. For all intents and purposes I'd dropped out of school. Remember, I was hardly getting out of bed. And then I found out I was pregnant. It was all just too much for me. I think if I'd stayed another moment I might have ended up like Parry."

"You didn't give me enough of a chance." Moonlight reflects in his eyes like bright, hard crystals. I take a chance and put my arms around his stiff body, trying to hold him. He doesn't relax any, but he doesn't pull away, either.

It seems like hours we stand, me holding him. After a while, he moves a bit, and I let him go.

"Thanks. I appreciate the hug," he says.

We manage to make our way into the friendliness of the pub, to a back table. Evan brings a Guinness and a glass of red wine from the bar. We sit quietly, glancing at each other and then awkwardly looking away. Soon one of the women behind the bar comes and asks us if we'd like something to eat. We both order chicken curry and a side of chips. I know it will come with mushy peas and overcooked carrots.

"And a carafe of your red wine, please," Evan adds.

By the time the dinner arrives, I am ravenous.

"Let's pretend I cooked it," he says, trying hard to be friendly.

I look at his hands as he pushes a first bite of food with his knife onto his fork, remembering what a good cook he was when we were young.

"Next time could you take the vegetables off the burner a bit sooner?" I tease, hoping to soften him a little more toward me.

He looks up at me and smiles.

Mushy vegetables or not, the meal is delicious. There is no french fry like a Welsh chip, crisp and greasy, moist in the middle. And as the Welsh are known to do at meals, we talk about the weather. A safe topic. Evan confides how it hasn't been this beautiful in Wales in more than a decade. He lets me into his world a little, talking about his life as a teacher and a bit of how the choir started.

"Several months after you left, I was in the pub one night. A bunch of us had had too much to drink for a change. We were carrying on, and it turned into song as it sometimes does—you know how that goes. You remember the old saying 'If you get two Taffys together they immediately form a chorus?' "

I laugh, remembering how my da would break into song when he had a beer and there were friends over.

"I think it was Jack Ratchet who said, 'Someone oughta start a men's choir. That might put us right if anything will.' Before I knew it we'd gathered thirty men. Then it was forty and we were using my classroom for rehearsals. Once we were going strong, we all seemed to get something out of it. It filled our need to do something for each other and the village. And the men liking it filled me up." He pushes his hair away from his forehead and leans back in his chair, enthusiastic and relaxed as he talks about how he has made his own way in the world. "Now we are fifty in number, with a waiting list.

"It's miraculous, really. Never in a million years did I think we'd perform outside of the area. We've been all over Britain and who knows what lies ahead?"

Despite his enthusiasm, and how much he has helped the village, I can see in his eyes how hard it has been for him. "How do you find the time with your teaching schedule?"

"Saturdays, Sundays and substitutes." He shrugs. "It's good, mostly—I am enjoying my life. Once in a terrible blue moon I get to thinking about how tied down I'd be if I were hitched to someone, babies running around. And then I realize that it's something I miss. Having not had my own children around." He pauses, looking down at his plate, realizing perhaps he has strayed to dangerous territory again. But he doesn't take it back; he just leaves it there. "What about you, Alys? How have you managed with all you've had to face? It's a terrible lot you've had to deal with, and now your husband's death."

I try to think how to answer. There isn't a simple answer to how I've managed, besides the many ways in which I guess I've learned to cope: denial, anger, regret and sadness.

I try to put some of it in words. "Before Marc's death, I guess I just lived, making an effort not to think about anything unpleasant, particularly not my past. I just plowed through. That's all I could do. I am beginning to see now it was a rather superficial way to get through life. Marc's death has somehow changed all of that. There doesn't seem to be anywhere for me to hide now. My defenses are down. It's hard, and I am awfully lonely sometimes. I guess that's my biggest lesson at the moment: learning how to be single. How to be in the world alone. That's hard. But I have Hannah, and since she's doing better, I guess it means, in some ways, I'm doing better. You know what they say about parents—'You're doing as well as your kids are.' "

"So I've heard," Evan says, without affect.

Damn. My turn for an insensitive moment on dangerous turf.

"Hannah actually decided on her own to go to sleepaway camp."

"Sleepaway?"

"For a month. It's kind of a wilderness camp. You know, hiking, rafting. No parents, just kids and counselors. Her idea, totally. I think she felt she needed a break from me, my heaviness, and from Los Angeles, the city in general—you know how it is. Initially I was against it, but she talked me into letting her go."

"You'd never find parents here letting their children go off for a month, I don't think. It's an odd concept, young children going off without their parents." He shakes his head. "And are you still writing?"

"Poetry."

"Ah, of course, I wasn't thinking. I knew that. Gram told me. Funny, Parry always thought you'd be a poet."

"He did, didn't he?" I warm, remembering.

After dinner we walk back to Evan's. It's been a very long day and I've had much too much wine. We've taken the roadway and I stumble on a rock. Evan puts his arm around me and helps me get my balance; he's so close I smell the familiar lavender soap he's always used.

"Steady there, Alys." He rights me by putting my arm on his forearm for balance.

"The sky is so lovely, as clear as any Colorado night."

"Is it? What do the Rockies look like?"

I tell him that they range around the state like arms, holding the sunrise and twilight, making me feel safe, or as safe as I can ever feel. "At sunset the light turns them violet, just like in the American ballad. Their 'purple mountains' majesty' is just that. In places their peaks and valleys remind me of Switzerland."

"You've traveled a lot, then?" he asks.

"Not nearly as much as I'd like."

"Hmmm. When we were young my wildest fantasy was about taking you to Fiji—I don't know why Fiji—maybe because it was so far away from here and so exotic."

This fantasy somehow surprises me. That he'd really thought about a life with me. Traveling. Leaving Aberfan for any reason.

When we reach the top of his drive, where my car is parked, he says, "I don't think you should drive back to Cardiff tonight. You've had too much to drink."

"I'm fine," I lie.

"You're not."

"I'll be fine. It's just a little jet lag." I look up at the moon, which has now risen, full, over the Aberfan hills, and seems to be shining down directly on us. Hannah sees the same moon on the other side of the world. "I need to call Hannah."

"So call her here. I've a wonderful little guest room. And you can get up early and see your mam and da first thing. I'm also on the telephone. When you left, hardly any of us were—do you remember? The whole village has come into the twenty-first century. You can actually call Hannah while sitting in front of a roaring fire," he says, imitating a very stuffy Englishman. "I won't take no for an answer. You've no choice, really, Alys. It would be absolutely dead-out irresponsible of me to let you on the motorway. I can't allow it."

For a moment, I continue to put up a fight, and then, as I had last night at Beryl's, I admit to being knackered—driving on the wrong side of the road in the dark is not nearly as tempting as the thought of a soft bed. Once inside, Evan points me toward the sofa near the fireplace. "The phone is just there."

"What is it, five or six hours' difference? I can never remember."

"I don't know," he says. "I've not called the States in some time." Not missing a beat, he continues. "Perhaps if you go through the operator, they can tell you. I'll just go now and make the bed up for you and get out some fresh towels."

As he walks away, I eye his strong shoulders, admiring how his jeans fit his bottom, remembering how much I loved him, loved to look at him. I am immediately embarrassed and surprised by these memories.

The camp operator tells me Hannah's group is off on an overnight; the owner of the camp has gone with them. She assures me that everything is fine. Next I call Dafydd. He's in a meeting, but I leave word with Barbara to tell him I'm fine and I'll call again.

The room is dimly lit, the fire still going, although now it is only red-hot embers. And the cottage is quiet. I kick off my shoes and put my feet up, resting for just a moment.

I hear Evan, from under a heavy fog, as he moves about the room, but I can't seem to get my eyelids to move. I feel it when he puts the blanket over me and tucks me in, but I am too tired to respond.

*   *   *

Evan takes me for my first driving lesson, unofficial of course, because I am fourteen, still way too young to legally drive. He is trying
to teach me how to steer, shift the gears and use the petrol pedal, all
at the same time. I keep confusing the brake with the clutch. It seems
a lot to learn in an afternoon. He suggests we take a break, go to his
house for biscuits and tea. It sounds good to me since I don't want to
go home—in fact haven't wanted to go home since Parry moved out.
He is living with Gilly, who none of us, even Evan, know that well, except to say hello. Evan has been trying to convince Parry to make it
up with Da. He thinks that would help Parry pull it together.

I follow Evan into the small kitchen while he turns on the kettle
and gets the cups out. We talk about the rules of driving, coming to
a full stop at a stop sign, things like that. I watch as he pours out the
boiling water into the kettle.

Outside, the sun is setting in a blaze of gold and saffron in the blue
cloud-scattered sky.

"Come and look, Evan." He puts the teapot and cups on the table
and comes over next to me.

"After all, there's still beauty, isn't there?" he says quietly, then
turns and kisses me, on the cheek. I surprise him when I kiss him back
full on the lips. Then his arms are around me and mine around his
neck, the two of us there in the sunset. When he touches my breast I
don't stop him, so he hitches my dress up and feels them both bare,
the nipples hard between his fingers. His hand slips awkwardly into
my panties. He hesitates, then begins caressing me. I have not done
this before but I want him so badly I lift my leg and he puts his finger
in and moves it around till I almost cry out, his tongue against mine,
mine moving just as fast around his. My body loosens against him—
his is hard against me. I pull him closer.

"Alys," he whispers. "Oh, Alys."

I've never heard my name said like this before.

Then, suddenly, he pulls away.

"Please don't stop," I say quietly, confused.

"Alys, I can't. It's, it's . . . You're too young. So young you are. I
just can't. I'm so sorry."

"You don't have to be," I say, embarrassed, pulling myself right. I
am afraid of what I am feeling and what I would have let Evan do.

My dress falls straight and I run my fingers quickly through my hair.

Evan smiles tentatively at me.

We sit down across from each other at the small table and sip our tea. We smile at each other, acknowledging what is new between us.

Awakened by movement in the kitchen, I forget for a moment where I am. The fire has gone out. There is a blanket over me. But then I remember: Evan's house, with daylight now coming through the opening in the pine green velvet drapes. I pull the blanket up around my neck and shudder down, thinking about how we actually started, Evan and me. One day I was living at home and the next I was more at Evan's than not. It wasn't till Gram told me I was making trouble for Mam by my actions that it even came to my attention I might be doing something that wasn't proper.

Then is not now. I sit up, run my fingers through my hair, try to straighten myself out a bit. I am in dire need of a shower. The front door opens and then closes. Footsteps move away on the flagstone. I get up, quickly fold the blanket on the sofa, cross the cold flagstones in my bare feet. At the kitchen sink I let the water run and cup it with my hands into my mouth. Through the window, I see Evan in his garden in the shining morning, picking something and putting it into a pail.

I wander into the cowshed, touching the tops of the leather couches as I pass, looking for my bag. I feel as if I have had a hard night sleeping on concrete. I am dying for a cigarette. When I find them, I light one, inhale deeply, immediately get dizzy. After a few more drags I snuff it out in the fireplace.

In the bathroom, the tiles are clean and white and cool under my feet. Evan has left a stack of towels on the counter for me. I take off my clothes, having been in them for two days, and run the water for a bath. It is strange and then not so strange to be standing naked in Evan's bathroom, looking at myself in his mirror.

I sneak a look into his medicine cabinet and glance at the tidy shelves, everything lined up and organized. There is no makeup remover, no perfume. Seems to be just as he said—he has made this life without a partner. I close the cabinet door quickly. The steaming bath feels good. I completely submerge, holding my breath for as long as I can.

I towel-dry my hair and tie it back. Then I put on my crumpled clothes and use my finger to brush my teeth. When I come out of the bathroom Evan is in the kitchen. He has started a fire. Cut flowers are arranged in a vase on the table.

"Morning, Alys," he says, looking up from his cooking. "You fell asleep on the sofa. I hope it was all right that I let you sleep. Did you find everything you needed in the bathroom?"

"I did," I say, remembering how easy we used to be with each other years ago. "Thank you."

"I'm making a quick omelette, and then I'm off to school. D'you like coffee or tea?"

"Coffee, thanks."

"I was wondering," he starts rather formally. "I imagine there's a lot for you to do while you're here, people you will be wanting to spend time with, but . . ." He pauses. "Well, what I mean to say is that it might be helpful if we could spend a bit of time going over things, getting to know each other again, perhaps clearing the air. I finish at half past three today. I could make you dinner, here?"

For a moment I hesitate. Having dinner with him alone in his house intimidates me. Thankfully, I remember I have promised to see Mam and Da.

"Mam. I promised Mam I'd cook them supper. I actually want to do a bit of shopping for them, cook a few meals they can have ready in the fridge. Try to take the strain off Mam a bit. Perhaps *you'd* like to join *us* for an early supper? I can't imagine they'd mind." I figure with my parents around we will stay on even ground.

"I'd like that," he says immediately.

"You didn't get to the guest room last night, but wouldn't it be a bit easier for you to be right here, steps away from your parents, rather than trekking back and forth to Cardiff? You've so little time as it is. There will be food in the fridge and a telephone at your disposal. I'll keep the fire going when I'm around. No strings attached." He raises his right hand. "I'll try to keep my attitude light."

I can tell how hard he is trying. Why I would think his dinner offer is dangerous, and not this offer, is beyond me, but I accept.

"I'd like that, Evan. Thank you for asking."

The drive back to Cardiff is easier than it was coming up. I know my way, straight down the M4 as if I've done it a hundred times. It takes me forty minutes. There are tasks to fulfill now, places to go

and people to be with. It is as if I am beginning some new phase of
an old life, moving into it, if only for a little while, getting the chance
to live with it in a different way. While I am checking out of the
hotel, I ask the concierge where I might find a supermarket. His idea
of a supermarket is a small shop in Rhiwbina that certainly has the
basic food groups: potatoes, tomatoes, onions, swedes, parsnips and
eggs, but not much in the way of herbs or other exotics. How spoiled
I have become, living in a place where I can drive up, park the car
and quickly get everything under one roof. Or maybe it's the other
way around. Maybe I am actually more isolated. Here, as I gather
paper towels, loo paper, cereal and tinned soups, I have a long conversation with the shopkeeper. Next door I have a nice conversation
with the butcher while he cuts me two legs of lamb—"from local
sheep"—and several chickens. "Do you want the chickens with their
heads on or off? With the feathers or without?" One of the legs of
lamb is an offering for Evan.

Down the road is a greengrocer with a larger selection of fruits
and vegetables and fresh herbs, and next door is a bakery. I love the
contact and brief conversation with each shopkeeper.

When I arrive at Da and Mam's, Mam doesn't seem to be around,
at least not downstairs. I put the perishables in the fridge and go upstairs to see how Da is feeling. He is propped up in bed watching the
telly with his oxygen mask on. He starts to remove the mask.

"No, no, Da. You don't have to take it off. I'll come closer."

But he pulls it up around his head anyway.

"Where's Mam?" I ask.

He shakes his head.

I wonder if she leaves him often. She can't possibly be with him
twenty-four hours a day. Perhaps she's gone off to the shop or next
door. She must have friends.

"The cemetery, most likely," Da says, quietly. "She does that
some mornings."

Of course. I imagine they all visit there often, if not daily. Poor
Mam. What must it have been like through all these years? The years
without Gram to steady her. The years when there has been no one
for her but Da.

Da moves his legs to give me room to sit on the edge of the bed.
All of my anger gone, I want to ask him about the bench, but

think better of broaching that subject just now.

"I've brought some chickens to throw into a soup," I say.

"She'll like that, Allie. She won't let on, she won't. Your mam's not good with saying so, but she's glad you've come," he says, his words coming out choppy with his heavy breathing. "She didn't think you would. She's spent a good many years being sorry. She's said out loud at least a dozen times that she didn't handle you properly. But she did her best. She was caught in a bind that choked her like everyone else. At first everyone blamed me. Later, everybody blamed themselves." He starts to cough.

I put my hand on his knee and then I lean toward him, pulling him up straight, thinking that might help him stop coughing. It does.

"It's been too many years without you she's had to make do with just me. You did the right thing, leaving here," he says. "When I've gone, take her with you, Alys. She deserves some better years. A fresh start. Away from the darkness here." This last bit comes out in a whisper.

What is he asking? In my wildest musings I have never thought about living with either of them again, least of all Mam. What would that be like?

While I am chopping the vegetables for soup, I try to imagine Mam sitting in the rocker in my kitchen, talking to Hannah, washing her clothes, hanging them out on the line—a view of the sea in the distance—walking along my stretch of the Santa Monica beach. She wouldn't actually have to live with me, would she? Perhaps just nearby. There are the Sunshine Towers, beautiful condominiums with a pool and sauna several blocks away from me. And in town, a bit farther away, are the rows of small bungalows for assisted living. But Mam would never allow anyone else to clean for her or cook her meals. I can't imagine it; she is too private, too much to herself, even with Da.

The front door bangs, followed by creaking up the stairs. A few minutes later Mam is standing by the kitchen door, her coat over her arm.

"Da says you're making chicken soup. That's nice."

I turn.

"He's not so good today," she says. I can hear the fatigue in her voice, the giving in and giving up to what is happening, what has been happening for months, having to watch Da fade, and having no control over it.

"I don't really know what to do," she says, laying her coat over a chair. "He's dying, you know." This seems so big for Mam to admit out loud, so revealing of her sadness.

"He's worried about you," I say.

"Me?" She's surprised, her hand on her chest.

"After . . . You know, I've been thinking. Da and I were talking about me taking you back to the States."

"No," she says immediately.

"No?"

"What in the world would I do there? My life is here. Everything I know is here. This is my home, Allie."

"I know, but it will be so lonely without him. Beti and I are in the States." Suddenly, I really want her there, for her and for me. "Our children are there. You could make a life."

She looks at me or, rather, through me. A long silence stretches between us.

"I could visit?" Her eyes settle in on me, hopefully.

"Of course you can."

"We'd always meant to, like," she adds. "Somehow time got away from us. Always so much to do round here, I guess. You know how that is." She bows her head. "I'd best help you," Mam says then, moving toward the counter where I've been chopping. "That is, if you wouldn't mind, like? Da will be wanting his tea sooner rather than later."

"I'd like that, Mam. I could use some help."

We make small talk about her trip to the cemetery. She says she goes about every other day. She tells me she is also trying to keep Gram's garden up in the back, at least the tomatoes, although she's hard pressed these days to find the time. As I am washing several sprigs of mint, she comments on how she's never thought of putting mint in chicken soup and how inventive I am. I tell her about my wonderful friend Elizabeth. I tell her about Elodie. Considering everything that is going on and not going on, we are very much at ease with each other.

CHAPTER FIFTEEN

While the soup is simmering on the stove, Mam goes upstairs to check on Da. I need air badly, a stretch, a look at the sky. I start out in one direction—up toward the cemetery—but almost immediately turn and walk in the opposite. Once again, it is like I am being pulled by something unearthly, and before I know it, I am standing in front of the Joneses' front step. I have to physically restrain myself, put my hand over my mouth, in order not to call out, "Hallie!"

I hesitate before walking up to the door, partly hoping no one will be home. When the door opens, I want to see little Niko on the stairs, his shy way of smiling just for me. But little Niko is no longer little Niko, and Mrs. Jones, no longer yellow-haired and unlined. She stares at me for a moment, then throws her arms around my neck.

"Alys dear!" she says squeezing me tight. "I can't tell you how wonderful 'tis to see you. Can you come in? Oh, do come in. Tell me absolutely everything about you, dear." She wraps me up in her arms and ushers me into the house I know as well as my own. "When did you arrive and how long will you be staying? Come in, come in. Mr. J is in the garden. He'll be so glad to see you, too."

The kitchen table is already set for two with a flowered cloth and colored serviettes in silver rings, two candles; I smell the comforting aroma of meat roasting. How have they managed after all they've lost to keep such friendliness and warmth alive? Why didn't I stay in touch with her?

The obligatory cup of tea, and then Mrs. Jones is sitting across from me, her warm hand on mine.

"How *are* you doing, Alys? Tell me all about your family. Your husband. What does he do? Tell me what it's like to live in the States."

I'm not so good at hiding things these days, and Mrs. Jones can see it in my face.

"Oh, Alys dear, whatever is wrong?"

I shake my head, not wanting to open it all up again. She rubs my hand. "Perhaps I can help?"

Before I know it, before I can shore myself up, I say, "He died. My husband. Quite unexpectedly almost a year ago now, while I was out of town. In front of our eight year old, Hannah. She had to handle the whole thing with him on her own."

"Oh my goodness, sweet Alys. How terrible. I'm so, so sorry. Doesn't seem to be easy for anyone, does it?" She leans over and puts her arms around me as I cry. "There, there. There now, dearie," she whispers. "I s'pose the good news is that if anyone knows how to comfort a child, it's you. D'you remember how wonderful you were with Niko? No one could have helped him through like you did. And of course, time helps. Not that we ever forget." She clicks her tongue and rubs my shoulders. "We never forget, do we? But we somehow learn to live alongside it."

"It was my fault," I whisper, surprising myself.

"What, dear? Your husband's death was your fault?"

I shake my head again and again. "No, Hallie's."

"Oh, Alys, sweetheart, it was nobody's fault . . ."

"If I hadn't insisted on buying our milk, if I'd let her do it instead of me, if I'd let her queue up with me . . ." I am sobbing.

"Alys, Alys . . ." Mrs. Jones has gotten up and is cradling me in her full, soft arms. "It wasn't your fault. Please you mustn't think this. My God, Alys, have you been carrying this around with you all these years? Dear, dear Alys." She rubs my back until I've stopped crying, then pulls a hankie from the sleeve of her cardigan.

She smiles at me. "Okay now?"

"I didn't want to do this. I'm so sorry."

"Now, now, Alys. I'm glad you did. Now it's out. It's terrible that you've been holding on to that all these years. You must know there was nothing you could do to save Hallie. It was her time, like. We know that. And so must you. It's been so many years now, and life is short enough, Alys. Let these thoughts go, please, dear." She pats my hand.

"And what about your children, Alys darling. How are they doing now?"

I catch my breath and then I tell her all about Dafydd and Hannah. Feeling better as we talk, I notice a vase of yellow roses on the sideboard in front of a photo of Hallie, confirming for me that Mrs. Jones must be the one who had put the flowers I saw on Hallie's grave.

Finally, I ask about Niko, who she says is living in Newport now. He and his wife run an ice-cream shop. "Homemade creams and ice lollies," Mrs. Jones says. They have two children; one, named Hallie, is four, and the other, named Gregory, two years old. "Harry and I see them about once a month."

Mr. Jones comes in from the garden, immediately cracks a wide smile and says, "My goodness me, it's Alys Davies. I'd know you anywhere. What a nice surprise. Why, you haven't changed an iota." He takes off his gardening gloves and hugs me up into his huge frame, lifting me off my feet like a child, putting me down squarely, taking my hands in both of his big ones and looking at me closely. "You look good, you do. Healthy and full of life." And so does he. He is not stooped by age, his shoulders still wide, his hair still a wispy blond, like Hallie's.

Mrs. Jones doesn't mention my outburst, but continues to stay close, her hand on mine now that I am sitting again. She listens as Mr. Jones asks me all about my life in California. He says how proud of me he is, how glad he is to see how well I am doing.

"And how's your father doing, then?" he asks.

"All right, it seems. Well, that's actually a lie. He's dying. Mam is handling it, or I should say, it seems like she is. But he's dying. He was a little better yesterday."

Mrs. Jones nods, her eyes full of tears. She shakes her head as if trying to change the subject.

"Are you here long enough for us to arrange a dinner with Niko and his family? I'm sure he would love to see you." We make a tentative date for next Monday night.

I hesitate before taking my leave, asking if it's okay to see Hallie's room. As we walk up the stairs together, I think I smell Hallie's familiar lemony scent, and a million memories flash through my mind. Mr. and Mrs. Jones have made her room into a guest room for their grandchildren. There are photos of the kids and their colorful crayon drawings are tacked on all the walls. Sitting on the corner windowsill, in a small silver frame, is a photo of Hallie when she was about six, standing tall and smiling.

Back at Mam and Da's, Evan is sitting with Mam at the kitchen table. Seeing them together gives me a moment's taste of what it would have been like had I stayed. Both their features live in Dafydd, and it's clear that no matter where I've gone or what I've lived, we are a family. I wish Dafydd were here. I miss him. And Hannah. Six more days until I return to Los Angeles and then another week before I fetch Hannah home from Colorado. I am not ready to leave any of these people and be alone again, to have to face the problems of Gabriella and Isabel.

"The soup smells wonderful," Evan says, in that way I remember he always had of making me feel I've accomplished the impossible. He rises and comes toward me, both of us hesitating a bit, perhaps because of Mam's presence. "How are you?" he asks, with some new warmth, perhaps also because of Mam's presence.

The affection I feel for him is caught in my body like a frog in my throat.

"Da's asleep," Mam says from her place at the table. "I've asked Evan if he will join us for tea. We could take our bowls up later and eat with him. I hope that's all right, Alys."

"Of course," I say, looking up quickly into Evan's translucent blue-green eyes and then quickly away.

"Did you have a nice walk?" he asks.

"I went round Hallie's."

"Ah." He nods, and nothing more needs be said. I can see he understands.

"Evan was just saying about your little girl, Hannah," Mam starts. "And I was wondering how she is doing without her father." Evan's presence seems to free Mam up. I don't know how to answer, still feeling vulnerable and teary from being with the Joneses.

Evan comes to the rescue. "I told your mam that Hannah is enjoying herself at camp in Colorado." Does Mam even know what camp is? As I found telling Evan, it is not a common thing to do in Wales, to send your child away to a summer camp. To send your child away anywhere.

"She must be a very brave little girl. To lose a father is a lot. Especially at her young age." She pauses and adds, "I was also thinking you are very brave, to have let her go away, I mean, during a time that must be ever so hard for you."

My eyes fill. "It *was* hard for me to let her go. But she is very strong and she was determined to go."

"It's both a blessing and a curse to have a strong daughter," she says, looking straight at me.

My body goes still.

"What I really mean is, hard as it has been without you, I'm glad you are strong-willed. It has been good for you." She bows her head and looks down at her hands. "But . . . I have missed you."

"Mam . . ."

Evan moves back, giving us room.

"Oh, Alys," Mam says, starting to get up. I put my hand over my mouth, embarrassed that I am falling apart in front of her, in front of Evan.

"I'm sorry, Mam. I don't mean to be crying. I know you have your hands full now. It's just . . ."

Before I can finish my sentence she is beside me, holding me. I am very small, crying in her arms. My body shakes and the tears keep coming until I feel I have dissolved in them, dissolved in my mother's arms.

Mam reaches into her apron pocket and gets her handkerchief. She wipes my eyes and holds it up to my nose, and like a small child, I blow.

"There, there, Alys," she says, patting my arm. "There, there. It is hard to be losing a husband and a father all in the same year. It seems utterly unfair that you should ever have to lose anything else again in your whole life." Her words open a place inside that has been shut down for a long, long time.

Later on we eat dinner with Da. He has been using the oxygen mask but while Mam feeds him it hangs loose around his neck. Da is relieved that Doc Rogers is coming again later. "I think I'll ask him for some painkillers," he says.

"Are you in pain now, Arthur?"

"A bit."

"Where, then? Is it something I can massage?" Mam's expression is full of her own pain. "Your da's not had much pain before now, then," she tells me again. "At least not in the lungs, coughing or short of breath, until just now. Others who have had the black lung have had pain sometimes for years and years, and trouble breathing. Right, Arthur?"

As I sit with them, tough as the situation is, and as many years as we have been apart, we seem to manage together. Mam and Da are in this hard time together. I can feel their deep partnership. And I feel mostly at home, with Evan, too, as if he has always been near, in the back of my mind, in the quiet of my heart. But now I can admit it out loud to myself. Of course, as soon as I do, the cold black terror surrounds me. Someone else can be taken away from me. Such a familiar feeling, this darkness rising, turning all hope away. It seems even more haunting in Aberfan.

After dinner, Evan asks if I want to go round the pub and have a drink with some friends. "You might remember Oscar Jeens. Worked in the mine with Parry and me. He lives with little Sophie Greenway."

I remember a lot about "little Sophie." She stuck her tongue out at me more than once when we were little and had turned her back on me when we'd gotten older. She was younger than I by a few months and, like Parry, drew beautiful pictures. Sophie had drawn a picture of all the children who had died in the disaster for their parents. Of course, I also remember that years later she'd had an abortion, and the father turned out not to be Oscar Jeens, who was her boyfriend back then, too. It was quite a scandal. When I'd found I was pregnant, it was because I knew she'd had an abortion that I'd considered one.

"It won't be a late night," Evan promises. "Just a few blokes from the choir and their wives. Might even be fun for you to see some of the old-timers." I wasn't at all sure about that.

As we leave the room, Da raises his hand, and Mam says, "Have a lovely time."

Outside, Evan takes my arm. It surprises me.

"Do you remember how to play darts?"

In the dark, smoky pub, someone is strumming a guitar. Evan leads me to the back, where a group of people gather round a small table. Two men toss darts in a corner.

As we approach the table, the men all stand, holding out their hands across it, transferring cigarettes to ashtrays or mouths to shake Evan's hand. The smoke is thick. Of course in California, smoking is banned in restaurants and bars. One black-haired man affectionately claps Evan on the back and offers him a cigarette. I think about having one, but don't. Evan introduces me to everyone, including "little Sophie" Greenway, who now has long red hair with a tightly curled fringe at her forehead and blue eyes made up in dark liner with heavy mascara.

"I remember you," she says. "You were just a snip of a thing when you left, and you aren't much changed except maybe your hair is longer and there's more of it." She smiles, appearing to be friendly, but I hear something else in her comment. Maybe I'm just being overly sensitive. "I like your boots," she adds, which makes me immediately uncomfortable since my casual clothes cause me to clash with the rest of the women, who have on silk blouses and nice slacks or skirts. "Where'd you get them? Texas? Montana?"

I wind my long, unruly hair into a knot at the back of my neck, wishing that I wore makeup, eyeliner, a skirt—anything that might make me look more formal. "California," I say. She eyes my jeans and T-shirt.

"What'll you drink?" Oscar asks me. I look around at all the bottles of ale and Guinness gathered on the table. I hate beer. Especially warm beer. "White wine," I say, and once again I'm embarrassed. Evan, seeming to sense my discomfort, steps in. "We've just had a huge dinner at the Davies house. I'll actually have a glass of wine as well."

As the group continues to order, Evan goes off to throw some darts. Sophie's friend Enid says, "You live in the States, like?"

"California," I say again, this time with a smile.

"California. That's why you're so brown. That's a long way from here. Is that where you went when you left here? Do you live anywhere near Hollywood?"

"Not too far away."

"Do you know lots of actors, like?"

"Not personally."

"Have you ever run into Paul Newman? He's my favorite. Is he still married to Joanne Woodward?"

"I think so."

"I love their salad dressing, don't you? They make pickles now and ketchup. And chocolate. I saw these small square bites wrapped up with a photo of Paul and that beautiful young woman."

"I think she's his daughter," another woman says.

"I don't know that for sure," the first one answers.

"Is the life easier there, being warm and sunny all the time? Is that why you left here?"

Before I can answer, tell them in fact that the Newmans live in Connecticut, Sophie adds, "It's Malibu I'd like to go to. I had a friend who told me there's a stretch of beach where all the houses are as big as Caerphilly Castle, with at least five bathrooms in each one. I hear the houses sit right up on the sand next to the ocean and there's nothing but one star living smack-dab next to another. Barbra Streisand and John Travolta. People like that."

"Where do you live, Alys?" Enid asks.

"Santa Monica."

"Is that close to Malibu?"

"Pretty close," I say, still trying to be polite despite the fact that both Enid and particularly Sophie seem to have it in for me.

"So why did you leave Aberfan?" Sophie asks challengingly. "That is, if you don't mind my asking?"

I actually do mind, so I say, "I needed to get away."

I glance up and catch Evan's eye. He's across the crowd and deep in conversation with Oscar and another man.

"I heard you left because you were pregnant," Sophie says.

Nobody else seems to have heard. I'm sure I turn beet red, but I look straight at her and ask innocently, "Where did you hear that?"

"I don't know—around," she says offhandedly, as if everyone knew.

I feel like she has just stuck her tongue out at me again.

"Another drink, anyone?" one of the men asks.

Several of the men have gathered around Evan. They whisper and laugh like small boys, and I sense they are talking about me. I am afraid that, like Sophie, they are saying terrible things. But Oscar looks over at me kindly, then clears his throat. It seems to be Evan they are on about because he puts his hands in his trouser pockets and tilts his head, looking down as if he's embarrassed. Almost immediately the men raise their voices and begin to sing. At first the words are unfamiliar; I only hear their deep, clear tones and see how the music gathers them into themselves, their arms around each other.

Evan finally joins in, entwined, his friends on either side, and I hear "Love Changes Everything." Evan looks straight at me as he sings and I blush. Everyone in the pub joins in, including Sophie Greenway, singing straight to me.

By now the pub is full; there is hardly room to stand. At the end of the song, everyone applauds. Almost immediately they begin another, and the attention is off Evan. He edges his way through the group toward me.

I hope he is ready to leave. The smoke is starting to get to me. He holds my gaze until he is close up.

"Are you ready to go?"

As we say our good-byes, I glance at Sophie and Enid over his shoulder, then follow Evan toward the door.

All at once we are out in the clean, open air. It is cooler and we pull closer to each other. The feel of his shoulder against mine and his voice go straight through me.

"Are you cold?" he asks, which saves me from having to comment on Sophie or Enid. He takes his cardigan off and wraps it tightly around me. We walk back up the hill in silence to Mam and Da's, where we've both parked our cars.

There is an energy between us. Crackling. I am nervous. When we get to the cars I start to walk toward mine.

"Why don't you leave yours here?" he asks. "Drive with me."

I stop. Why not? I can easily walk up here tomorrow morning. I'll be doing that anyway. But I don't like the idea of not having a way out if I need one. Not being able to leave Evan's house if something unforeseen should arise.

"No, I'll drive it down now."

"That seems rather silly, doesn't it?" His tone immediately changes the charged atmosphere.

"I'd just rather have it near," I say stubbornly.

"All right, have it your way as usual, Alys." And he gets into his car and slams the door. I follow him in my car down the hill and around until we are at the bottom of the drive. He gets out to open the gate. I follow him up his dirt road and park next to him. He comes over to open my door. Somehow I know he will apologize, and he does.

"Sorry, Alys. I didn't mean to jump all over you."

"It's okay."

"Come on, then. Let's have a nightcap before you try out my guest room."

Once we are inside, Evan starts a fire. Then he pours out two glasses of red wine, handing me one and pointing to a comfortable overstuffed chair near the fire. We haven't said a word, as if neither of us is willing to chance saying anything else that might upset the other. I sit. He sits. He raises his glass to me; I acknowledge him, raising mine.

"So," he starts.

I look at him, a half smile.

"How are you doing now, on your third day? More time with your mam and da, seeing the Joneses—is it what you expected?"

My eyes travel around the room. How does it feel being back, seeing Beryl, seeing my parents, Hallie's parents, being here now with Evan?

"You know," I start, "it's oddly comforting. All of it."

"Really. I would have expected you to say it was difficult. Or that you'll be glad to go back to the States."

"As I said, Evan, in all these years I haven't spent a lot of time going over things. It was too painful. But the one thing that has come up for me again and again is your face: your delicious smile, the way it immediately used to comfort me. We have both suffered—not just you. You act like you are the only one of us that felt anything. It's beginning to make me feel nuts. You don't say what you mean. You just kind of bash me. What's that kind of behavior called, passive-aggressive?"

"Sorry, Alys."

"No, you're not. You're actually not sorry, Evan. Why do you keep saying you are?"

"Because I'm trying to be sorry. I'm trying, but when I look at you I remember how deeply I loved you, how the thought of you ever leaving me was so terrible . . . and then you did. I remember how much you hurt me, how it about killed me. And now here you are, in front of me as if none of it ever happened."

I sigh. I don't know how to deal with this. Of course a part of me realizes it's not really just anger. It is his sadness, his disappointment. I understand that. But it's relentless, the weight of his inability to forgive me.

"Okay, so if you felt so much, why didn't you come after me?" I ask quietly.

There is a long silence. The fire is roaring with gunshotlike cracks.

"I wanted to. Every day for weeks, and then months. By the time I'd screwed my courage to the wall, you'd already gotten together with Marc."

"But that was more than a year after I got there!"

"I know." He looks into his wineglass, draining it of every drop. "I counted every minute, every hour and every day of it. I felt so betrayed by you, it sucked the life out of me, it made me immobile."

We are back to where we started in this conversation. Stuck. It has been a very long time since I have let myself feel the depth of my own sadness about that long-ago time. And about Evan. Strangely, in this long moment between us, I do not feel the excruciating loneliness that I remember. When I look up, Evan is staring at me.

"It was a hard time," he says.

"For both of us," I say.

He nods. "For both of us."

He shows me the guest room, which is up a narrow stone-walled spiral staircase and has fire engine red walls. The windows are small. He tells me one looks out over the field behind the house, and the other looks out into the garden. Evan lifts my suitcase up onto a stand near the washbasin. He turns on a light near the full-size brass bed, illuminating a beautiful patchwork quilt.

"How in the world did you ever get the bed up here?" I ask.

"I didn't. The farmer's wife left it for me. It's one of the permanent fixtures in my life here."

"I guess so." I laugh.

Evan leaves me to unpack and get comfortable. I note that the ice has been broken. There is definitely less tension in the air.

Back in front of the fire, watching the embers, talking a little about our careers, he tells me how wonderful it has been, being a part of so many children's lives, watching the population of children regenerated, living through it all. He must be revered by all the parents. I tell him how grateful I've been to Hannah's teacher, who has been so supportive and understanding through the past difficult year. He asks me about my own career, and I embarrassedly admit that I haven't been able to write much of anything in the last year, even though I have a manuscript due to my editor.

Before we go off to our separate quarters, we agree to have dinner together tomorrow night, here.

"I'm home from school early tomorrow. No meetings in the afternoon for a change. You have yourself a full day with your parents. I'll pop that little leg of lamb you brought into the oven. We'll eat about eight?"

"That sounds so nice."

"Good," Evan says.

"Thanks for letting me stay here," I say.

"Not a problem. I hope you sleep well. It's a great sleeping room, the red room. I've always slept like a log in it."

"I'm exhausted."

Chapter Sixteen

The next morning, I am up early. Unlike a Colorado morning, the flat, gray light of a Welsh morning does not stream through the window. Rather, it presents itself—it just is, somehow.

I put on my shorts, jogging bra, a T-shirt and sneakers. The house is quiet. I can see Evan's car from the window so I tiptoe down the stone stairs—hoping not to wake him—through the library, through the mudroom and outside. I walk up behind the field to the right until I am along the ridge of the hill. In the distance there is a bit of sun through the dark clouds.

I notice that my senses are heightened. I take in a deep breath and do a few sun salutations, bending low and reaching high, and then I start a slow jog up along the ridge path. It is a splendid morning, brisk, and the low fog sits on the hills like a soft coverlet. The view is altogether so familiar, and yet it is as if I am seeing it for the very first time. In the distance there are many more single cottages tucked in, smoke curling out of their chimneys.

What would I have been like had I stayed? Would Evan and I have married? Would we have more children? I pick up my pace and then for the next thirty minutes I am in my routine, thinking about nothing but the soft, cool air, my feet hitting the ground, a loose jaw, and my breathing. Before I know it I am back at the bottom of Evan's drive. I can see his car has gone. I am relieved. Mostly since Marc's death, I've gotten used to quiet mornings. Mornings without much talk. Hannah is definitely not a morning person, nor am I.

And the cottage is all mine. There is a fire going, and Evan has left me a note on the breakfast table under a vase of orange poppies:

> Berries and bread. Help yourself to anything and everything.
>   Evan

Walking around his house, touching his belongings, looking at the life he has made for himself makes me feel as if he is still in my presence.

I fix myself some coffee and berries and call Dafydd, leaving a message saying I miss him and am having a fine time. I don't tell him I am so glad I came by myself or how wonderful these few days away from responsibility and parenting are beginning to feel. I also don't tell him I have checked out of the Angel Hotel and am now staying at his father's house. But I do say that I hope he has been in touch with Hannah, that I am longing for news of both of them, and that I will try him back later.

It's too early to visit Mam and Da, so I drive into Merythr to find something typically Welsh for Dafydd and Hannah. It has bloomed into a gray summer morning, the chill just under the warmth of it.

I pass an older woman who is wearing a blue raincoat with a plaid scarf tied around her head; gray hair escapes out the sides of the scarf and in the front. The size and shape of her remind me of Gram. As she passes, I see the canvas bag on her shoulder is full of vegetables and a loaf of bread. I touch the shilling hanging from the silver chain around my neck and long for my grandmother. I turn and watch her back as she disappears into the crowd.

"Come shopping with me, Alys." Gram is gathering her money and her canvas tote. She throws me a cardigan. "You choose Sunday dinner. Anything your little heart desires."

"Lamb," I say immediately. It is dear, and we don't get it often, but lamb is my favorite.

"Lamb it will be, then."

"Do they kill the lambs when they are very little?" I ask while we make our way down the hill to the coach stop. "How do they do it? Does it happen fast? Do you think the lambs know they are about to die?"

"They are probably too young to know what's coming. But it is a kind of sad part of life, to grow them for this end. Maybe if we think about what a special treat it is to be able to take their body into our own, it is easier. Seems like each of us has a time on this earth, and each of us spends our time and then we move along. Even little lambs."

Gram puts her arm around my shoulder, so I balance myself against her as we walk. It is still hard for me to move quickly.

"We don't have to walk so fast, Alys. I'll keep up with you. We're not in any hurry."

In Merythr I stand outside the butcher shop while Gram chooses the meat. I cannot think about the sweet little creatures in the field behind Auntie Beryl's as the same lamb we eat.

When Gram comes out, she tells me Mr. Goshen has said hello and he has a good job for me mincing meat whenever I am ready.

"That's disgusting," I say. Then I see the smile around Gram's eyes and know she is having me on.

"I have a surprise for you," Gram says. She steers me down Saxon Street and round a row of high wooden bookshelves filled with books outside of the library, where a fair is on.

We stop in front of Stouffer's Jewelers. "Here we are, then." Gram holds the door while I go in.

"Rosemary and Alys Davies! Good morning to you both," Mr. Stouffer says. "It's just finished. Just now, in fact. I've just put it in its box. Come, Alys. Come have a look."

Mr. Stouffer places a small black velvet box on the counter in front of me.

"That's for you, Alys. From your loving gram," he says.

Gram puts her arm around me and says quietly into my ear, "I believe it kept you safe. And I believe it will always keep you safe."

There in the box, lying on the soft black folds, is my shilling, the one I was holding on to when the tip slipped. It is mounted with a silver band and hung from a silver chain.

I am searching each face on the walkway, as if one of them might hold some clue to my own feelings about the past, and my future.

In a quiet café, seated at a table near the window, I order ham-and-cheese quiche and a glass of white wine. I begin a letter to Hannah.

"Alys?" A voice behind me interrupts my thoughts. It is Sophie

Greenway, with a tall, elegantly dressed middle-aged woman who looks vaguely familiar.

"I thought that was you, then, Alys!" Sophie says. "Are we interrupting your writing? We were just going to sit down for a bite"—she points over at another table—"when I saw you over here."

My God, she wants to join me. "Well, actually, I'm writing a note home to my daughter and—"

"Oh, so you do have a child," Sophie says, as if she's caught me red-handed.

I put my hand under my chin and stare her right in the eye. "Yes, Sophie, I do. In fact, I have two children." I reach for my glass of wine. "And you?"

"I thought so," she says. "No. No. I don't have any children. Never wanted them. Most of the town knows that, like." She pauses. "You know, I hope you didn't get me wrong last night. I wasn't trying to start anything. It was just I was wondering if what I'd heard was true. Like you said, rumors aren't the nicest thing in the world. Sometimes they can cause a lot of problems."

"Yes, well . . ."

"So would you mind?"

"Mind what, Sophie?"

"Us sitting down with you? Getting to know you better, like."

And I see she means it. That perhaps she hasn't meant to be unkind at all; her way is just different from mine. Moving my papers into a pile, I say, "Please, join me."

"You sure, then?" the other woman asks.

"Of course," I say, forgiving Sophie.

"We'd love to," Sophie says brightly, ignoring her friend's reluctance and pulling out a chair for herself and the other woman. "I 'spect you remember my aunt Gilly?"

"Gilly?" I repeat, recognizing the name but the memory still not jogged.

"Auntie Gilly, this is Alys Davies, just back from the States."

Auntie Gilly looks uncomfortable as she holds out her hand to me. "Glad to meet you after all these years. You must be Parry's little sister."

It has been so long since I have been referred to as "Parry's little sister" that I spend a few moments just feeling it.

They settle themselves and a waitress comes by to take their order. I order another glass of wine.

"Oh my God," I say, finally getting it and then blurting it out. "Are you the Gillian Parry lived with after . . ."

Before I finish my sentence, she nods.

Her presence conjures Parry for me more explicitly than anyone has, and I feel him with us at the table.

"Your mother didn't think much of me," Gillian says. "Even now, all these years later, me with my own three children and a husband of nearly twenty-three years, and she still won't look at me directly when I run into her on the road." Her eyes go all sad and liquid. "D'you mind me talking about him?"

I have to think for a moment, but then I say quickly, "Not at all." I know it's time. It strikes me how when one starts to try and put things into perspective with regard to one's past, very often every part of that past will present itself.

"For such a long time I have longed to be able to talk about Parry with one of you," Gillian says. "If your mother understood, I suspect she would have been grateful. I would be pleased to have any of my children loved as much as I loved your brother." She takes a sip of her lemonade and then says, "May I speak bluntly?"

I nod.

"Your brother was hurting so bad and he needed a lot of coddling, he did—and I was able to give it to him for a time. Things had gone so sour for him in the world. Not just with your da, but he felt like he had made all the wrong choices. He could talk to me. I listened without judging him.

"I'm sure your mam thought it was all about sex," she says. "But I was six years older than Parry. Twenty-five, I was when he lived with me. And it was not sex he was after. It was my place and maybe a bit of mothering. He needed safety and somewhere he could just be. My parents had built a small room over the garage for my nana, but she died early on and so they gave the room to me. It was completely private. And it made things easier for Parry. He didn't have to face your da.

"Perhaps the reason your mam won't look at me is she blames me. D'you know, to this day, I blame myself. I wish I could have known what I know now. Perhaps I would have been able to talk some sense into him." Her eyes fill with tears.

"I felt the same way. Evan did, too." I put my hand on hers. "But none of us could have saved him." This time I believe it a bit more myself.

"Maybe," she says.

When our food arrives, we eat our lunch without another word about Parry. Gillian speaks about her children. They are twelve, fifteen and twenty-two. Her husband is an architect and she is a painter. She tells me Parry taught her.

Turns out Sophie has been living with Oscar for twelve years and he won't marry her.

"Says the idea of marriage is just too frightening, he does. Like I said, I don't want children anyway. I've known that since I was a little girl. Too afraid I'd lose them somehow."

We certainly have that in common. Part of me wants to know what else Sophie has been through since the disaster. If she has nightmares, day terrors. What more we might have in common.

"But I'd like to be married. A wedding dress and brass candlesticks . . . you know, all that 'settling down' stuff."

"What do you do, Alys?" Gillian asks.

"I write poetry."

"Like Dylan Thomas?"

"I wish." And then, we all recite in unison what every Welsh schoolchild learns in his primary years:

> Do not go gentle into that good night,
> Old age should burn and rave at close of day;
> Rage, rage against the dying of the light.

"He was an amazing poet," I say. "And proud to be Welsh, he was."

"And you?" Sophie asks.

I am a little more used to her direct style of inquiry now. She doesn't intimidate me. So without too much thought, I say, "I'm proud as well. I suspect we've both come through a lot since we were little, Sophie." She nods.

I have faced up to something with Sophie, who to me represents the villagers and how some of them must have felt about my leaving. I can see I was terrified of that response, and now I feel I am among old friends. What we have in common is our home, the place we were born out of, its history, what tore us apart and the place it takes up in our hearts.

As before, when I get to Mam and Da's, Mam is in the kitchen. "I was just wondering where you were, like," she says. I kiss her on the cheek. She puts her hand up to the spot I kissed and smiles at me.

"It was kind of you to make so much chicken soup. Your da's loving it, he is. He actually had a bowl of the broth for breakfast. He seems that much better today, he does. And I think Doc Rogers was pleased with the way he looks. Hasn't taken one of the painkillers Doc left. Not one." Mam seems actually hopeful. But just as I am about to hold on to that, she adds, " 'Course I'm not getting my hopes high, remembering with your gram, like, out at Beryl's. Just before she sank to the lowest level, she had a few good days. A few days, one after the other where it almost seemed she might be coming out of the woods. Even Beryl felt she was on the road to recovery. And then, just as we were breathing a sigh, she passed."

Mam is chopping vegetables, making salad. "Would you like a bit?" she asks.

I shake my head. "I've just had a piece of quiche in the village."

"Oh, you went to Merythr?"

"I was searching for something typically Welsh for Dafydd and Hannah. I found a Welsh flag for Hannah and a wooden love spoon for Dafydd." I think of telling her I met Gillian and decide against it.

"Both Welsh." She smiles.

We are making small talk again. But now it is sort of a relief. Almost normal.

"Your da was sleeping the last time I looked in, but you go on up now and have a look. If he's awake, you have a nice chat with him. I'll bring you up a cup of tea. He's so glad you're here."

The stairs creak in the usual places. I sit down on the top of the landing, outside Parry's room, and take in the house. Even under the circumstances, nothing seems as bad as it was when I lived here. I peek in the room and see Da asleep, the oxygen mask over his face. As I watch him for a moment, an immeasurable fatigue overtakes me. I sit down in the chair near the window, cross my arms over my chest, close my eyes and fall into a deep, peaceful sleep. It is late afternoon when Mam wakens me to tell me Evan has called. Da is still sleeping.

"Don't worry, dear. He needs his rest. When he wakes in the night, I'll let him know you were here. You just go on back to Evan's. It's so nice, the two of you being able to spend some time, isn't it? He's cooking a delicious meal for you now. Go on, then."

Da's forehead is cool when I kiss it. I whisper that I'll see him tomorrow. I hope so.

When I get back to the cottage, Evan is also in the kitchen. He has cut small red potatoes into fours and arranged them around the lamb. He has smothered the lamb with sliced onions and poured last night's red wine over it and cut rosemary from his garden. The smell is wonderful.

"I've probably stuck too much garlic into it. I didn't even think to ask if you liked garlic. I can't remember."

"I love garlic." There's that charge again in the atmosphere. Everything I touch seems alive. I am aware in the moment of being drawn to Evan and I am careful, hesitant in my actions, afraid that somehow something I might do or say will cause him to pull away.

After he has poured me a glass of wine, he turns. "I have some great news." His eyes are shining and his right leg is rhythmically tapping. He hands me my glass.

"What news?" I ask.

"In the post today, a letter from the queen."

"The Queen of England?"

"She's interested in hearing the choir. She's considering us for a royal performance on the anniversary of the disaster," he says. "She wants us to perform before the Court this fall, and I quote"—he moves to the kitchen table, where he has safely laid the letter on top of a place mat, and reads from it—" 'I'm told you are the spirit of Aberfan.' "

He raises his glass as he moves toward me. "Alys, I'm terribly excited. No, actually, I'm over the moon."

"My God, Evan. It's incredible. What exactly does it mean?"

"Well, I guess it means that all of us go up and sing for Her Majesty's people. An audition of sorts." He shrugs. "If they like us, then we sing for her and the whole Royal Court on the anniversary of the disaster. It will possibly be televised. There will be lots of publicity. I can only imagine. On top of it being a splendid opportunity, it will be an amazing experience. Imagine, Buckingham Palace. I'll have to borrow a tuxedo!"

He is very handsome. His blue eyes really shine and there is a clarity about him that was there even when he was a boy. He knows what he wants and he has gone after it. He was like that with me. He didn't give up until he thought he had me.

There is a lot I know about Evan, and a lot I don't know. I find myself moving closer to him, wanting to touch him, smell him even. Yes, everything draws me in.

"What is it, Alys? Is something wrong?"

How can I possibly answer that question?

"Not a thing."

"Oh. It felt for a moment as if you'd lost interest in what I was saying."

"Not at all. In fact, quite the contrary. I was fantasizing for a second on exactly how a performance at Buckingham Palace might really catapult your choir's career. You could end up going on tour, even coming to the United States," I say brightly.

But I have said the wrong thing, I can tell immediately. The energy between us is still alive, but he has pulled away. I swallow and put the glass down on the sink.

"Yes. Wouldn't that be something. I could visit. Meet Dafydd. Hannah." But his tone has gone flat. He turns away, back to the lamb. "Into the oven with this now.

"I thought I'd make a tomato salad," he says, changing the subject. I watch him washing the tomatoes, then slicing them in silence, placing them on a small platter and sprinkling them with olive oil, salt and pepper.

We are complicated together. There are so many years we have not known each other. But the comfort is there, the comfort of our early years together, as if somehow they have been there all along, silenced, but waiting to be reawakened, to be noticed.

Evan turns back to the stove, adjusting the oven temperature. He picks up his wineglass and pours more wine into it, then quietly walks past me. "Let's go up to the field. Bring your wine, Allie."

I take a sip of wine and pour several inches more into the glass.

I follow Evan up the stone path, past the poppies, which have all bloomed now and are full, their black tongues wagging; past the daisies and the trellised honeysuckle, smelling so sweet it is almost sickening. The North Star shines. Up to the top of the garden and beyond, to the meadow, we go. Evan sits on the picnic table, a shadow against the fading light.

"Remember when we used to come up here and picnic?" he says when I am within hearing distance.

"Yes," I answer. I lean up against an old wooden beer barrel that Evan uses to catch rainwater.

"Come sit next to me, Allie. Do you mind? The view is so spectacular from here."

I pick my wineglass up off the water barrel and go sit next to him. We are so close our arms and shoulders are touching. My heart is beating in more than just my chest.

"D'you see that small speck of cottage over there? I looked at it before this one became available." He sighs. "But I wanted this one. I have always wanted this one. I was willing to wait and it paid off.

"I'm awfully glad you're here, Alys. It's a wonder to see you again, to have the opportunity to try and sort some of our hard stuff out. D'you know what I mean?"

I am almost afraid to breathe. "I do." And when I turn to look at him, it seems the easiest and most natural thing in the world for me to just reach over and kiss him. He kisses me back, just as gently, and then he pulls me up into an embrace, folding me into him. Soon I am undoing his tie, unbuttoning his shirt. His eyes on my eyes as I push his shirt down his arms and onto the table, feeling the mass of hair on his chest, running my hands through it.

He pulls my T-shirt over my head and looks at my breasts and again into my eyes. "Is this okay? Are you all right with this?"

I put my fingers on his mouth to quiet him. "I think I started it, didn't I?"

He kisses me again, lifting me off the table and into his arms. And then we are both struggling to get our trousers off as quickly as we can. And before I know it we are down in the tall grass. Half sitting, I wrap my legs around his waist, drawing myself as close to him as I can, my chest against his, holding him, his strong muscular back, feeling the long-ago familiar shape of his head, his ears. My face so close I smell the faint scent of the lavender soap and I kiss him again. He moves me so he can inch my panties off and I guide him, feeling his warmth as he slips inside me. His hands embrace my buttocks firmly as he pulls me toward him, kissing me back. Then he lays me back on the grass, his arms cushioning me, and goes so deep. I am completely lost in Evan. After a while we are both crying.

And then, under the moon, we sleep, naked in the field. Several moments, a half hour later, I awaken and roll onto Evan. In this quiet dark I feel as close to him as I have ever been to anyone.

"Do you miss him?" he asks, so quietly.

I wait for Marc's presence to manifest beside us. Instead, there is emptiness, as if I am the sand as the sea pulls away from it.

"I will always miss him."

"It was a stupid question. I shouldn't have asked it. Of course you will always miss him. How could you not?" Evan pulls away, if only slightly. I have ruined the moment for him. He wanted me to say something else. I turn and wrap myself around him there in our field—legs, arms, shoulders.

"It wasn't a stupid question. You can ask me anything you want. I might not always have an answer. At least not immediately, but it feels good that you want to know me now. I want to know you, too, Evan."

Putting my lips on his for only a moment, I am not surprised at how quickly I am wet and ready for him. When he is inside me again, I pull his buttocks to me, arching up so that he goes so deep I feel myself begin to disappear. I sit up and wrap my legs around his waist, pulling him toward me until we are both sitting. When I put my arms around him, I feel light and free. And it is all fire and I am burning, burning, not at all afraid. Through a long tunnel I hear him say, "Alys, I love you. My God, how I love you." I can see his face in the faint moonlight, in our field. It is beautiful. Evan is so beautiful. I try to come back to him but I am throwing myself through the waves again and again, until there is one I can ride, and it is so wild all I can do is hold on for dear life.

CHAPTER SEVENTEEN

As the dark really takes hold, the temperature drops. After our dinner, we wash up and Evan gathers our sleeping gear to the back field.

At dinner I had asked him if he knew how many stars there were in the sky. It is a rhetorical question, but he goes along with me.

"You know, I've wondered that myself. I've a map of them. We could sleep out tonight if you like. Count them. I happen to have one of those subzero sleeping rolls in case the temperature drops."

I think he is kidding, but before much time passes he gathers a flashlight and binoculars and his star map. But by the time we get out, the sky has hazed over a bit and we can't see all that much. We locate the Big Dipper, Cassiopeia and Orion, his bow and sword so bright I feel I can almost reach out and touch him. As Evan points out the constellations for me and begins a favorite story about "Leo the Lion" his mam used to tell him, I roll closer to him. Soon, the two of us, tucked up snugly in Evan's sleeping roll, fall asleep. The next thing I know, I am pulling the bedroll over my head to escape the misting rain on my face and neck, like someone is watering us with a watering can.

"Have we ever made love in the rain?" Evan asks, kissing my neck. "Let's just open the roll and do it right here."

By the time we gather everything up, we are both drenched to the bone, slogging ourselves and all the gear down the hill, with Evan shouting at me not to forget the flashlight or the pillows.

Despite the fact that I don't sleep in the guest room but rather in Evan's bed, it is a wonderful night's sleep.

The next morning is Saturday, and after a good long sleep in, we build a fire, I mix up some griddlecake batter and Evan picks blackberries from the garden. The sun begins to come out from behind the few clouds left from the night before. The batter made, I luxuriate in front of the fire wrapped in an old Oxford shirt of Evan's, thinking about how incredible it is that we have this time between us to begin to feel things out. No, it's much more than that—it is like a gift from the gods. We've discussed the possibility of a hike before I go over to my parents, or even more lovemaking. Looking out the kitchen window, Evan says, "For goodness' sakes, there seems to be someone walking up the drive! Two someones to be exact. I'm not expecting anyone. Don't move a muscle, Alys. I'll deal with them."

It doesn't even occur to me to put a robe on, expecting Evan will handle it. Chase the intruders off. He's gone for quite a long while. I sit quietly, not a serious thought in my head for once, watching the flames chasing each other. Then the door opens and Evan comes in. "Alys . . ."

The way he says my name, I turn quickly and see Dafydd and Hannah.

"Seems your children missed you, Alys." Evan's smile says everything.

I am stunned. For a moment we just stare at each other. And then I shout, "Ohmigod!" Hannah runs into my arms like she used to when she was five or six, grabbing me and burying her head as far between my breasts as is possible. Hard to believe, but she is taller than when I left her in Colorado less than a week ago, and sturdier. "What's going on, sweetie, Dafydd?"

Dafydd stands quietly, a kind of smirk on his face. "Sorry, Mom." He shrugs. "Hannah was homesick."

It takes me a moment to fully grasp what he's said. "Homesick? Oh, sweetie, no."

And then I stop and ask as calmly as I can, "What exactly do you mean, 'Hannah was homesick'?"

"I mean, Hannah was homesick." He stands there, all six feet of him, with his hands in his pockets now, a sheepish grin on his face. I realize he is playing with me. He wanted to come on this trip and so he found a way.

"Why didn't someone from the camp tell me?" While I say this, I pull Hannah close to me; she smells of something sweet, oranges. I rub her back in the spot that's quieted her since she was a baby.

"I tried to call, but you'd checked out of the hotel. You didn't leave your parents' phone number. There are twenty-four pages of Davies in the South East Wales area. I didn't know how to reach you. I wasn't sure what to do, so I just thought, Well . . . it was one of those occasions where I just used my 'better judgment,' as you would say." He smiles at me, straightening out his tweed sports jacket and adjusting his gray trousers.

"Better judgment? Ten hours on the plane and four thousand miles of traveling, not to mention the expense." I realize I am standing there in my underwear, my bare legs hanging out of one of Evan's old shirts, and Hannah and Dafydd have never before laid eyes on Evan. Hardly the perfect moment to be a sanctimonious parent. "Good thing I hadn't gone back to the States, huh. Well." I don't know what else to say. "I suppose you've both met Evan."

Evan nods. I hug Hannah closer. "Thank goodness you're safe." Dafydd comes over and puts his arms around me and gives me one of his air kisses.

"Where are your suitcases?"

"They're at your parents'." Dafydd smiles.

"Oh my God, you've already met my parents? How?"

"Well, just your mom. Your dad was sleeping. We took a taxi from Heathrow to Paddington Station, a train to Cardiff and then another taxi from Cardiff to Aberfan. The first door we knocked on—Garland, I think their name was—they knew where your parents lived."

"A taxi? The Garlands?" I say, disbelieving. It's not the taxi, of course, or the Garlands that astonish me. How, where did Dafydd get the—well, balls, to just hop a plane and come, to locate Mam and Da? What must she think of me now, my two children arriving on their doorstep, neither of them knowing where I am? And then I remember all the things my family has lived through in this small town that didn't do them in. And of course this won't either.

"Your mom said we could stay with her. She didn't think Evan had enough room for all of us," Hannah says, eyeing me suspiciously, her voice more grown-up than I remember. "She showed us your room. I asked her if she had any of your stuffed animals or other stuff and she said that she'd kept a small box with some of your favorites. She's going to get it out of the attic so I can look through it." I can't believe Mam still has anything left of mine.

Hannah looks first at me and then at Evan, up and down, her eyes squinted. "Are you staying here *alone* with Evan?"

Fortunately my open suitcase is in the guest room, although my clothes from yesterday are strewn out all over Evan's floor. I rub Hannah's head and try to ignore the question.

"Not exactly, Hannah," Evan says, covering for me. Thankfully, he diverts her attention. "Do you like cats?"

She nods.

"Would you mind terribly helping me over here for a moment?" She moves slowly toward Evan. "I have these three wild kitties that live outside but need feeding. Could you take their bowls out for me? I'll bring the food."

Dafydd stands in front of me looking guilty. Next to Evan, the likeness is uncanny: the blue-green eyes, the dark hair, the height— even the way they stand, kind of balancing on one foot.

When the door slams behind Hannah and Evan, I ask Dafydd, "So?"

"What do you mean?"

"I mean, exactly what happened, Dafydd?"

"Apparently she called home for two days straight, leaving messages on the machine. Then she called me," he explains, pausing. "She was tearful, wanted to go home. That same afternoon, not being able to get ahold of you, her counselor called me. We agreed she should try to stick it out. They started out on a three-day backpack trip, and by the second night, Hannah wanted out. The next morning, the camp director called me to say he'd gotten her to agree to stay the course of the backpacking trip, but it was his feeling that she was having a very difficult time being separated from you. Then *I* tried to find you and couldn't." His worry and anger are evident.

"But I called the camp two nights ago. I spoke to someone . . . How come no one said anything to me?" I'm backpedaling and he knows it. "And I called *you* several times," I say.

"Yes, I got your messages, Mom, but you didn't mention you were leaving the hotel. You didn't leave a number. It's so unlike you."

Shit.

"I was worried when I called and they said you'd checked out. So, being her guardian in your absence, I asked the camp to put her on a plane and send her to me."

"Dafydd. Omigod—are you telling me Hannah flew by herself? To New York?" I grab the back of the rocker. "That's not just one plane—it's two."

"She's almost nine, Mom. Plenty of children fly by themselves at an even younger age. I arranged for an escort."

"How did you get time off?"

"I took it. I felt this was . . . well . . . kind of an emergency." He looks me straight in the eye.

I think about the conversation we'd had the night before I left Los Angeles for Wales. "You used the opportunity. I told you I wanted to do this on my own."

"Okay, okay. I'll agree. I *seized* the opportunity." He smiles at me, almost wickedly. "Kind of caught you with your pants down, didn't we?" He laughs.

"Dafydd, that's neither appropriate nor funny," I say sternly, trying to stifle my own smile, angry at myself for all the years I haven't managed to keep the boundaries between parent and child somewhere in line.

"Sorry," he laughs. "I couldn't help myself."

I know this blasé act is a front, but I play along with it. "I think I'll just go put some trousers on. Perhaps you should go get to know Evan or something."

My anger is rising. I feel like a complete idiot as I slither into the bedroom. I grab my leggings and T-shirt from the floor and quickly push everything else under the bed. Why didn't I leave a forwarding number at the hotel? What was I thinking, or not thinking? What kind of mother am I? I knew it was too soon to leave Hannah. I let her talk me into it. I quickly pull the cozy up on the bed and fluff the pillows and look around to see what other signs of me there are in Evan's bedroom.

I try to pull myself together and get out there, but before I can move, Hannah is peeking in at the door.

"Are you mad at us, Mommy?" She doesn't move from the doorway.

"Mad?" Yes, I'm mad, totally over the top, but I can't tell her that. "Oh, Hannah, no, I'm not angry. The only one I should be angry at is myself for not leaving a number when I checked out of the hotel. Come here, sweetie." I put my arms around her. "I am so sorry." Her small body next to mine makes me realize how much I have missed her.

"Your mom seems really nice. We couldn't see your dad 'cause he was sleeping. We left all our stuff there, but Dafydd told her we had to wait and see what you said about us staying there. Are you really staying here?"

I bite my upper lip and nod. Hannah looks around the room. Her eyes rest for a moment on my backpack. Somehow I missed it in my search. "In this room?"

"Well, yes, Hannah," I finally say. After all I am an adult, able to sleep where and with whom I want to sleep, right? And then, quickly changing the subject, I add, "You must be hungry and tired. Let's get some breakfast for you right now.

"I'm so glad to see you." I kiss her on the neck. "So you actually flew by yourself? Were you scared?" We hold hands as I usher her out of the bedroom, thinking about 9/11, thinking about terrorists the world over.

"Not even a little bit, I swear. I can't believe you've never let me fly by myself. It was soooooo much fun. The flight attendant from Denver to New York kept asking me if I was all right and giving me lots of nuts and pretzels and Cokes. I had two desserts.

"On the little flight from Durango to Denver I told the flight attendant that I was scared and so she sat next to me. When it got bumpy she explained everything about hot air rising and mixing with cold air. She pointed out the sound the wheels make when they go up and come down and all that stuff. Next time we fly together, I'll explain it all to you."

In the kitchen, Dafydd is sitting awkwardly on a stool. He keeps changing the position of his legs and readjusting his shoulders, and Evan seems to be listening intently while he stirs the griddlecake mixture, nodding his head as Dafydd talks. Evan looks up when we come into the room.

"Dafydd is just filling me in on their adventure. You know he called Beti to fetch Hannah's passport, but she didn't have a key, so she had to climb in one of the upstairs windows. Then apparently she couldn't find the passport in your desk where it should have been, right, Dafydd?" Dafydd nods. "And she was rummaging around when the neighborhood security folks saw a light on. Knowing you weren't home, it seems, the guards came in and threatened to arrest Beti. Finally, Dafydd called a neighbor, who came over to clear her with the security company. Then the whole crowd of them began looking for the passport, including the officer. When they found it, Beti rushed it by FedEx to Dafydd. I'm impressed." He shakes his head in amazement. "S'pose we should ring your mother and let her know they arrived here safely? Can you imagine her opening her front door and finding her grandchildren there on her stoop with their bags?" He laughs nervously.

"That's probably not so funny, Evan," I say rather gruffly.

"Oh, it is, too! They're here safe and sound." He runs his hand through his hair. "It's amazing, really."

"Dafydd," I interrupt. He turns toward me, waiting for me to complete my sentence. And then I don't know what to say. "Well," I finally manage.

"Well?" he says.

"What's your plan?"

"Plan?" He looks confused.

"Yes, now that you're here, what are you going to do?"

"I don't have a plan, Mom."

I can feel myself begin to slide inside. I am so angry with him, as if it is Dafydd's fault Hannah was homesick. His fault that I didn't leave a number.

"I was hoping *you'd* have one," he says, sounding just as angry.

"Okay, okay. So why don't we have some breakfast?" Evan says quickly. "I suspect your children are exhausted, with the time change and all. We need some food. Then we can talk about a plan. I've no doubt, Alys, that your mam and da will be wanting to spend as much time with your children as they can. And I know I'd like that, too."

"Yes, well . . . this isn't exactly how I envisioned the two of you meeting after all these years. Or you, either, Hannah." I put my arm around her.

"Plans are sometimes that way—that's the adventure of life, isn't it!" Evan says a little too buoyantly. "Here we all are, extraordinary as it is," he adds, clapping his hands together just like a third grade teacher would.

"Yes, here we are," Dafydd awkwardly agrees. We stand quiet for a moment.

Evan breaks the silence. "I think the occasion calls for some griddlecakes. What do you think, Alys?"

I shake myself free. "Yes, griddlecakes."

"I like your house," Hannah says to Evan somewhat grudgingly. "It's cozy."

During breakfast Hannah tells us about her experience at camp. She tells us about her bunkmate and how she said "shit" and "fuck" all the time. She tells us about how they'd hiked up the bottom of Engineer Mountain and it had started to thunder and lightning and they'd camped out in tents in the pouring rain.

"I just suddenly didn't want to be there. I wasn't that scared or anything. I just wanted to come home. I tried to stick it out. I really did. I thought I was going to be able to. But I couldn't. I just couldn't do it. I missed you, Mommy."

Evan, who is sitting next to her, leans over and touches her hand affectionately. "I'm glad you're here, Hannah."

"Thanks." She moves her hand quickly away, then turns her head and looks at me, squinting her eyes again a little, waiting for me to say something. A moment later, looking at Evan, she quickly adds, "I'm glad I'm here, too." Then she looks away.

At breakfast, across the table from one another, Evan and Dafydd seem to stumble a bit in their conversation until they find they have music and soccer in common.

"I don't play rugby, but I play soccer," Dafydd says. "D'you think Wales will ever qualify for the World Cup? I'm surprised they haven't already."

All through breakfast, they fire away at each other.

"Sting's my all-time favorite. The guy's a genius. He's always one step ahead of everybody else, despite his age," Dafydd says.

"His age? Despite his age?" Evan smiles. "Goodness, I haven't noticed that talent fades with age. There's Sting and there's David Bowie and Philip Glass. They've all gotten better with age, don't you agree? D'you know Glass' work?" Evan asks. "What about that Virginia Woolf movie? Wasn't that score something!"

"Relentless," Dafydd answers, sounding just like Marc.

After breakfast, Dafydd goes into the guest room and lies down. Hannah is totally wired. The difference in my children.

"You look exactly like Dafydd," she tells Evan, a little friendlier now. "How come you and my mom never got married?" She doesn't wait for an answer. "I told my friend Abigail that my mom got pregnant out of wedlock and my brother was the result. But Abby didn't know what wedlock was, so I don't think she understood the story." She is talking too fast.

"How in the world do *you* know what wedlock means, young lady?" I ask her.

"I read it somewhere. Probably *Little Women*. Probably Jo said it, you think?"

She asks Evan if he's had any girlfriends since me. He looks embarrassed for a moment, but then tells her he's had one. Hannah's eyes get big. She says, "Won't she be angry that my mom's here?"

When he tells her it was a long time ago, Hannah nods. "Do you have other kids?" she asks.

"No, Dafydd's it."

She nods again.

"Hannah!" I say. "Stop. This is rude."

"I'm just checking things out." She seems just a tad too comfortable with everything, the other shoe hanging around somewhere, waiting to drop. Then she asks if she can have a tour of the whole "little" house and the garden.

"Certainly," Evan says. "But I rather you didn't refer to it as 'little,' " he says, sniffing in twice and lifting his head in that way the British do when they want to show distaste toward something. "It's not *so* little a cottage, you know. I'll show you some of the work I did on it. It's over three hundred years old. There wasn't even an inside toilet when I bought it."

Evan takes her around the house. I don't know what to think or exactly how to move forward. I do the washing up and put another log on the fire.

When they come out of the library, Hannah announces, "There's tons of room. I think Dafydd and I should stay here."

I look at Evan. He raises his eyebrows. "She's decided she wants to sleep in the library, and Dafydd can have the red room." That's where he's napping now. "Perhaps it would be easier on your mam, with your da and all."

Despite the fact that my suitcase is in the red room, I am uncomfortable because now I am sure Hannah understands I am sleeping in Evan's room.

"Please, Mommy," Hannah begs. "I want to be with you." She says this looking first at me, and then at Evan. I wonder if what she really means is that she wants to guard me.

Evan moves toward me and puts his arm around my shoulder. Hannah watches every move carefully.

"Relax, Alys," he says.

I step away from him in embarrassment. "I'd better call Mam. She'll be wondering what's going on. By now Da will be up and I told her I'd come over this afternoon and—"

"Alys," Evan gently interrupts. "You and I planned a hike for this afternoon, remember? They won't mind. We'll go over directly after. Now, while Dafydd naps, why don't you rest? I'll show Hannah the garden and then maybe we'll all be ready for that little hike. Something easy. We could show them around the village a bit, or walk up the back way to your parents'."

I stand still. "I'm not exactly comfortable with all of this."

"I can tell," Evan says quietly.

Hannah rolls her eyes. She asks Evan, "Do you have a TV?"

"I'm sorry. I don't."

"Figures." She glares at me. "Do you have a CD player?"

"I absolutely do, and I've lots of CDs—rock 'n' roll, the Beatles. You'll find something you like, I bet." He is trying so hard. "In the library, and it's fairly simple to operate. In fact, it's on, I think. Just waiting for a new choice." She goes off to find it. "Holler if you can't figure it out." He watches her leaving, then turns to me. "I think it's pretty interesting that the two of them should show up now."

"Oh, yeah, perfect timing," I say.

"It's kind of brave of Dafydd to come after you explicitly told him you wanted to do this trip alone. And clearly, Hannah needed you."

"I'm sorry, but the timing stinks."

"It is what it is, Alys. You're a mother, after all. Why do you have to be comfortable with it?"

"Because I do. I feel like I'm in kindergarten again and I just want to stamp my feet."

He laughs. "So go ahead, stamp them. No one's looking but me." He starts to put both his arms around me.

"Don't, Evan."

"Why?"

"I don't know. Hannah . . . Dafydd. I just feel so . . . cornered, I guess. Finally, you and I have a bit of a chance to begin to sort through some things together. And I was looking forward to sifting through my own feelings about everything. Now I have to add my children into the equation. I know that sounds self-centered and selfish, but I didn't want to have to worry about my children. That's why I didn't bring them.

"I was beginning to see the possibilities of putting some things behind me and exploring others, not to mention being with you—like this, alone, undressed. Now, with my children here, my trip becomes something entirely different. Trying to make them comfortable, looking after them. You know, I always want what's best for them. It's second nature to want to see everything through their eyes—even Mam and Da—*especially* them, really. And they'll want to know all about my past. I'll have to go through all the hard things I've managed to shield them from: the cemetery, Hallie, Parry. I become 'Mom,' as you point out. Something I was trying to have a little break from. I don't want to be Mom right now. I want to be . . . oh, I don't know. But not Mom. We won't have an opportunity to be together, at least not in the same way. I just don't think I'm up to it." And I start to cry.

"Oh, is that all?" he says, putting his arms around me, and this time I let him.

"It's not funny. I'm serious."

"I know you're serious. But it is kind of funny the way you turn everything into the most unbelievable drama. There's enough going on in your life as it is without blowing things completely out of proportion. Let some of this stuff go."

Of course, he doesn't know the half of what's going on in my life. But I can already feel myself calming down, and it makes me mad that he has that kind of power over me. Always did.

"How can you be so utterly calm? First I descend on you, and now my children. You must be thinking we are here to eat you alive."

"Alys. In a million years I certainly never expected to have the opportunity of you in my life, let alone in my bed, again. Nor did I expect to have your children in my house. But can you imagine what it must feel like for me to finally be able to meet Dafydd . . . and Hannah? 'Omigod,' as you would say. She reminds me of someone, her strength, her independence. She even looks like you looked back then. She is completely willing to tell you what she feels and needs. And even if your amazing daughter isn't so keen on me, I respect her for letting me know exactly where I stand. To have all of you in my house, is the most—let's see, how can I say it without sounding completely daft? Having all of you here is the most deeply comforting thing I have experienced since I was very small and living in my own parents' home.

"I wonder," he continues. "Couldn't you just let us be whatever it is that we are becoming in front of your children? What could possibly happen other than for them to have to deal with sharing you?"

I start to pull away.

"Wait. Don't pull away. Pulling away is my job," he says, teasingly. "Couldn't you just relax enough to enjoy this? If you look at it, we all actually win. Dafydd gets an opportunity to know me some, which he says he's been desirous of for years. I get an opportunity to know him, which I have been desirous of since he was born. And you and I both get to comfort Hannah. Not to mention they'll get to know their grandparents and Auntie Beryl. If you were able to look at it from a bit of a different tilt, the next several days could be an unbelievable adventure."

"You don't get it, Evan. Perhaps for Dafydd it's not as relevant—he's older. But my being with you will be hard for Hannah. She's already watchful and uncomfortable. Consciously or unconsciously, she wants me to continue to be completely devoted to her father. This is complicated."

"Oh. I hadn't actually thought about that. You might be right. But if we are to move forward a bit, wouldn't it be wise to show at least some affection toward each other in front of them?" Evan asks.

"I don't know. These are not questions I wanted to think about just yet."

"Yes. I can see that. I hear you. Well, whatever happens down the road between us—I guess having your children here will slow it down a bit. In the end, maybe it will buy us time and save us any further possibility of heartache."

"Maybe," I agree.

Evan is giving me exactly what I need and have longed for through this terrible, long, lonely year. It occurs to me that perhaps somehow what's happening here is similar in a way to what Gabriella offered Marc: an unconditional, easy, really safe place to love.

"Come on, Allie, what do you say I just take your clothes off and ravage you right here on the kitchen floor?"

I laugh.

"Come here. I promise I will be sensitive. I'm just trying to take what we've got, no matter that it's not exactly what or when either of us might have imagined it."

We hold each other.

"Shall I call your mother and tell her everyone's staying here and we'll all be over to throw some supper together a bit later? Is that all right?" Evan asks.

I nod.

When we finally get over to my parents', Da seems not to be doing as well as he had been yesterday. His eyes look more sunken and his breathing is raspier. But when he finds out that Dafydd and Hannah have shown up on his doorstep unexpectedly, he smiles and pulls his oxygen mask up. "Alys, you're joking? You must be joking?"

Apparently Mam hadn't told him.

"I'm not joking, Da. They're downstairs right now."

When he hears the homesick Hannah story he laughs out loud. "Not a bit like her mam, huh, Alys? Mind of her own." Before I can respond, he says, "Having you show up is absolutely wonderful, but your children—ah, Alys, I am already in heaven. Bring my grandchildren up immediately. I've not a moment to lose."

"Stop it, Da."

"Stop what, Allie? Should I be pretending with you that I'm going to live forever? You and I both know what's what, and if I'm not allowed to have a bit of fun with it, what is left for me?

"Get the children, Allie," he says sternly, starting to cough with his exertion. "And, by the way, have we any of that gorgeous chicken broth left? And I wouldn't mind a touch of whiskey if Mam has any about. This calls for a celebration, don't you think?"

In just a few moments, Dafydd stands near Da's bed, and Hannah's right up next to him. With my permission, Mam has given Hannah the teddy bear I got from Princess Margaret after the disaster. She is clutching it close. I am surprised, after all she and Dafydd have been through this year, that neither seems put off by the oxygen and other hospital paraphernalia.

"Thank goodness, *finally,* a TV," Hannah says when she first walks into the room and spies it. Then she goes round the room picking up photos, asking questions about each of them. Before long, Da and Mam are telling my children all about my childhood. Mam tells Hannah how naughty I was when I was five and six.

"Alys loved to go into the shops with me. One day I'd taken her to the Tesco. I let her out of my sight for less than a moment, truly, less than a moment." Mam laughs. I hadn't seen her so animated since I was a small child. She is as I remembered her when I was little, very little, her eyes full of light, everything about her relaxed. "And she'd grabbed a tin of tomatoes from the middle of one of those high pyramids, the middle, like, and the whole thing came down around her. I heard her wailing from the back of the shop, and my heart stopped. By the time I got to her, there were people gathered from everywhere trying to comfort her. And there she sat among dozens of tomato tins. Lucky for her, and me of course, it hadn't come down on her head. It would have made mincemeat of her."

Hannah picks up another photo. "Who's this?" She brings it over to Mam.

Mam looks at it and says as she points, "Well, that's your mama, and that's your mama's little friend Hallie."

The picture was taken just days before the disaster.

"She and Mommy were best friends, right?" She looks at me. "Until she got buried, that is."

You could have heard the brush of a bird's wing, it was that quiet. I don't remember ever telling her that.

Everyone seems to have stopped breathing.

"I'm afraid that's true," Evan says, stepping up to Hannah and putting his hand out for the photo.

"Did you know Hallie, Evan?" She is challenging him, making certain he knows me as well as he appears to.

Evan nods.

"What was she like?"

My throat begins to close up. I tell myself to take a deep breath.

"They were a pair, all right. Your mother and Hallie. Inseparable. Hallie was a bit of trouble, she was, always on the edge of it. Bit of a daredevil, too. She liked to break the rules. She had a laugh that was contagious. Once she started, the whole crowd around her would go off, too." He looks at me, puts his hand over mine. "They were a wild pair, right. Hallie and Allie."

"Whatever happened to the little one?" Da asks. "Brother, wasn't it? What's he doing now? I've forgotten."

"Niko," Mam answers. Her whole tone has changed, she is solemn, unsmiling, her posture stiff. She inhales audibly three times.

"He's married with two kids. He and his wife own an ice-cream shop," I say. Mam shoots me a questioning look. "Remember, I stopped over at the Joneses' house," I remind her.

She nods. "In Newport," Mam adds.

"You must have really been sad," Hannah says in a small voice.

"I was so sad," I say.

"For a long time, huh?"

Dafydd moves closer to Hannah, puts his hands on her shoulders.

"I was sad for a really long time, Hannah. But now I have you." She smiles at me.

Mam clears her throat.

Evan rubs my shoulder.

Da adds, "It was a long time ago, Hannah. Time has helped us all to forgive life's harder moments. I am grateful for that."

Hannah moves toward Da and pulls herself up next to him. I am envious of their easy, unconditional acceptance of each other. And so quickly.

"Did someone say something about chicken broth?" Da asks.

"Oh, I almost forgot," I answer. "I'll just get it now."

Down in the kitchen, warming some of the leftover chicken soup and making a salad, I remember that yesterday it felt strange to be a grown woman preparing a meal for Mam and Da in the kitchen in which I grew up. Today, somehow, it doesn't feel so strange to be a grown woman in my mam's kitchen, preparing a meal for my parents, my children, and Evan. I think how Marc would have fit right in. He could easily have been a friend of Evan's.

I hear footsteps and half expect to turn and see Marc. But it is Dafydd, come down to help, he says.

"So I know it's a personal question." He pinches some of the sliced tomato. "And you don't like personal questions. But what's up with you and Evan?"

I take in a deep breath and say quietly, "I don't know."

"Mom, this is me you're talking to. Come on. You can do better than that."

Facing him directly, and almost without thought, I say, "I think I'm either falling in love with him, or I am in love with him. Some of it feels very new, because it is new, and some of it feels like it's always been there."

"You're kidding, right?" He is smiling in disbelief. He runs his hand through his thick hair. "You think you're in love with Evan?" He walks around in a small circle. He snags one of the carrots I'm shredding for the salad and crunches off a bite, shaking his head at me. "Let me just get this straight. This is too much. This is like, like, I don't know what it's like." He breathes in deeply and throws his head back slightly and I think how unbelievable genetics are. "I don't know whether to be upset because it's only a year since Marco's been gone or to be totally relieved that my mother has found some happiness after all she's been through, and it happens to be with my father."

"Dafydd . . ."

"This is weird."

"Dafydd."

"Or to be completely freaked out because . . . are you going to move back here? Are you going to live in Aberfan?"

"Wait . . ."

"Mom, this is just too weird. You've only just met him. I mean, I know you knew him in your youth, but . . . this is so fast . . . this is . . ."

"Wait! Stop it, Dafydd. You're making this into some cheap, predictable Hollywood film. Please. I'm having enough trouble as it is with all of it."

Dafydd looks at me as if he doesn't know me, like I'm not the same person who left the States a week ago.

"Then tell me, Momma."

"I don't know, Dafydd. That's the truth. I didn't come over here to reunite with Evan. I came over here to see my father before he died. To see my mother. To face what I wasn't able to face a million years ago because I was too young to fully understand it. I came over here to try and put some of the jagged pieces of my life to rest. And now I have all these feelings and I don't know what to do with them.

"There's so much about my past I haven't shared with you or anyone. And now you guys are here before I've had a chance to bring myself up to date with it, to understand where I am with all I left behind, now.

"Here's what I know for sure. Marco was the best friend I've ever had. I loved him. We had a good relationship, which as you witnessed was not always perfect. He raised you, not like you could be his own, but like you absolutely were his own. And then in a way, the three of us had Hannah." I want to tell him about Gabriella, about Isabel. I'd like Dafydd to know, and on the other hand, I don't want him to know.

"But he died," I continue. "And that threw me into a deep black hole. A place that was so familiar. And when Hannah went off to camp, and I got the letter from Mam saying Da was ill, I thought it was time for me to go back and . . ." I start to cry, quietly.

Dafydd puts his arms around me. "Oh, Mom."

"So when I say I don't know, I really don't know."

"Okay. Okay."

"You did the right thing, fetching Hannah. You did. I probably should have brought both of you with me in the first place. You should have met Evan years ago. I should have come long before now. I'm sorry, Dafydd. I'm so sorry."

"Mom, it's okay."

"I wish my da weren't dying," I say stupidly. "I want you to know him. I want you to know Mam, too. And Auntie Beryl."

"It's not too late. We can have a start, can't we?"

I pull away from him and hold his face in my hands. "I love you, Dafydd."

"I love you, too, Mom."

Together we bring the salad and six bowls of chicken soup up to Parry's old room. Hannah has managed to get them to turn the TV on and the four of them are watching the BBC news. Actually, the three of them are watching. Hannah is stretched out on the bed next to Da, fast asleep. Evan is sitting on the floor with his back against the bed. Mam is in Parry's desk chair with her feet propped on the foot of the bed.

Evan helps Dafydd hand the bowls round.

"I think we should let her sleep," Evan says, nodding his head toward Hannah.

Later, walking back to Evan's, Dafydd carries Hannah down the road in the light rain. She opens her eyes briefly. I am already worrying about the sleeping arrangements, but Evan whispers to me that he'll use the sleeping roll and camp on the floor in the kitchen area near the fire. Odd that I have managed for twenty years without him, but after last night I don't like the thought of not sleeping next to him. But considering the consequences of my children's reactions, it is probably wise.

We tuck Hannah up on the sofa in the library, and with all the high emotions of the day, I find I am completely shattered. Dafydd is wide-awake and so, it seems, is Evan. When I go off to prepare for bed, I hear the two of them on about soccer again, and then big American films versus independent foreign films. I wonder if Evan has seen any of the films that Marc scored. I wonder if they will talk about Marc. Despite Dafydd's feelings about my relationship with Evan, they seem initially easy together, lots of common ground between them to build on.

"Good night," I say from the library door before going in to kiss Hannah. The two of them, like bookends, look up.

" 'Night, Mom."

Evan smiles.

In the library, I bend to kiss Hannah on her cheek, but she pulls me toward her.

"Don't go, Mommy. Rub my back," she whispers. It is an old request. "I miss Daddy."

"I miss him, too."

"No, you don't. And neither does Dafydd."

"Of course we do."

"Dafydd has Evan and you have your dad. I don't have anyone. I'm the only one who doesn't have a dad. And I'll never have a dad again. Even if you marry Evan, he won't be my dad. He won't. No one will be."

I stay quiet. Here is the other shoe, dropping.

"Suzanne, at camp, has two dads. That's all she talks about. I hate her. Every night she told these stories about her birthday parties and stuff, and about what good friends both her dads are. She has a dog, too. I tried not to listen and one time I told her to shut up. She said she was going to tell on me and that I was mean."

I rub her back lightly.

"She told me I was just jealous 'cause I didn't have a dad. I hate her. Anne Foley, our bunk counselor, told me I should try and get along." Hannah starts to cry. "I don't want to get along with her. I hate her."

"It must have been very hard," I say, lying down next to her and taking her hand.

"If you marry Evan," she starts, "he probably would never have a dog. I bet he doesn't even let the cats in when it rains. I can tell."

She yawns and turns over. "Scratch lightly. Under the T-shirt. Don't leave till I'm asleep."

CHAPTER EIGHTEEN

The house is dark except for a small light over the kitchen stove. Wide-awake, I sneak out of the library, putting on my boots and a Polarfleece of Evan's hanging near the door. I rummage in my purse for the pack of cigarettes and a box of matches. The door scrapes on the flagstones. The cool night air is a relief against my face. I walk up the pathway toward the field, the stars hanging huge and bright, the grass dew-wet from the rain earlier and the smell of jasmine climbing up the side of the cottage, still strong as it was last night. At the top of the field I sit down on the picnic table and light a cigarette. In the distance the glow of the village seems festive. Tomorrow, Evan's choir will be singing at the Welsh Baptist Chapel. And later, we'll take Dafydd and Hannah up the valley to meet Auntie Beryl.

What would life in Aberfan be like for me now? After all, I certainly can write poetry anywhere. I try to imagine myself waking up, making breakfast and taking Hannah to school. She would get used to it—children adjust more quickly even than adults. She would grow to love Evan. He would be one of the teachers at her school. What would it be like to come back to this cottage to write? An ordinary day, the quiet dailiness of life here, Hannah and Evan together.

I pull deeply on the cigarette, looking up at the sky, up beyond the clouds, through the stars, straining to see beyond all we know: the sun, the moon, the solar system. I wonder about the fine line between life and death. Maybe it is just a gauzy piece of silk that separates the two? Is Marc still somehow within my reach? Are the dreams I have the unconscious workings of my own psyche, or are they moments when my spirit actually interacts, connects, with his?

Over the last year, so often when I've needed Marc I close my eyes, and a quiet, a spaciousness that is so still and full surrounds me, and then the answer is there, his answer. Is it really Marc, or is it what I know about him? How I know he might advise or respond?

Once, months after Hallie had gone, when I was up at the cemetery, I thought I saw her. Just a flash of corn yellow and the blue blaze of her eyes and then her smile. Afterward I felt quiet, satisfied. I hadn't told anyone, ever, afraid they'd think I was losing my mind, like some said of the mams and das who were losing theirs, having conversations with their little ones and imagining their presence. But for a long time afterward I hadn't missed Hallie so much, had felt her near me.

Gram believed that God resided in all natural things—even rocks and running water had a soul. She was definitely an animist.

I pick up a handful of small rocks, roll them around in my hand. Looking at them.

> *Where does love go*
> *after the body love lives in, dies?*

A line from one of the many poems due to my editor in a month. Most of them about Marc. Eight about surviving Marc's death, and the newer ones about going on without him.

I am worried about Hannah, about what it will be like for her to grow up without Marc, about whether she will be able to call him up in her mind's eye as she grows older.

After Parry died, I went through a period where I couldn't remember what he looked like, or the way his voice sounded, or his smell. I became desperate. I would open his cupboard and go through his clothes, holding them up to my nose, trying to catch his smell. I slept in his T-shirts.

I miss my garden and the ocean, my morning run along Ocean Avenue and the view of the sea through the palm trees, the homeless shadow man who hits me up for change. But when I think about the house, taking Hannah to school and coming home to do dishes and write—going back there, to what I have called home—it seems as foreign to me as the possibility of living here. It is obvious, after all these years I still know nothing of life and even less of love.

"Alys . . ." It is Evan's shadow in the pale moonlight, although it could easily be Dafydd. "Are you all right?" His voice is deep and always reassuring. It resonates inside of me. It is all of what I remember and filled with some new possibility. He moves toward me, slowly, hesitating. "Do you want to be alone?"

The question seems larger to me than what Evan wants to know. And I wonder if that's really what I want, to be alone. I've been alone for far too long as it is, longer than just the year that Marc has been gone. Perhaps longer even than the years after Hallie and Parry died.

"No."

He comes toward me and stands next to the table. He touches my hand. "You're cold," he says.

We sit together for several moments. And then he says, "This is very hard for me." His voice is so quiet.

"What?"

"To explain what I'm about to explain."

"Oh."

"It's not just about loving you—which I have felt in some fashion or another forever. I know you and your family filled some urgent need for me after I'd left my parents' home. And later, after the disaster and Parry, we filled a need for each other. And it was all important. Utterly important, at least to me. But it's more than that."

I'm not sure what he is getting at. But I stay quiet.

"A few years ago, when I was involved with Shirley." (It is the first time I have heard her name.) "Well, actually I guess it was seven or eight years ago now. She pressed me to marry her, which I was prepared to do, mind you. But she started to talk about having a child, about what our child would be like. She wanted to make a family with me. I went cold inside. I had to ask myself how I could possibly marry her and yet not want to have children with her.

"I reminded her how many hours a day I spent with children. Told her I wanted to be able to come home to a quiet, tidy house. That I couldn't commit to having another child of my own. It seemed overwhelming to me. I couldn't imagine getting up at all hours of the

night, not being able to sleep in on the weekends or travel during the
summer months, make my own way.

"So we ended it. Just like that. Almost immediately she moved
out. Several months later she moved away. To Bristol, I think. And
there I was, all alone again, and somehow I didn't mind. I was actually grateful to her.

"After she left, I began to build this new feeling inside which was
all about me in the world, alone. I bought the meadow and then the
cottage came up for sale. I renovated it and then decorated it. And I
must say, I've enjoyed the last several years. I've found some peace.
I've actually begun to enjoy my life.

"And then you reappear out of nowhere. Oh, don't get me wrong.
You know I kept up with you through Gram. And perhaps I didn't
truly give up on you until you'd married Marc and I heard you were
pregnant again. Probably no coincidence that it was about the time
Shirley and I got involved. But your reappearance certainly has
turned my world around.

"These last several days with you I've had to come face-to-face
with so much of my past. It's an incredible surprise, an unbelievable
miracle to be with you again. I love you. It sounds almost ridiculous,
since I've not anything more than a simple sense of who you are now.
But for whatever reason, I can say it without a moment's thought. It
seems rather easy to me, straightforward and true. And that's all very
well.

"But when I met your children, when I walked out into the drive
this morning, put my hand in Dafydd's and looked into Hannah's
eyes, something else came alive in me.

"And"—he pauses, looks up into the sky—"and I want to be able
to love you out in the open, in front of the world, and have you love
me back."

A shiver runs up my spine. I would like to look away from his intense stare. But I don't. I stay with him.

"I want to spend the rest of my life with you. Oh, Lord, I've probably said it all wrong, I'm sure."

I continue to stare at him, unable to say anything. I bite my upper
lip. Evan has poured his soul out to me. I have heard him. Part of me
has even felt it. But the truth is, the news is so good that I cannot
hold it inside all at once, but know I must come to it in pieces.

"Alys . . . have I said too much?" he asks. "You don't feel pressured, do you?" He laughs.

"No," I say, meaning yes. I give him a look.

"Hmmm, well, what do you say we forget all this for now and go inside? It's getting cold out here."

He takes my hand and leads me down the stone pathway.

"Incidentally, you should figure out a way to quit smoking," he whispers. "It's a totally disgusting habit. It makes you look like a scrubber and it smells, not to mention what it does to your lungs. It's very unattractive."

This makes me laugh and breaks the tension that presses in on my chest.

We sleep together for the last several hours of darkness. I don't care if either of my children catches us. In the morning, by the time Hannah and Dafydd get up, Evan and I have both showered, separately. I have decided we will all go to church and hear the choir, watch Evan conduct.

"It is really just another day," Evan says, smiling.

"Yeah, right. There is no such thing for me as just another day in Aberfan." And there is no use in pretending that everything is just the same between us.

After breakfast Hannah feeds Evan's wild cats. I am washing up the dishes when Dafydd comes into the kitchen.

"I keep forgetting to ask you about this woman who called me." He fumbles in his trouser pocket for a moment and then hands me a slip of folded paper. "She called me last week. She said she was going to be in New York soon and wondered if she might see me. She said she was an old friend of Marc's."

I unfold the paper. In Dafydd's sweet slanted cursive, it reads *Gabriella Purdue.*

"Oh, Lord," I say under my breath.

"Isn't she the singer who sang 'And Then Came Love' from *The Yellow Door?*"

"Yes," I say, casually as I can, trying to recover from my surprise, wondering if she has said anything else to Dafydd, told him anything. "It's just . . . that . . . I haven't seen or heard from her in a very long time," I lie.

"What do you think she wants?"

I shrug. "What else did she say?" I ask finally, as innocently as I can.

"Nothing, just that Marco had told her all about me and that she wanted to meet me. How do you think she got my work number, anyway?"

"Is it that hard to get?"

I am furious. She has crossed a line. How dare she call Dafydd. How dare she use Dafydd. It is more than a threat. It is war.

I try to smile at Dafydd as if nothing is going on inside. I hate her. I hate Marc.

"Hannah," Dafydd calls out as he leaves the room.

I get a cigarette from my purse in the entry and light up, taking a deep puff, wandering into the kitchen, leaning on the windowsill, hunched, my arms crossed over my chest, dragging in hard.

Evan comes in quietly and puts his coffee cup in the sink. Seeing the lighted cigarette in my hand, he turns and says sternly, "Come on, Alys. What are you doing? I told you I don't like you smoking. And since this happens to be my house, I definitely do not want you smoking in here. Particularly not in my kitchen. Put it out, please."

I glare at him.

"Come on, put it out."

This is a facet of Evan I do not always like: the meticulous, fastidious homemaker.

"Oh, fuck you, Evan," I say quietly.

"I beg your pardon?"

"I said, fuck you."

"How dare you? What in the world have I done to deserve this? I think you owe me an apology."

"For what? An apology for what? I'm so sick of all of this. You think you know me. Who do you love, Evan? What do you really know about me other than at one time I turned my back on you and . . . all of this? See how enormously self-centered I am, Evan. I smoke! How in the world could you ever trust me? How could you trust anything about me?"

Evan is quiet.

I can't believe I am taking this out on Evan.

I throw the cigarette in the sink, where he runs water over it.

"I'm sorry, Evan."

"Alys?"

I begin to sob, covering my face. Evan comes around and stands in front of me. I am unable to speak, unable to do anything but cry. If this is some debt, some unpaid bill because of our union, our marriage, that I am now responsible for in Marc's absence, I will not pay it. I will not bear this brunt, either emotionally or financially, nor will my children. I stagger to the bathroom and vomit into the toilet until there is nothing left but sour bile. And then I am sobbing again, choking, completely out of control, my head in the toilet.

"Alys," Evan says quietly outside of the door, "can I come in?"

When I don't answer, he opens the door a crack and closes it behind him.

"Alys, what is it?" He kneels down next to me, touching my head. "What's happened? Tell me, please."

"Evan, what's happened?" Dafydd asks, sticking his head into the bathroom. "Momma, what's wrong?"

He comes over and kneels next to me.

"Please, Mom, what's happened?"

Hannah knocks.

"Why's Mommy crying? Mommy?" When I don't respond she comes and puts her arms around my shoulders and scoots in behind me, close. "Mommy, what's wrong?

Now there are four of us in Evan's small bathroom.

"It's not about her dad, is it?" Dafydd asks Evan.

"I don't know." Evan moves me away from the toilet. He puts down the seat and gathers me up on his lap, holding me in his arms like a child. At first I am stiff and then I release into him.

Dafydd says, "Hannah, why don't you and I take a little walk around the village? We'll be back in an hour or so, Momma." Hannah holds on to my blouse.

"Come on, Hannah," Dafydd urges. "Evan will help her."

After they've gone, Evan carries me into the living room. He holds me in the rocker in front of the fire, continuing to hum the old Welsh lullaby, the same lullaby Gram sang. I close my eyes and fall into the rocking motion, then a kind of light sleep. When I open my eyes, Evan asks, "Do you want to talk about what happened?"

"It's too awful," I whisper.

"Too awful to talk about? Or do you mean too awful to talk about with me?"

"Both," I say.

"Alys," he says, looking sad.

I touch his face. He hasn't shaved yet, and the stubble that shows dark like a shadow is rough beneath my fingers.

"I was a terrible wife," I say so softly. Evan puts his ear right next to my mouth as if he hasn't heard me. I say it again, this time a bit louder: "I was a terrible wife."

I close my eyes and tell Evan everything.

"Oh, Alys."

"I might be able to understand another woman. But another child?"

Evan is quiet, his head down. "I understand how you must feel, Alys. Please don't take this in the wrong way, but I really do understand how awful you must feel."

I look at Evan as if I am seeing him, or at least his pain, for the very first time. How can he think that what I did to him is the same? I continue to look at him. And as I reach deep down inside, I see that it is the same.

I bow my head, crying again, this time more quietly. And then, looking up, I say, "I am so sorry, Evan."

CHAPTER NINETEEN

Dafydd and Hannah still aren't back when I've finished with the dishes, so, having recovered some, I start over to see Da and Mam.

I go the back way along the ridge, looking out over the whole valley. Noticing, as always, the hills—how they roll into each other like the smooth curves of a woman's body, the tantalizing iridescent glow of green against raw, rusted bracken weeds, the touch of a late-morning breeze making waves of the greenery. This is the land I am from, what I grew up looking at and loving before the disaster ruined it all for me.

Up ahead, two people walk toward me. The figures disturb my horizon. I do not want to share it with anyone. I want to hoard this beauty as my own. As they get closer, they become Hannah and Dafydd. Hannah runs toward me, her hair blowing out behind her like a blond veil. Dafydd has his hands tucked deep in his pockets. I will never be able to look at him in the same way because now he will always remind me of Evan.

When he gets close, he smiles. "Hi. You're okay?"

Hannah throws herself on me. She has grown. I hold her, closing my eyes for a moment and breathing in the possibility of the two of us staying here with Evan, forever. Something inside opens, but it is still dark and scary. "I'm okay," I say, in answer to Dafydd. The three of us continue to stand, looking out over the hills, together.

"I can't believe you grew up here, Mom," Dafydd says. "It's just magnificent. Not wild like the Rockies, or rugged like the Santa

Monica Mountains, but man, it's sure a force all its own. I don't think I've ever seen anything so gorgeous."

"It is, isn't it?" I feel proud, as if by being Welsh I get to take credit for this glory.

"If you're feeling better, Mommy, Dafydd wants to pack a picnic and go for a real hike up and down some mountains. Can we?" Hannah asks. "And what about visiting Auntie Beryl?"

I pat her back. "That's a great idea. In fact I'm feeling much, much better, sweetie."

When I say I'd like to quickly visit my parents, they tell me they are just coming from there.

"He's sleeping," Hannah says. "And Mam's going to rest, too. They had a long night."

"His breathing is off," Dafydd adds. "But he seemed in good spirits, before his nap. They showed us more photographs. Your father told us all about the village."

"And lots about the disaster," Hannah adds. "More stuff than you ever said. Like how many of your friends died and how you almost drowned in the sludge, too. So sad, Mommy."

For a moment I am concerned Da has revealed to Hannah how Parry died. "Parry?" I ask.

"He told us about what a great artist Parry was," Dafydd reassures me.

"Your mom fixed us tea and biscuits. She's like you, Mommy. She thinks food will cure anything."

Dafydd smiles and puts his arm around my shoulders. Turning a bit away from Hannah and moving closer to my ear, he says, "I understand why you had to leave."

When we get back to the cottage, we find Evan napping on the sofa in the cowshed. He sits up, sleepily. "So do we have a plan?"

Packing a lunch together, we seem, in our own way, a family. There is already so much between us, a shared history, something we could all grow into.

We ring Beryl. "What? Your children are here? My goodness, Allie, did you expect them? No, of course you didn't. My goodness, what you must all be experiencing! How wonderful for your da. And your mam. What am I saying? It's wonderful for all of us! How soon will you come, will you be here?"

Our plan is to get to her around three p.m., when she will be back from market, which gives us time to make the long detour to Hay-on-Wye, a small medieval town on the English border. It is the long way round—two hours away from Auntie Beryl's, but supposedly magnificent.

Along the narrow high-hedged lanes, I tell stories, point things out. We laugh a lot. From the backseat Hannah leans forward a bit, between Evan and me. She affectionately pets Evan on the arm as he is shifting gears. I watch her putting her reservations about him away—at least for the moment. Evan answers Dafydd's and Hannah's questions elaborately, throwing his own tales of valley life into the mix, until Hannah announces, "I have to pee."

" 'Spend a penny,' " Evan quotes an old adage. "When I was growing up, Mam would give me a penny 'just in case.' The public loo cost a penny back then. Now it's a bit more—ten pence, I think, maybe twenty by now."

There's not a public toilet in sight, so we stop at a viewpoint turnout—Hay Bluff—at the end of a single-track road. Sheep are scattered in with the view of a sweeping stretch of hilly, open land. Hannah thinks she sees ponies. I walk her to a clump of windblown trees leaning low. She crouches behind them while I stand in front waiting for her. In the distance I can see the steep slopes of the Black Mountains.

Hannah emerges triumphant and wanting lunch. "Why can't we just eat here? I'm starved."

Before I have a chance to answer, Dafydd and Evan come trudging toward us, Evan with the rucksack on his back.

Between the two of us, Evan and I have made the most delicious sandwiches: thinly sliced cheddar cheese, avocado and tomato on whole wheat bread; baked ham, Swiss cheese and honey mustard on baguettes. We have berries from the garden, chocolate bars from Evan's stash and salt-and-vinegar crisps. Maybe Dafydd is right. I do think food will solve almost everything. Clearly Evan does, too.

After lunch we find the Book King, whose empire of books is stretched on bookshelves up and down the side of the main road for several hundred yards.

"Alys Davies," the bookseller says. "Poetry, huh?" He motions for me to follow him to one of the back stalls. I can't believe it, but there, among works by Walt Whitman, Emily Dickinson, Anne Sexton, Dylan Thomas and a hundred others, are two of my own books, *Under the Sycamores* and *Pressing for Time*. He asks, "Would you mind autographing them? I sold one a while back and probably could have gotten a good quid more if it had your signature in it."

I write:

Wales will always inhabit the deepest valley of my heart

Corny, but true. I sign my name.

After the Book King, I take over the driving to Auntie Beryl's while the others sleep. For the first time in a very long while, I feel content. In this moment, I am with everyone I need.

When we get to Beryl's, Evan greets her with "Our gypsy mama." She is waiting for us outside in front of her flower-strewn walkway. Evan picks her off her feet and hugs her.

"More like a gypsy grandmamma. My bones are aching today," she complains, smiling.

Auntie Beryl is dressed in one of her bejeweled full skirts, frayed a bit at the hem. Braided and wrapped around her head is her signature scarf.

"This is Dafydd and Hannah," he says, waving them over. Dafydd eagerly stretches out his hand. Hannah, more reserved, touches Beryl's skirt.

Dafydd is amazed at the cottage's low ceilings. "And I thought Evan's doorways were low. This must be under five feet. My God, people must have been tiny in the old days."

"Old days?" Auntie Beryl says, walking straight under the front door. "The Welsh aren't a tall bunch, are we, Evan?"

"Speak for yourself, Beryl," he teases, ducking to enter.

Beryl has fixed us a proper tea with small sandwiches. She has made Welsh cakes. "Which I am famous for all the way from Mt. Snowdon to Aberfan," she tells Hannah. And next to the cakes, a bowl of fresh butter, another of clotted cream and a third of raspberry jam. The tea is hot and strong. My children and Evan dig in as if they haven't eaten in weeks.

"I hope you and Hannah are giving your mother a real run for her money. When she was little she didn't know the meaning of the word no, and she was forever running off and hiding herself away, scaring her mam and da, not to mention her sweet gram. They'd be looking for her everywhere, they would."

"What about Evan?" Hannah asks.

"I didn't meet Evan till he was nearly seventeen, but as far as I can remember, he was nearly perfect. He *is* nearly perfect." Beryl winks at me. "Although I don't think his parents would agree. Times were different back then, sure enough, but rumor has it he ran away from home when he was about sixteen—didn't you now, Evan? Wasn't that 'bout the time you started working down the mine?"

"You ran away from home?" Hannah's eyes are wide. "Why?"

Evan looks at me, and I can almost hear his mind working. "Well, I . . . I wanted to be a miner. It seemed like a romantic way of life. And as it turned out, it was the only decent job available to someone who hadn't yet taken their O-levels. I wasn't near ready to take mine."

"O-levels?" she asks. "What's that?"

"Exams you take to graduate from high school. I didn't take the exams, so I didn't graduate."

I've heard this partial invention. It's the story he tells everybody.

"My parents had put their law to me. I couldn't continue to live with them and go down the mine. They wouldn't allow it, too much of a worry. Out of sight, out of worry for them. Or something like that." He looks over at me again and I smile, reassuring him that the real story is safe with me.

Auntie Beryl puts her arms around me and says quietly in my ear, "How have you made out with your father?"

"It's been good. Much more than I expected. You helped. Our talking helped."

"And your mam?"

"There, too. Really fine."

"I'm coming down tomorrow to see them both."

Beryl tries to talk us into spending the night, but by early evening Hannah is complaining about a tummyache and sore throat and has found her way to my lap. She is a bit peaked. Her head is warm. She hangs on me, heavy and whiny, a sure sign she is coming down with something.

"Why don't we start home?" Evan says quietly. "It's probably better to be awake and at home than to intrude on Beryl."

"Your house is not our house," Hannah sasses. "He doesn't make our rules, Mommy. I want to stay here. I'm tired."

Evan just smiles and handles it. "What about the kitties? Who will feed the kitties if we don't go tonight?"

She buries her head under my arm.

Back at Evan's quite late, I tuck Hannah up, and surprisingly, she asks if Evan will sit with her for a while. I use the opportunity to sneak out into the meadow for a cigarette. Dafydd finds me.

"Why are you smoking?"

I shrug. "It's just for now," I say.

"You know, Mom, you seem happy here, with Evan. You get along so well. Why don't you just stay a while?"

"It's not that easy, Dafydd. I wish it were," I say quietly.

Once again I choose to sleep with Evan, and I am in his arms when I awaken in the middle of a nightmare:

A woman is standing in the middle of a dance floor, where a combo is gearing up on the stage. Her husband is trying to get to her, but is moving too slowly. Soon he is lost in the wind as the storm breaks. Heavy taffeta, satin and silk, sized and rubbing together like the crack of autumn leaves. When the sax blows its first notes, the crowd pushes off.

"My God!" he shouts, as she's lost in the blur of carousel colors. "Somebody help her!"

She holds her arms in front of her, whirling around and around, faster and faster, her arms and legs and head melding together. She closes her eyes, and for once she's not thinking of anything other than the hot, wet air, a pure whisper whipping her into that whirl. As the band plays on, her husband, still crazy to get to her, does a do-si-do. Her dark mouth opens and her long teeth shine like the moon's white sails against the black bay of night. "Kiss me!" she cries out. Her husband, desperate now, reaches out his arm just as the last horn brays and grabs her wrist as the lights go on. The woman falls to the floor, her face breaking into a thousand bits of glass. Quickly then, her husband reaches into his back pocket for a brush and dustpan and, bending low, sweeps her up, nodding to the crowd as he turns to go.

I switch the little night-light on.

"What's going on?" Evan asks, turning over toward me.

"A nightmare."

"Bad?" he asks, and yawns. "What can I do?" He looks at me then.

I am naked and suddenly shy. "I'm sorry."

"Nothing to be sorry for. I can sleep with the light on if need be. Sometimes I think I could sleep standing up."

"I mean, I'm sorry for leaving you," I whisper. "I never stopped loving you."

After a long moment Evan says, "I'm sorry for not going after you."

He continues to stare at me. "You know, you're more beautiful than you were as a teenager, if that's possible."

"Stop, Evan. You're making me feel self-conscious."

"I'm in love with you. Wow. Even in the middle of the night I'm in love with you," he says, sounding surprised.

"This isn't love—it's obsession," I tease back.

"You're probably right," he says, laughing. "But it's also love, Alys." He leans toward me and puts his arms around me. Soon his hands are caressing my breasts and he is kissing my neck. Before I know it we are rolling around on the bed and I am as fierce as he is in helping him find his way inside of me.

Afterward he says, "Now I suppose I should apologize?"

"For what?" I ask.

"For seducing you."

"You never have to apologize for that."

He turns the light out, and then, this time at my initiation, we are at it again, more slowly and gently. I am feeling him from the inside out. That scary dark place inside me is nowhere to be felt.

The next morning, before first light, Hannah comes into Evan's bedroom.

"Mommy, I don't feel well." She stands by the bed while I gather my wits about me. Next to me, Evan awakens and pulls himself to a sitting position. We are both naked under the cozy.

"You're actually sleeping with him?" she says. "That's disgusting."

Now I see she hasn't understood what is going on between Evan and me. Or, if she does on some level, the bald reality of it staring her in the face is quite different from what she has imagined. Leaning toward her, I put my lips to her forehead. She is burning up.

"Come on, sweetie." I pull on a T-shirt as I herd her out of the room back toward the library and her bed.

"I don't want to go back to that bed. I want to go home."

"Does anything else hurt besides your throat?"

"Everything hurts. My throat feels like I swallowed a razor. My ears hurt, too. Mommy, why are you sleeping with him? I can't believe it. It's wrong. You're still married to Daddy. I can't believe this. What would Daddy say? How could you do this to Daddy? He would never do this to you!"

Little does she know.

Just as Hannah plops down on the library floor and starts to cry, Dafydd comes out of the guest room. Evan emerges from the bedroom, sweats on, pulling on a shirt.

"What's going on?" Dafydd asks. His hair is sticking out and he is rubbing his eyes like a child.

"Hannah has fever."

"She was sleeping with him, Dafydd," Hannah says. "Mommy was sleeping with Evan. You're only supposed to sleep with your husband." Now she is sobbing. "It's not fair. What would Daddy think?"

"Oh, Hannah honey," I say.

"I'll make some tea," Evan says.

Dafydd pulls Hannah onto his lap. "I want to go home," she says as Dafydd pats her back.

I am crouched on the floor, next to both of my children. I don't know what to say. When Evan waves me over, I move toward him reluctantly.

"Let Daffyd handle it. I suspect he'll know what to say."

Like Hannah must have felt, I don't like Evan telling me what to do with my children.

Hannah says again, "But she's still married to Daddy." Dafydd just holds her.

Evan is pouring mugs full of tea.

"I'll give Hannah hers," I say.

He puts two teaspoons of sugar into each mug and stirs them.

Then, looking rather sternly at me, he says, "That's all right. I've got them. Go put some pants on." He grabs up three of the mugs and goes to sit next to Dafydd and Hannah.

Evan puts his hand on Hannah's forehead. "You do have a fever, poor little girl." He rubs her head. "But it's not too high. What about I run a cool bath for you?"

Hannah just stares at him.

"Sometimes when I've a fever, a cool bath brings it down and then I can sleep. I bet if I run it, your mother will sit with you."

"Okay," Hannah says quietly.

How does he know what to do when he's never had children? Then, of course, I realize Evan has had hundreds of children, and they've all been Hannah's age.

While the bath is filling, I quickly dress. Evan comes back into the room, where Dafydd is seated on the floor next to Hannah.

"What time is it?" Dafydd asks.

"Half past five," Evan tells him.

"What day is it?"

"Monday. What time is your flight?"

"Eight p.m. But I've decided I'll stay another day if that's okay."

I'd forgotten that Dafydd was to leave today. I exhale. My flight is booked for Wednesday evening.

"Why don't you all stay an extra couple of days?" Evan asks. "That way we won't have to rush through the next day and Hannah will have time to kick this little bug." He looks at me sadly, then at Hannah. "Hannah sweetie, your bath is ready.

"Alys, do you want to sit with Hannah? You could read her the beginning of *The String and the Harp*. It's my all-time favorite book. Takes place in North Wales. You'll love it, Hannah. So will you, Allie."

"I'm going to call Doc Rogers," I say quietly.

"Why don't we see how she is after her bath and some sleep?" Evan says, patting my arm.

"It could be strep. If it is, it needs to be treated immediately." I can feel myself moving into a place of high anxiety. "Strep is serious if you don't catch it quickly."

"It could also just be a sore throat," he comforts. "It's the middle of the night. She's been doing a lot on very little sleep."

"You're right. She shouldn't have made this trip. She should be back in Colorado."

"Oh, right, Mom," Dafydd says. "Sick out there alone on the prairie with all those coyotes and bears," he says facetiously. "Sounds much better than being here, in a warm house"—he yawns—"with us."

I glare at him.

"Hannah. Would you let me have a look down your throat?" Evan asks.

I feel the way Hannah must. I want to say, *Who the hell do you think you are? What if she is really ill?* But part of me is relieved I don't have to deal with this on my own.

Evan uses his flashlight to examine Hannah's throat. "Aha! It's so dark down there. Oh, that's interesting. . . ." he teases.

"What?" Hannah asks.

"It looks like . . . Mars," Evan says.

"Mars? What does Mars look like?"

"You don't know what Mars looks like?"

"Uh-uh."

"Well, it's red. But there's no life. No mountain peaks and . . . wait! No pus!"

"You're disgusting, Evan!"

"Hannah. Take your bath. I guarantee you . . . if you bathe in that frigid water, let your mam read a bit, and go back to sleep, you'll wake up feeling like a million quid."

"What's a quid?" Hannah asks.

"Hannah." Evan points. "The bath."

Hannah gets up and walks toward the bathroom.

"Alys." Evan points again.

"What if it is something more—"

"Alys."

"I'm going."

"Can I go back to bed?" Dafydd asks.

"See you all later," Evan says. "I'm going out to howl at the moon."

Once Hannah has bathed and I've put her back to bed, I'm completely shattered, and I fall asleep in the large chair in front of the fireplace. An hour later—it feels like seconds, actually—Evan wakes me to tell me Mam is on the telephone. I slowly open my eyes, still groggy, my head hurting.

Mam's voice is shaky. "Doc Rogers is here with Da. You should come. He's . . . Please come, Alys, quickly."

"Oh, Mam," I say, holding the telephone for a second after Mam has rung off. It is happening too fast. I thought I would have more time. Evan holds me. In his arms I feel safe. I want to stay there.

"Go, Alys. Hurry," he whispers. "I'm perfectly capable of coping with Hannah, and if I need help, Dafydd will cope with me," he says, reading my mind yet again.

CHAPTER TWENTY

Early-morning drizzle, daylight just coming on around the edges, and I arrive at my parents' house in less than three minutes. It is so quiet. I take the old stairs two at a time. In Parry's room, Mam is standing near the bed, facing the door, crying quietly, no noise, but her body shakes. She looks so young, her hand over her nose and mouth, like a small child. At first I just stand there.

"Forgive me," she whispers so quietly I can barely hear her. "Forgive me all those years I was unable to stand beside your da. I was scared and weak. I was wrong. I let him down. And I let you and Parry down."

"No, Mam, you didn't." I start to go to her, but then hold back, giving her space.

"He was a good man, Allie. A kind man. He didn't deserve what the villagers gave him. Afterward, everyone knew it. They made amends to him, afterward. But it was years after the tribunal and mostly too late. Anyway, he's finally free from it all," she whispers.

Doc Rogers is just removing a stethoscope from Da's chest and putting it into his pocket. He shakes his head, reaching over to remove the oxygen nasal prongs from Da's nose.

"Ah, Rita. Those were long-ago years, they were. I 'spect Arthur forgave those early reactions after the disaster. We were stunned as he was and none of us acting in our right minds, like. True, though, he paid a price too dear for coal. Dearer price than any of us, he paid. A good strong heart, Arthur had, now quiet."

Da does look now as if he is sleeping peacefully. I wonder if he really is free of it?

Had I kept Da so deeply hidden in me, buried like my past, that I'd somehow missed the heart of him?

So often, I wanted to just lie down—like Parry did, like Da is lying now. Perhaps everyone in this village experienced some of these same feelings. The lyrics to a song by Dar Williams pass through my head:

> *And when I chose to live,*
> *There was no joy.*
> *It's just a line I crossed.*
> *It wasn't worth the pain my death would cost*
> *So I was not lost or found.*

Coming back here now, being able to look at the truth of my past, is like a second chance.

I go to Mam then, hold her, rubbing her back, smoothing her hair.

"Thank you for coming, Alys." She touches my cheek softly with her hand. "Da was so happy to meet your children, finally. He was so glad to see you have grown into a fine woman then. And I'm awfully grateful to have all of you with me now."

Dafydd stays for the funeral two days later. Beti, Colin and the kids come over from the States. I am surprised at how many people show up in Bethany Chapel. Neighbors and old friends. The Joneses, Niko, the Garlands. So many people I haven't seen since I was fifteen. The village rallies round Mam. Reverend Land goes on for a while about what a decent and kind man Da was. How he looked after his family and the needs of the village in the best possible way he knew, and that the villagers had done him a disservice, initially, in pointing the blame at him for the disaster. "But that is behind us now, by many years.

"He was a good friend to me and to all of us. I will be remembering him for his good heart, his patience. Even with all his own trouble, he moved graciously through his life.

"Let us bow our heads and keep a moment of silence in his memory," Reverend Land concludes.

Evan rises from the left front pew. "Ladies and gentlemen," he begins, speaking softly but looking out over the group of us. "Twenty years ago, after this village had suffered through the bleakest of times, I went to Arthur Davies and told him I wanted to start a choir in memory of all of us who suffered through the disaster and lost so much as Arthur had. You'll remember, none of us had much heart left at the time. All of the monies the village collected through donations went to clearing up the slag, building the community center and erecting the new playground. Of course we were all grateful for these monuments." Evan clears his throat and I can tell he is on the verge of tears.

I put my hand on Hannah's knee and the other one on Dafydd's, thinking of the distance we've come since we last sat together at a funeral.

"I gathered a few men, who gathered together a few more, and finally we made a number of us, Arthur, one of the first," Evan continues. "And we practiced until we had voice and song that lifted our own spirits and, we hope, the spirits of the village. And when we needed anything, Arthur Davies gave it to us: His generous donations helped us start up the choir."

Mam leans forward from her place behind me and pats my shoulder. " 'Twas what you sent us, Alys."

I am confused for a moment, and then realize they'd never used the money I sent for themselves, but passed it on to Evan and the choir.

"And finally, he helped secure our first public presentation right here in this very chapel.

"Arthur didn't know that in August we will give our first Royal presentation before the Court at Buckingham Palace. But it is my hope—no, it is my belief, that his generous and gracious spirit will continue to guide us in song, forever. And when we sing before the Queen, he will be there with us."

As if on cue, the members of the choir in attendance stand and sing Da's favorite:

> Far away a voice is calling,
> Bells of memory chime,
> Come home again, come home again,
> They call through the oceans of time.

We'll Keep a Welcome in the Hillside,
We'll keep a welcome in the vale,
This land of ours will still be singing,
When you come home again to Wales.
This land of song will keep a welcome and with a love
That never fails, we'll kiss away each hour of Hiraeth,
When you come home again to Wales . . .

Sunday afternoon in the pub: Hallie and I under the table, our fort. Watching their feet, swinging back and forth—Mam and Mrs. Quiggly, her black sling-back shoes, Mrs. Burton's red shoes and Mrs. Jones in her fancy sandals and her hose with the dark toe band showing. Their laughter, earsplitting, hitting high loud notes. Da and his friends raise their glasses, the clinking, the ring to them. Their own laughter, raucous. Peeking out from under the table, I see them, all of the men, their heads together, and then their voices, loud and clear, like water rushing down a riverbed, their voices together into one voice 'tween them.

We'll kiss away each hour of Hiraeth,
When you come home again to Wales.

After the choir has finished, Evan looks out at all of us and says, "May God be here, and inside each of us, now and forever. Amen."

Hannah holds my hand. Dafydd and Mam both reach over and put their hands on mine, like the game we played as children, one hand on top of the other. And on top of all our hands I feel Gram's. In that moment I surrender to something more than I can see. I look around at the many familiar faces from my childhood, sharing this sweet, sad moment with my family. A small blue jay flies into the chapel. It flaps its way to the front and lands quietly on the lectern, and when the singing stops, it flies out again.

At the cemetery, in a light drizzle, a group of us stand while Da, in a plain pine box, is lowered into the ground. Mr. Lennitt, who worked down the mine with him, hands Mam Da's headlamp and lunch pail.

"Finally I cleaned out his locker for him," Mr. Lennitt says, his head bent low.

Mam places them on top of the coffin.

"Was Da a miner, too?" Hannah asks. I love that she calls my father Da.

I nod.

After the crowd disperses, Hannah asks, "Where's Hallie?" We move through the rows of white arches, my children quiet as I point out my friends. Dafydd stops and reads each memorial placard and looks at each photo that adorns the many gravesides.

When we get to Hallie's grave, Hannah asks, "Don't you still miss her?" and I know she is thinking of Marc.

The deep, dark place inside me opens again and I say simply, "Yes. But now, mostly, I have found a place for Hallie to rest inside of me. She is never far away. Sometimes lately, when you and I are horsing around, hanging out, it reminds me of how it was with Hallie. I mean, you remind me. We were the same age as you when it all happened. I know she would have liked you."

"That would be funny, wouldn't it, if we were all the same age, and friends?" Hannah presses closer to me.

Dafydd asks, as I knew he would, "Where's Parry?"

We stand uncomfortably at Parry's grave, none of us saying anything. When Evan appears, he grabs Hannah up and puts his arm around Dafydd, shaking us out of our quiet and grief. "Now this is someone you both would have loved. When I tell you there was not a woman in the village who wasn't mad for him, and not a man who wasn't envious, and all the little children gathered at his feet, I am not exaggerating. He was the smartest, the wildest, the best of all of us, and he would have loved every inch of both of you, not to mention that you . . ."

"Are both exactly like him!" Dafydd fills in quickly.

"How did you know what I was going to say, you lucky sods, you?" Evan says, slapping Dafydd on the back. "Nothing like genetics!"

I have moved to Gram's graveside. We all stop and stare quietly at the words on her stone:

LET THE RIVER RUN THROUGH US
AND EMPTY INTO OUR HEARTS.

"That's beautiful," Dafydd says, looking up at me.

"Your mam wrote it," Evan says. "It was part of a poem she wrote for your gram."

I look at Evan, and he reads the question on my face.

"Because I know everything about you." He winks.

Later that evening we all go back to Mam's. Many of the neighbors bring food and drink. Someone has brought a lamb with all the trimmings, chips and many plates of overcooked vegetables.

And Evan is right. Hannah's sore throat has gone quickly, the fever broken after her long nap the day Da died.

In bed that night, after we make sweet and very quiet love, he says, "Why are you leaving me again?"

On top of him, I kiss him on his eyes and his nose and then deeply on his mouth.

How can I leave this man who seems, in almost every way, everything I've always wanted? "I have to," I say. "There's still so much I have to unravel."

"But why can't you unravel it from here?"

"Because I can't. I have a life back there," I say sadly. But also just around the edges, there's that familiar feeling of being cornered like some wild animal. "And Hannah has a life. School starts for her soon. I can't just stay." He starts to pull away and I stop him.

"I am not leaving you forever. Just for now. Come to Los Angeles. Come see how I live. I want you to know what *I've* grown into. You could come back with Hannah and me." And the moment I say it, I know the impossibility of the request.

"In August I have the Royal Court appearance."

"Well, perhaps I can figure out a way to come back for that. Or you could come after that."

"After that, school starts. And then the anniversary of the disaster."

There is a long silence between us.

"I am not leaving you in the same way," I say.

"Why does it all feel so familiar?"

"Please, Evan, understand. I need to be where I lived with Marc so I can figure out where to put him and his other family. I need to reexamine all the stuff that has occurred in my life that until now I wasn't willing to look at. Separate it all out and see where it ends and I begin." I don't mention that there is still a large part of me that is paralyzed by the thought of living in Aberfan.

I want to ask him to come live with me in Los Angeles, but I know it is as much of an impossibility as it is for me to stay in Aberfan. Just the same, I need to hear him say it so that he will know, this time, that it is not all my fault, my leaving him.

"After you have finished your performances, *you* could come live with me?"

Another long silence. We don't say any more.

We put Dafydd on the bus early the next morning for Cardiff. His plane leaves in the evening from Heathrow to New York.

"I'd like to come in August for the Buckingham Palace ceremony," Dafydd tells Evan before he leaves. "I want to know what she keeps in that purse of hers."

"I'd love to have you come," Evan replies, looking straight at Dafydd despite the fact that I stand between them. "Why don't you come a day or two early so we can go round London together? I've a friend in Soho who will loan us his flat."

They shake on it.

After Dafydd is gone, I walk the long way to Mam and Da's, everything feeling completely different from the way it did even a day ago. The sky has clouded over and it is dank and cold, now a typical dreary Welsh morning. I have a sudden feeling of wanting to be done here. To be on my way. The once wide-open space and grand view of the valleys are again closing in on me, and I know in part that it is my way of trying to block the pain.

An hour later, when I am sitting at breakfast with Mam, Beti says, "I've decided to stay on for a fortnight. You're looking tired, Allie. You go on home, then. Colin will go with you and the children. Get Hannah back to school on time. I'll bring Mam home with me soon as we've tidied everything here. It'll be good for her to have a time away with all of us in the States."

As I pull my own loose ends together at Mam and Da's, I try to include Evan in everything. He puts up a friendly front, but it seems an effort for him even to have a full conversation with me. He is already moving far, far away, tuning me out, the distance between us becoming as wide as the great blue-black Atlantic and Pacific oceans.

On the morning Hannah and I leave, he makes us a big Welsh breakfast with heaps of fried bread, thick rashers of bacon and fried eggs.

"So if your book is due to the publisher in August, you must have a lot of work ahead?" Evan asks.

"I do."

"August is a big month for all of us," he says, dishing out the food.

"It'll be a whole year then," Hannah says. "A whole horrible year since Daddy died."

"Yes," I say. "A whole year."

Evan gives me a long look and I am hoping that he finally understands why I am having to leave, why even coming back for the ceremony in August will be hard. I am thinking he can see that my life is not only about me.

As I have arranged, Mr. Jenkins, from the car service, knocks promptly at three o'clock in the afternoon.

"Ms. Davies," he says, bowing low. "I trust your trip home has been a good one?"

I nod, once again fighting back tears. Mr. Jenkins gathers our bags and puts them into the boot of his Daimler.

"Lovely car," Evan says.

"Come with us, Evan," Hannah pleads. "We've got lots of room in our house."

He rumples her hair, as has become his habit, and crouches down to give her a hug. "You take care, lovey."

Then it is time for us. We stand face-to-face, not knowing what to do.

"Will we speak?" I ask.

"Of course we'll speak."

We wrap our arms around each other, both tentative. I kiss him. "I love you."

He nods, a small smile on his face. "Me, too."

As Mr. Jenkins turns the car around, from the backseat I see that Evan stands watching us as the car moves down the drive, his hands in the pockets of his jeans.

Field after field passes away as we move away from my home.

PART III

Chapter Twenty~One

E van.
    There is not a blue-sky fall day that he isn't in my thoughts. I dream of him, write him poems and letters, call him.

At first he is so distant, I wonder if he is trying to put me off.

"Evan?"

"Hello, Alys."

"How are you?"

"I'm fine."

"How's the choir going?"

"Fine."

One-word answers. I know he is hurt, responding from that hurt. In the old days I might have given up. But I can't stop myself, can't cut him off; he is there all the time, inside me, amazing and frightening.

Each morning I ask myself the same questions: Can I go back? Can I live in Aberfan? And each morning, the answers, hard as they are to bear, are no.

Then, one afternoon while I am watching Hannah in a soccer game, she has a breakaway and is running down the middle of the field. I am jumping up and down, shouting her on, and I actually look around for him, for Evan. I realize there is no one on earth with whom I would rather share this moment. When Hannah kicks the ball into the goal, I know I have to figure something out.

Marc's absence is still a black-and-blue bruise I touch tenderly and often.

Since our return, I have packed up his scores and donated them to the UCLA Film School. His clothes, those Dafydd couldn't use, I gave to a local synagogue, and I packed up most of the photos that hung everywhere in our house. There are still many of him hanging in the library and in Hannah's room. I keep circling back and finding less and less of him and myself where we once were, together.

Last week, in my garden, I planted artichokes, and it excites me to think about the future possibility of digging into their sweet hidden hearts.

My latest book of poetry comes out in the spring, and already there are book parties planned in California and a small tour in the Midwest and the Northeast to look forward to. Getting back to work has helped place me in the world again. I feel less insecure and more as if there might be some future for me.

Mam flew back with Beti. She stayed with Beti and her family for a week and with Hannah and me for three weeks. Her presence in my home filled me with a deep pleasure, healing all of us, filling up the sad space in each of our lives. She loved our mountains and the sea, the warm air and bright sun. We took long walks, during which I really opened up, telling her about my feelings for Evan and the conflict of not being able to live in Aberfan, having made a life and a home in America. I asked her a lot of questions about her own experiences after the disaster, and how she was able to stay with Da.

"I can't really explain all of it, Alys. It was such a tough time."

"But did you ever think about leaving him, or leaving Aberfan?"

"No, I never really did. It may have passed through my mind, but I couldn't have done that. It was too many years we'd been together, too many nights. It would have been too hard for either of us to start over.

"But don't compare us, Alys. That would be very dangerous for you. The truth is, I may not have actually moved out of the house, but I certainly moved away emotionally. And I guess that meant I moved away from you, too." She puts both her arms around me. "I hope I still have some time to make that up to you."

I am so grateful for this apology, for how aware Mam seems to have become. Any small sore spot left inside me seems smoothed. My own experience has taught me how hard it is when your world falls apart to take care of anything outside of yourself. Perhaps if Mam had been more attentive I'd never have learned how to reach inside and take care of myself.

"Leaving all of you back then seems so selfish now," I say sadly.

"Like your gram used to say, 'You just can't take things out of context—sometimes you miss the whole reason for an action.' It was just too hard for you to stay. You've said it's even hard for you now. Maybe when you get yourself clear of these latest tragedies you might feel differently?" Mam smiles and pats my cheek. "Home will be there. And I bet Evan will, too."

A shiver runs through me.

Home. Such a huge concept. It seems like I've been looking for home a long time. I know it is more than just a place, Los Angeles or Aberfan—more than any one person, Marc, my children, even Evan. In the past, home has been the place that opens for me when I feel afraid, lonely or brokenhearted. It is the place where a poem begins for me. It is a wild place, a place more often now of great romance, as light and bright as an angel's wing, a place I am just beginning to feel good in.

A week before Evan and the choir's royal audience at Buckingham Palace, I am pruning the lemon tree. I think how well Hannah is doing now that we are back—particularly considering we've only just passed the year anniversary of Marc's death. Work left on my poetry book isn't creative as much as line editing. I wonder if I could sneak away for a long weekend for Evan's big day this Sunday. The more I think about it, the more desperate I am to be in London for the performance. I call Elizabeth in Durango and ask her to come stay with Hannah. I intend to surprise Evan, and hope Dafydd won't feel encroached upon. I pack my bag, excited about the possibility of being there with Evan, imagining a long walk in Hyde Park, perhaps a rowboat ride on the Thames, a candlelighted dinner at some small Italian restaurant in Soho. I imagine the three of us together, Dafydd and his parents. I let the full possibility of us as a family roll around in my head and then in my heart. I look for the telltale signs of guilt and fear and I am surprised at how little of either there seems to be. But a night before I am to travel, Elizabeth calls to say she's broken two ribs in a river rafting accident and she won't be able to help out.

I have, of course, done an endless amount of thinking regarding

Gabriella and her relationship with Marc. In fact, in the last months, it feels like it has consumed my every waking moment.

I loved Marc—that's for sure. I loved being with him. But because I'd run from home and hadn't ever really faced what I'd run from, I was in many ways emotionally frozen, my soul reined in tight. And while Marc grew, I struggled to keep control in order to hold on to the small amount of safety I felt I had. And as Marc tried to penetrate, I became less penetrable. In the beginning, Dafydd stood between us. And later, Hannah. They were my foils. With them in the forefront of our relationship, I didn't have to push deeper.

I was so young. *We* were so young. Despite the fact that somehow we'd just missed each other, Marc and I had managed with all our love to raise remarkable children.

And now there is Isabel. Not my child, but Marc's child. And because of all Marc and I had been together, I begin to feel that Isabel is owed the same chance as Dafydd and Hannah.

So just after Mam leaves, when Gabriella rings me up, I am prepared. She is in Los Angeles. Before she plunges in, I surprise her by asking if she will meet me for a quick dinner at an Indian restaurant in Beverly Hills.

I arrive an hour early and nervously window-shop, finding myself in front of the map store, Marc's favorite. Inside, I scan the walls, moving up close to a map of the Côte d'Azur. I locate Nice, where we spent a splendid fortnight when Hannah was two while Marc worked on a Steve Morgan film. Such luxury, being in Europe together at the expense of a movie company. The continuous stretch of clear blue water, white sand beach and warm sunshine was magical. I remembered the open-air market spread for what seemed miles with stacks of fresh fruits and vegetables. Each morning, we consumed rich steaming café au lait with a fresh warm baguette. In the evenings, while the sun set over the sea, we spooned thick, rich bouillabaisse and sipped the light local pinot noir in small cafés on the edge of the Mediterranean.

Knowing now that Gabriella was already ensconced in Marc's life, I have to wonder about that trip and then, of course, every trip after that. But I stop myself from going any further. No matter what the story might have been, Marco and I were still together. What we experienced in Nice was ours—mine now. I buy the map, perhaps meaning to fortify myself with something of Marc's presence in the face of his lover.

A turbaned man in white trousers and a long white silk shirt bows me through the door. Gabriella is seated in the restaurant's brightly lighted foyer, waiting for me. She is more beautiful than I remember. She is wearing a black suit, the jacket open, and a tight white lace blouse that shows off her figure. Her long burgundy-black hair is pulled up in a chignon. She wears a double strand of pearls and her lips are clenched, like the opening bloom of a red tulip. She is definitely a stereotype of Latin beauty.

"Hello, Gabriella," I say, as casually as if I'd met her just days before. In her presence I have an almost physical memory of all those years I didn't *consciously* know anything was going on, when Marc was half there with me, behaving as if he were tired, overworked, unavailable. Nine years of her in my life without actually knowing it. In a weird sort of way, we are sisters.

"Hello, Alys." She stands up, stretching her long, elegantly fingered hand toward me. I see a diamond ring on her wedding finger and wonder if Marc gave it to her. Years ago, when Marc asked me if I'd wanted a diamond, I'd laughed and said, "Me, diamonds? I don't think so."

Gabriella's eyes are black, her long lashes made thicker by the heavy black mascara she wears. She leans toward me, her hand firmly around mine, her smile crinkling her eyes a bit near the temples, making her beauty a little less forbidding. "Thank you for suggesting this," she says.

I wonder at our differences—her low, resonating voice and flamboyant presence, while I am small, almost mouselike next to her, dressed in my short black skirt, tweed jacket and cowboy boots.

The maître d' leads us downstairs to a corner table.

We immediately order drinks: for me, a glass of cabernet sauvignon, and for Gabriella, merlot. She raises her glass and I raise mine. Exactly what are we drinking to? I wonder.

After several moments she says, "Well, Alys . . ." Her Portuguese-accented English is beautiful. I sip on my wine and nod, still not speaking.

She glances down into her glass when the turbaned waiter appears again, giving each of us a menu.

Gabriella's threat has stared me in the face since I left Wales. I have decided to tell Dafydd about her, so if she should call again, he will know why. But I haven't yet.

The way I come to their story now is different from when I first found out. There's something that makes me believe their situation was, as Gabriella herself told me, "not meant to hurt me." Perhaps it was as simple as Marc needing more than I was able to give him, and then Gabriella presenting herself. She was everything I wasn't; she filled in with all the emotion and flamboyance I didn't have. Marc fell in love with her, but maybe not out of love with me.

"How are you, Gabriella?" I ask, noting that it's not just a polite inquiry. I am really curious.

She looks at me, waiting perhaps for my animosity to rise, but I say nothing else.

"I am still struggling but"—she shrugs, shaking her head—"I'm a little stronger."

I nod. "So am I."

"Please, Alys, it was not what you must think. I want to tell you."

"I don't need to hear."

"But I need to tell. Please."

I don't know if I am strong enough for the details. But I let her tell me.

"In the beginning, our relationship was as casual as you can imagine. Neither of us took it seriously. After all, we were both married," she said. "It was . . . how do you say it? A moment, a fling. And then, when Marc made another trip to Rio, and still another, I gave him my ultimatum. I wanted him to choose."

She continues. "He wouldn't hear of it. He all but laughed at me. I was furious he wouldn't divorce you. Furious. By then I'd fallen deeply in love with him and I wanted to be with him morning, noon and night. He'd already told me, warned me in fact, that he would never leave you, how you'd suffered enough in your life and he would never be the cause of further suffering for you.

"After we'd been involved for some time, it became obvious to me it wasn't only because he didn't want to hurt you, but much more complicated. He was an honorable man, a loyal man, yes. But he admitted to me he couldn't leave you because he loved you. And then there were Hannah and Dafydd to think about." She raises her hands as if to say, *That was it.* "And so it was I had to learn to make do. He made it crystal-clear that if I wanted any of him, I had to learn to live alongside you."

I swallow, holding myself together, hearing much as I had imagined it.

"I had no choice. It was that or nothing." She smiles halfheartedly. "I will tell you, though, he always felt he loved you much more than you loved him. He once said he didn't think you were able to love too deeply because of all you'd been through as a child. Whatever the reasons, I'm sure what I got from him was not nearly what you had of him."

I know what she says is true.

"I don't know how you imagined us," Gabriella says. "But I can assure you it was not at all what I wanted, particularly in the beginning. I mean, the beginning after I fell in love with him.

"At first I would have done anything to have him to myself. Anything. And then things changed for me. The more I concentrated on Isabel and was with Marc when he was with us, the less you and your family disrupted my life. Of course, if I allowed myself, I could get wildly jealous and then not speak to Marc for days at a time," she adds. I lift an eyebrow and she answers the unspoken question. "We spoke to each other a few times a week—mostly just to say, 'Hello. How are you.' "

"What about *your* marriage?" I ask.

"Oh, that." She rolls her eyes. "Yes, I was married to Carlos Romeros. If you could call it a marriage."

Carlos had been at the dinner party Marc and I had thrown years ago for all of his Brazilian "network." He was movie star handsome, with dark hair and wild black eyes. His voice was smooth, like twenty-five-year-old Scotch, maybe even smoother, a born crooner. He was one of the most popular singers in Brazil.

"I was so unhappy. Carlos did not know the meaning of the word 'faithful.' During our marriage he had dozens of affairs, many of them with my friends—my so-called friends. It seemed every time I looked around he was involving himself with someone else. There was nothing between us anymore, not even our careers.

"Then Marc called and asked Carlos to recommend a woman singer for the title song for a film he was doing. Carlos recommended me," she said, laughing bitterly. "Always so generous, my Carlos.

"It took us several days to do the recording. And during that time, we got involved. I pursued him. He was a treat for me. Then he became everything. And you must remember I am a Catholic, but I was so sure I could convince him to leave you, I filed for divorce. My mother did not speak to me for a long time. Later, when Carlos and I were finished, Marc still wouldn't consider leaving you.

"Somewhere in between his first visit to Rio and the others over that next year, I got pregnant. When I found out, I didn't tell him because you had just had Hannah and I was afraid he'd make me do away with mine, or that he would abandon me all together. I was six months pregnant before I confessed. He was furious.

"But"—she pauses, and waves her hand in that way to show how things always work out—"as time passed and after he saw Isabel, he relented a bit and he got used to the idea. What he never got used to was being away from you and Hannah. You were his 'life partner,' he called you. Even now, with Marc gone for a year, and having just said what I said about being able to put you out of my thoughts, I can feel the jealousy."

With Gabriella's telling, I begin to understand the mess Marc had gotten himself into. She is like a tropical storm. She whips you up, takes you in and beguiles you with her warmth and charm, her soft beauty. She seems to have no hard edges anywhere—in every way, a complete contrast to me.

The waiter appears again. I am not hungry in the least, and I say so. Gabriella orders Tandori chicken, curried vegetables, dal, potatoes and raita.

"You'll have some of mine," she says. "You must. My goodness, you're so little. You American women are always so concerned about your weight, no? Why do you all want to be so skinny? No breasts!"

I actually laugh.

"You know, as it is, I have been quiet about Marc. There are few people who know that Isabel is Marc's daughter. He wanted it that way. Now that he has gone, we seem to have lost many of the people who used to come around. I am feeling very alone. And so is Isabel. For her to know that she has a half sister would make things easier, I think. And perhaps even for Dafydd and Hannah. It would be another one for each of them to talk to about Marc."

I stare at her, and as the anger rises again, I don't try to hide it, letting it live fully out in the open between us, for just a moment.

"I guess you don't agree."

I don't answer.

"Isabel feels so alone, and sometimes she is so angry with me. I must admit I've had a hard time working. Mr. Meyers made it clear that Marc had not taken care of either Isabel or me in his will. But perhaps since some time has passed, I might appeal to you again." She looks straight at me and then quickly away.

"Isabel is quite good on the piano. She also sings. Where she goes now is a preparatory school for musically talented students. But it is very expensive."

I think about the small private school that Hannah attends.

"Do you want to see a photograph of Isabel?"

It seems like we are raising the dead. But part of me feels butterflies in my stomach, some strange form of excitement.

When Gabriella holds out the photo, I gasp. Isabel has bright eyes and a soft jawline; her smile is so familiar.

"She's like him, isn't she?" Gabriella exclaims as if that is the real prize she holds, her daughter's likeness to Marc.

I can feel my eyes fill.

"She looks like your Hannah, too, doesn't she?"

I continue to stare at the photo. Yes, she looks like Hannah, but she also looks like Marc's sister's and brother's children. She is a real Kessler.

"Her birthday is two days before Christmas."

"But, Marc, how can you be gone the week before Christmas? This is Hannah's first Christmas."

"I've no choice, Alys. I don't set up these film schedules. We've been over this a million times. I'm a hired hand. Why does this come as a surprise to you? Dafydd will be here. I'll be back Christmas Eve at the latest. I promise."

He arrives a full day late. Christmas night. I've cooked a goose and we are all around the table. Beti and Colin, their children, Dafydd. I am sitting at the table nursing Hannah when he comes in, flustered, red in the face, tired from the flight.

"Merry Christmas," he says, his arms full of packages, which he carefully places under the tree.

My disappointment is huge and when he comes to the table and leans over to kiss me, I give him my cheek instead of my lips.

Beti fixes him a plate while Dafydd rushes to the tree to find the gift he has lavishly wrapped for Marc.

Everyone is so glad to see him. Our eyes meet briefly over Hannah's head, across the table.

"So I am wondering again if there might be some way you can help?"

I think about my last conversation with Ed. How he had outlined my own expenses. "If you're careful, you'll be all right," he'd told me. "Your stocks are doing well and we're managing to put some money aside each month for a college fund."

"I hope to be working again soon. But, well, you must know how that is. It is quite difficult. I try to be available to Isabel and I don't like to leave her with the help."

I imagine her staff. Marc had once said we'd have a magnificent life if we lived in Brazil. Does she have a cook? I would like to have a full-time cleaner, an occasional baby-sitter, but I've never wanted a cook. How could I get through my life without cooking?

"You will think about it?"

I glance at the photo of Isabel still on the table. We are very different, Gabriella and I, but we are in the same mess. Marc hadn't meant for me to find out. Marc hadn't meant for any of this to happen. But it has. And here we are.

"Yes, I'll think about it," I say quietly. I look at her hand, the diamond. If it was mine and I was in her position, I'd sell it. But I am not Gabriella.

"Thank you," she says.

I wait for a moment. I wait for her to say something more. Anything. But she says nothing.

As I drive home, I wonder at how Gabriella didn't ask me a single question about my life. It is as if my life, my grief, doesn't exist. Marc's death only affects her.

Sometime during the first week in November, I awaken in the middle of the night in a panic.

I turn on the light and try to figure out when I can go back to

Aberfan for another visit. Sooner rather than later, for it is suddenly clear to me that while I am busy looking for myself "out there," putting my life in order, I might in fact miss Evan again. I glance at the clock; here it is four in the morning, twelve in the afternoon in Wales. Evan will be at school, and he has no answering machine.

I get up and put on a flannel shirt. It has been raining for several days. In November the house is cold. I walk through it, past the tall windows looking out on the canyon, past the Chinese wardrobe in the dining room, where Marc's ashes have been stored for over a year. In the living room, I turn on the outside lights and slide open the double glass doors, looking down into the vast space below where the coyotes are yelping. A low fog is hanging over the canyon cliffs. I am a little older now than Mam was at the time of the disaster. I want to move into the muscle of my life. I have more than enough proof of how short a life can be.

Back in the house, I call Dafydd. It is after seven a.m. in New York.

"Sweetie?"

"Hi, Mom."

"Did I wake you?"

"Not really."

"Listen, I want to scatter Marco's ashes. It's time."

"Okay. When?"

"This weekend."

"Oh, Mom. Can't it wait until I come out on business? I'm right in the middle of a million different—"

"I haven't been able to move ahead. I need to get on with my own life. I need to put Marc somewhere. I can't have him hanging around in the dining room anymore."

Dafydd laughs.

"I'm serious."

"I know you are."

"And there's something we need to discuss," I add.

"About what?"

"About Marco."

"What is it?"

"Not now. When you get here."

"Okay."

"This weekend, okay?"

"Okay, Momma."

I'd thought about gathering a group, having some of the same folks who'd spoken at the memorial service trek up the hill with us in order to say a few words; but in the end, it is just Dafydd, Hannah and I.

"Isn't it against the law to throw ashes just any old where?" Hannah asks. "I can see it now. We'll be spending Thanksgiving in jail."

"Stuffing and water," Dafydd adds.

We decide to hike to a spot in Temescal Canyon where as a family we'd hiked millions of times. We know the spot where we want to fling the ashes: about three miles up there is a view of the ocean in one direction and the Santa Monica Mountains in the other.

Hannah complains the whole way. Dafydd worries if we don't hurry he'll miss his twelve o'clock phone conference. Hannah continues to worry we'll get caught by the "coppers." Dafydd's feet hurt and he is getting a migraine.

By the time we reach the spot, I am ready to throw the two of them off the cliff with Marco. So much for family. It serves me right for coercing them. I should have come by myself and just dumped the ashes.

We sit down and I open the blue velvet bag. Immediately I see that the brass box is screwed down tight with small brass screws. Why haven't I scoped out the box before? Luckily I have put my Swiss Army knife in my bag. With it, I try to jack the screws out. They won't budge. I use the awl on the knife and try to pry it open.

"Someone's coming!" Hannah whispers. "I knew it. We're done for now."

I put the box under my bag and sit on it. It is a dog walker with half a dozen dogs.

"Howdy. Beautiful day, isn't it?" the fearless leader says as he pauses for a moment, taking a water bottle from his rucksack and pouring the water into a small blue bowl. Each of the dogs has a lap. One of them comes over to me and puts his face on my knee. I rub his head. I am afraid they might sniff Marc out, but after each of the dogs has a little drink, they start on their way.

I try the awl again. "Help me, Dafydd."

"Ah, please, Momma. I'm not very good at this."

Which one of us *is* good at this?

Dafydd takes the box.

"I'm going to keep watch, okay?" Hannah says.

Seconds later she calls out, "Someone's coming!"

It is an older woman. She has binoculars around her neck and is carrying a bird book. She pauses right near us and puts the binoculars up to her eyes. "Oh, my goodness, it's a red-tailed hawk. The markings on the tail are unusual. We've actually been tracking them."

I find a loose cigarette in my bag and put it in my mouth. I'm not starting up again; this is just a little slip because of stress, grief. It won't last. Just a stray left over from the really tough days.

"Would you like to look?" the woman asks. Her head whirls around just as I strike the match. "You can't smoke up here. Didn't you see the sign down there? This is a no-smoking area!"

"Sorry," I say, stubbing the cigarette in the dirt. I pick the butt up immediately and roll it in a tissue, then put it in my pocket so she won't accuse me of littering. "That's the only one I have, I promise. I don't really smoke."

She shakes her head, not seeing through on her offer to show me the hawk, and quickly walks away.

After she's gone a distance, Dafydd hands me the box. "Here. It's open. Careful. The screws are all loose." Clearly, mine are, too.

"Hannah. We're ready."

The three of us gather round the box. "Which of you wants to start?"

"Start!" they both say at once.

"No, thank you," Dafydd says immediately.

"Me neither," Hannah says.

"Okay. But don't you want to at least look at them?"

They both shake their heads.

The wind is light, but it's blowing. Dafydd says, "Careful the ashes don't blow back in your face like they did in *The Big Lebowski*."

I tell them I think I should move a distance away from the path and just empty it over the side of the cliff. "Any objections?" They shake their heads. "Shall one of us say a few words?" They both shake their heads again.

"The fewer the better," Hannah says. "Let's do this quick, before we get arrested. Daddy wouldn't mind. He always said he hated small talk."

I walk up the path about ten feet and lean way over the side, the box poised to be emptied. For a moment I feel the pull of the space below and start to tremble, begin to lose my balance. I steady myself with the help of a nearby tree trunk and catch my breath. I put my hands in the box, feeling the ashes, feeling the light sandiness, feeling Marc, what is left of him. I lean closer and smell the sweet, pungent smell, take a finger full, and lick some of the ashes.

"This is the last time I will hold you. The last time we will stand together like this . . ."

Then, handful by handful, I start to throw him off the cliff. When I am through, I stand for what seems like the longest time with the empty box, and then I take my wedding band from my trouser pocket.

"Thank you for saving my life," I say, and heave the ring like a heavy rock, as far as I can.

"Momma? Are you all right?" Dafydd calls.

"Mom? Let's go!" Hannah is nervous.

I am covered in dust, my black trousers splotched in a fine gray coating of it.

Just after we return from the flinging, Dafydd and I are in the garden sitting on the two chaise longue chairs on the lower deck, looking out over the pepper trees that Marco loved so much and, beyond that, the miraculous view of the sea.

"Marc had a lover," I say simply. "A longtime lover."

"Oh, Mom . . ." Dafydd replies, as if it is something I might have imagined.

"Gabriella Purdue."

"You're kidding." He lifts his eyebrows and takes off his sunglasses.

"I'm not. He also had a child with her."

"No."

I nod. "Her name is Isabel and she is just a bit younger than Hannah. I found out a few months after Marco's death."

I reach over and put my hand on his knee. "Someday I'll have to tell Hannah, but not now."

Dafydd's face is full of pain. "Why? I don't get it."

I shrug. "I was not the perfect wife. He might have been lonely. He was not the perfect husband." My eyes fill with tears. "You know, I don't think there is such a thing, really. A perfect marriage. But I think, all things considered, Marco and I did a pretty good job of it. Mam says, 'It takes a long time to make a perfect marriage.' "

Dafydd's eyes fill.

"He loved you very much, Dafydd. You know, sometimes I teased him that he'd really fallen in love with you first."

Dafydd smiles. That is an old story among the three of us.

For weeks after my meeting with Gabriella, I go over the papers she's sent me about Isabel's school. I don't ever have to be best friends with this woman, who had in some ways given Marc what I was unable to—but finally, I know I have to acknowledge what had come out of that relationship. Their child. Isabel. And so, I write Gabriella and tell her I will help pay for Isabel's education for as long as I can. I let her know I have told Dafydd about them and what I am doing, but Hannah is still so young, I hope I will be able to stave off telling her for a few years—until she is a bit older, perhaps, and more settled with all that has come to pass.

This morning, Hannah sits at the piano, practicing for her recital tomorrow. She is playing Mozart's "Rondo Alla Turca." One phrase continues to trip her up. She stops, starts again and slowly moves over the phrase another time.

And here I am, too, on this glorious fall morning in November, in my kitchen slicing tomatoes from the garden. Welsh-born and living at the tip of America's Pacific Ocean, still wondering how I came to be saved and what I will do, finally, with my saved life.

Gram used to say, "No one knows when the final tap on the shoulder will come. So luxuriate in every moment!"

I have just cut up a full, flat plate of tomatoes. There are six in all: one a papaya orange, another kiwi green with three black stripes. Imagine that, designer tomatoes. My favorite are yellow, the size of marbles. There are three shades of red, with seeds so petulant that when I bite into them, they squirt and run down my face, my chin, and onto my shirt, a taste that I imagine worms taste: dark, rich earth. Dirt—what I remember eating when I was six, walking through my gram's vines, the ones that grew upside our fence, just picking one tomato straight off and biting into it. Sometimes in the late California summer, when I eat a tomato, the only thing I see is Gram's face, a sunbeam reflecting off fine dark hair framing high cheekbones, her smile and slightly yellowing teeth, her long thin arms around me. She is my whole world and everything I know and love, in that one bite of tomato.

"Lord!" I look down at the knife, the tomatoes and then at my finger, where the bright blue-red of my own blood drips. I put my finger in my mouth.

Hannah moves over the same phrase in the rondo.

My finger is bleeding quite badly now. It stings from the vinegar and lemon. I mop it with a paper towel. I go to the phone and dial Evan's number. He answers on the second ring.

"Two eight two nine," he says.

"It's Alys."

"Hello, Alys."

"Listen, Evan. I'd like to come over after Thanksgiving."

Silence on the other end.

"Elizabeth will stay with Hannah while I'm gone."

Still, silence. I can taste the blood from my finger. It is running down my throat.

"Evan, please."

After another moment, he says brightly, "Well now, this is sort of a coincidence. After Thanksgiving sounds fine, but I'd actually like to see you sooner if that's possible. I just bought a ticket to L.A. to arrive next Monday. I was going to ring you this morning to ask if the timing was all right for you. I can't stay too terribly long, but—"

"Next week?"

"I'm having a bit of a hard time without you."

I can feel my face breaking into a smile. "Just a bit?" I am so excited.

"Well, perhaps more than a bit. I thought I should see how you live, as you suggested. No strings attached."

"Omigod, that's the best news I've had in . . . maybe ever," I admit.

In the background Hannah goes over the Mozart piece for the twentieth time, this time with no mistakes.

"That's lovely," Evan says. "Is it Hannah?"

"It is."

"Give her my love," he says. "Tell her I'll be seeing her soon."

Perhaps I will always feel the quiet ache that the Welsh call *Hiraeth*: a longing for something indefinable, unattainable. Maybe in my case it is my home I will always be in search of, but more likely it is probably my buried innocence, and I will always be digging out.

But there is also the keen possibility of my being able to live boldly in the treasure of my saved life, *"to kiss away each hour of Hiraeth,"* as the song says—a growing faith that home is in every moment and everywhere I go, and that I can harvest those experiences that connect my life with other lives.

A lofty thought for first thing in the morning, but one I'd like to grow into.

Photo by Joyce Ravid

Katherine Leiner is a longtime author of children's books. She has two children and lives part of the year in New York City. *Digging Out* is her first novel for adults.

DIGGING OUT

❖

KATHERINE LEINER

This Conversation Guide is intended to enrich the individual
reading experience, as well as encourage us to explore these topics
together—because books, and life, are meant for sharing.

A CONVERSATION WITH
KATHERINE LEINER

Q. It is hard to imagine a more devastating accident than the tip slide in Digging Out, *which claims the lives of 116 children. What inspired you to write this story?*

A. When I was a young teenager, living in a bright southern California beach town, I read about the Aberfan disaster. I couldn't fathom the devastation, the loss. I became obsessed with it. Like many around the world, I sent whatever pocket money I had. And coincidentally, years and years later, I married and lived in Caerphilly, Wales, for some time—right down the road from Aberfan.

Q. Because Alys is a survivor of such a tragedy, her story is unique. But in other ways, her challenges are common ones. What are the larger themes that make Digging Out *appealing to a wide audience?*

A. Suffering is part of life. In fact, the Buddha says life is suffering. Some of us seem to have more of it in our lives than others. The common thread of challenge for all of us is that there are ways of dealing with our suffering, ways in which to "dig out," to live life, despite the suffering, with passion and hope. In her late thirties, Alys realizes that it is time for her to "move into the muscle of her life." All of us have ways in which we are digging out. The hope is that we do it sooner rather than later. But sometimes later must be good enough.

Q. Auntie Beryl's bohemian wardrobe and outspoken manner make her a wonderfully vivid presence in the Davies family. Who is your favorite character?

A. Parry was my favorite character. I loved his passion. I tried every which way not to have this young man die—but die he did. He was the one in the family who really understood what it would take to live alongside all that loss. And I guess he just couldn't figure out a way to do it. I think Parry lost all hope and therefore couldn't fathom the possibility of forgiveness, and so continuing along in life seemed overwhelming to him.

Q. How much of Digging Out *is based on your own experience?*

A. The only part of *Digging Out* that comes out of my own experience is the fact that I met my second husband in high school, we had a long marriage, and he died quite suddenly when he was rather young.

Q. You've written children's books for years. What made you want to write an adult novel?

A. Because I have been writing for children for so long, I wrote the first draft of *Digging Out* for young adults in the third person. It didn't work at all. When I found Alys' voice, I knew the book was an adult piece, and as I continued, I began to see how it was also about my own inner world, much in the same way all my books for children have served to enlighten me about a particular aspect of my own emotional life.

Q. Are you working on another project?

A. Writing for adults is totally delightful, and although I am continuing to write for children, I am hard at work on my next novel for adults.

Q. What are you hoping readers will take away from their experiences reading Digging Out?

A. Loss is hard, for all of us, young and old alike. And we all experience it to varying degrees throughout our lives. I believe that mostly we have the means of moving through loss, and my hope with *Digging Out* is that the story presents a character whose life has been so emotionally difficult and yet she finds the courage and the strength to move through it. I think it was Robert Frost who said, "The only way out is through." Dealing with loss to whatever degree we can helps us to move through it.

QUESTIONS FOR
DISCUSSION

1. What could be the various meanings of the title *Digging Out*? In what different ways was Alys buried? What tools does she use to "dig out"?

2. Alys discovers her deceased husband, Marc, has had a child out of wedlock. Based on what we learn about him in the book, what do you think this tells about his character? What does Alys' reaction say about her? Can you imagine why Marc's affair may be partly a reaction to Alys' behavior?

3. In some ways Parry is the most passionate figure in Alys' life. How does the loss of this dark "hero" color, or not color, Alys' relationship with men?

4. How does the early loss of Hallie affect Alys' ability to form strong bonds with other women her age? What role does female friendship play in her adult life? Might stronger, deeper bonds with women help her other relationships?

5. Should Alys and Evan get married? If yes, where should they live?